MW00389618

The Roar of the Lions

The Roar of the Lions

Wes Brustad

The Roar of the Lions

© Wes Brustad 2013

This book is a work of fiction. Named locations are used fictitiously, and characters and incidents are the product of the author's imagination. Any resemblance to actual events or places or persons, living or dead, is entirely coincidental.

Published by
Lighthouse Christian Publishing
SAN 257-4330
5531 Dufferin Drive
Savage, Minnesota, 55378
United States of America

www.lighthousechristianpublishing.com

Author's Note

Many of the characters and incidents in this book are actual historical personages and events. At the same time, this is a work of fiction requiring the imagination of the author be brought into play to keep the story moving forward.

Daniel, Nebuchadnezzar, Amel-Marduk, Neriglissar, and Amytis among others lived in Babylon in the sixth and seventh centuries B.C. That Nebuchadnezzar suffered a period when he acted and thought he was an animal—most likely a steer or bull—is both historical record and recorded in the Bible (Daniel chapter 4). For most of us, it was an act of God. Others call it boanthropy, a mental illness in which a person is resolutely convinced they have become an animal and acts accordingly.

Nowhere is it recorded what happened during the time of Nebuchadnezzar's transformation. All that is known is that one day he ruled the greatest city in the known world and oversaw an empire of unheard of proportions; the next day he no longer had the capacity to rule and was removed. Somehow the kingdom held together during the time of his incapacitation, even in the face of many pretenders to the throne. When he regained his senses, he returned to his throne and a kingdom greater and stronger than ever.

What happened?

This is a story that tries to answer that question.

THE BABYLONIANS

Look at the nations and watch—
        and be utterly amazed.
For I am going to do something in your days
        that you would not believe,
        even if you were told.
I am raising up the Babylonians,
        that ruthless and impetuous people,
        who will sweep across the whole earth
        to seize dwelling places not their own.
They are a feared and dreaded people;
        they are a law to themselves
        and promote their own honor.
Their horses are swifter than leopards,
        fiercer than wolves at dusk.
Their cavalry gallops headlong;
        their horsemen come from afar.
They fly like a vulture swooping to devour;
        they all come bent on violence.
Their hordes advance like a desert wind
        and gather prisoners like sand.
They deride kings
        and scoff at rulers.
They laugh at all fortified cities;
        they build earthen ramps and capture them.
Then they sweep past like the wind
        and go on—
        guilty men, whose own strength is their god.

Habakkuk 1: 5-11

Chapter 1
THE DREAM
572 BC

"What does it mean?" reverberated the screams throughout the palace. "Someone tell me what this is about" yelled Nebuchadnezzar as he careened off the door leading to his bedchamber into the anteroom, his nightclothes in disarray. The four palace guards who had been on duty tensed, knowing their very lives were at stake if they said or made the wrong move. They stood at attention, eyes straight forward, as their squad leader approached the King to find out what was wrong.

"My Lord, what happened?" He beckoned two of the guards enter the King's bedchamber to search for intruders. The other quickly stepped to the doorway leading to the family sitting room to seal off their space.

"Get my astrologers and wise men here now! And all the magicians! I've got to know what I just dreamed," roared Nebuchadnezzar. "What in all the gods' names does it mean?" He brushed aside the guard at the doorway and ran into the large sitting room, his eyes wild with panic. Servants began to pour out of the doorways to tend to the King's orders. They had never seen him this distressed and were immobilized with fear. Like the guards, they knew the wrong move could be fatal.

Into the chaos stepped Amytis, the servants quickly making way for her. She had seen this before. After forty-two years of marriage, she was well aware that her husband's fears were deep rooted and very real. Moreover, she knew they were likely related to the supernatural and unknown as he had never been intimidated by anything or anyone in the physical world.

How ironic, she reflected, that superstitions could bring the most powerful ruler in the world to his knees.   She strode directly to Nebuchadnezzar, taking both his arms in her hands, "What is going on, darling?   Why all the commotion?"

"They're after me again! Why can't they leave me alone? Why can't they talk to me straight? Always in nightmares. I'm going crazy! Do any of you understand this? I can't take this! It's all crazy!!"

She clung to him, holding him as she would a young child, "It's okay...it's all right." For a moment, Nebuchadnezzar slumped against her, the tension starting to release. But his fear did not subside.

He suddenly broke free of her and circled the room, shouting at those present, sometimes striking them in anger, "What am I supposed to think? Someone tell me what it was about!"

Amytis pointed to a servant and ordered, "Gather the King's wise men. Go to each one's house and tell them to come without delay. Go quickly. And make sure Daniel knows as well."

"I want Amel here . . . at once!" screamed Nebuchadnezzar. "He needs to hear what this is about. If I'm going down, he'll be going down too. Go get him!" With that Nebuchadnezzar strode back into his bedchamber and began pounding the walls until his hands began to bleed.

"You heard the King," said Amytis to a nearby guard. "Go to Amel-Marduk's palace and wake him at once. Bring him back quickly but warn him about the King's state of mind. He deserves to know what he's walking into." She turned and ran to Nebuchadnezzar, grabbing his arms to stop his relentless pounding. "My Lord...my love, please stop. You're damaging your hands! Calm down. We've sent for the wise men, even Daniel. And Amel-Marduk will be here momentarily. Please . . . you need to get dressed to receive them."

~

Amel-Marduk had worked late into the evening putting the finishing touches on the gold lions flanking the Procession Way, a mile long boulevard that began at the Ishtar Gate and ended at the giant three-hundred foot ziggurat which towered over the city. He still stood in awe of this pyramidal temple that he had designed and built with his father, Nebuchadnezzar. Standing on the top level, one could see for miles into the surrounding desert and hills. Most fun, however, was looking down from the shrine onto the streets of the city of Babylon where people resembled ants scurrying about. Seven levels, each forty feet or so high, made up the ziggurat. Each level was painted a different color suggesting a permanent rainbow covering the city's sky scape. It was appropriately named Etemenanki which meant "the house of the frontier between heaven and earth."

Everything about this project demanded excellence. The gold lions provided the sense of awe essential to connote the sacredness of the street leading to the complex of temples surrounding the pyramid. He had 120 of them to place in equal intervals. The most challenging work was placing them in the right sequence. It had been very tiring to compare the faces and body contours of the lions so that each placement perfectly heightened the feeling of fear and veneration as one got closer to the Temple of Marduk.

Needless to say, Amel-Marduk was beat. After a light supper he had tumbled into bed and fallen fast asleep. The voice of his head servant urging him to wake up was distant at first but grew louder as he shouted in his ear and tapped his arm. Amel struggled to shake off the deep sleep which had engulfed him, making every attempt to understand what this voice was telling him. As he rose to a seated position, one arm supporting him to keep him from lying back down, he rubbed his eyes and saw that in addition to his servants his bedchamber was occupied by several of the King's palace guards.

"What is going on?" he groggily asked. It looked dark outside. Why were they waking him? More to the point, why were they in his private bedchamber before he had the chance to get dressed? He looked at his clothes. He was still dressed as he was when he left his work with the lions and returned to his palace.

Instantly he came awake, springing out of bed to question his servant, "Are we under attack? Is the King all right?"

The captain of the King's guard stepped forward, speaking quietly, "No, my Lord, there is no attack. But the King is not well. He seems to have suffered a nightmare that has greatly disturbed him. He is calling for all his palace counselors to assemble immediately. He specifically wants you at his palace."

Amel locked eyes with the captain to ascertain the truth of what he said, then, in turn, looked at the faces of every man in the room. No one flinched. Maximillan, his head servant, whispered, "It's true, my lord. The King is not well. You must go to the palace at once."

~

There was more than one palace in Babylon. The official palace grounds covered almost thirty acres including six palaces and the King's royal stables, home to his prize horses and livestock. The royal palace which housed Babylon's administration and was used for ceremonial and state functions was located directly on Procession Way. The King had long ago ceased to live there.

When Nebuchadnezzar decided to build for his homesick wife a palace that resembled the treed mountainous landscape where she grew up, he designed and built his residential palace with the hanging gardens on the banks of the Euphrates river directly to the west of the original palace. Between the two anchor palaces, the King and his son, the Crown Prince Amel-

Marduk, built a third palace where Amel lived with his family and servants.

Within a short time, three other palaces—all smaller in scope—were built for each of the King's other children. They all sat within the carefully guarded and protected palace grounds. In the wee hours of the morning these were only looming shadows as Amel left his home to walk to the King's residence.

The King's palace was in an uproar. All the candles and lanterns were lit, the kitchen was bustling, and the servants were running helter-skelter as they ushered in the royal officials and counselors who had been summoned in the middle of the night. All were on edge as they heard the wailing of Nebuchadnezzar from his personal quarters. Something had gone very wrong.

Amel ran up the steps leading to the palace's main entry. No sooner had he entered the large outer anteroom then he was met by Antiosyss, the high priest of the Temple of Marduk, the chief of the Babylonian gods.

"Your highness," Antiosyss said, "the King is troubled by powerful demons. He has had a bad dream! It has badly terrorized him. He wants to know what it means. I came as quickly as I could and have brought my priests to help."

Brushing past Antiosyss, Amel continued on through the outer courtyard into the public receiving room which was filling rapidly. A quick survey of the room told him his father had not yet entered. He exited the room and walked across the inner courtyard headed for the four tall, muscular and well-armed guards at the entrance to Nebuchadnezzar's personal quarters. Recognizing the Crown Prince, they parted to let him enter. He moved on to the sitting room where his mother stood trying to bring some order to the scene.

"Oh, Amel, am I glad to see you," exclaimed Amytis. "Your father had one of his awful dreams. Whatever it was, he can't shake it. He wants his wise men and every counselor in the palace to help him figure out what it means. He's been calling for you and Daniel since he woke up. He won't calm down."

"Let me talk to him," said Amel-Marduk as he strode to the King's bedchamber.

Once inside, he found Nebuchadnezzar seated on his bed, his head in his hands, alternately muttering and screaming: "Why does the tree need to be cut down? Why are the gods tormenting me?"

"Father," Amel softly spoke, "may I enter?"

Nebuchadnezzar turned to look at him, his eyes wild with fear, and asked "My son?"

"Yes, Father, I'm here, replied Amel. "What can I do?"

"Amel, I'm glad you're here," said Nebuchadnezzar as he rose from the bed and went to grasp Amel-Marduk tightly. "I don't know why, but there's something very eerie about what I saw tonight." He started shaking as he continued, "I may have offended the gods . . . I don't know . . . it's as though everything I've built—our empire—is about to crumble. I have a very bad feeling about this."

Amel grabbed his father by both arms, firmly enough to stop the trembling, "Look at me, Father. We're not under attack. All is well. We'll get to the bottom of this. All your magicians and wisemen are in the receiving room eager to help. They can answer your questions and explain the whole thing."

"Good...that's good," replied Nebuchadnezzar. Straightening up, he grabbed his formal robe and put it on, then picked up his scepter, the powerful symbol of his kingship. Somewhat calmed, he looked at Amel, "Let's see if we can find out what this is all about. If nothing else, Daniel will know."

Upon their entrance, the room grew silent. The speculation and bantering stopped, as no one wanted to be conspicuous and face the wrath of the King's anger. Nebuchadnezzar walked towards his throne, but then stopped in the middle of those assembled. In the loud voice the courtiers had come to fear, he bellowed, "I had a dream tonight that has terrified me, and I don't know why. That's why you are all here. I want to know why I am frightened. I want to know what this dream means." He slowly began to turn, looking everyone directly in the eyes, "You know such things. You study the signs and the spiritual world. "

He paused, then began again in a voice of cold steel, "I demand an answer... or each of you will die."

The silence was deafening. No one moved, blinked or looked anywhere but straight ahead. Amel walked up to the King saying, "My Lord, let's sit as this may take some time to fully unravel." He took Nebuchadnezzar's arm and began walking to the throne. He, too, surveyed the roomful of people looking for some sign of affirmation that someone could provide the right answers. His eyes darted like daggers, cutting to the very core all the pretenders to the throne. While he did not believe in this mumbo-jumbo of spirits and the netherworld, he knew his father needed to hear from one of them some explanation that made sense and would restore his emotional sanity.

They reached the throne where Nebuchadnezzar sat facing his retinue. Amel stood at his side, not as before but with a new presence that commanded their total attention. The silence grew in volume until Beltekasmer, the dominant magician and interpreter of dreams of the court, knelt before the throne to ask, "My King, may I have a word?"

Nebuchadnezzar stared at him for what seemed like an eternity, then said in a voice not much above a whisper, "It better be good. Speak."

"I want to help you, my lord," Beltekasmer replied. Gesturing with his arms to encompass the room, "All of us do. But we need to hear your dream before we can interpret it. If it pleases you, I beg you to share your dream, then we can explain it to you."

Turning to Amel, Nebuchadnezzar said, "Shouldn't they be able to know it already if they're in touch with the spirit world?" Nebuchadnezzar lived in fear of supernatural powers and was convinced the gods granted divination to all those claiming to access that world. His question was genuine.

Not one to give any stock to the spirit world, Amel smiled and replied, "It would be better for your wise men to hear it directly from you. If you want an explanation of your dream, you should tell it in your own words."

That is a credible answer, Nebuchadnezzar thought. Maybe his son was ready to follow in his footsteps. "You speak well, Amel. They should hear it from me."

He rose from his throne and looked around the room, speaking carefully and with dread, "I was lying in my bed, and suddenly there was a tree in the middle of the empire. An enormous tree that grew larger, stronger and taller until its top touched the sky. Everyone on earth could see this tree. Its leaves were beautiful; its fruit sufficient to feed everyone on earth... even all the animals who took shelter under it and the birds which lived within its branches.

"As I was gazing at this incredible tree, I saw someone come down from the heavens—a messenger of the holy God. He called in a loud voice, 'Cut down the tree and trim off its branches. Strip off the leaves. Scatter the fruit. Let the animals escape from under it. Give the birds time to flee from the branches.' Then he ordered that the stump, roots and all, be bound with a chain of iron and bronze and left in the field."

Nebuchadnezzar's voice had grown louder as he re-imagined this vision. He began to shake with fear, his eyes ablaze with the terror known only by a man who has come to the edge of an abyss. He found the going now much tougher.

"And then it seemed like the tree became a human. The messenger said that he—the stump—would be drenched with the morning dew and live among the animals...that his mind was to be changed from that of a man to that of an animal for seven years. What are we talking about? The stump of a tree who suddenly becomes human and then turns into an animal? It's all crazy...makes no sense."

Nebuchadnezzar shot upright out of his throne, grabbing his head in both hands and screamed: "The gods must have sensed my questions because the next thing I heard was an announcement by several messengers...I think they were holy ones. They emphasized that this verdict was final and that it came from the Most High God who is sovereign over all kingdoms that men create. And he said that the true God easily gives these kingdoms to anyone he wishes . . . nobility toppled in favor of the lowest common man!"

Nebuchadnezzar was shaking uncontrollably by now and failed to take sufficient breaths as he spoke. He was so frightened by this vision, he retreated back into his frenzy, "So what is the interpretation of this dream? Speak!"

No one dared to open their mouth. They didn't have a clue what this meant.

Suddenly he realized Daniel was not in the room. "Where's Daniel?" he asked Amel who shrugged that he didn't know. "Where's Daniel?" the King thundered in a loud voice to the entire assembly.

The silence in the room grew heavier.

"I want Daniel here—now!" screamed Nebuchadnezzar. "He knows more than all of you combined. And he isn't afraid to tell me the truth unlike so many of you slithering scum. If Daniel has disappeared, then I am fearful. You all should be fearful. This empire may well be in danger."

"My Lord," said Laconius coming forward through the King's court. "Daniel had to travel to the Fifth District to resolve a water dispute. He is a full day's travel away from the capital." Laconius served as the chief aide to Daniel and was well known by Nebuchadnezzar and the entire royal court. He had the same virtues as Daniel; when he spoke, it was always in truth.

"Well, go get him immediately," commanded Nebuchadnezzar. "Take a squad of my guards with you and good horses. He must return at once."

"Yes, my Lord," bowed Laconius who then backed away from the throne to exit the palace.

Nebuchadnezzar was both terrified and furious. He began to shake and rant like he did upon awakening from his dream. He stormed into the assembled court advisors, wise men and courtiers accusing each one of them of disloyalty and insubordination. There was no rhyme or reason to his charges. It was clear he was on the verge of losing his mind. Everyone looked down and slid to fold into the outer walls of the room.

"So Daniel isn't here! Let me see how powerful each of you is. Do the spirits talk to you?" screamed Nebuchadnezzar in the face of a court magician, continuing to harass and frighten people around the room.

"STOP . . . my Lord." Antiosyss stepped from the crowd towards Nebuchadnezzar. "Your problem is that you have aroused the wrath of the gods. They are tormenting you. The only way we can stop this is to cleanse the palace of the evil that has been unleashed and beg our great god Marduk to bring you understanding, oh King."

"No, don't bring Marduk into this!" screamed Nebuchadnezzar as he ran for the wall and began beating it with his hands. "Gods, demons . . . more gods . . . more demons! No more! Just tell me what my dream means," wailed the King.

Amel crossed to his father, pushing Antiosyss aside, "Get out of here!" He took the King by the arm and led him to the entrance to his private quarters all the while shouting to Antiosyss, "You pretend to have power and access to Marduk, but you are nothing more than one of us...simple humans living in a real world. Leave . . . now!"

Antiosyss, unprepared to have his authority challenged, was caught speechless. He froze in place trying to make sense of how he, the high priest of the great Babylonian god Marduk, had been so readily dismissed.

"Guards," screamed Amel, "take him away right now! I want him and his priests out of the palace!" He pulled Nebuchadnezzar through the doorway out of the receiving room. Immediately three guards filled the entry, their spears crossed. The captain of the palace guard signaled four guards to escort Antiosyss out of the palace. They moved rapidly, picking Antiosyss up so fast he had little chance to object.

No one else moved. Once the assembled counselors were certain the King had left and would not be returning they quickly dribbled out of the palace in pairs and threes, speaking softly to each other in not much more than a whisper. They were glad to get out alive. Front and center in their minds was what happens next. If there is no interpretation, what would the King do?

~

Leading his father to his favorite chair in the sitting room, Amel ordered the servants to fix some food and a soothing drink. Nebuchadnezzar would not sit, continuing to rant and chase ghosts in the room. Everyone but Amytis and Amel had left the room; the servants occasionally peered around the door posts to see what was happening.

"My Love, please be calm," begged Amytis putting her arms around him. "All this will be explained when Daniel arrives. You know he always seems to know these things," she cooed. "There is no need to worry about this when we'll have an answer in a day or two."

Nebuchadnezzer whirled to face her, "A day or two?! We may have lost our empire in that time. No, we cannot wait. I'll go find him myself." He strode to his bedchamber to change his clothes.

Having entered the room unnoticed as Amytis was trying to calm Nebuchadnezzer, Dorcas approached Amel asking, "My Lord, let me help. I believe Abednego and I can reassure him that the kingdom is safe and that he will learn the truth once Daniel returns. He may listen to us."

If it were not for the fact that he completely trusted Dorcas, a Jewish slave assigned to his palace for the past twenty years, Amel would have summarily dismissed such a request. But this was a woman in whom he had complete faith. She was the only person in the kingdom whom he could trust with his doubts about the superstitions of Marduk worship. Lately, he had even been revealing to her his apprehensions about the relationship Antiosyss was nurturing with Neriglissar, his brother-in-law. He had smelled a rat and looked to her to help him bring clarity to the situation.

"It's worth a try," he said. "But I don't know about Abednego. What can he do?"

"He's Daniel's close friend. The King knows him well and respects him for his integrity. Please, I think together we can bring peace to his mind."

Willing to try anything, Amytis crossed to Amel and grabbed his arm, "Let them. It can't hurt, and we aren't helping him."

Turning to one of the servants by the door, Amel ordered, "Get Abednego. Tell him the King has need of him...now!"

"He's right outside," said Dorcas. "He was in the room and saw it all. As I was coming into the palace, he caught me and urged me to ask you if we could pray with the King."

Pray? Amel thought this was all nonsense, but then his father did believe in the super-natural world. Maybe this would calm him.

"My Queen . . . my Prince," said Abednego who had just come to the entry of the sitting room led by one of the palace's servants. "I cannot interpret the King's dream, but God will work through Dorcas and me to quiet him if you permit," Abednego bowed.

Knowing this was probably the best chance he had to restore normalcy in the palace, Amel gestured to the King's bedchambers, "Go...but if you excite him further, I'll . . . I'll . . . just don't make it worse."

Dorcas and Abednego quickly crossed to the bedchamber's door and entered to find Nebuchadnezzar lying face down on his bed, his arms beating the blankets and wailing, "Stop tormenting me!" He looked at them wild-eyes, "Why does this frighten me so badly?"

They moved to the bed, one on each side, and gently placed a hand on each of his shoulders. "My King," softly said

Abednego, "we are here to help. We will call on the most high God to relieve your spirit . . . to bring you peace."

Nebuchadnezzar propped himself up and looked at Abednego as though he was an apparition, "Can you interpret my dream?" He rose to his knees and grabbed Abednego by his shoulders, "What does it mean? Tell me!"

Abednego took the King's arms in his hands and looked directly into his eyes, "No, my Lord, I cannot interpret your dream. Daniel, who is coming, will do that. But I can pray to God who gave you this dream to restore calm in your heart and mind. And He will do so if you wish it."

"Please let us pray with you," Dorcas pleaded.

Hearing her, Nebuchadnezzar whirled around to see who else was in his private bedchamber. She looked familiar to him, but he struggled to place her until he saw Amel directly behind her, "You're Amel's servant? Is that why you're here?"

"Yes, she is my servant, father," verified Amel. "But I didn't bring her or ask her to come. She came on her own to help us. There is no one more trustworthy in my palace."

Perplexed by everything that had happened to him tonight, and now to find a servant and one of his civil administrators asking to pray with him to a God for whom he had built no temple in his kingdom dumbfounded him. He stared wildly from one to the other, his mind racing. Would a God he did not worship—moreover a God he never acknowledged—help him . . . especially if this same God sent him this nightmarish dream to terrorize him? Yet, it seemed like they wanted to help him, and Amel obviously thought they could. Maybe they can.

Dorcas took one of his hands in hers and began to pray, "Merciful God, ruler of the universe, look down on us with favor. Restore peace to the King, I pray."

Abednego who had slipped to his knees by the bed looked upward, his face shining as though lit by candles, continued, "God of all power . . . of all spirits and all gods, we beg your mercy to be bestowed on the King. May he know you and the depth of your love for him. Touch his mind, his body and his spirit with your almighty mercy."

Nebuchadnezzar's head turned upward trying to see this powerful God. Without warning, the tension visibly left his body as he slumped down on the bed. He began to weep as the great terror within him sloughed away. He rose on his knees, gratefully taking the hands of Dorcas and Abednego in his and whispered to them, "I am no longer afraid, and I don't know why. Thank you for praying for me. Whoever this God is, I need to build him a temple." Abruptly, a darkness invaded his mind. With urgency in his voice he said, "But I still don't know what the dream meant. I must know."

"You will know when Daniel returns," said Dorcas. "Rest in peace until then. He will give you the answers you seek."

Suddenly very tired, Nebuchadnezzar let go of their hands and fell back on his bed. "I must get some sleep." He looked at them, "Thank you for your prayer. And I thank the most high God for His peace."

It was all surreal to Amel who had watched his father morph from a screaming madman into a man overcome with peace and gratitude. What happened here tonight? How did a dream give rise to such terror? Crazier still, how did these two people—his servant and the Administrator of Water in his father's court—have the power to bring calm to it all?

He escorted Dorcas and Abednego to the door and through the sitting room to take their leave. Amytis who joined them took their hands and said, "Thank you." She began to weep in gratitude, "Thank you for such divine help."

Amel called over a guard, "Escort these people to their homes." Turning to Dorcas and Abednego, he admitted, "I don't understand what happened tonight, but I thank you for being here." He abruptly turned and went back to check on his father.

As Dorcas and Abednego left the palace, she asked, "May we check on him tomorrow? Will you come with me? Until

Daniel returns, I think we need to stand ready to re-assure the King."

Abednego smiled, "I'll come with you, but I think God is taking control now."

~

The sun was setting when Amel-Marduk stopped his work crews for the night. He stood dead center in Procession Way, taking in the symmetry and grandeur of the wide boulevard he had created. The gold lions were a brilliant touch, as the rays of sunset danced on them, each one a slightly different hue. He was fatigued having not slept the night before. He had never seen his father come apart at the seams that way. When he finally returned to his own palace a little after 3:00am, he couldn't sleep. So he rose before sunrise and went back to work staking out the lions. Sleep was overtaking him, however. It is time to get some rest, he thought. He mounted his horse and rode home.

The first words he spoke when he entered his palace and saw Dorcas supervising the evening meal were, "Has Daniel come yet?"

"No," she replied, "but if Laconius rode through the night to where he was working, I think it's likely he could be here sometime tonight or in the morning."

Amel ordered up a bath and wearily walked to his bedchamber to get out of his dirty clothes. The bath seemed to melt all his worries; the steaming hot water felt good on his tired muscles. Fully relaxed, even the tensions of his mind began to release. Sleep was now a prize to be desired. He let himself doze for a few minutes, then shook it off as best he could to towel himself and put on clean clothes. His robes felt particularly good compared to the sticky, tight clothes in which he worked.

Dorcas was waiting for him in his sitting room with a cold drink of his favorite nectar. "Thanks," he said, taking the tumbler and draining it in one swallow. She poured him another tumbler full from the pitcher on her tray. He sat in a large, cushioned chair, motioning her to sit across from him, "I have never seen my father so afraid! This is a warrior—a fighter—who never feared anything. Something totally frightened him...almost to the point of death. But, there was nothing! Just a crazy dream. What was that all about?"

Remaining standing, Dorcas answered, "Maybe God was trying to get his attention."

"What are you talking about? You're sounding as crazy as the King. There is no God. All this business about the gods, spirits, demons, and the supernatural is utter nonsense."

"You didn't think that way when Antiosyss tried to save your family," Dorcas answered gently.

Amel flinched at the mention of his family. He would never forget the accident. During construction of a third palace for Nebuchadnezzar, a large stone the size of two horses slipped loose from the work crew and rolled one hundred feet down hill, crushing his wife and two sons. Recalling the horror of that scene, tears sprung to his eyes. His boys were to follow in his footsteps as rulers of Babylon after he succeeded his father to the throne. In an instant, all his hopes and aspirations of a living legacy came to a jolting stop. Not to mention losing his wife, the love of his life. He had vowed after that never to invest his emotions in anyone again. The pain was too great. Recalling that deathly scene, he felt he was once again on the brink of slipping into an abyss. Would this memory never die?

"I would have done anything . . . believed in anyone, if my boys and wife could be restored to me," he mumbled. "I wanted Antiosyss's incantations to work. I was caught up in thinking the god Marduk was powerful enough to bring life back to the dead." He lifted his head and looked at her, smiling cynically, "But it was all hocus-pocus wasn't it? Antiosyss is a charlatan and Marduk is a myth. There is no spirit world. There's nothing but the real world in which we live."

Dorcas put her tray down and sat directly across from Amel. "You are right about Marduk and all the priests who try to make him and the other gods a reality. But there is one most high God who is real."

"Where was he when my family was killed?"

"I can't answer that. Maybe Daniel can when he returns."

"Dorcas, I'd love for your God to be real because I'm at my wit's end with Antiosyss and his schemes to frighten my father. Antiosyss would like nothing better than to lord it over him. I'm convinced that he's colluding with Neriglasser to somehow bring the King to believe that the throne should become his! Antiosyss must be destroyed. I wish I knew how to do it."

Amel suddenly realized he has spoken too much. "Forget all this, Dorcas. This is dangerous talk that will only get us in trouble."

"My Prince," she replied, "by now you know you can trust me. I have never betrayed your confidence and I don't intend to. You are right to take note of Antiosyss's efforts to sway the King in favor of your brother-in-law. Neriglasser has obviously promised Antiosyss something if and when he takes over the throne."

Amel looked at her hard. She didn't flinch but returned the stare. He had grown to trust her, but this conversation took his trust to a new level. She really was loyal . . . maybe the only one he could trust.

~

"Start placing the bricks for the walkway between the lions," Amel ordered his foreman. "We've got them in perfect line so make sure your men don't knock them out of kilter."

He got up from his knees where he had been diagramming in the sand for his construction supervisors how the walkway would bend and flow along Procession Way. He shielded his eyes from the hot, midday sun to look down the Way at the ziggurat. A smile crossed his face. His father would be pleased with the outcome of this project.

His reverie was broken by the sound of a galloping horse approaching him. Zocor, the Captain of the King's palace guard, came to a sliding stop beside him. "Daniel has arrived back in the city. I thought you'd want to know immediately. He's in his quarters cleaning up."

Without a word, Amel swung up on the spare horse the Captain had brought, and together they raced down the Way towards the King's Palace. "Does Daniel know what's going on?" asked Amel as they rode.

"He seems to have got the gist of it from Laconius. He didn't ask us any questions so I guess he knows as much as we do," replied the Captain, adding under his breath, "and I hope a lot more."

They turned in at the side gate before reaching the royal palace that bordered Procession Way and rode along the avenue that connected five of the palaces. They dismounted at the entrance to the King's residence, tossing the reins to two servants at the ready. Amel rushed up the steps to the grand foyer, then slowed, opting to wait for Daniel before he entered the presence of his father. He barked at a servant, "Go to Daniel's house and ask him to hurry. Tell him I'm waiting here for him."

He strolled outside the entry at the top of the grand steps that led from the ground up to where he stood. Designing this to be the grandest of his palaces, Nebuchadnezzar had constructed at the palace's entry a large marbled patio standing higher than the other palaces on the grounds. Only the ziggurat and the Temple of Marduk stood higher in the city. From here he could see many of the great buildings his father had built in Babylon. For once, however, he didn't enjoy the moment. He was anxious for Daniel to bring some order to the chaos that had enveloped the palace. Curious to see how his father was doing, he went back inside to find Amytis coming to greet him.

"He's in his bedchamber, still mumbling about that dream, his eyes crazy with fear," she said. "Daniel can't get here soon enough."

Amel hugged his mother, drawing her close, "I hope Daniel can satisfactorily interpret his dream . . . that father won't dismiss him as he did the other wise men."

"He will," whispered Amytis, "Your father trusts Daniel to always tell the truth. If he says he can tell your father what it means, the King will believe him."

A guard entered the foyer and saluted, "Daniel has arrived. He's coming up the steps."

Amel let go his mother and crossed quickly to the entry then started down the steps to meet Daniel. He grabbed Daniel by both arms, "I'm so glad to see you. I know you had a long, hard journey through the night to be here. Thank you for getting here quickly."

"No, no, I had to come as fast as possible. I have heard that the King is . . . well, let us say quite frightened by one of his dreams." Daniel smiled at Amel, exuding a calm and serenity that the palace had been missing for almost forty-eight hours. "I am but a servant of the King. It is not for me to concern myself about other things when his very health is in danger."

I'm so relieved you're here, Amel thought as he grabbed Daniel's forearm in greeting. "He's in his bedchamber. I think we should go see him without delay."

They walked up the steps to the foyer where Amytis met them. Bowing to her, Daniel softly spoke, "Your Grace, I'm so sorry for all this disturbance."

She took his hand and led him to Nebuchadnezzar's private quarters talking all the way, "I've known this man for forty-two years and I've seen him upset by a lot of things, but never so badly as this. Daniel, you have to calm him down. He's blinded by rage because no one can tell him what his dream means. Whatever you do, give him an answer but don't set him off again! I can't take any more of this!"

They entered Nebuchadnezzar's sitting room. They heard the King mumbling incoherently in an adjacent room. Amytis whispered to Daniel and Amel, "You both stay here. I'll go bring him out."

She disappeared into Nebuchadnezzar's bedchamber
where they heard her tell the King, "Sire, Daniel is here. He's
just arrived and is waiting for you in your sitting room."

"He's here? Good. He'll make sense out of this
nightmare."

Nebuchadnezzar strode through the doorway towards
them, eagerly grabbing Daniel's forearm in greeting. Daniel
knelt before his King. "No, don't worry about that,"
Nebuchadnezzar pulled him back up to his feet. "You've got to
solve this mystery. I've never been so frightened by a dream. I
know . . . I feel . . . look, it is all bad to me right now. There's
something ominous about this, and I've got to get some answers."

He found his chair and sat, motioning to Amel and
Amytis to join him in seats on either side.

"You probably should start at the beginning and tell
Daniel what exactly you dreamed," she softly spoke as she took
his hand in hers.

"Yes, yes," Nebuchadnezzar leaned forward in his chair,
"None of my astrologers and magicians can interpret it for me,
but you can. You can because the spirit of the holy gods is in
you."

Without any histrionics, he softly repeated every detail of
his dream as he had told his wise men two nights ago. When he
finished, he looked deep into Daniel's eyes and pleaded, "Tell
me, Daniel, tell me what this nightmare means."

Daniel did not move for what seemed like hours but was
only seconds. His calm demeanor was replaced by a perplexed
tension, his eyes straining to find understanding. As he struggled
to sort things out, the elements of the dream began to create a
terror within him and he began to think, is God that angry with
Nebuchadnezzar? Has the Babylonian empire finally ended?

Nebuchadnezzar came out of his chair and grabbed Daniel
by both arms, "Do you understand any of this?" And then more
urgently when Daniel did not immediately respond: "Talk to me.
What's happening?"

Frightened by what was beginning to become clear in his mind, Daniel's complexion paled and his knees weakened. He sagged, only remaining standing because Amel saw what was happening and leaped from his seat to support Daniel. Regaining control of himself, Daniel stood tall and apologized, "My King, my Lord, forgive me. I should not have weakened like this." He began backing away, not looking at them, "I cannot tell you what I have just seen. It will do no good for you to know. I should take my leave."

No one in the room had ever seen Daniel in this state of uncertainty before. The man who never backed away from speaking the truth, whether it helped or hurt, now refused to speak. The shock was enough to bring Nebuchadnezzar out of his depression and reclaim his leadership. He straightened, looked Daniel hard in the eyes, and commanded, "Daniel do not let the dream nor its meaning frighten you. I am ready to accept the truth I know you know. Now, tell me what this is about."

Dropping eye contact with the King, Daniel looked up to the ceiling and whispered to himself, "Almighty God, empower me...let me be strong...let my words be yours."

Looking back at Nebuchadnezzar, he saw a King who was no longer a pool of self-pity and who was ready to confront reality. A calm befell Nebuchadnezzar. Amytis came over to stand by him, holding his arm in hers. Amel let go of Daniel and stepped back to give him space.

"My Lord and King, if only this dream and its meaning applied to your enemies." Daniel paused, looking into the faces of each of the royal family. "But that is not the case. The tree you saw which grew large and strong, reaching to touch the heavens above and visible to the entire earth...with beautiful leaves and abundant fruit to feed everyone . . . its full and long branches providing shelter for the animals below and nests for the birds above . . . you, O King, are that tree. You have become great and strong; your greatness has grown to reach the sky above and your empire extends throughout the earth. Never have there been so many lands and people conquered to create the kingdom you now control."

Amel began to relax, gladly seeing that Daniel was acknowledging his father's vast power and position. This should put the King at ease, he thought. Noo matter what else Daniel says, we all know he is still in control and nothing can harm him.

Daniel continued, "You, O King, saw an angel—a holy one—come down from heaven. You heard him correctly when he said 'Cut down the tree and destroy it but leave the stump, bound with iron and bronze, in the field with its root in the ground.' And, yes, this angel did say one more thing, 'Let him be drenched with the dew of heaven and let him live like the animals until seven years pass by.'"

"I know all this," Nebuchadnezzar interrupted. "But what does it mean? I don't get it."

Amytis squeezed her husband's hand and said, "Let him finish. He will tell us. And do not be afraid. Even Daniel knows you are invincible."

Daniel winced at her words, knowing that what he said next would make her words a hopeful wish at best and a lie at worst. He plowed forward, "This is the interpretation, O King, and this is what the most high God is telling you. You will be driven away from people to live with the animals. You will eat grass like cattle and live in the fields, awakening each morning drenched with dew. This will go on for seven years. Only when you acknowledge that the most high God is sovereign over the kingdoms of men—and that includes you—and can do to anyone as He pleases will you re-enter your palace."

"Oh, come on," snorted Amel. "This doesn't help make sense of anything. Daniel, what you're saying is crazier than the dream itself!"

Daniel lifted his hand to quiet Amel and now spoke in a quiet, steel-edged voice, "The command by the angel to leave the stump of the tree and its roots in the ground was not an after-thought. It means that your kingdom will be restored to you when you acknowledge that God in heaven rules even you, King Nebuchadnezzar."

No one spoke. Even Amel, who dismissed all this as supernatural nonsense, was silent as he reflected on Daniel's words.

The quiet of the room was broken by Daniel who approached Nebuchadnezzar, kneeling before him. "My Lord and King, you have allowed me to advise you in many things these past years. Please . . . I beg you . . . please accept my advice today. Confess your pride. Acknowledge that God—and only He—is sovereign. And, I say this with gratefulness for all the kindnesses you have shown me. Renounce your sinful ways by being kind to the oppressed. There are so many people whose burdens you can remove and can make whole. It might be, if you change your ways, that your prosperity will continue and none of this happen."

"Father, this is just stupid," snorted Amel. "You're the supreme ruler. You have nothing to apologize for...to anyone." Turning to Daniel, he said, "Daniel, I respect you for your integrity, great intelligence and wisdom. I'm sorry that you are indulging in the myths of the spirit world. I thought you, of all men in this court, would refrain from this claptrap."

"Amel, stop," Nebuchadnezzr's voice snapped like a whip in the room. "Daniel is speaking his heart. You and I both know he can't do otherwise. Whether what he says is true or not, he believes it and continues to be honest even when it could bring him harm."

Nebuchadnezzar stepped close to face Daniel and took his face in his hands, "You are the most honest man I know. Thank you for speaking forthrightly to me. You will be richly rewarded. Now, go get some rest from your journey."

The King turned to Amel saying, "Look at Daniel and see the face of honesty...a man you can forever trust. Would we all have that character." With that he turned and strode back into his bedchamber.

Amel crossed to Daniel and placing his hand on his back began to usher him to the door leading into the foyer, "You are a courageous man. You don't mince any words. I cannot believe this mumbo-jumbo about the tree and angels and my father becoming a bull, but that's all right. You brought him back to his senses and restored calm to the palace. We all thank you for that."

At the doorway, Daniel stopped and bowed before the Crown Prince, "My Lord, God works in mysterious ways. I beg you to keep an open mind about His sovereignty."

Amel stared at him, looking puzzled yet cynical, then quickly walked through the foyer and down the palace steps.

Chapter 2
THE SCAM
572 BC

Within a few weeks, things began to settle down as life at the palace returned to its normal pace. Although disturbed by his dream and Daniel's warning, the King was able to shrug it off and once more began to work with his son on the various building projects they envisioned for their capital city, Babylon. After constructing the hanging gardens for Amytis, other challenges paled by comparison. But the Procession Way that Amel had just completed seemed once again to jump-start their creative juices. Their immediate focus was the re-design of the central market.

Rumblings within the King's court persisted. Nebuchadnezzar's emotional breakdown revealed a soft spot that gave courtiers courage to openly jockey for greater power. Fed up with these insubordinations, Nebuchadnezzar decided to play a heavy hand and elevated Daniel directly under him to rule his vast kingdom which now included Mesopotamia, Syria, Phoenicia, Israel and northern Arabia. For all practical purposes, Daniel was in charge of the Babylonian government; everyone in the hierarchy answered to him. To soften the blow, Daniel established a Governing Council composed of approximately thirty leaders from the city representing the military, priesthood, farmers and growers, merchants, and the King's court. Unfortunately, it didn't stop the insolence; it only exacerbated it.

At age sixty-two, Nebuchadnezzar began moving into his statesman years, tired of going to war and dealing with all the affairs of governing the millions of people who inhabited his lands. He had long ago determined that Amel-Marduk was to succeed him and now he had the perfect teacher to train the Crown Prince in the ways of governance affairs. When Amel was in the palace with Daniel adjudicating disputes, dealing with the distribution of water, or evaluating policies proposed by the court's wise men—astrologers, magicians and princes—the political undercurrents remained calm. No one would challenge his succession to the throne.

Amel left the palace grounds early one afternoon to check preparations for the central market reconstruction which Nebuchadnezzar had completely entrusted to him. He was glad to be out in the sun and away from the endless details of administration. I'm a builder, not a governor, he thought. And while I can fight with the best, I'm not a warrior at heart. He stood on a platform that had been built for him to oversee the project and felt completely at ease. He and his father had Daniel running the kingdom. There was no one better. So let him do what he does best and I'll get back to creating this great city, he reasoned.

"Did Daniel release you early today?" a voice boomed behind him. He whirled around so fast he almost lost his balance to see Neriglissar, his arms resting on a rung of the ladder, caustically smiling at him. "And why in damnation are you re-building this market which is quite serviceable?! It all seems a waste to time and money to me," his brother-in-law snorted as he lifted himself up onto the platform. "Do yourself a favor with the priests who matter the most to your father. Work on their temples. Do you think I'd waste my time making their temples grander if there wasn't a pay-off?"

"Daniel doesn't release me. I release him," Amel shot back. He never liked Neriglissar who had married his oldest sister, Princess Kassaya, twenty-three years ago. Neriglissar was a leading courtier in Nebuchadnezzar's court who gained the King's favor by his fierce action in combat and his unswerving willingness to lead his men into impossible situations only to win the day and advance the Babylonian empire. He had been a bur in Amel's side ever since he fought with Nebuzaradan, the

Commander of the Imperial Guard, to destroy and capture Jerusalem.

As Amel softened his position with people, Neriglissar hardened to become more like Nebuchadnezzar. Each year he grew more power hungry, gathering people into his inner circle whom he could use to advance his plans to usurp the throne upon the demise of Nebuchadnezzar. He was swift to deliver justice to those who crossed him and quick to curry favor with those who could further his plans. Unscrupulous and untrustworthy, he had no friends...only people who owed him or feared him.

"Hey, I'm just kidding. But you really ought to spend time beautifying some of these temples in the city. You'll make a lot more friends that way."

"For one who doesn't buy into religious superstitions, why do you worry about appeasing the priests?" replied Amel. "You ought to go find a war to fight. You're a much better warrior than a designer or builder."

Neriglissar stood by Amel looking down on the market and across the southern axis of Babylon. He didn't respond. Both men took in the magnificence of the city. Finally Neriglissar broke the silence, "We really should, you know."

"We should what?" asked Amel as he turned to face his brother-in-law.

"We should go back to battle. It's been three years since Tyre fell. We're getting soft. There are more lands to conquer...more treasure to build our wealth. Look to the north and west of us. They're not our friends, you know."

"You know my father's not interested in opening up another battlefront when we are enjoying the most peaceful time in our lives as a nation. You're a great fighter, brother, but you might want to expand your skills away from the battlefield," said Amel as he started to climb down the ladder.

Neriglissar stopped him with his right hand, "This is the best time to take the offensive. No one is thinking they'll be attacked."

"Daniel wouldn't consider it," replied Amel as he continued downward. "Neither would my father without Daniel's concurrence."

"And that's exactly the problem," hissed Neriglissar who bent over the edge of the platform to get Amel's attention. "Where are the people who built this kingdom? The warriors, the fighters? What's a former Jewish prisoner doing running our country? And I mean *our* country. It's all wrong."

Amel looked up at Neriglissar with growing disgust. "Do yourself a favor. Go work on some temples. Daniel's not going anywhere, and neither are you."

"Daniel's not invincible...and neither are you!" retorted Neriglissar.

Realizing his voice had grown louder, Neriglissar scrambled down the ladder to join Amel. Stepping directly into his path, he said, "I deserve better. You didn't defeat Jerusalem. You didn't topple Tyre. I did. And I will get my due." He turned abruptly and walked off, gathering his entourage that had been waiting for him on the streets below.

~

Irritation at Daniel's rise to second in command of the Babylonian empire turned to hate as Neriglissar rode back to his palace tucked in the northeast corner of the palace grounds. As he reflected that his palace was an after-thought . . . not included on the central avenue of royal residences within the palace grounds . . . his anger grew.

His encounter with Amel-Marduk reminded him that he, the greatest warrior in the kingdom, no longer had direct access to Nebuchadnezzar. He was therefore denied the necessary platform from which to claim the throne upon the King's death. Nebuchadnezzar had acknowledged his greatness years ago when he gave his oldest daughter, Kassaya, in marriage to him as a reward for his feats on the battlefield. His inner dialogue erupted into spoken words catching his lieutenants off guard, "Amel is no leader. He couldn't possibly take command and rule with the relentless force of his father."

"Sire?" questioned an aide not understanding Neriglissar's intent but certainly his anger as this wasn't the first time it had spilled out publicly. "It may be better to talk of these things in the palace and not on the streets."

Neriglissar scowled at his own carelessness and replied, "You're right." The light banter that had been taking place among his soldiers stopped. They knew well their leader's volatility; no one wanted to trigger it. Their silence allowed Neriglissar to wallow in his bitterness.

Surely, he thought, there must be a way to thwart Daniel's power. I can't kill him. The King would never forgive that. He is a scrupulous man of integrity. It would be hard to find any shady dealings to exploit. How can I do away with him?

"Wait." Neriglissar abruptly reined his trotting horse to a stop as the rest of his party collided with each other at the sudden halt. He turned to them, a smile coming over his face: "I want to see Antiosyss. We're going back the way we came . . . to the ziggurat. He's probably there."

As an idea began to form in his mind, he picked up the pace and put the horses into a cantor. Those on the streets recognized the mark of royalty and quickly scattered as the horses swept by. When they reached Procession Way, he slowed to a walk to take in the splendor of the boulevard. He had to admit that Amel's gold lions lining the wide expanse were quite stunning. With this recognition the bile he held for Amel bubbled up and his mission took on greater import.

When they reached the ziggurat, he inquired of the priests at the foot of the steps where Antiosyss might be found. "He's in the Temple of Marduk making preparations for tomorrow's ceremony," replied the senior of the two priests. "I'll be glad to go find him for you."

"No," said Neriglissar, "don't interrupt him. Tell him I'd like to have him join us for dinner tonight in my palace. No one else . . . just my wife, me and him. It will be the usual evening meal hour." He waved his hand to those with him to follow as he turned his horse, "Back to my palace."

~

The main course had just been served when Antiosyss picked up his cup of wine to toast his hosts. "To long life," he said. Taking a sip, he replaced the cup on the table and began to eat, "Tell me, my friend . . . I know there is a reason we are together this evening. What is on your mind?"

Kassaya laughed, "You know my husband too well, Antiosyss. I'm surprised that he made it this far into the evening without taking you into his confidence."

"I'm honored by your remark, Princess. Surely you know that I—that the priesthood—holds your husband in highest regard. You would both be such wonderful successors to the throne."

"Antiosyss," spoke Neriglissar slowly, "I need your advice. You are not only a wise man but one who has the ear of the spirit world and Marduk himself. For what I seek, I need every power I can call upon."

A servant entered to fill the wine cups. The conversation stopped until he had completed his task. As he was leaving, Kassaya said to him "Leave us alone until we call for you."

He bowed, "Yes, your highness," and exited.

"I thought you didn't take our religious beliefs seriously," smiled Antiosyss.

"Ah, but I do," demurred Neriglissar. "It wasn't all a waste of your time to instruct me in the ways of Marduk and temple worship. I'm certainly no priest, but I've learned a bit. Not every battle can be won by might alone."

"So, speak. How can I help you?"

"It's Daniel," Kassaya spit out. "This new position my father has granted him puts us ever farther away from the throne."

"Yes, we have a common enemy," smiled Antiosyss as he took another sip of wine.

Neriglissar leaned forward, now intently focused on Antiosyss. "Daniel has to be stopped. How, is the question? But an idea began to dawn on me today. If we could somehow discredit his integrity his power base might begin to weaken. Even the King's confidence in him would be shaken. The question is, as I said, how can we do this in such a way that it cannot be traced back to us."

"I, too, have been thinking along the same line. You know, one of the most contentious issues for the people is food . . . its availability and price. Since the near famine we suffered eight years ago, this topic has never been far from the minds of all, courtiers and common folk alike." Antiosyss paused to let this thought sink in.

"Go on," encouraged Neriglissar.

"Everyone can use a little more money, no?" asked Antiosyss to which Neriglissar nodded in assent. "What if we made it worthwhile for our largest farmers to contrive a grain shortage in the upcoming harvest? We haven't had a rainy growing season. It wouldn't be that difficult to conceal a good portion of the upcoming harvest. If we can make it more profitable for them to store the harvest than sell it, they will gladly do so."

"But what does this have to do with toppling Daniel?" asked Neriglissar. "It would be hard to pin this on him."

"No, no, not the food shortage," said Antiosyss. "That is but the set up for what we do next."

The three talked late into the evening, every idea feeding on each other. A plan was coming together that spelled trouble for Daniel.

~

"You want me to do what?" asked Leandrus, the major grower in the Babylonian region.

"Look, you win three times on this deal," explained Gormen. "You put half of your harvest in storage and sell the rest. Your taxes are delayed...cut in half because your sales are half of what they would otherwise be. You hold the grain for a few months and then parcel it out on the market and pay the rest of your taxes then. Because food will become scarce, you get a better price when you do sell it. On top of this, I give you a silver shekel for every twenty bushels of grain you store."

"But what if I get caught? What if the authorities start investigating and find my storage sheds?" replied Leandrus. "Then I stand to lose big."

"They're only going to know if you tell them," retorted Gorman, tired of endlessly reciting the plan to the farmers on his list.

This was Gorman's third day convincing the growers to join in the plan Antiosyss and Neriglissar had designed to precipitate a food shortage. He didn't know where the plan came from; all that mattered to him were the two shekels of silver he pocketed for every farmer he recruited. He had been approached by a casual acquaintance, one of the sub-rosa bosses in the central market, to take on this assignment. If he kept his mouth shut, convinced the farmers to take the bribe, and didn't talk about it to anyone, he figured he'd move up a few levels in the city's underworld.

"Everyone's in on this," Gorman insisted to Leandrus. "Build a few hidden storage facilities, hide the grain for a few months, and then when the politics shake out a few people who aren't especially liked by the court power structure you can put the grain back on the market. No one will even care that you were part of a cabal because by then they all will be happy with their winnings."

Gorman paused, then pulled out a mina of silver worth 60 shekels and put it in Leandrus' hands, "Take this as a down payment. You have a lot more to come."

Leandrus felt the weight of the silver burning into his hands. I've never had this much pure wealth before in my life, he thought. I want to do this.

"What if I get caught?" he spoke up. "What if the authorities find my grain before everything plays out as you describe?"

Gorman folded his arms in front of him and smiled confidently at Leandrus. "The people I represent are more powerful than anyone who could be looking at you. Trust me, you don't need to worry about that."

Leandrus had a lingering doubt or two but could not take his eyes off the silver in his hands. With the extent of his land holdings, he could easily make tenfold of what he had in his hands. The risk was more than worth it.

"All right, I'm in. Let's hope this thing gets resolved quickly so we can empty the storage bins by next spring."

~

As the early summer harvest was gathered, the markets realized much less product than in previous years. Questions were raised, but quickly deflected by the growers giving as reasons a scarcity of rain and excessive water run-off during the winter and spring months, crop damage by pests, and an unusual fungal disease. As prices increased and availability of food shrunk, it wasn't long before the people of Babylon began to protest to the merchants who, in turn, complained to Shadrach, the Administrator for Agriculture in Nebuchadnezzar's court. They had suffered crop shortages before so this wasn't all that unusual. But given that the fields looked pretty healthy leading up to harvest time, he sent several teams of men into the countryside to investigate.

They reported the same results whether they went east or west, north or south. Something had happened this year to result in a shortage. Since the losses were apparently universal, it didn't occur to them that anything other than natural causes underlay the problem. Shadrach, in turn, reported to Daniel that the food supply was jeopardized for the year and encouraged him to pursue alternatives, specifically recommending sending a delegation to Egypt without delay to negotiate a major grain purchase.

Daniel and the delegation returned to Babylon three months later, worn out from the trip but pleased with their results. They had managed to structure a deal whereby grain shipments would be coming to Babylon weekly, subsidized by the government to maintain previous year's prices. Calm once more settled over the kingdom as a crisis had been averted.

The day he returned, Neriglissar and Antiosyss enjoyed an evening of specially crafted beer served with a sumptuous meal. There was never a food shortage in the palaces of the ruling class elite. Lifting their glasses in a toast, Antiosyss couldn't contain the smile that spread across his face, "To a most successful plan." They downed a sizeable portion of the liquid, very pleased with themselves.

"It's time we unfold phase two," said Neriglissar withdrawing a document from under his robes. "Here is a decree sent to all the growers asking them to withhold one-half of their crops from market signed by none other than Daniel himself."

"Is the signature and seal an excellent copy?" asked Antiosyss. "You know the King's aides and the Governing Council are going to examine it carefully when Daniel denies any knowledge of this."

Neriglissar rose to hand the document to Antiosyss. He stood drinking his beer as Antiosyss held the paper into the light looking for any sign of fraudulence. He ran his finger over the seal of Daniel's office. It felt authentic and certainly appeared official. Handing it back, the high priest nodded his head quite pleased with the results. "Excellent. There will be no question of its legitimacy. What are you going to do with this?"

"I'm going to get it to Nolter—you know—the most vocal merchant in the central market. I'll use several people so it cannot be traced to me. I suspect once he opens this, we won't have to do a thing but watch Daniel fall from grace. Nolter is a hothead and isn't going to keep this silent."

"Good plan, my friend," Antiosyss concurred, "a good plan. We should be done with Daniel in a few days." Antiosyss refilled their beer tankards as Neriglissar sat back down to finish his dinner, both fully satisfied with how well their strategy to discredit Daniel was playing out.

~

"I thought for once we had someone whom we could trust!" shouted Nolter. "Daniel has not only betrayed us who manage the central market, but he's put all of our people at risk at his gain," he continued as he waved the document wildly in the air further exciting all the merchants who had come with him to protest to Shadrach. He thrust it into Shadrach's hands, "Look at this! Is that not his signature and seal? He caused the grain shortage so he could make a deal with Egypt to benefit himself."

"Treason," shouted several of Nolter's colleagues.

"Does the King know about this?" yelled another.

"He sold us out! I wonder how long he's been conspiring with the Egyptians?"

Shadrach was transfixed on the decree in his hands. He could not believe what he saw. Daniel simply would not do this. What was going on? He stood up and in a terse voice loud enough for everyone in the room to hear said, "I tell you right now that there is an explanation for this. Daniel would never take a bribe . . . would never hurt the kingdom." He started to leave, then turned at the doorway to face the angry merchants, "I will get to the truth of this and I will report back to you."

"It's pretty obvious, isn't it . . . Daniel's no dummy. He's probably been doing this for some time, right under our noses," snorted Nolter as he snatched the decree from the hands of Shadrach. He turned to his friends, "Let's not wait for more lies from the Governor. We need to open this up for everyone to see, and take it to every member of the Governing Council. This needs to go directly to the King."

~

The court was in an uproar over the next two days. Nolter and his group showed the decree to everyone they could find who had a position within the royal palace and the Governing Council. Their anger was unrequited. They were on a mission to unseat a traitor. That he had personally gained was of no consequence to them. Daniel's crime in their eyes is that he had robbed every one of them in the process. This was unforgiveable.

Seizing the moment, Neriglissar leaped into the resulting political frenzy to lobby the King's councilors and courtiers in support of Daniel's ouster. Playing a more sinister role in the background and only surfacing to act when needed, Antiosyss preyed upon the fears of the supernatural that ruled many of these men's lives. They didn't meet much resistance since nearly everyone who had access to the royal palace held some sort of grudge against Daniel, given he had shut down the corruption that had previously ran rampant. The few exceptions they encountered were easily convinced to go along with the majority when threatened with a loss of court position or bodily harm. Nothing was overt; rather, it was implied that certain protections they enjoyed could easily be removed leaving them exposed to the disgruntled masses eager to exact revenge.

Word traveled fast to Amel-Marduk who dismissed the whole thing as but another attempt to unseat Daniel. He had been through a number of these over the years, although he did admit to himself that this one had some teeth given the decree that they kept talking about had Daniel's seal and signature. He still trusted Daniel implicitly. If he had asked the growers to reduce what was available for market, he reasoned Daniel had a legitimate purpose. At that moment, he was more focused on new design ideas for the central market.

Nebuchadnezzar's close relationship with Daniel prevented anyone from telling him what had transpired until the entire Governing Council was of one mind and could approach him in force. The palace servants and the courtiers had seen in the past what happened to messengers of bad news, especially when they were wrong. Better to keep quiet and let the King hear from a source he could not easily dismiss.

By the end of the second day, there remained one hold-out. Polynices was a wealthy patron of the court who had never needed to engage in anything other than honorable behavior as his wisdom and good business sense had enabled him to amass a considerable fortune. He enjoyed significant favor with Nebuchadnezzar and had supported Daniel from the beginning of his rise to power as he valued the Governor's integrity.

Tired of the uproar at the palace, Polynices returned home early in the afternoon. He was seated in the courtyard of his spacious house, calmed by the babbling water of the fountain as he reflected on the chaos at court. A servant interrupted his thoughts to announce a visitor. The high priest of the temple, no less, wished to see him.

"Bring him in," he instructed the servant, his mind racing to grasp what this could be about.

He rose from his chair as Antiosyss entered. The two men grasped arms in greeting. "Please, make yourself comfortable," Polynices gestured to a divan adjacent to where he had been seated. "Some nectar for my guest," requested Polynices of his servant.

"That will not be necessary," Antiosyss curtly spoke to the servant. Remaining standing he added, "Leave us alone. No interruptions." He took his eyes off Polnices to hurl a dangerous glance at the young man who suddenly had become quite frightened. Upon his exit, Antiosyss turned back to Polynices, both his silence and stare significantly lowering the temperature in this outdoor oasis.

Finally he spoke, "Have you no fear of our god, Marduk? Do you realize you are taking on the supreme ruler of the spirit world as well as the entire priesthood by your refusal to call Daniel to account for his treasonous actions?"

Neither man moved. Polynices had no doubt that the supernatural world and Marduk, its leader, were anything less than real. He had no idea Antiosyss had entered the fray to remove Daniel, and that meant he—Polynices—was no longer engaging in court politics. This had escalated into something much more terrifying.

Polynices was the first to avert his eyes, swallowing with effort. His body shifted backward to put some space between himself and Antiosyss. He had been slammed by the growing evil that Antiosyss's aura was exuding. He recognized his family and very being were in imminent danger if he made the wrong move. As much as he respected Daniel and wanted to do the right thing, it was not going to be at the expense of losing his wealth, his position and even his life.

"What do you want me to do?" His words came out as barely a whisper.

"Join with the others. This is going to the King tomorrow. We must be unified."

Again, neither man moved. It was Antiosyss who made the first move this time, crossing to stand with his face directly in front of Polynices's face, less than two inches apart. "Do you understand?" hissed Antiosyss.

Unable to bring a sound to his throat, Polynices nodded his assent, then dropped his eyes to the ground. Antiosyss abruptly turned and left the house.

~

Daniel and his supporters had not been living in a cocoon since Nolter and his fellow merchants erupted. They knew the decree he was bandying about was a fake. What they didn't know is why the farmers had such a low crop yield. Shadrach, in particular, took it upon himself to get out of the city and spend time talking to the growers in the fields nearby Babylon. He was determined to get some answers.

Late in the afternoon of his second day, Shadrach dropped in on a large farm owned by a man he knew well and liked. He hoped he could learn something from him; for the past thirty-six hours he had come up empty.

"Samir," greeted Shadrach, "it's good to see you. How is your family?"

Smiling broadly, Samir replied, "All is well, sire . . . all is well."

He was glad to see Shadrach whom he respected. Since Shadrach had become the Administrator of Agriculture, the farmers had fared well. The black market had been minimized, pay-offs to officials had ceased, and the lot of farmers in general had risen within the social fabric of the kingdom.

They talked at length as they relaxed under a shade tree in the front of Samir's home. When the conversation finally got around to the recent harvest and the shortage of grain, Samir began to grow noticeably cooler. Something is up, thought Shadrach. If I'm going to make any sense out of all this, Samir is probably my best chance. He decided to cut to the quick.

Shadrach let the conversation lull into silence, then he leaned forward to look Samir in the face, "Samir, what is going on? Tell me the truth, my friend. No incriminations. I just want the truth, and I am certain you know it."

Struggling to keep his composure, Samir asked, "What do you mean?"

"I know you're hiding something from me. Our relationship has never been clouded, but today there is a storm in our conversation. Do you not think I cannot sense this? Evil is soon to attack the highest level of our kingdom. What will result can only be very bad. I don't want that. You don't want that!"

Samir couldn't respond for fear of dissembling in his emotions. He opened his mouth to speak, but only swallowed hard. His eyes were wide with fear at being found out. What would happen to him, his farm, and all like him? It was too much for a simple farmer to handle.

"Do you know what is going on back in Babylon?" asked Shadrach gently.

Samir looked up at him, shaking his head no.

"A very just and fair man—Daniel—is being accused of ordering you and all the farmers to put half of their grain in storage at harvest time. Did you receive this order? Did you see it?"

He paused to let it all sink in before continuing, "You do not want to see Daniel removed from his governorship. If he goes, everything you loathed from the past will return. The bribes . . . the corruption . . . disrespect of your family. All of it comes back." Again . . . a pause. "Do you really want that, Samir?"

Samir suddenly stood up. "Come with me," he said as he strode at a fast pace into his fields. They walked for almost a half a mile before they came to a large mound of earth. Samir walked around to the narrow end and began pulling aside the wood slabs that were somewhat hidden under the dirt. As he threw the last couple of pieces aside, Shadrach's eyes had adjusted to the dark inside to see bushels and bushels of grain concealed within the mound.

"Unbelievable!" exclaimed Shadrach. "Is this what you did with your grain at harvest?"

Samir nodded, "We were told to do so."

"By who?"

"He said it came from high authority within the palace. What could I do? None of us really had any option."

"There's more to this than just an order, Samir. You've been honest with me to this point. Don't hold anything else back," urged Shadrach grabbing him by the shoulders.

Samir froze. Revealing the pay-off he received to conceal the grain could mean the end of his life. What to do? He broke away from Shadrach afraid to speak.

"If you really believed you were being given an official order, I will support and defend you. But I have to know all that transpired. What accompanied this order to make you act on it?"

Samir remained silent. Shadrach tried another tack. "Whatever it was, I will not hold it against you. You were obviously lied to because this did not come from my office and I am in charge of all agricultural affairs. So someone acted illegally, and whatever he or they did cannot be held against you."

"They gave us one shekel of silver for every twenty bushels of grain we concealed," Samir said almost inaudibly. "I knew this was probably not the right way to do things, but he kept persisting that this came from royal authority." He paused, his eyes downward in shame, "Besides I had never seen real money like this before in my life. I couldn't say no."

Shadrach gave a low whistle. This was real money. Whoever supplied it had enormous resources. There was no reason for the King to do this, and it was hard to imagine that Amel-Marduk would take his eyes off his building projects to get involved in such a scheme. Pretty interesting, he mused. I've got to get back to Babylon. Daniel will help sort this out.

"Samir, thank you for telling me the truth. Don't worry. You will not suffer any consequences. I give you my word. And please let the other growers know they must come forward of their own accord. If they do, they will not be punished."

They walked back to Samir's house where Shadrach met those accompanying him to return hastily to the city.

~

"The King, his highness King Nebuchadnezzar," bellowed the palace guard Captain.

The room grew quiet as Nebuchadnezzar walked into the room and proceeded to his throne. No one could remember when the room had been so full of people. Usually it looked quite large with only the thirty or so councilors and wise men present at most deliberations. Today, there must have been several hundred men crowding the walls.

Nebuchadnezzar did not sit as was his normal custom. He surveyed the crowd with a scowl and said, "The smell of blood must be in the air today. Like lions, you come to feast," he laughed cynically and then sat down calling out, "What is the first issue of the day?"

No one moved as no one wanted to be recognized as the provocateur to challenge the King's highest appointed official, Daniel.

"Well," exclaimed Nebuchadnezzar loudly, "you're all here to see someone die. Get on with it."

The King's councilors and wise men looked from one to another and with the movement of their eyes rose in unison to approach the King.

"My Lord, we have discovered a most serious grievance and threat to the kingdom." It was impossible to distinguish who was speaking.

"Speak up. And come forward so I can see who is talking," said the King.

The group moved together as one to approach the throne. Mysonus, their spokesman, stepped to the center, "My Lord," said Mysonus, "it has come to our attention that the grain shortage of this fall was contrived to the benefit of one man."

He took the decree out from his robe and held it up for the King to see. "Our growers were ordered by decree signed by that man to put one-half of their harvest into storage. This resulted in the necessity to negotiate grain shipments from Egypt to sustain our people until the next harvest. This same individual who ordered the concealment then profited substantially from the Egyptians for helping them sell their surplus grain to us."

"And who is this man?" thundered Nebuchadnezzar.

Taking more courage by the King's interest, Mysonus replied, "My Lord, he is none other than Daniel."

The King neither moved nor spoke, his demeanor unchanged. Those bringing the accusation began to whisper affirmations among themselves, congratulating themselves for revealing a contemptuous traitor within the King's inner circle.

"Quiet!" commanded the King, rising from the throne. The room froze. "Do you know the truth about this? Do you have any idea what happened and who did it? You are all so quick to condemn the one honest man in the kingdom. Are you so filled with jealousy and hatred that you can no longer see anything clearly? You rush to judgment because it pleases you, not because it is what is right for the kingdom. You disgust me!"

By now the entire group who had approached the King had melted back into their seats. Everyone else in the room was immobilized, their backs deep into the walls, no one wanting to be there any longer. The King was angry, and it wasn't directed at Daniel.

"Give me that decree," Nebuchadnezzar ordered Mysonus.

Stepping forward, Mysonus bowed and handed the decree to the King. "Sire, it appears to be official in every regard."

"Are you all so blinded by your greed and envy that you could not recognize an obvious act of sabotage?" snarled Nebuchadnezzar. "Are you that stupid?! And you are supposed to be Daniel's Governing Council?"

Holding the decree in front of him, he proceeded to break it up into tiny pieces. "This is what I think of this decree. It is so obviously phony, and none of you had the clarity of mind to consider its absurdity. What do we have here? A council of idiots!!"

Nebuchadnezzar stepped down from his throne onto the main floor where his councilors sat. As he moved, no one remained in his chair. He began circling the room, looking in the eyes of all who were gathered as he spoke.

"I heard of this two days ago from Daniel himself. He sent Shadrach into the farms to investigate. Last night, we heard what had taken place. Daniel made the effort to uncover the truth," he roared. "Which one of you even thought to verify this lie? No, you were all too busy lapping up the drivel, and truth be damned!"

He stopped in mid stride and turned to Zocor, the Captain of the palace guards, "Bring in that worthless piece of dung."

Upon his signal, the two guards at the entry parted the crowd in front of them with their spears. Through the doorway came two other soldiers dragging a man who had been flogged within an inch of death, his blood and pieces of flesh dirtying the floor. Gorman, barely conscious, attempted to lift his head to see the King as he was thrown to the floor. It was a horrible sight. Several of the bystanders in back slipped out the door barely able to contain the vomit rising in their throats.

"I'll tell you what happened . . . just like I have to tell you my dreams that you don't ever seem to know. This human scum paid our farmers one shekel of silver for every twenty bushels of grain they put in storage and kept from market. Not only that, but he then received two shekels of silver for every farmer he coerced." Nebuchadnezzar paused to let this information sink in. "Now that's a lot of money by the time the plot was fully unfolded. Not many people in this kingdom have that much money unless . . . unless it was a group effort."

The murmurs started immediately. "No!" "We had no idea." "Not me," emanated from the assembly. What was to celebrate the revelation of a traitor had turned into a nightmare with the possibility of imminent death for many in the room.

Nebuchadnezzar let the panic in the room mount as he returned to his throne and sat. He raised his hand for silence and spoke quietly in a steel-edged voice, "This man did not do this on his own. Unfortunately, by the time the guards found the man who hired him, he had been killed, leaving no scent on the trail to the top of this cabal. We may never know who was involved. This much I know. If and when I do find them, death will be too good for them."

He leaned back in his throne, and waved his hand dismissively, "Now, get out. All of you."

~

Within the dark recesses of the Temple of Marduk huddled two men, each carefully scanning the environs for those who might overhear their muted conversation.

"Will your men talk?" whispered Antiosyss.

"No. They wouldn't know what to say even if they were apprehended and tortured," replied Neriglissar. "Everyone in the chain has been killed. They were killed for reasons far removed from our scheme by unknowing men in my command. The trail is stone cold. Nothing can be traced to us."

Antiosyss rose from the stone ledge on which he was seated and gripped Neriglissar's arm in pledge, "This was a noble effort on our part. Daniel must be destroyed if we are to rise. Let us continue to plot his demise."

Neriglissar smiled wanly as he returned Antiosyss' grasp, "Yes, the fight will go on, but it's more difficult now and we must be much wiser. Daniel is stronger than ever. This has only increased his stature in the eyes of the King and the people."

Antiosyss gestured around him to the altar before a large statue of Marduk. Atop it, a fire burned brightly. They were in the sacred chamber of the temple where only death lurked and none but the highest of the priesthood hierarchy dared enter. Together they stood, facing the essence of evil. Antiosyss took Neriglissar's arm and steered him towards the foot of the altar. He knelt as did Neriglissar.

Looking up at the statue of Marduk, the high priest said, "Next time, we bring the powers of the spirit world into play."

In a loud voice, Antiosyss prayed, "Marduk, supreme being of the spirits...we call upon you for your wisdom and strength. We surrender to your almighty power." He swayed into a trance-like state, then fell limp on the altar. Startled, Neriglissar leaped to his feet moving quickly backward from the terrifying image above him, his mind racing.

Chapter 3
TRANSFORMATION
571 BC

Narseniah sashayed through the market, stopping every
now and then to look more closely at the fruit she was ostensibly
purchasing. Every man's eyes were on her, her full figure
illuminated beneath her transparent silky robes. Her sheer beauty
commanded attention, and she loved it. Nothing was left to
chance. She had long ago learned how to play her charms on the
lustful desires always burning in men's hearts.

Her eyes searched the aisles in front of her as she looked
for Laconius. She knew he came once a week to the market with
Daniel's kitchen servants to sample the produce himself and
oversee their buying for the day's meal preparation. She had
never met him, but she knew who he was. It was time for her to
get into action and get close to the second most powerful man in
the empire.

There he was. A dozen stalls down. She paid for the
grapes she put in her basket and hurried through the crowd to join
him as he was looking over a beautiful display of vegetables.

"When were these picked?" he asked the merchant,
pointing at some eggplant.

"Excellent choice," smiled the merchant. "These were
picked yesterday and brought to market early this morning. I've
never seen such wonderful color and texture." He picked one up
to hand to Laconius.

Before the exchange could be made, Narseniah stole the
eggplant out of his hand and brought it to her nose, "He's
absolutely right. The scent is extraordinary and the body
beautifully configured."

Both Laconius and the merchant looked at who had interrupted them, pleased to see such a beautiful woman interacting with them. This type simply did not come to the market.

"Not nearly as beautiful as you, my lady," smiled Laconius.

"No truer words were ever spoken," confirmed the merchant. "It is my pleasure to serve such a lovely and wise woman."

Narseniah looked seductively at them, confident she had them both in the palm of her hand. To the merchant she said, "Please wrap up three of these for me." Then she looked at Laconius with a playful smile, "I know who you are."

Yielding to her charms, Laconius laughed, "And who am I that such a pretty lady would know, let alone approach?"

"You are the Governor's chief aide," she said. "I seldom come here, but when I saw you in the crowd, I had to meet you. Besides, you stand out so it wasn't hard to see you." She gestured to the throng surrounding them, "Not one of these comes close to sharing your handsome features and stature."

"Why...thank you. And who are you, beautiful lady?" grinned Laconius, fully captured by her charm.

"My name is Narseniah. You may have heard of me. I am the daughter of High Priest Antiosyss."

A frown fell over his face hearing the name. This was not lost on Narseniah who quickly added, "But I'm not like him. I stay away from the temple. That's not for me."

The smile returned to Laconius' face. "I'm glad to hear that, Narseniah. Your father is a very powerful and dangerous man. It must not be easy to stand apart from him. I applaud you if you are able to do so."

She paid for her produce, took the eggplants from the merchant, and turned to walk away. She stopped after two steps and turned back to flash a seductive smile at Laconius, "I do . . . and . . . thank you. I hope we see each other again." She quickly walked out of the market leaving Laconius to stare at the backside of the most beautiful woman he had ever seen. His mind was awash with feelings and desires, not all of them virtuous.

~

The beat of the drums grew louder and faster as the flames of the fire on the altar leapt toward the grotesque image of Marduk suspended from the stones high above, their shadows flickering on the walls of the cavernous inner sanctum of the temple. The priests who surrounded the altar were swaying back and forth, caught up in the frenzy of the moment. Antiosyss had leaped onto the altar to dance wildly in and through the flames as he incanted Marduk to manifest himself to the assembled faithful.

Neriglasser moved out from the hidden alcove where Antiosyss had placed him to watch the temple ceremony. Most ceremonies in the temple were never open to those outside the priesthood. He had been cautioned to remain unseen but his view was blocked, and he wanted to see for himself what powers his friend possessed. He could feel an evilness in the room, and it frightened him. Yet, he had to stay to see if any of this was real. If Marduk could be summoned to de-throne Daniel, I'll become a believer and use him, he mused.

"Aye—eeh!" came a shrieking scream from the back of the room. A person split the concentric circles of swaying priests and careened towards the altar.

Antiosyss stopped dancing to stand motionless atop the altar. He lifted his arms and commanded, "Silence!"

At the bottom of the steps leading up to the altar knelt a figure clothed in black, its hair on fire. The figure rose and threw off the robes that encased her. She stood naked, her hair continuing to flame without destroying a single hair.

"Narseniah," whispered Neriglissar to himself. He had met her a few times in Antiosyss's quarters within the temple and, like all men, had been enchanted by her beauty. But standing completely nude only forty feet away from him, she shook him to his core. His eyes were riveted on her.

Antiosyss signaled the drummers to begin again, their rhythms slow at first but then increasing in tempo. Narseniah started to dance, deftly using the altar steps to enhance her poses. She was all over the room, dancing in and around the priests who formed the first circle surrounding the altar; she leaped back onto the steps, then down to sweep through another circle of priests until she had worked her way to the back of the room and then forward again. As the drums quickened, her dance became more intense and possessed. Flames began to protrude from her fingers, her jumps taking her higher than humanly possible.

What is this about? thought Neriglissar, never taking his eyes off Narseniah. This is not normal. This woman has powers like I've never seen!

The drumming reached a frenetic pace, humanly impossible to sustain. Narseniah sprung onto the altar to join Antiosyss, each on either side of the flaming fire. Without warning, she fell rigid into the inferno, her head caught by her father who slowly lowered her body to rest on the blaze. She reached her arms out toward the statue of Marduk and screamed, "I am yours. Take me!"

Antiosyss abruptly signaled the drums to cease. All motion and sound stopped. After a full ten seconds, Antiosyss quelled the flames simply by the motion of his hands. Narseniah lay on the burning coals, drained but her eyes wild and alive. She slowly stood, her nakedness glowing without evidence of a burn mark on her body or a single singed hair.

"Great is the power of Marduk," shouted Antiosyss.

"Great is the power of Marduk," echoed the assembled priests.

"And great is the power of Narseniah," she exclaimed.

"Great is the power of Narseniah," murmured the priests.

"Great are the powers of Narseniah," mumbled Neriglissar who stood transfixed and unable to move by what he had just witnessed. She is undoubtedly the most beautiful woman on earth he thought. But she is also the most frightening person I will ever know. He turned and exited the room by the tiny corridor in which he had been concealed.

~

Laconius began to look forward to his visits to the central market which were now enhanced by his encounters with Narseniah. Often they would stroll through the various stalls together, assessing the produce and making small talk. Beside the fact that he was deeply smitten by her, Laconius enjoyed the envy of other men who saw them together. Never in his life did he expect to engage the attention of such a beautiful woman, and he was not going to let anything prevent this relationship from blooming.

One morning Narseniah casually mentioned that she was curious about his God, "You don't have a temple for him. How do you worship him?"

"He's not confined to any space," replied Laconius. "He's everywhere . . . all the time. We can pray to Him anywhere . . . in our homes, on the streets, even right here in the market."

"But don't you have special ceremonies to conjure up his spirit? How do you show him honor?"

"Daniel says we honor Him with our lives . . . the way we live and conduct ourselves with others."

"That's a bit difficult to understand," she laughed. "You don't see him. You don't have a temple for him. You just . . . you just imagine him out of the air and he's there?"

Laconius knew what he believed but she was asking questions he felt uneasy answering. Daniel could field her curiosity, but he would stumble and the last thing he wanted was to lose the confidence of this woman who infatuated him.

An idea popped into his head, "You need to meet Daniel. He can answer anything you ask. Would you like to?"

"It would be an honor to meet him," she said. "But how can I? Would he even give me the opportunity? I mean, he is the most powerful man in the kingdom next to the King." She giggled and grabbed his arm, "Just to see his home and where you live would be a thrill."

~

Pleased that he could do something for her, Laconius arranged for her to come to the house to meet Daniel after lunch one day before he returned to his duties in his offices in the royal palace.

"Tell me, Laconius, who is this woman you want me to meet?" asked Daniel. "Where does she come from? What is her name? There's no problem having her visit us, but I'd like to know a little more about her."

"She is the most beautiful woman in the world," gushed Laconius. Suddenly blushing, he quickly added, "But she's also very smart and sincere." Not knowing how Daniel might take this next piece of information, Laconius hesitated then continued: "She says that she is the daughter of Antiosyss."

"You're not serious! Do you know who Antiosyss is?" exclaimed Daniel.

"Yes, he's the priest of the Temple of Marduk, but hear me out, sire. Lately, we have been talking a lot about God. She told me she and her father have little in common and . . . well, to be honest, I can't answer her questions any longer. I thought you could help her."

"That's all good and well, but you must be very careful, Laconius. Antiosyss is not pleased that I am Governor of the land. He would like nothing better than to see me destroyed. This is not a nice man, but he is very clever."

Swallowing hard and now very uncomfortable Laconius replied, "I know. I was startled to learn whose daughter she is, but her interest in knowing more about our God . . . well, it won me over. She has so many questions! I can't begin to answer them. I told her you could though, and when I suggested she needed to talk with you she got very excited. If she wasn't seeking answers, I don't think she'd consider coming here."

There was a knock at the outer door. Daniel gestured to the entry. Laconius took his leave of Daniel to escort Narseniah into the house. They entered the dining room to find Daniel rising from his chair.

"Sire, this is Narseniah," introduced Laconius. Daniel gave a slight nod as Narseniah politely bowed before him in respect of his governorship position.

"Very nice to have you in my home and to meet you, Narseniah," said Daniel. "I know your father."

Narseniah froze. Did he let me in his house just to expose me and belittle me? She collected herself and said, "He's a very powerful man with some. Not to me. I do not believe in the ways of Marduk. I don't really know what I believe in anymore."

"Laconius tells me you have an interest in God Almighty...that you have many questions?"

"Yes, my Lord. I do. I am honored to meet you and to be in your home." Her eyes took in all of the room and the corridors beyond. She couldn't believe her fortune at making it into the house of the man she was determined to bring under her powers. This was easier than she had ever hoped for, thanks to Laconius' unchecked desire for her.

"Well, then, have a look around," replied Daniel. "I really should be heading back to the palace anyway. Perhaps we can schedule some time on another day in the late afternoon or evening when we can talk at more leisure. Nothing gives me more pleasure than to talk about the wonders of our good God, especially with those eager to know truth." Daniel turned to Laconius, "Let's find some time for the three of us to talk in the next few weeks."

"What a nice man," Narseniah remarked as Daniel exited. "Please, let's do find time for us to talk. But now, Laconius," she said as she grasped his arm in hers, "show me this wonderful house."

~

The kingdom settled back into its normal routine once the contrived food shortage scare was exposed. There was some jockeying for power within the Governor's Council which was swiftly dismissed thus cementing Daniel's position and power. In matters of empire affairs, the path always ran through Daniel leaving those who would affect royal policy on the strength of their own position impotent and more frustrated than ever.

At first, Daniel was suspicious of Narseniah. But each time they discussed the nature and ways of God, she came back with more questions probing deeper than most of his devout Jewish friends, all of whom had been taken captive with him thirty-three years ago when Nebuchadnezzar first conquered Israel. Whereas his friends' faith was steeped in their culture, Narseniah's curiosity seemed Godly-inspired and sincere. His respect for her grew daily as did his comfort with her presence.

Narseniah began to be a regular visitor to Daniel's home as her pursuit of truth and inquiring mind appealed to Daniel's mentoring instincts. Cool to her at first, the house staff soon warmed to her charms and accepted her. It did not go unnoticed by Daniel that Laconius had more than a passing interest in her, and that was pleasing to him as well. Laconius had served him well for almost ten years. He was more of a son than an aide at this point. To see him take a God-fearing wife would be more than he ever dared to hope for, and so he encouraged the relationship.

Narseniah never lost sight of her objective throughout her charade. She was determined to bring Daniel under her control and was prepared to extend the subterfuge for as long as was necessary. It was clear to her that Daniel relied a great deal on Laconius who was an able administrator in his own right. With this reliance came a great deal of imbued power. Laconius held the key to her plot to usurp Daniel. She had always flirted and teased Laconius knowing that she triggered unspoken and unseen lustful urges. She knew this because it had been this way all of her life with men. She easily recognized the signs and knew how to play them. So now she started to move aggressively . . . touching him when they were alone, wearing provocative clothing that sometimes revealed more than it concealed, and offering endearing comments openly suggesting she had reciprocal feelings for him.

Her chance came unexpectedly one evening when she learned Daniel was gone for the night on business to a neighboring town. She had enjoyed dinner with Laconius and the house staff in the kitchen. Laconius was escorting her to the main entry to take her leave. In the hallway, she grasped his arm holding it tightly, the bottom of her full breast burning into his forearm.

"I want to see your private quarters," she whispered. He looked at her surprised. "It's all right, Laconius. I just would like to know where you sleep so I can imagine you when I lay down at night."

This was a bold move on her part and both of them knew it. She pressed the issue by leaning into him, her lips at his ear cooing: "Please, everyone is busy cleaning up and no one is here to even see us."

His mind was a whirlwind of emotions and images...excited and sexually alert but tempered with guilt for what he was thinking. She was so stunningly beautiful, and it was obvious she was interested in him.

"Why not?" he quipped, steering her in a direction away from the entry foyer of the house. They made their way through the grand central sitting room and past Daniel's chambers to arrive at his personal quarters—spacious and well accented.

"This is it," Laconius spoke as with his hand he swept the room for her to take in. "I am very fortunate to have this."

"But you also earned it and deserve it," Narseniah whispered, playing to his sense of ego. She crossed to his bed, turned and asked, "Do you mind if I sit down?" Not waiting for his response, she took off her outer robe and lay down seductively.

Laconius was riveted to her. So many feelings were throttling through his body. He couldn't take his eyes off her. Moreover, his mouth refused to work. He couldn't speak to answer her. He stood, his eyes filling with a longing he had long attempted to deny.

Narseniah was completely aware of the effect she was having on him. It was going well. She slowly rose from the bed, took him by his hands and led him to where she had just laid, turning him to sit down. Backing away from him but never breaking eye contact, she found the door to the room and proceeded to shut it. She stepped back to him, removing her clothing piece by piece until all that was left was skin.

"I've always wanted you since we first met," she smiled seductively. "Do you like what you see?"

The lump in his throat had become a boulder. He swallowed hard, his passions ignited beyond the point of no return. He lifted his hands and reached for her.

~

Life forever changed for Laconius. His innocence had been replaced by a burdensome guilt but even more by an overwhelming lust to possess Narseniah. She knew she finally had a potent wedge in Daniel's life that was hers to leverage at the right time. She was smart enough to know she had to play Laconius carefully. If he suspected her interest in him was strategic to accomplish other purposes, he'd turn on her in a minute.

Laconius stayed away from the market for the next few days, embarrassed at the thought of confronting Narseniah. He didn't know whether to apologize to her, speak endearingly to her, or just pretend nothing happened. His emotional confusion did not go unnoticed by Daniel and the rest of the household staff. When Daniel finally asked him if all was well on the third evening following the seduction, he realized he needed to get back into his routine and, most of all, confront Narseniah.

Early in the morning, he timidly set off for the market, still not knowing how he should act if he saw her. It wasn't long before he felt a familiar touch at his elbow.

"I've missed you, Laconius," softly said Narseniah. He nervously turned, his eyes looking at the ground as his mind raced for what to say. His eyes came to rest on her feet, then took in her beautiful body section by section until he was looking directly into her eyes.

"I love you," she mouthed the words, disarming him completely.

Trembling slightly his heart answered her, "You are the most beautiful woman I have ever seen. Can it be my good fortune that you truly care for me?

"Yes, Laconius. You are very special to me, now more than ever after our night together."

Relief flooded his face followed by a broad smile, "I didn't know what to say or how you would feel. I was afraid to find out and so I stayed away." He wanted to embrace her but was afraid to show any emotion in the public market. He put his hand on her back and directed her towards an alley feeding out of the trade arena. "Let's find somewhere we can be alone . . . away from all this," he waved at the merchants.

~

It was obvious to all that Laconius had a new lease on life. He was more charismatic than his old self, cheerily greeting each task from dawn to late evening. He seemed to gain significant efficiencies in administering Daniel's personal affairs to the point where he began to be entrusted with issues at a higher state level. He was now included in some official meetings in the palace offices where his opinion was sought and valued. Narseniah, of course, was once again a regular presence. Her beauty, which knew no equal, combined with her desire to please brought added vitality to the daily routine of Daniel's home and offices. She had yet to find the opportunity for her next move and so was patiently building her relationships for when she needed them.

At the end of another warm day, Narseniah was waiting outside by a column leading into the palace area where the Governor's offices were located. Laconius was due to pass that way and she wanted to use the remainder of the afternoon to probe for opportunities she might use to discredit Daniel. It was such a lovely day that she began to doze as she rested against a stone pillar.

What felt like cold stone encased her upper arm and squeezed painfully as she heard a snake-like hiss, "What is your business here?" Before she could turn to see her antagonist, he continued, "Don't turn to look at me. I know who you are. Why are you at the Governor's office? I know it's not for anything good." And then he laughed, vicious and guttural, relaxing his grip on her.

Narseniah jumped and whirled around to see Neriglissar sneering at her.

"So speak," he commanded.

She had seen him in the temple meeting with her father on more than a few occasions. She had heard he was furious that he no longer had direct access to the King but like everyone else had to go through Daniel. Because her father was able to see Nebuchadnezzar at will given the King's fear of Marduk and the world of the supernatural, she had always suspected Neriglissar of teaming with him to regain power.

Not so innocently she said, "I know what you're up to with my father. So what's your business with Daniel?"

"I hate the man," he spit. "But it interests me that you are here. All I can imagine is that your father is using you to pursue a plot simultaneously with the one we have in motion."

"So what if he is?"

Neriglissar moved to put his face directly in hers, their bodies touching. "Don't double-cross me."

She didn't blink, knowing if she flinched first he'd have the upper hand. Their lips almost touching, she spoke without emotion, "I have my own plan. It does not include my father."

He smiled, still very much in her face, "I told you I was interested in why you were here." His hand gripped hers so hard her eyes began to tear as he continued, "Let's you and I work together. We'd make a powerful team."

"I don't need you," she smiled back at him through her tears. Behind him, she saw Laconius exiting the palace offices to approach the steps leading to the street below. She turned to wave at him, saying to Neriglissar, "Do you know who that is?" He turned to look then shrugged.

"That's Daniel's trusted aide . . . and my lover." Tapping him on the chest and flashing her sweetest smile, she clucked, "I have my own plan. You aren't in it."

Neriglissar watched her run like a little girl to Laconius. So outwardly innocent and beautiful to a fault . . . but inwardly evil to the core. She was a force to be reckoned with he reflected. He needed to prompt Antiosyss to act quickly with the King. Their plan was to frighten Nebuchadnezzar with revelations from the god Marduk elevating Neriglissar to equal status with Daniel. He would be in charge of all military forces; Daniel would remain the authority for civil affairs. They thought they had some time, but now they had competition.

~

Again, it was serendipitous. The opportunity to capture Daniel's attention fell into her lap when she heard through Laconius that Daniel was bringing Amel-Marduk, the Crown Prince, to his house for dinner that evening. It was the King's desire that his son learn the nuances of governance under Daniel's tutelage so that he would be in position to take over the empire at such time that Nebuchadnezzar passed on. Amel had agreed to take one day each week away from his building projects to work with Daniel in the Governor's offices dealing with the endless affairs of the kingdom. They had encountered a rather thorny problem that morning that required more discussion than they had time for during the regular course of the day, and so they agreed to continue their business at dinner that evening.

Laconius returned to the house earlier than usual to supervise and prepare for their royal guest. It was highly unusual for any member of the King's family to eat and be entertained in other than the royal palaces. Laconius could not afford any mistakes if his boss was to remain in high regard in the palace.

As he scurried around the house barking orders to the staff, Narseniah tailed behind. They were standing in the main dining area discussing seating arrangements when she asked Laconius what he had in mind for after dinner entertainment that evening.

"What?" he looked at her dumbfounded. He hadn't given this a thought, but now realized how important it was to the success of the evening. "I don't know. I was focused on the meal itself and didn't think about it. What should I do?"

"What if I were to entertain with some songs and dance? I have long worked with a couple of musicians who also perform regularly in the palace. They're exceptionally good, and I have also performed at many temple events. I can't do a long program but I think it will be entertaining."

"A short program is fine . . . if you really think you can do this. I like it. I mean, we have no alternative, but if we did, I'd still like it," exhaled Laconius with noticeable relief.

"Good. Then I need to be off to get the musicians and to rehearse. I'll be back easily in time."

Narseniah couldn't believe her good luck as she hurried down the streets. This was going to be a show that both the Crown Prince and Daniel would remember the rest of their lives! Marduk is good.

~

Amel-Marduk and Daniel had finished dinner and had fully resolved all the issues they had brought with them from their troubled morning. They were both in good spirits, relieved that nothing remained unsettled. Laconius entered the dining room to announce, "We have some very special entertainment for you tonight in the sitting room. I thought a short program would be pleasing to settle the food before you return to your palace, my Lord."

Daniel laughed, looking at Amel, "I didn't know about this. Leave it to Laconius to think of everything."

"Some music would be quite welcome right now," agreed Amel. He rose from his seat and with Daniel went into the adjoining room.

They were seated at the end of the large room which Laconius had re-arranged to allow for a performing space for the musicians and Narseniah. He gestured for the musicians to take their place, then proudly introduced "My Lord, please enjoy your evening."

The musicians began to play and through the entry at the opposite end of the room stepped Narseniah, beautifully, but not provocatively, dressed. Her stunning beauty proceeded her to the delight of both men who applauded before she sang a note. Knowing she already had them in the palm of her hand, she sang with confidence.

After Narseniah's first number, Amel leaned in to Daniel to ask, "Isn't this the daughter of Antiosyss at the temple? I believe I've seen her before."

"Yes," replied Daniel, "she is. And she is a wonderful singer. I had no idea she could perform this well."

"Another, please," requested Amel.

For the next twenty minutes, Narseniah charmed the men with several lovely songs, each one garnering more applause from her small audience than the one before. Laconius remained in the room, watching in total admiration. He thought, this was one of the proudest nights of his life. How grateful he was to

Narseniah for not only saving the night but making it an incredible success.

She finished her last song and offered two dances to conclude the evening. She asked for their leave to make a quick change of costume. Amel was in particularly good spirits as he had enjoyed a good deal of wine in addition to his food. While Daniel did not partake of the grape, he, too, was pleased with the evening and the obvious pleasure his guest enjoyed.

The musicians once more started to play, focusing the men's attention to the performing area. A new Narseniah revealed herself in a costume usually reserved for belly dancers the King routinely enjoyed in the palace but seldom seen elsewhere. Nothing was left to the imagination. Her ample and perfect figure was fully revealed and, when combined with the seductive dances Narseniah knew all too well from temple ceremonies, the effect on her audience was startling and in stark contrast to the music she had previously performed.

She saw Amel begin to smile with delight. She pressed forward with everything she had. There was no turning back now. She was finally going to get what she wanted and that was to seduce Daniel and thus shatter his championed integrity. That she was also getting the Crown Prince at the same time was nothing short of fantastic.

"Stop this!" shouted Daniel, rising abruptly from his chair.

Amel looked at him, wondering what had prompted this outburst. That Daniel was angry was evident by his red face and pursed lips. He glanced at Laconius who was as bewildered as him.

"Stop this. I smell evil in this house . . . a stench directly from the pit of hell . . . from the temple of Marduk!"

He turned to glower at Laconius, "What are you trying to do to my home, Laconius? This is not entertainment. These are the very ceremonies performed before Marduk with the priesthood. I'll have none of this in my house."

61

Daniel turned back to Narseniah, "Go!. You've violated my trust. Leave my home." He apologized to Amel, "I am truly sorry for this, my Lord. I had no idea."

Narseniah didn't flinch. Rather, she signaled the musicians to restart, stripped off her costume and began to re-enact the altar ceremonial dance which drove the passions of men to the breaking point. Amel could not take his eyes off her. Daniel, on the other hand, was so horrified that he stood up, grabbed a cloth off a table near him, and rushed to cover her.

"I asked you to leave," he shouted. "Now I command you to leave. Laconius, call the guards to remove this woman."

He pushed her towards the door and not kindly. She was the devil incarnate to him and he wanted her gone as fast as possible. Laconius rushed to get her out of the room.

Amel watched the entire scene completely captivated by Narseniah's beauty and sensuality. He had never entertained any thought for any woman since the death of his wife whom he loved dearly. But . . . this woman . . . she was unlike anyone he had seen. He was completely seduced by her. All the lusts and passions he had long ago quelled were now bubbling over, taking control of his mind and body.

Daniel was so upset and angry that did not recognize what was going on in Amel's being. "I cannot believe this happened in my house," he said to Amel. "You must forgive me – us—for this...this despicable behavior. I ask for your forgiveness and for forgiveness from my God."

Amel had begun to return to his senses and saw how distressed Daniel had become. He laughed, "Don't worry about this, my good friend. This is no problem to me. I ask you, please, put it all out of your mind. We had a wonderful dinner, good conversation, and excellent music. And I, honestly, enjoyed it all."

"No, Sire. It was the work of hell. I don't know how long it will take to clean the air and the very walls and floors of my home after tonight," sadly answered Daniel.

Amel by this time had risen to take his leave. He grasped Daniel's arm in friendship and bid him goodbye. As he left the house, all he could see was the incredible naked body of Narseniah beckoning to him. He tried to shake it off and mounted his horse to ride back to his palace with his guards. Her image was cemented firmly in his brain. He had to see this incredible, seductive creature again.

~

The streets were empty as Narseniah made her way back to her house adjacent to the Temple of Marduk. The coolness of the cobblestones was welcome to her bare feet as she felt she was burning up from the emotional and physical exertion of her performance. She smiled thinking of the impact she had had on Amel-Marduk. She recognized the look of desire; his face was flushed with it. So she lost Daniel, she thought; if I pick up the Crown Prince instead, I'm ahead of the game.

She quietly opened the door to her home and slipped inside. Waiting for her was Synthora, her aide and best friend.

"Did he take the bait? Did he lie with you?" she eagerly asked.

"No," beamed Narseniah as she took Synthora's hands in hers and sat them down on a couch. "Daniel threw me out of his house."

"What?" exclaimed Synthora, rising...now very worried about future implications.

"Oh, sit down, Synthora," laughed Narseniah as she drew her back to sit on the couch. "I couldn't have fashioned a better evening. Daniel had invited the Crown Prince for dinner so I got two for one. While Daniel was aghast at my performance, Amel-Marduk was totally mesmerized. He couldn't take his eyes off of me once I re-entered the room to dance. I mean, think about it," she said as she jumped up. "I'm much nearer the throne than I thought I'd be after tonight."

As understanding flooded over her, Synthora began to laugh with Narseniah, rising to grab her hands. They giggled and danced around the room like the little girls they once were.

"So what's our next move?" chuckled Synthora.

"We'll figure it out tomorrow," replied Narseniah. "Right now, I want something strong to drink. I just want to enjoy the moment."

~

So wrinkled with age and a life given over to demon-possession, Marlee looked like she was barely one step ahead of death and smelled even closer. Her magical powers were widely known. Her ability to harness the supernatural combined with her wizardly persona made her a fearsome presence. One did not involve her unless for serious business.

Narseniah couldn't bear the stench emanating from Marlee, and so their meeting was held outside in the courtyard. She decided she needed to capitalize on the momentum from the night before. She wanted the most cunning and devious mind to strategize her next move.

"I don't think you should waste time on the Crown Prince right now," clucked Marlee. "You have him in a good place. When you need to call on him, he'll come panting like a dog."

"Are you serious?" asked Narseniah. "I thought that if I pressed things with him, he'd be able to get me to the King."

"I agree," chimed in Synthora. "Why shouldn't we focus on the Prince when Narseniah has so obviously enchanted him?"

"All I want is a chance to be in the presence of the King," said Narseniah. "Give me that opportunity, and I can seduce him, Once he's under my spell, I'm in the seat of power. Whatever I want, I know I can get him to do. But the man is getting old. I need to be a fixture in the palace before he dies."

"So, let's take a direct approach," growled Marlee. "Let's not aim for the banquet room. Let's aim for the bedchamber. If you can ply your sensuality and charm on him in his most private quarters, don't you think you'll fare better?"

"Why . . . sure, I guess. But how do we make that happen?"

Marlee beckoned the two women to come closer. She whispered, "We go for the Captain of the palace guard. You first seduce him. He, then, gives you entry into the King's bedchamber because he—not Amel-Marduk—is the King's gatekeeper. And if for some reason there is any trouble . . . say the guards have second thoughts and bar you . . . or, say, the King himself does not surrender to your charms and has you arrested . . . will not Amel-Marduk come to your defense? If he wants you, he'll overcome anything that might befall you."

The two younger women rolled this idea around in their minds, recognizing the plan's brilliance. "Do you know Zocor, the Captain of the guards?" Synthora asked Narseniah.

"I do," snapped Marlee before Narseniah could answer. "I'll set you up with him. We'll use the temple. I'll invite him as an insider to observe the altar ceremony. If you give the performance of your life, he'll be consumed with a lust that can only be satisfied when I bring you to him. The rest is easy. Let him taste of your fruit over a few weeks and he will do anything for you."

~

Bringing Zocor, the Captain of the King's palace guard, under her spell was far easier than Narseniah imagined. Obviously, Marlee had exercised her powers on him as well because the man was a smitten puppy in her presence. His needs were simple, and she knew how to satisfy them. Within a few days of their flowering relationship, she had gained access to the King's residential palace on the river but was always careful to avoid the royal palace on Procession Way and Daniel's presence. Zocor could not believe his good luck at wining her favors and freely bragged to his men of their sexual exploits. They were always eager to see her which gave her free rein to roam at will in the palace except for Nebuchadnezzar's private quarters.

One night as they lay in bed after another round of love-making, Narseniah casually asked, "Would you ever let me see the King's personal quarters?"

"There's nothing to see," replied Zocor.

"But I'd like to say I've been there," she said. "I'd like to see him as well, if that were possible." She turned over onto her stomach, her head propped in her hands.

He sat up and swung his legs over the side of the bed as he looked back at her, "What are you saying? I'm not enough for you?"

She laughed, rising to her knees as she let her robe slip off her shoulders to the bed. "Isn't this made for a king," she gestured towards her naked body.

Zocor stood and looked at her in disbelief, "You want him too?"

"Think of how you would win his favor if you brought me to him in his bedchamber. He would hold you in the highest regard thereafter. You'd enjoy a status higher than his inner circle of wise men and advisors. And think of how you and I would become the most formidable alliance in the empire next to the King as we would be blessed with his special favor." The words tumbled out of her mouth, her ideas erupting faster than she could physically articulate them.

"I don't intend to share you," angrily spat Zocor.

"Is part of me better than none of me?" taunted Narseniah.

"What's that supposed to mean? Are you threatening me?"

"No, not a threat. Just promise of a great future for us if you look at things with detachment. Where's the soldier in you, Zocor? You're a warrior . . . a strategist they tell me. So, I'm offering you a plan to advance your position and keep me at the same time. Am I missing something here that you see and I don't?"

Zocor didn't know how to respond. It was obvious she was ambitious and wasn't going to be stopped in her quest to gain favor with the King. Either he could work with her or take the chance of losing her and maybe his post if she chose to turn on him.

"I don't care about him," said Narseniah as she jumped off the bed and came around to grab Zocor's arms. "But I do care about power...about having the opportunity to rule...to not fear what others can do to me." She squeezed his arms so hard he winced at the pain. "Don't you want that too? It's ours for the taking."

There was no turning back. She had cast her lot, and his was but to follow.

"Maybe you're right," he whispered, unable to look into her eyes which were ablaze with raw ambition. He didn't dare deny her. To do so meant the loss of lustful fulfillment not to mention jeopardizing his very career if she turned on him. He pushed back from her as he came to grips with reality. He continued backing to the doorway, then, nodded his assent, "You're right."

~

A perfect day was drawing to a close as the sun sank slowly into the western skies. It had been a good day. Nebuchadnezzar was pleased with the reports that had been brought him from all sectors of the empire, and he had enjoyed an especially satisfying afternoon reviewing and making suggestions to the plans for the central market renovation that Amel had developed. Life was good.

His favorite place in the entire kingdom was on the rooftop veranda of his palace where he could stroll at will by himself surveying the city he had created. The golden rays of the late afternoon sun danced like gold flakes on the spectacular architecture that made up the core of the great city of Babylon.

The waters flowing down the hanging gardens he had built for his wife gurgled peacefully beneath him.

To the south towered the multi-colored ziggurat and beyond that the immense Temple of Marduk. While it did not have the height of the three-hundred foot tall pyramid, the temple stretched four-hundred seventy feet in length and its grounds spread over sixty acres. And more temples scattered throughout the city...he had built many to satisfy the whims of the priesthood and almost as many palaces as he experimented with new construction techniques.

His gaze on the horizon brought to mind the massive care he had taken to fortify the city. Not content with the outer wall which in itself was thick enough to turn a four-horse driven chariot around in a circle, he had constructed two inner walls as a safeguard should attacking enemies pierce the outer. Guard towers were stationed every sixty-five feet along the outside wall, giving his army ample warning of oncoming attacks. Moreover, a moat fed by water from the Euphrates surrounded the city. He had designed nine gates that led into the city. As he turned to look north, he settled on his favorite, the Ishtar gate, built as a homage to the goddess of fertility.

Was this not the strongest and the most beautiful city on earth!

He leaned against the parapet looking down on the recently finished Procession Way, his eyes then caught by the sparkling waters of the Euphrates as they passed under one of his father's greatest design and engineering achievements, a four-hundred foot bridge spanning the two major sectors of the city. He chuckled to himself when he remembered that underneath the bridge Nabopolassar, the first King of Babylon, had built a tunnel over fifteen feet wide and high enough for any military apparatus or wagon to pass through. Probably over-kill, he laughed; but some day it might come in handy.

The scene was overwhelming and intoxicating. He lifted his hands to take it all in reveling in what he had created. The words tumbled out of his mouth although no one was there to hear, "Is not this the great Babylon I have built as my royal residence by my mighty power and for the glory of my majesty?"

The words had barely left his lips when he heard a voice coming from above. He swung around to identify the source. This was impossible because he was at the highest point of the palace and the closest adjacent skyscraper was more than a half mile away.

"This is what is decreed for you, King Nebuchadnezzar, because of your arrogance and pride. Today, your royal authority will be taken away from you. You will be driven away from living with people instead to live with the animals of the field. You will eat grass like cattle. Seven years will pass by until you acknowledge that the Most High God is sovereign over the kingdoms of men and that He can give them to anyone he wants, anytime he wants."

Immediately Nebuchadnezzar sensed a physical transformation overtaking him. His arms began to itch. When he pushed his sleeves up to scratch them he saw a mantle of hair pushing through his skin to cover his body. Suddenly very frightened, he began tearing his clothing off only to find this phenomenon happening over his entire frame. Blood began to ooze from where he had scratched. He looked at his fingers which now appeared as claws due to the enormous sudden growth of his nails. Wildly running towards the door leading to his bedchamber, he tried to call for help but only heard a loud bellow emanating from his throat. Panic set in.

~

Narseniah was tingling with excitement, her arms awash in goose bumps. It had only taken five days for Zocor to find the right time for her to make a move on the King. Nebuchadnezzar had opted to relax by himself and had ordered the servants out of his quarters leaving only the palace guards at the entry. He had dined early and advised Zocor he wanted to sit on the outdoor veranda off of his bedchamber to enjoy the cool breezes in the setting sun. It seemed like the perfect opportunity to make her move.

As pre-arranged by Zocor, she slipped past the guards at the entry and made her way through the King's outer rooms to the bedchamber. Nebuchadnezzar had left the veranda and was walking back and forth in the vast bedchamber, taking his clothes off and letting them lie where he shed them. Narseniah stood silently at the doorway, hidden by the columns. Something was wrong about his behavior that frightened her. His action became more agitated. No longer was he removing his clothing as much as ripping them off himself as though they were ropes or chains that bound him. As he did, he was snarling and making grunting noises. From time to time, he would lower himself to the floor to walk four-legged on his arms and legs.

Something wasn't right. Then it registered. As he bared parts of his body, he looked more like an animal than a man. He was covered with hair which terrified him the more he ripped his clothing off. His movement grew more animated and hysterical as did his vocalizations. Narseniah was watching a man morph into a beast right before her eyes. As terrified as she was, her eyes were riveted on him. She edged out from the column that hid her to keep the King in her eyesight as he crossed back out to the veranda. Without warning, he whirled around to race back into the bedchamber where she now stood. He attempted to ask her what she was doing there but only a loud bellow like that of a bull came out of his mouth.

Narseniah screamed, running for the entry to escape what she feared was a wild animal. "Help! Help me!" she screamed as she collided with the guards who had come running.

They let her pass between them out of the King's quarters while they ran through the sitting room into the dining area to find Nebuchadnezzar on all fours prowling around the room like a caged animal. He was bellowing loudly at them, but they didn't understand what he wanted. In fact, they didn't even know if this was the King as he looked nothing like what he had before. They braced themselves at the doorway, their spears pointed at him to stop him from charging.

By now the Queen and the entire palace staff had tumbled into King's quarters, alarmed at what they were hearing. More guards arrived, their job now to contain Nebuchadnezzar to his quarters until they could figure out what to do. Zocor had shuttled Narseniah out of the palace completely and had sent some of his men to get help. He had seen the King at the height of his anger a year before after his crazy dream. At that time, no one but Amel-Marduk and Daniel had been able to quiet him. He waited for their arrival as he watched Amytis carefully negotiate the King's bizarre movements in order to get close to him to calm him. What on earth had happened to the King? He hoped beyond all hope that Narseniah was not the cause of this.

Within the hour, Amel arrived and entered the dining room where his mother had managed to sit in a chair next to Nebuchadnezzar who remained on all fours. When the King saw him, he roared like a bull and went to him. Almost afraid to leave the protection of the soldiers with their drawn weapons, Amel hesitated then broke through their ranks to approach his father . . . if, in fact, he could even call this beast his father.

He spoke gently, "Father, what has happened to you? I want to help. Tell me what happened."

Nebuchadnezzar rose to stand, his arms striking the air like the front legs of a horse, attempting to communicate but only able to make the noises of an animal. As he did so, he recognized he was not being understood by either his son or his wife. In frustration, he collapsed on the floor drooling and lowing like a bull. Amel was frozen in place. Never in his life had he seen anything this incredulous and sub-human. He couldn't speak; he couldn't move. His mind was racing, what to do?

"It's all right," came a familiar voice from behind him. Daniel had arrived and had entered the dining room. "The dream is being fulfilled."

He patted Amel-Marduk re-assuredly on the back and stepped to Nebuchadnezzar, kneeling to look him directly in the eyes, "You're all right, my King. The dream you had one year ago is now unfolding."

Nebuchadnezzar looked at Daniel, the noises coming from his mouth subsiding and his body noticeably relaxing. He looked from Daniel to his wife and to his son, then to all the guards and staff huddled at the doorway. With a heave, he got up on all fours. Daniel quickly rose to stand with him. The King moved to Daniel and gently pushed against him in the direction of the doorway.

"You'd like to go out?" Daniel asked.

Nebuchadnezzar nodded, understanding that the only communication available to him was to use his body as he had lost his ability to speak. Daniel walked ahead of him, the guards parting to let them pass. Zocor signaled his soldiers to stay ahead of the King and Daniel to make a protective human corridor as they made their way out of the palace and into the gardens. It was eerily silent. By now, hundreds of people involved in the affairs of the palace were running to see what had happened, not knowing what to make of this or how to act to serve the King.

"Don't let this become a spectacle," Daniel said to Zocor. "Have your guards move everyone back inside. The less who see this, the better."

Nodding his assent, Zocor barked a few commands to his men who immediately cleared the outside grounds of onlookers and secured a private zone for the King.

Daniel proceeded to a grassy meadow fenced on all sides where he asked Nebuchadnezzar: "Is this where you'd like to be . . . at least for tonight?"

Nebuchadnezzar nodded his head and let out a gentle bellow. He began to graze like any of the horses and cattle in the King's barns. As they watched in disbelief, Daniel asked one of the servants to go to the barn and bring back some grain. Nebuchadnezzar was now relaxed and oblivious of the people staring at him. Amytis went to talk to him, but he simply ignored her as he did Amel. The servant returned with the grain which he gave Daniel who approached the King, placing it on the ground. Nebuchadnezzar scampered over to it and began to enthusiastically eat.

Daniel backed away and sought out Zocor, "Let him stay out here tonight. Make sure you have guards around the meadow so he doesn't get out. We don't want to lose him. Tomorrow, we'll bring him down to Rymen who can put him in a field where he won't injure himself or get hurt by any of the animals."

"Yes, sir," replied Zocor, too stunned to question any of this.

Daniel saw Amytis and Amel-Marduk standing near Nebuchadnezzar, their faces in shock. He approached them and said, "My Lady and my Prince, this is all very alarming and unusual, I know. The most high God has acted, fulfilling the promise of the dream. We can't begin to fathom or understand this. We can only accept it and make the King's life as comfortable and safe as possible. As bizarre as this sounds, he's better off out here tonight than in the palace. Zocor will see to his protection."

Amytis began to sob, clinging to Amel who held her tightly, "I don't understand why this is happening," she cried. "I just want my husband back again."

"I know," Daniel gently replied. "Let God work His plan, and it will happen."

"Let's go back inside, mother," said Amel. They left the meadow and returned to the palace. The guards quietly took up positions around the meadow as the King quietly munched his grain.

~

Daniel and Amel walked back into the palace, both knowing they had to act quickly to contain this situation and strengthen the governing infrastructure that was already in place. Once word leaked about the King's inability to rule, every pretender to the throne would be in motion building his power base while simultaneously discrediting Daniel's authority. Moreover, with the apparent demise of the leader who single-handedly built the Babylonian empire, an hysteria was likely to break out that could unsettle the general populace further confusing authority.

"My Prince, you must assume the throne this very night," advised Daniel. "We must convene the Governing Council first thing in the morning to explain that the King has been taken with a serious illness and that you as Crown Prince are in charge until such time that he has recovered."

"That's all good and well as long as you continue in your position as Governor," replied Amel. "I can't assume the throne without you; I have far too much to learn yet."

"Right now, you need to take over your father's role as King of this nation," urgently said Daniel as their pace quickened towards the palace. "I can only do what the King tells me to do, but I cannot be the king. You are now the King."

Daniel stopped in full stride, grabbing Amel's arms. "And you must act like the King starting now! No apologies. No gentleness or inadequacies even suggested. If there is anything other than the bravado and forceful nature of your father exhibited in the palace and throughout the land, your enemies will destroy you."

The two men locked eyes, motionless. Amel slowly nodded, understanding the severity of the struggle for power that would soon ensue and his need to disarm it by a combination of a well thought out strategy and sheer force of personality.

"I understand."

As Daniel let go of his arms, Amel grabbed his right arm in pledge saying, "We do this together. You stay right where you are governing the kingdom; I'll guarantee your authority."

Again, they paused, both taking in the partnership that had been outlined.

"I, too, understand. We do this together...for the King," replied Daniel.

Chapter Four
CONFRONTATION
570 BC

The royal palace was in full operating mode with the rising of the sun. Daniel and Amel had been there for an hour preparing for the Governing Council and summoning all members to its meeting that morning. The palace guards had also roused Rymen, the King's chief herdsman, from his sleep and escorted him to the palace in the dark.

Rymen lived in a modest house located next to the royal barn, south of the King's palace. The barn was surrounded by grassy pastures stretching in all directions and irrigated daily from the Euphrates River and the canal bordering the palace grounds to the south. Only prize breeding stock was housed here. These horses and cattle were the pride of Nebuchadnezzar who delighted in showing them to visiting dignitaries and guests. An abundance of shade trees grew throughout the pastures to provide cover. The animals were regularly rotated from pasture to pasture so the green blanket of grass was always lush and never looked worn.

A gentle man of fifty-one years of age, Rymen devoted life to caring for the King's precious livestock. In all his years on earth, the King had never spoken to him nor had Rymen seen the inside of the royal palace. Now to be dragged out of bed to appear before the King for no reason he could think of . . . he was scared to death! His knees shook uncontrollably as the guards escorted him up the steps to the palace.

"Come in, Rymen," smiled Daniel as he walked to the doorway to welcome the herdsman. "I'm sure you're wonderingwhat this is all about. Let me tell you, you have nothing to worry about. We have called you here to ask for your help."

"My Lord," said Rymen as he entered the room and saw the Crown Prince. He dropped to his knees before him.

"Get up," ordered Amel. Rymen obeyed, still quite confused by the grandeur of this environment not to mention being in the presence of two of the most powerful men in Babylon.

"We have a problem," Daniel began. "The King has been struck down by the most high God as He had promised one year ago in a dream. There's no need to go into all that except to tell you that he thinks he is now an animal."

Rymen's head snapped to look at Daniel, not quite sure he had heard everything correctly.

"He thinks he's a cow . . . a bull!" said Amel in frustration. "I don't know what he thinks he is but he's acting like one of the cattle in your herd."

"My Prince," said Daniel gently, "I think we need to go back to the beginning and explain it all. Rymen deserves to hear it and ask any question he might have."

"Agreed," said Amel. "Rymen, come sit down. We want you to understand what is happening because you are now in our confidence. None of this must get out to anyone else. Do you understand?"

Rymen's head was spinning. What were they talking about? He could only nod his head and sit, hoping it all made sense to him shortly.

After they had told him everything from the dream Nebuchadnezzar had one year ago and the condition they found him in last night, Amel found Rymen's eyes and looked into them deeply, "I want you personally to take care of my father for however long it takes until he is restored to his normal self. Find a safe pasture for him that is hidden from view. He needs to be safe from others and, more importantly I suspect, from himself. The pasture and barn in which you place him will be well guarded. Zocor will see to that."

"Can you help us?" asked Daniel. "You will be solely responsible for the care of the King. Don't ever forget, he is still the King whether he acts like an animal or not. He deserves the best care."

Bewildered beyond belief but comprehending the situation and the charge that had been placed on him, Rymen looked at both men and nodded his head, responding to them shakily, "I have to be truthful with you. I am frightened by all this. But I give you my pledge that I will care for the King as I would for one of my own children. He will be safe and comfortable."

They rose and bid Rymen good bye. The guards escorted him back to his house and the royal barn. Amel followed Rymen with his eyes and said, "That's a good man—a humble man of the earth. I feel good about him. He'll take good care of my father."

~

Zocor was waiting in the outer foyer as he, too, had been summoned. He had been up all night personally keeping his eye on the transformed King, but grew more confused and concerned with each hour by the strange situation into which he had been thrust. If anyone knew that it was he who had arranged for Narseniah to be in the King's private quarters last night, it was possible he was going to be accused of instigating the whole incident. Albeit tired, he was on his toes when called into the room by the Crown Prince.

"Zocor, as you are well aware, major changes are taking place," spoke Amel. "The King is seriously ill and incapacitated, and I am assuming the throne until he is well. I shall expect you to carry out my commands as though my father were issuing them. Is that understood?"

Swallowing hard, Zocor nodded, "Yes, Sire." He wasn't that familiar with Amel-Marduk as he hadn't spent much time in the royal palace and had no interest in the affairs of government.

His mind was a whirlwind. Obviously they didn't know about Narseniah's presence in the King's palace last night. And in all the ruckus that resulted, his guards who let her pass likely forgot about her.

A kaleidoscope of thoughts dizzily revolved in his brain. It looks like I'm off the hook for that stupid blunder. But what's going to happen now? The Crown Prince seemed strong enough, but could he command authority over all those who aspired to power, especially Neriglissar? Do I trust him to hold onto the throne? If I align with him and he is toppled, what happens to me?

Daniel could see the internal struggle taking place in Zocor, but he knew this was Amel's battle to fight alone. Amel would only earn Zocor's allegiance if he was sufficiently strong to command his respect.

"Look, Zocor, I need you to fully understand what is happening," said Amel. He looked to Daniel for help, "Daniel, tell him what's going on . . . from the dream up to last night."

After Daniel had fully briefed the Captain of the Guard and assured him that this strange illness had an end although possibly not for seven years, Zocor breathed a little easier. At least there was some reason for what had happened last night to his King.

"It's very important that others don't see the King," Amel said to Zocor. "They can know he is sick, but if they see him in the fields acting like an animal they will assume he's forever lost his mind and challenge my validity to access the throne. We know he's going to recover, and now you do too. Your job is to protect him . . . shield him from being a spectacle and ensure his safety. He is still the King." He paused, then, asked, "do you understand?"

Zocor struggled for words to respond but was unable. Daniel stepped to him, placing his hand on his shoulder and said, "Captain, your King trusted you to be in charge of the palace guards. Honor that trust. He needs your vigilance now more than ever."

Zocor nodded imperceptibly and Daniel pressed on pointing to Amel-Marduk, "Our young King also trusts you to serve him as well. Honor that trust, and he will honor you when all this is past us."

Having made up his mind to stay the course with the King and his family, Zocor drew himself to attention and saluted Amel with his arm thrust forward, his hand balled into a fist, then brought it to lie across his chest, "My Lord, I understand. I pledge to serve you faithfully."

"Good. I shall count on you today and every day," said Amel, relieved the personal safety of himself, his father and his family was ensured. "Work with Rymen to take care of my father, then, come back. We are assembling the Governing Council to explain the situation. I'll need you here to show a strong, unified presence when the others arrive."

~

Facing the court's wise men, councilors, military officials, and ruling bureaucrats who made up the Governing Council was a formidable task. Other than Daniel, there was not one man in the room that Amel could trust. They were all foxes in the hen house, particularly now that Nebuchadnezzar was incapacitated. His intimidating presence was the glue that held the kingdom together. Amel knew he had to come out of the gate with no less strength of personality than his father.

The throne room was buzzing with speculation and typical palace gossip as to why they had been called together at such an unusual hour in mid-morning. Normally, this group never met until the afternoon. Mysonus, the elder of the wise men, was deep into a hushed conversation with Beltekasmer, probably the most politically astute of the magicians and astrologers with whom Nebuchadnezzar surrounded himself. At the other end of the grand hall laughing at a joke Polynices had told him was Nebuzaradan, Supreme Commander of the Imperial Guard and a formidable figure. Antiosyss stood dead center, directly in front of the King's throne. Never one to remain on the fringes, he knew Nebuchadnezzar feared his ability to exercise supernatural powers and so positioned himself where he could best dominate discussion and control decisions. At his side was Neriglissar, a division commander and therefore subservient to Nebuzaradan but clearly the superior warrior.

Daniel entered the room unannounced and took his seat below and to the right of the throne. The room quieted noticeably in deference to his position.

The palace guards sprang to life, smartly snapping to attention at the four entries to the room and signifying the King's entrance was imminent. Everyone who had been seated rose to their feet; all talking ceased. In strode Amel-Marduk wearing a robe usually worn by Nebuchadnezzar. Heads turned; the gossip resumed but in subdued tones. Amel walked directly to the throne. He stopped and turned to face the court, speaking in a loud, commanding voice.

"My father, the King, is seriously ill." The murmurs re-started at this news. "I have assumed the throne and his position until such time he is well again and can return to ruling Babylon. Meanwhile, the affairs of this empire will continue uninterrupted. Daniel will remain my Governor; you will continue to serve in the court."

He looked slowly around the grand hall, catching the eye of every faction leader and political force with his hard stare. He resonated power and an unrelenting grip on the authority of his right to rule in place of his father. It was a power play of extraordinary finesse. He asked no questions; he just assumed his role. Too intimidated by his brazenness, the courtiers acquiesced. He grabbed their submission without hesitation and pressed on. He sat on the throne as the others continued to remain on their feet.

"This has all happened very quickly, so we will likewise re-structure our governance quickly to lend experienced judgment to my rules and decrees. As you know, this body was convened by Daniel to advise him as Governor of the kingdom.

My father put up with it but never considered you part of his decision making process. He kept that authority for himself and only himself.

Amel paused to let that last reality sink in, then, continued: "Because Daniel values your input, I, too, will listen to you. But understand there is only one person in this room who makes decisions. Me, and, of course, Daniel to whom my father and I delegate the normal administration of the kingdom.

"There are over thirty of you and that is too many voices guiding decisions. I am simplifying it as of now to draw upon the experience and wisdom of the kingdom's most trusted leaders. I am asking Mysonus, Nebuzaradan, Polynices, Shadrach, Meshach, and Abednego to join with Daniel as my inner circle of advisors. These seven men will assist me on a daily basis. I will, of course, continue to rely on this Governing Council for input as we discuss the larger issues confronting our empire."

His stern demeanor didn't invite discussion or questions. He was fully in charge, and not one person doubted it.

"So then . . . you are dismissed. We'll convene this larger body in several days when we are ready to discuss whether or not to extend the borders of our southwest sector through war, economic pressure or treaty. Those in the inner circle of advisors, please stay behind as I have a few issues to raise with you."

Amel dismissed them with a wave of his hand. But they didn't move. Instead, they broke out talking in small groups re-hashing what had just happened.

"I said, you are dismissed," Amel abruptly stood and loudly ordered. " Leave! Now!"

He looked around the room for Zocor until he found him, then thundered, "Zocor, clear the room. This meeting is over."

The room quietly emptied in seconds. Amel had won the opening battle, but he had made more than a few enemies as a result of excluding them from his inner circle. Power was the currency of choice with this group. To not be involved in decision-making meant to lose it.

~

"I am insulted...no, furious," shouted Neriglissar to Antiosyss as they made their way from the palace through the central market to a little tavern where they could talk discreetly.

"Shhh. Keep your voice down," cautioned Antiosyss. "Big ears are not always readily seen, but . . . ahhh . . . just keep your voice down."

"I cannot believe Nebuzaradan was selected over me. Amel knows better. I thought we were friends. After all, I am virtually his brother and a member of the royal family.

"Don't think I'm all that happy either," snapped Antiosyss. "I'm the leading priest in the entire kingdom, and I was shut out."

By now they had reached a tavern and quickly found a quiet corner where they could talk. "I'm not going to take it," said Neriglissar. "I don't know which one of them put this group together, and I don't much care. As of now, they are both on my top two list to destroy."

"Who do you suppose drew up the inner circle list?" queried Antiosyss. He quickly added, "I mean . . . I'm curious."

"It doesn't matter. It is done and we are out. It's our destiny to change things."

They sat in silence, mindlessly drinking their beer, looking for answers. Antiosyss looked up at Neriglissar and whispered, "Daniel." He smiled cynically, then, in a louder voice repeated, "Daniel is responsible for this. I never liked the man. He always thought he was better than anyone else."

By this time, Neriglissar was just downright angry. He felt betrayed. As the King's son-in-law and the leading warrior in the land, he should have been included. Now his objective was to get even. It was important that his power and position be properly respected. The thought of partnering with Antiosyss to lay low the partnership created by Daniel and Amel grew on him as he knew there were unholy powers to call upon by the priest when needed.

They each sat in unhappy silence sipping their drinks. "Let's get them," Neriglissar slammed his fist down on the table.

"Do you have any ideas?" asked Antiosyss.

"No," he replied, "that doesn't matter. What does matter is that we agree to work together. The ideas will come once we have our alliance in place. I'll do everything in my power to get rid of them." Neriglissar stood up, paying the tavern owner more than he needed.

"Agreed," replied Antiosyss. "I say we tackle Daniel first."

"Makes no difference to me. I just want them both gone." Neriglisser pushed back from the table and stood up. "I have to go. My men are waiting."

~

The transfer of power from father to son was virtually seamless given that both men had delegated the governing of the kingdom to Daniel. The citizenry of the Babylonian empire had no idea what had befallen Nebuchadnezzar as Amel-Marduk with the help of Zocor and Rymen successfully managed to keep hidden the King in his animal state. For the most part, the palace servants and guards who had witnessed Nebuchadnezzar's metamorphosis kept silent. The few who were compelled to gossip were soon discredited as their colleagues refused to corroborate their stories. As far as the Governing Council was concerned, Nebuchadnezzar was ill and the Crown Prince had stepped in to take over for his father.

The one wild card was Narseniah. She had seen something completely in-human and so bizarre that she couldn't get it out of her mind. Yet, she knew that such a morphing couldn't be real. Did she actually see the transformation of man into animal or was she imagining it? Maybe the King was convulsing and therefore the bellowing sounds? Maybe he had taken violently ill causing his skin to burst into hairy splotches. Maybe she had imagined the entire scene! One thing that did concern her was that she had been in the palace when the King went crazy and she could easily be blamed for it. And so she had kept out of sight, hoping her presence that evening would be forgotten in the chaos that ensued.

For the next several weeks, Narseniah stayed close to home and the temple seeking to learn of any rumors about her that might fall on her father's ears. She didn't suggest anything to Antiosyss, and it didn't appear that he had heard anything. She did, however, notice that Neriglissar seemed to be spending more time at the temple in quiet conversations with her father. Whereas in the past, he might be seen once a year at the temple for a major ceremony, now Neriglissar was coming and going several times a week. She surmised something was afoot, but her overriding concern was her own safety. Perhaps it was time to seek out Zocor to find out what the palace was thinking.

She waited for him at the palace rear entry used only by the guards and servants. She knew it well because this was how he had arranged for her entry that fateful night one month ago. Sitting on a bench in an area where the servants often took brief breaks from their duties, she didn't draw attention and blended into the shrubbery around her.   When Zocor finally emerged late in the afternoon, she rose and quickly fell in step with him from behind.

"Zocor," she said quietly, "we need to talk."

Caught off guard, he whirled to see who was speaking to him. When he realized it was Narseniah, he tightened. As much as he was pleased to see her and once again give loose rein to his lusts, he was equally anxious that their secret not be revealed.

"We shouldn't be seen together," he said as his eyes scanned the terrain to see who might be watching.

"Has anyone mentioned my presence in the King's bedchamber the night he fell ill?"

"No. No, it seems to have been forgotten what with all the excitement that took place that night," he answered. "That's why we can't be seen together right now or ever. If one of my guards sees us . . . well, it could trigger his memory. And who knows whom he might then start talking to which could raise a lot of questions. You need to go right now. Stay away from here."

"So they don't know about me? They don't suspect me/"

"No . . . not a mention. We must keep it that way," Zocor said, then turned and abruptly walked away.

"Good," Narseniah said under her breath. She, too, turned and quickly left the palace grounds. Her secret was safe. She could once again surface, now to take aim at Amel-Marduk. He would be easier pickings than the King.

~

"We've been talking about this for four months, and we're not any closer than we were when we first started," complained Neriglissar. "How can a man be so wise to anticipate our every move?"

They were sitting in the garden of Neriglissar's palace, a wonderful residence he could claim only because of his marriage to Kassaya, Nebuchadnezzar's oldest daughter. Antiosyss took the peeled orange from the plate of fruit between them and bit out a juicy hunk, the juices squiggling down his chin. It had been a delicious lunch in spite of their heated conversation of how to take down Daniel. All their efforts thus far had totally failed. Each time they initiated a deception or trap hoping to discredit Daniel, he countered with the finesse of an expert swordsman.

"These things take time . . . strategic moves can't be rushed," soothed Antiosyss who signaled one of the servants hovering in the background to refill his goblet. By this time both men were used to speaking openly about their plans to topple Daniel. While at first their meetings were whispered conversations in dark corners of the temple, they were now over bounteous meals, usually in Neriglissar's palace.

"It's time to make a bold move. We're unable to pierce him politically. We need to find a way to kill him," said Neriglissar glad that he had finally articulated what he had been thinking for weeks.

"Have you lost your senses?" incredulously asked Antiosyss. He looked at the servants who waited in the garden for their bidding and leaned into Neriglissar whispering, "Be careful what you say when others are around."

"Don't worry about them," laughed Neriglissar. "They're loyal to me. If they weren't, they know what would happen," as he moved his arm with his index finger pointed at his throat in a slicing gesture.

"Still . . . one can't be too careful," countered Antiosyss uneasy that others could be privy to such treasonous remarks.

He took a drink from the goblet one of the servants had re-filled and faced Neriglissar, "Maybe we've been going at this the wrong way. Instead of trying to trap him politically, perhaps it's time to call upon the spirits and take this into a different dimension."

Ignoring Antiosyss completely, Neriglissar continued on with his own thoughts: "I command a good portion of the Imperial Guard. It would be a simple thing to ambush Daniel as he leaves Babylon on a trip to the provinces. We could easily create an emergency in any sector . . . in fact, let's use the southwest sector where the Crown Prince is concerned about the security of our borders. We create a disaster so serious that it demands Daniel's presence to resolve. Since it's a journey of many days, we will have ample opportunity to ambush him and his small retinue of guards."

He turned to Antiosyss well pleased with his plan. "I will use my most trusted men. This is so opportune, is it not? Daniel can be gone quickly and no one need know what happened."

"I don't want to go that direction," said Antiosyss. "At least not yet. Better to call upon the powers of Marduk and use the gods to stop Daniel."

"You know that's all contrived," snorted Neriglissar. "You haul out Marduk and his powers regularly to intimidate everyone. That may give you power with people, but you and I know it's a myth. Marduk can't help us."

"Don't you ever demean me like this again," said Antiosyss who had shot out of his chair waving his finger at Neriglissar. Displeased with this dismissal of his position and power, he hissed, "You have no idea of the power I can bring into play. Power that can strike you or any man to the ground if I so wish and Marduk is in agreement."

Not ready for this angry response, Neriglissar stood and lifted his arms in a gesture of apology while trying to make amends, "Forgive me. I over-stepped my bounds ...I truly am sorry. I take back my suggestion. Let's do it your way."

Ruffled but knowing his only hope to gain a ruling foothold in the empire was through his alliance with Neriglissar, Antiosyss extended his hand in friendship. "I accept your apology. We are in this together and we must not let our alliance be fractured." They grasped each other's arms in a truce.

"Call on Marduk," said Neriglissar. "Let the gods lead us, and may it bring us a quick victory."

~

Loyalty was one thing; good gossip another. The servants of the palaces within the King's family were close-knit and, in fact, often changed positions with each other giving them broad access to the ruling class of Babylon. The conversation overheard at Neriglissar's palace was too good to leave untold. Within a week, Dorcas who served in the palace of Amel-Marduk heard the story which by then had become amplified. Alarmed that Daniel was in imminent danger, she approached Amel-Marduk one evening as he was eating dinner.

"My Lord, may I speak," she entered the dining room as the Crown Prince was finishing his meal.

"Go ahead, Dorcas," he replied. "You know you are free to talk here."

She proceeded to tell him of the conspiracy hatched by Neriglissar and Antiosyss and the impending danger to Daniel. He was fully aware of Antiosyss's anger at not being included in the inner circle of advisors, but Neriglissar's hostility caught him by surprise. He hadn't considered a threat to his authority rising from within his family. At the same time, he always knew Neriglissar aspired to the throne and harbored a consuming lust for power. He should have been more alert to this danger from his backside.

When she had finished, he calmly spoke, "Thank you for sharing this with me, Dorcas. The plot probably isn't as far along as what's been told to you. You know how these stories grow with each telling. Yet, I suspect these two men do have an alliance and that they would very much like to get rid of Daniel." He paused and smiled at her, "If he goes, I am that much more vulnerable to them. So it all makes perfect sense."

"You have to stop them!" she blurted out, then realized it wasn't her right to tell the Crown Prince what to do. "I'm sorry, my Lord. It's just that . . . I can't bear . . . it would be horrible for everyone if Daniel were to be killed. And you must not . . . ." her voice trailed off into silence at her embarrassment of revealing her feelings for him.

"Dorcas, come here," gently said Amel as he rose.

She walked to him, her head down in submission, and stopped before him. Amel took her hands in his and said, "Thank you for trusting me enough to tell me about this plot. I should have been more aware, and I will henceforth." His voice grew in urgency. "Look at me." She lifted her head to look at him. "I'll warn Daniel about their plans, don't worry. We will all be more alert to what they might try next. And our alertness will keep us safe, thanks to you. Keep your ears open. If you hear any more, sort it out . . . sift out the obvious fiction from reality. Then always know you can come to me. I appreciate your being my eyes and ears in quarters I simply cannot have access to."

She nodded, forced a smile, and left.

That is quite a woman, he mused to himself watching her leave. She's strong, attractive and smart . . . and very courageous. She is truly a special woman.

~

Egyptian forces were provoking the integrity of the Babylonian borders in the southwest province with greater frequency drawing the attention of the full Governing Council and Imperial Guard. At this point, Amel-Marduk did not want to engage in war. At the same time, the peace enjoyed by the empire was being disrupted by the tensions rising from the growing number of border conflicts between the two nations. Action was required.

In a meeting of the inner circle of advisors prior to the convening of the Governing Council, Nebuzaradan proposed that Neriglissar take two battalions of the Imperial Guards to the area in question and forcefully put an end to the conflict. He reasoned that in acting with strength, the Babylonian empire would overpower Egypt's challenge and expunge any thought of war they might harbor. His argument was powerful. The entire Governing Council endorsed it unanimously. Within two days, Neriglissar and his troops left Babylon for the southwest sector.

While he disliked the prospect of war, Amel-Marduk was glad to have Neriglissar out of the city for a few months. He hoped there would be some pause in the conspiracy and that Antiosyss wouldn't act on his own.

Unbeknownst to Amel and Daniel, Antiosyss, too, was pleased with Neriglissar's departure. The high priest needed time that Neriglissar was unwilling to give him . . . time to prepare and conduct the ceremonies that would please the gods and time to design a spectacular public event that would solidify his supernatural supremacy in the hearts and minds of the citizens of Babylon. These things could not be rushed.

The Akitu—the empire's most important agricultural holiday festival—was four months away. It always took place immediately after the barley harvest in March at the time of the spring equinox. The twelve-day festival consisted of private and public rituals. The only public events which the majority of people could enjoy, however, were two processions. On the seventh day, the King led the idol of Marduk out of the temple to the Shrine of Destinies, where the fate of the people was divined, followed by a grand procession to the Akitu Temple outside the city's gates. Following a three-day banquet reserved only for the upper echelon of Babylonian society, a second procession returned everyone to the city of Babylon in grand style. That left the average person with only a couple of parades to watch.

Antiosyss knew that the Babylonians cherished this holiday as it was an opportunity for them to thank the gods for the harvest. More importantly, it served to ensure that the subsequent growing season would yield abundant crops. Antiosyss knew he needed to create a spectacular ritual that most of the people who lived in the capital city could see.

The King was central to all activities of the Akitu festival, and Antiosyss had no desire to elevate Amel-Marduk in the eyes of the people. With Nebuchadnezzar indisposed, however, the Crown Prince would have to step in. This would only make it more difficult when it came time to overthrow him.

The answer came to him late one sleepless night. As the spiritual leader of the kingdom, he had the authority to amend rituals and ceremonies if he could sufficiently justify the changes to the people. Because the King was ill, he would dispense with the twelve-day ritual of Akitu and propose a new Feast of Marduk. He reasoned that he could sell the idea on the basis that the gods would not be pleased if the King were absent from the normal proceedings demanded by the Akitu. Rather than take that chance, better to celebrate a feast dedicated to the god of all gods—Marduk! No god could take umbrage at this.

It was the perfect solution. Neriglissar would probably be back in the city in four months enjoying the accolades of another victory on the border. That would give more credence to both of them. In the meantime, in Neriglissar's absence, he—Antiosyss—would have a free hand to design and create an event giving him center stage during the most important and highly anticipated week in the Babylonian calendar.

~

Narseniah again felt secure enough to participate in the spiritual and political life of the city. She had identified Maximillan, Amel-Marduk's head servant, as her next target. If she could compromise him, she stood a good chance at gaining direct access to the Crown Prince. Like her father, she thought she would do better this time by invoking the spirit world to assist. She returned to her role in temple ceremonies, much to the pleasure of the priests who had missed her sensual presence.

Pleased to see Narseniah again in temple activities—because he recognized the power she wielded with men—Antiosyss began to see her as a tool to unseat Daniel. Given her zeal for the spirit world of Marduk and her willingness to be inhabited by demons, he had every reason to think she could be the foil to pierce Daniel's spiritual cover. He was unaware she had failed to seduce Daniel and thus had no hint she would be anything but helpful.

He also suspected another arrow in his quiver was going to be Coaster, an emerging priest in the temple. He didn't know where Coaster came from; he certainly had not recruited him. It was as though one day, he was there. The man pulsed with evil, so strong a putrid stench emanated from his body. His eyes were yellow, snake-like. Tall and imposing, with arms and a chest that filled most doorways, his fingers were unusually long and serpentine, more feminine in character than male. Androgynous with no obvious gender, most people kept their distance from him. It was uncomfortable to be near him, and yet his persona was of such magnetism and other worldly power that no one could take their eyes off him when he was present.

It wasn't easy spending time with Coaster but Antiosyss stayed the course, getting to know him by often eating with him or by engaging him in brief conversation. What he began to realize is that this was no mere man. With each encounter he sensed sinister supernatural powers that pushed and strained to be released, evidenced by quirky body movements and sudden releases of hate so intense they took form as white, hot vapor. Antiosyss looked forward to these meetings because of his own desire to be consumed by the spirits. It was terribly exciting to see in Coaster the realization of what he wanted to become.

One evening after an intense temple ceremony, Antiosyss asked Narseniah to join him and Coaster for a libation in the high priest's preparation room. She had seen Coaster in action, but had not yet had occasion to meet him face to face. The idea of being with him now was exciting. While she, too, stood in some awe of the man's persona, she was never afraid or offended by him; rather, she felt an attraction as though he were a kindred spirit. The thought occurred to her that maybe Coaster was the edge she was seeking in her quest for power.

Coaster appeared unusually warm, sweating profusely which was not that unexpected after such a physical ceremony. He couldn't get enough beer, draining tankard after tankard willingly poured by Antiosyss.

"You better go easy with that," laughed Narseniah. "We might have to leave you to sleep in here tonight if the beer goes to your senses."

"Nothing touches my senses," snapped Coaster as he slammed his tankard down on the table top. "I have no senses. I have no need of senses." His character had instantly changed and the room was pervaded with a growing coldness that caused the hairs on the back of their necks to rise.

"I was just joking . . . making a joke," said Narseniah as she struggled to regain her composure.

"Oh, I get it," smiled Coaster. The chill evaporated as fast as it had materialized. "Sometimes I get confused." He paused as both Narseniah and Antiosyss stared quizzically at him. "I don't like to be challenged."

"She meant nothing," spoke Antiosyss. "She admires your powers and your ability to channel Marduk and his demons."

"Yes, I am amazed by your commitment," said Narseniah. "You let yourself become an instrument of his minions . . . and it lifts you to a higher power! I want that for myself."

Pleased to have two new and eager disciples, he drained another tankard then asked, "How can I help you? Antiosyss, you first; let me connect you to the spirits you seek."

This was phenomenal thought the high priest. I have been thinking of bringing my daughter into our plot and here we all are. This is the rest of the team I need to finally get rid of Daniel.

Looking directly into Coaster's piercing yellow eyes, he said, "I want to unseat Daniel from his governorship so I can bring down Amel-Marduk. You can help me do this." He turned and gazed at Narseniah, "Both of you."

"I hate Daniel!" Coaster exploded. Now extreme cold fell on the room . . . so cold that it physically hurt. Coaster rose to his feet and began roaming the room, yelling, "I hate everything about that. . . that . . . that self-righteous, arrogant man! He needs to die! I want to kill him myself, rip his heart out . . . tear his head from his body."

The rant went on for several minutes while father and daughter edged towards the walls fearful of the uncontrolled anger and suffocating hate that took over the room. They watched in total terror the transformation of Coaster's human body into a writhing serpent-like form, fire flashing from his mouth and fingers giving way to spikes that extended from his hands and feet. Unable to breathe, they finally collapsed.

Antiosyss came to first. He gasped for air, and when his respiration approached normal he looked around the room. Coaster was nowhere to be found. Narseniah was lying in an opposite corner from him, life-less. He crawled across the floor to her, every move difficult. Every muscle ached.

She was just coming to as he reached her. Her eyes blinked open, looking at him, "Are we still alive?"

In spite of their seemingly awful situation, Antiosyss chuckled and replied, "Yes. Yeah, we're alive all right. Maybe now more than ever."

Narseniah started to move, pushing up from the floor to sit, her back against the wall, "I've never seen anything like that. What an awesome force! Would we could tap that."

"We can. And we will," softly spoke Antiosyss. He slowly lifted himself off the floor to his knees, then stood, extending his arm to help her up. He looked at the empty doorway and said, "That was the power and person of Marduk himself. That can be ours."

Narseniah gripped her father's arm tightly, her voice almost inaudible, "And he hates Daniel more than even we. Can that be?"

Antiosyss grinned broadly and nodded.

~

As the Feast of Marduk drew closer, Antiosyss and Narseniah sunk deeper into the powers of hell with the help of Coaster. The three were now the highlight of every temple ceremony, improvising on tradition and creating an excitement among the priesthood never seen before in Babylon. As they spiraled downward, their plans to topple Daniel began to take shape. Everything keyed off the upcoming Feast. With the days growing fewer, their urgency intensified.

In the southwest province, things had gone well for Neriglissar. After a couple of serious battles with the Egyptian border forces, life settled back into the occasional skirmish. It became clear to all that Egypt had lost heart in expanding its territory. Leaving a few troops behind to shore up the border guards, Neriglissar gathered his battalions to return to Babylon where he was received with a hero's welcome. A potential jolt to the empire by an unfriendly neighbor had been stopped in its tracks.

Amel-Marduk convened the Governing Council in a rare morning meeting to honor Neriglissar prior to a city-wide celebration in which he and his troops would parade along Procession Way to the ziggurat for a ceremony capping the day's festivities. The royal palace had not seen such energy in years as members of the Governing Council, military commanders, and the pillars of Babylonian society crowded into every crevice hoping to share in this moment of the kingdom's greatness.

The throne room was awash in the din of small talk and speculation as those present waited for the Crown Prince to appear. Neriglissar waited in a holding room elsewhere in the palace so he could be introduced to the crowd with great pomp and circumstance. The palace guards appeared without warning and struck their spears loudly on the marble floor in three successive raps. Quiet instantly fell over the room as Amel-Marduk entered and made his way to the throne where he turned and faced the assembly. He waited until he had their full attention, then extended his right arm and thundered, "The Babylonian Empire remains as strong as ever. Long live King Nebuchadnezzar!"

The room joyfully exploded with cries of "Long live the King." This was a day of celebration and the outburst could not be held back. Amel let the merriment continue, smiling as he watched Nebuzaradan accept congratulations and appreciation for the fine work of the Imperial Guard.

The trumpeters who flanked the room sounded a fanfare that quieted the assembly. Amel-Marduk looked at Nebuzaradan and said, "Commander, we congratulate you on a quick victory in the southwest sector."

He raised both of his hands towards the large doors that gave entry into the room and said, "And now we honor the warrior who led our troops into harm's way and emerged victorious."

The trumpets sounded another flourish as the doors swung open to reveal Neriglissar standing resplendent in full armor set off with festive splashes of color in plumages and a draped robe. Nothing could contain the celebration that erupted and continued as Neriglissar made his way through the room, receiving homage from those who pressed in upon him.

After what seemed like half of the morning, Neriglissar finally reached the foot of the throne and ceremonially bowed to the Crown Prince saying, "All is well, my Prince. Peace once again reigns throughout the empire." The celebration started all over again, but this time was cut short by Amel who with the help of the trumpeters once more hushed the room.

"Neriglissar, we honor your victory and that of your troops," said Amel.

Turning to the Supreme Commander, the Prince said, "Nebuzaradan, a word from you to begin."

Making one speech after the other, the leading men of Babylon jockeyed for a moment of shared glory with the hero of the day. So the morning went, each man heaping on more hyperbole.

And then like a bolt of lightning shattering the calm of the day, a voice sounded above the fray, "It no longer makes any sense that Neriglissar is not in the inner circle of advisors. The King surely would agree that he belongs there. I propose he be admitted at once as a testament to his strength and service."

Amel's smile froze on his face as he searched the room to find the offending voice. To interfere in the ruling authority's decisions was next to treasonous. As the crowd began to fade back against the walls, he saw standing in the center of the hall Beltekasmer, the dominant wise man in the court who had been shamed by Nebuchadnezzar for his failure to correctly interpret the King's dreams.

"My Lord," Beltekasmer said as he approached the throne, "this man—this commander—has surely earned the right to be in the highest ruling authority of the kingdom."

Voices offering support for the idea came from all corners of the room as men mumbled endorsement without fully coming forward to identify themselves. Neriglissar seized the opportunity and stepped towards Beltekasmer. "Thank you, wise sir, for your endorsement." Turning to face Amel, he continued with a solemn expression on his face, "It would be an honor to join your inner circle of advisors." Again, the affirmation of the mumbling crowd pervaded the room.

Furious and taken back by this affront to his authority, Amel was speechless. He saw Daniel rise from his seat to speak which triggered him into action. Looking directly at Beltekasmer, Amel slowly rose from the throne and said, "Only because you are favored by my father and are in his service, I am not removing you from Babylon today. You have stepped beyond your bounds. Be glad you still have your life."

"My Prince," said Neriglissar in a tone just short of condescension, "he was only trying to be of help. I, myself, never knew why I was excluded from your inner circle; and now when I am clearly a key player in the affairs of the empire I am more puzzled than ever why you would not welcome my loyalty and knowledge."

"Do you not understand that this decision is neither yours nor anyone's in this room to make," roared the Crown Prince turning his full attention to Neriglissar.

Remembering that this was a celebration for the man he was now upbraiding, Amel collected himself. He realized this was not the time or place to cross swords with Neriglissar.

"I am pleased with your victory, but that is not a license to rule. I will hear no more of this matter. Go on . . . all of you. We honor a great military hero today, nothing more. Zocor, open the doors and clear the way for the celebration to continue."

Amel stepped off the throne and brushing past the two men left standing in the center, he led the procession outside and down the palace steps to his waiting escort. Nebuzaradan quickly hustled Neriglissar in the same direction, hoping the parade would let everyone return to their senses.

~

It was a beautiful day for the festivities. People thronged both sides of Procession Way to cheer their nation's leaders. Amel dutifully rode the point position, escorted by his most trusted Palace Guards. The Supreme Commander of the Imperial Guard, Nebuzaradan, and his top generals followed.

The roar of the crowd, however, was reserved for Neriglissar. He milked every ounce of their enthusiasm with smiles and shouts of, "thank you." As Amel heard the rising acclaim accorded Neriglissar behind him, he knew he was up against a formidable foe not to be taken lightly. Dorcas' warning rang loudly in his ears.

The ziggurat ceremony was standard priestly stuff and of no interest to Amel who longed to be elsewhere. He finally saw his opportunity when he made a congratulatory speech high up on the fifth level of the ziggurat so the crowds below could see. He saluted Neriglissar for his outstanding service, and then drew attention away from him to focus attention on the King by extolling the great role of Nebuchadnezzar's many victories in building the empire.

"Today," he said, "is a time to take pride in our heritage and in our King as we thank those who have served him faithfully through the years."

The re-direction of the crowd's affection worked as the formal celebration ended, allowing Amel to return to the palace grounds. He went directly to the pasture to spend some time with his father. Amel still did not know if Nebuchadnezzar understood anything he said, but he re-capped the events of the day as he leaned on the fence watching his father graze. When he got to Beltekasmer's treasonous remark, he noticed Nebuchadnezzar quit eating and became somewhat agitated. The King walked on all fours towards the fence where he was leaning and bumped it hard with his head. Amel jumped backwards. The King continued to bump the fence while bellowing loudly. It was as though he were telling Amel something. Finally, he quieted down and returned to his grazing.

"I heard you, father," whispered Amel to Nebuchadnezzar. "I'm not going to lose the throne. It will be there for you when you're ready to return."

A peace settled on him as he watched his father. He was beginning to realize the pressures that came from being king in addition to understanding how much energy and perseverance was required to stay on top. It's good to be king, but it isn't easy.

"I thought I'd find you here," came a voice from behind him. Amel whirled to find Daniel walking down the path toward him.

They both leaned on the fence and gazed in silence at Nebuchadnezzar contentedly eating the luscious grass Rymen worked diligently to maintain. It was peaceful. The clamor of the day was now distant.

"I told him about what happened today," Amel nodded towards Nebuchadnezzar. "I think he understood. He told me to rule with confidence." Then he laughed and looked at Daniel, "At least, I think that's what he was trying to tell me."

"He probably was, and he probably did," answered Daniel. "You did well, Sire. You handled it like the King you will be."

Amel turned and began walking away from the pasture, gesturing for Daniel to accompany him. "We must be very careful as we go forward. We have serious enemies who will stop at nothing to remove us."

Chapter Five
ESCAPE
570-569 BC

All was on schedule, mused Antiosyss as he stood looking up at the ziggurat. Preparations for the new Feast of Marduk, one week away, proceeded at a frenetic pace as the temple priests and their servants prepared for the major event of the religious year. They devoted special attention to the external facade of the edifice and the surrounding gardens and particularly to Procession Way as this was where the populace would gather to witness the climatic ceremony of the day. A sizeable platform had been built on the steps over one-hundred feet high where an ornate altar was in the final stages of construction. Antiosyss had opted to take the ceremony outside to allow thousands to participate. He expected the entire Procession Way spanning one mile to be full of Babylonians drinking, eating, dancing and enjoying the entertainments that the priesthood had planned for them. All was orchestrated so that as night fell on the city, the specially designed torch lights that ringed the ziggurat would give it a surreal glow, offering a superb context for the final ceremony. He tingled at the thought of one-hundred thousand people focused on the magical powers he planned to feature that night.

"It's going well," said Neriglissar who stood by his side. "Where do you plan for the Crown Prince and the Governing Council to be for the ceremony?"

"I hadn't thought about it, but, I guess, down front on the street below the altar," answered Antiosyss.

"We have an opportunity to pit the people against Daniel and we must take advantage of it," returned Neriglissar. "Think about it. I know the whole idea of taking the ceremony outside of the temple is to show everyone the supernatural powers you command. And with Coaster and Narseniah, who would want to go up against you . . . against us?"

Antiosyss smiled at the expectation of the moment and simply nodded.

"So let's not only position our strength but simultaneously diminish Daniel," continued Neriglissar. "Everyone in power will be invited to the evening's ceremony. But not everyone will attend. You know already Daniel will not be present, and most likely not his three cohorts Shadrach, Meshack and Abednego. They abhor Marduk and the very notion of acknowledging, let alone bowing, to a god other than their own imagined deity! If there are reserved seats for every leader in a place that can be seen by all, their absence that evening will speak volumes!"

"Brilliant," quietly acknowledged Antiosyss. "I can play to his empty chair as unworthy—and fearful—to stand before Marduk," a cruel smile covering his face, "and, by extension, unable to stand against us."

"Build a platform for the Crown Prince, Daniel and the Governing Council just below and surrounding the altar. But it has to be high above the crowds—at least three stories high—so they can be easily seen," Neriglissar ordered, grabbing Antiosyss by the arm and climbing the steps. "Come here, I'll show you."

~

The mood within the inner circle of advisors did not match the beautiful spring day that had graced the city outside or the excitement bubbling throughout the citizenry. The Feast of Marduk was now only two days away. Having special seats of honor high on the platform inflated the egos of half of those assembled. They could not believe nor understand that the other half had chosen not to attend.

In the throne room where the inner circle gathered for a meeting, a heavy silence lay in the room. Nebuzaradan could not sit any longer and rose, pacing as he spoke, gesturing animatedly. "This circle—we—cannot afford any more gaffes. We sent Neriglissar to war. He came home a hero, and we excluded him from senior leadership. He's now allied with Antiosyss. I know it. Why give them more fodder for the fires that smolder within them and their followers? If we do not appear as a unified body at the biggest event of the year honoring a god whom everyone in this empire fears, we'll be lucky to have our families still supporting us. It's just not worth the risk to the kingdom!"

"Preposterous that you should think this event is beneath you," scoffed Mysonus. "Daniel, your absence will give credibility to their accusation that you are out of touch." Turning to Shadrach, Meshack, and Abednego, he snorted, "And don't think the three of you won't be in jeopardy too."

Daniel opened his mouth to retort but Amel cut him off with a wave of his hand, "I've heard enough. Thank you for your insights. I need to think this through. We'll meet tomorrow to resolve this."

The seven men stood up and exited. "Daniel," Amel spoke. "Stay behind. I want to discuss something with you." The Crown Prince motioned for Daniel to sit back down. When the last man had left, he sat back, his eyes resting on Daniel whose head was bowed.

"Why are you doing this? What is so wrong about being present at this city-wide celebration? Don't you understand that you will be adding momentum to a coup already in place against you? If you and these three are not in your places with the rest of us who make up the highest body of authority in the land, you undermine my authority."

Daniel's head pivoted to return Amel's hard stare. "My Lord, it is not my intent to bring you dishonor; at the same time, I cannot and will not dishonor the most high Lord God. My presence at the Feast signals that I embrace Marduk and all the demonology that goes with it. That I cannot and will not do."

"I can't afford to lose you, Daniel. Neither can my father."

"As difficult as it may seem to understand, I am persuaded that my God will prevail in all this. If you need to remove me from the Governorship, I well understand your position. So be it. We must both do what we believe is right."

Amel rose, heavy on his feet with a burden he did not want to bear, "You are the most honest man in all of our empire. It was never my intent to remove you." He paused, then, nodded at the door, "Go. I know your integrity will not permit you to unfold a false cover story. You will be truthful to a fault about the reason for your absence. May your God help me."

Daniel rose, bowed to the Prince, then took his leave. As he exited the room, he heard Amel mumble, "The war of the gods. Why do people get caught up in this nonsense?"

~

It seemed like there wasn't a family or household not on the streets enjoying the Feast Day. The priests had hoped that Procession Way would be full, but they were not ready for all the side streets around the temple to be jammed as well. The city came to a standstill; all commerce simply stopped. But no one cared. There was more than enough to eat and drink amply supplied by the priests with help from the royal family. Bands played on every street corner giving way to spontaneous exhibitions of dance, magic tricks, and acrobatics.

By late afternoon, the city of Babylon was tired but not out. The word was out that a spectacular finale to the Feast would take place after sunset. No one wanted to miss it; no one went home. Rather, those on the side streets began to push their way onto Procession Way to get a better view of the ziggurat. A crush of bodies paved the grand avenue.

Amel-Marduk had cleverly brought with him his mother Amytis, his brothers Marduk-Sum-Lisir and Nebudaren, and even his sister Kassaya. They occupied the four empty seats left vacant by Daniel, Shadrach, Meshack, and Abednego in the area reserved for dignitaries. Amel had asked Antiosyss to broaden the platform for honorary guests so it could include the full Governing Council with their families. With several hundred people on the platform beneath the altar, he knew it would be difficult to notice the absence of any one member.

As furious as Neriglissar was that his scheme to call attention to Daniel's absence had been foiled, Antiosyss was ecstatic with the crowds packing the streets for his culminating performance. As far as the eye could see from the top of the ziggurat, tens of thousands of people focused on his stage. Anticipation shimmered in the air.

As the sun sank beneath the horizon, lighted torches were placed in standards along Procession Way, creating a flickering ribbon dividing Babylon into two equal parts. Trumpets sounded from high above both the temple and ziggurat echoing down Procession Way to the Ishtar Gate and back. The bell tones were elongated at first, giving the mass assembly time to quiet down; then they increased in frequency, rolling back and forth between the temple and the ends of the grand boulevard until the music became as one harmonious brass choir.

As suddenly as they had begun, the trumpets stopped. Flash pots ignited shooting flames upwards from the four corners of the ziggurat to frame the pyramid in the darkened sky. Chanting in low guttural sounds, hundreds of priests recruited from temples in all parts of the city and carrying large oil torches emerged from the gardens climbing the ziggurat steps. As the first of them reached the altar they peeled off to encircle the ziggurat with light. A second group of priests circled beneath the first group on the level where the Governing Council were seated, and a third formed a final ring of light on the level below that.

When all the priests were in place, they chanted in unison, "Marduk, Marduk, Marduk." The trumpets blarred another fanfare

Watching from his position within the ziggurat behind the altar, Antiosyss smiled at Coaster and Narseniah standing by his side. "This must be fantastical. You step out first. I'll join you at the altar." With that he shoved them out into the exposure of the bright light of hundreds of torches.

Coaster circled the altar twice then leaped down to the platform where the Governing Council sat. He had a long train to his robe that whirled like a tail behind him with a life of its own, darting here and there to flick in the faces of Babylon's intelligentsia. He approached the Crown Prince and bowed low. With the snap of his fingers, his hair caught fire as did both his hands. Displaying them to the crowd, he next jumped in one spectacular move onto the shoulders of one of the priests, his face fully in the flames of the torch the priest carried. While the flames burned brightly, his face remained unscathed. He proceeded to leap from the shoulders of one priest to another, making his way completely around the ziggurat as the crowd roared its approval.

A whoosh of flame coming from four large pots of oil placed on the peak of the ziggurat illuminated Narseniah held high by two tall men, their chests bare and wearing only loincloths. She was beautifully clothed in multi-colored translucent robes, giving her the appearance of being on fire. She jumped from her perch to slide down a long pole taking her to the altar where she began to dance. The trumpets were replaced by drums which now pounded out an infectious rhythm quickly picked up and duplicated by the crowd. Sensuality reigned as she removed each veil, letting it drift onto the Governing Council below. The drums quickened their pace. Her dancing intensified until she was a color wheel of motion.

Coaster had made his way around the building to rejoin the action. The drumming was now at lightning pace, without warning colliding into silence. Narseniah arched her back upwards and screamed. Coaster hoisted her high above his head. She lay horizontal, suspended in space—even as he lowered his arms. Suspended in air, she slowly floated downward to the altar on which Coaster stood, unassisted. The magic in the air was now so palpable that the thousands watching did not move or speak.

Once more the priests began to chant, "Marduk, Marduk, Marduk." The large idol of Marduk, brought over from the Temple, slowly rose from the pyramid's apex to stand high in the sky. With the flames of the four large oil pots flickering on its bronze surface, Marduk could be seen for miles around the entire city and countryside.

It was Antiosyss' turn to take center stage.

The idol opened to reveal Antiosyss standing on a platform that extended from Marduk's waist. His white robes stood in contrast to all the colors seen heretofore. He raised his hands and the chanting stopped.

"All powerful Marduk," he yelled with all that his voice could sustain, "we bow to you."

He leaped off the platform to the rooftop ledge, his robes a dazzling reflection of the flames that surrounded him. He turned and bowed to the idol seemingly suspended in the sky. All the priests brightly illuminated by their torches quickly followed him as did the masses thronged below, awe-struck by what they were witnessing.

Out of nowhere a twenty-foot high, blazing torch appeared in his hands. He turned to face the crowd and screamed, "Marduk must be honored—a sacrifice to his glory!"

With that he cast the torch downward, directly at Narseniah lying motionless on the altar. It landed in the two-inch gap between Coaster and Narseniah, strikiing deeply into the wood. The crowd gasped, convinced Narseniah was being offered as a sacrifice.

Vaulting off the roof, Antiosyss soared through the air to land like a spear below the frontal piece of the altar. He clapped his hands and the drumming began, this time accompanied by the chanting of the priests, "Marduk, Marduk, Marduk." He turned to face the altar and gestured to both sides. Two spears slightly shorter than the torch he had thrown from the roof were vaulted into the sky, each braced by the two large, bare-chested men who had assisted Narseniah. The pointed spear heads atop shone brightly in the flames of the hundreds of torches still held high by the priests.

Standing completely still in front of the throne, Antiosyss slowly levitated upwards until he was even with the top of the altar on which Narseniah was lying. He took her by her hand and lifted her to stand with Coaster, one at each end of the large ceremonial edifice. The drumming and chanting once more quickened in pace. Satisfied that the masses were ready for the climax, Antiosyss extended his arms in a superhuman gesture to grab Narseniah and Coaster, both fully ten feet away on either side of him. He lifted them up to where they were standing at his eye level. With one motion he flipped them into the air to soar upwards forty to fifty feet, then to fall, landing on their backs dead center on the two long spears circumventing the altar. The spears pierced both bodies, and they came to rest where the blades merged into their wooden shafts.

Flames burst out of the mouth of the idol on the rooftop as though accepting the sacrifice. Antiosyss stepped to the rear of the altar and turned to face the crowd. He signaled the men who were holding the poles to lower the bodies to the altar. The drumming and chanting once more stopped. Antiosyss leaned over each body, and then pushed the spear blades outwards, his arms once more elongating. With the spears removed, he reached down to take the hands of Narseniah and Coaster. As one, they rose . . . very much alive.

The silence over the city was deafening. The fear and terror that swamped the streets was thick enough to cut with a knife. Babylon had just witnessed something never before seen that was not possible . . . yet, it seemed real.

"Marduk reigns," screamed Antiosyss, completely exhausted but exhilarated that the ceremony had been successful beyond his dreams.

"Marduk reigns," joined in Narseniah and Coaster.

"Marduk reigns." The priests' chant was picked up by the thousands of people flooding the streets of Babylon.

~

They sat in the coolness of Neriglissar's palace garden . . . simultaneously exhausted and invigorated. The Feast had gone well . . . beyond their wildest expectations. It had taken over four hours to make their way through the jubilant crowd from the ziggurat. People refused to clear the streets; they wanted to revel in the magic shared collectively. Even now, in the early hours of the morning, they could hear people still singing and dancing in the streets.

Put off by Coaster's foul stench, Neriglissar had placed his chair in the farthest corner away from him so he could enjoy the fresh air of the pre-dawn breeze. Antiosyss sat next to him with Narseniah on his other side.

"You are very scary people to be with," quipped Neriglissar as he held his goblet out to be filled by a servant. "Intimidating . . . but wonderful allies to have on my side."

"Your side?" snorted Coaster who was draining another tankard of beer.

"Does he always drink this much?" Neriglissar whispered to Antiosyss.

"Don't question it," replied Antiosyss just as quietly. "Leave him alone. He's not what you think. In fact, he is many . . . many demons fighting for supremacy. They are unpredictable and can be destructive if provoked. Let them settle. One will eventually take control."

"Aren't you afraid he'll decide one day to take you on? Get rid of you?"

"The possibility is always there," replied Antiosyss. "But if you recall what happened tonight, Narseniah and I are not without our own supernatural powers. Tonight was a real test of how far we were able to go in our own quests for supernatural power. I think we proved ourselves equal to Coaster."

Neriglissar instinctively withdrew into his chair, wondering if it was such a good idea to have invited these people to his palace to bask in the afterglow of the day's events. At the same time, he knew that without their bizarre powers a successful takeover of the kingdom would be futile. By teaming with the powers of the netherworld these three brought him, success was not only possible but guaranteed. Who could stop what they could put in motion? They defied the laws of nature itself.

"I've been thinking, said Neriglissar, changing the subject. "Our plan to expose Daniel's rejection of the Temple and Marduk himself by his absence at the Feast failed. I don't know if the Crown Prince knew what he was doing or if fate just collided with our plans, but we're right back where we were four months ago."

"Can you say that after what you saw tonight?" incredulously asked Narseniah. "I'd say we are in a better place than ever to be rid of Daniel. Can he withstand the powers we now wield? I think not. What we have to do now is come at him through a different door."

Antiosyss smiled at Neriglissar, "I told you she would be helpful to us. Coaster is sheer power, but Narseniah . . . she's both smart and formidable."

"What are you thinking?" asked Neriglissar.

Narseniah stretched, now beginning to tire from a strenuous day. She drew closer to the two men.

"Only three men in Babylon believe in Daniel's god . . . Shadrach, Meshach, and Abednego. They are key voices in the inner circle of advisors. I suspect they are of weaker character than Daniel. They must now be our targets. If any of them loses integrity, Daniel is weakened. When they go down, a quick move on Daniel by Coaster leaves Amel-Marduk with a big hole in governing the empire."

Narseniah smiled seductively kneeling between Neriglissar's legs while sliding her hand under his robe, "Do you think they can defend against the spirits in us? Do you think they can tame Coaster?" She left both her hand and her words suspended in silence.

She abruptly stood, "So let's now attack on another front."

Energized by the new idea, they spent the next couple of hours plotting how to best eliminate one, or all three, of Daniel's closest colleagues. As they fortified themselves with beer, wine, and food, their voices and bravado swelled, unknowingly revealing their scheme to the entire servant staff of Neriglissar's palace. The first light of dawn arrived as they put the finishing touches on their plan. Once again, Neriglissar felt good. Although they had been foiled at the Feast, they were back on track.

~

Stories about their masters' behavior and schemes were the most treasured morsels of servants' gossip in any palace. They were never contained to one residence. In fact, they quickly spread among the servants of the royal family. It was only a matter of a few days before Dorcas learned of the plotting in Neriglissar's garden. While most servants loved hearing and re-telling stories about the weird and bizarre Coaster who convulsed throughout the night, disintegrating every living plant he touched and members of his body morphing in and out of inhuman manifestations, Dorcas zeroed in on the plot against Shadrach, Meshach and Abednego.

What she heard frightened her. As soon as Amel-Marduk returned from the royal palace that afternoon, she apprised him of the growing conspiracy. While he previously had dismissed the supernatural, he was now on his guard. After what he had witnessed at the Feast of Marduk, Amel knew he and Daniel were up against powerful forces. What he saw was real. It was not natural. This stuff happened in spite of it being utterly impossible. So when he heard her story, he took it seriously.

He asked Dorcas to gather all the palace gossip daily and to report to him new developments of the plot. Because of the relentless determination of the cast of characters behind the conspiracy, he knew they were relentlessly determined to act and that it was only a matter of time until they did. He needed more specifics. What were they going to do and when did they plan to do it? He wanted to be able to give Daniel and his three aides ample warning.

~

Spring gave way to summer and the heat that came with it. With Daniel's help and his inner circle of advisors, Amel-Marduk had been ruling for over one year with barely a ripple in the empire's waters. As far as the people of the Babylonian empire knew, King Nebuchadnezzar was still on his sick bed. In truth, he was very much alive in a secluded pasture and barn watched over by Amel and Daniel together with Rymen and a few trusted servants and guards. That they had kept his condition secret was due to their diligence and discipline.

Amel and Daniel never took their eyes off Neriglissar and his band of conspirators, knowing their thirst for the throne was not satisfied. Through Dorcas they managed to keep abreast of the various maneuvers this group initiated to spark a misstep by Shadrach, Meshach or Abednego who respectively oversaw the agriculture production, road system and supply of water that kept the kingdom running. They finally settled on Abednego as their primary target because the supply and delivery of water was most critical in a desert land. Try as they might, however, every effort to trip him up seemed to be effortlessly parried. They finally concluded that Daniel, and thus his allies, had an information source who was privy to their plans and that they needed to speak less freely in places where their schemes could be overheard. The meeting place of choice became the High Priest's preparation room in the Temple of Marduk.

Employing their new demonic powers in temple ceremonies and spectacles, Antiosyss and Narseniah were busily engaged intimidating Babylon's populace. They reasoned that the more the people feared Marduk, the more they could control them. Since the vast majority of the Governing Council and the leading commerce and military leaders worshipped at the temple, it was a plan that seemed to make good sense.

Neriglissar, meanwhile, spent his time building loyalty within the Imperial Guard reaching out to garner support and goodwill from the commanders who were his peers as well as from the generals and captains who were his junior in battalions other than those which were under his direct command. If nothing else, he reasoned that at the appropriate time when the empire was in crisis he could rally the fighting forces to overthrow the Crown Prince and take the throne.

The odd man out was Coaster. As easily as he could have aligned with Antiosyss and Narseniah, he did not have the patience to build a constituency. He certainly wasn't welcome in Neriglissar's environment. He decided to take matters into his own hands. His plan was simple and direct: kill all who stood in their way. He was tired of the political schemes which never worked. Once dead, he reasoned, his enemies posed no problem.

Thought gave way to action. He targeted Meshach.

In the opening hours of the new day when men sleep most soundly, Coaster invaded the home of Meshach by easily leaping through an opening in the corridor that led to his bedchamber on the second story. He didn't know the lay of the house, nor did he care. But he did know enough to conclude the sleeping rooms would be located above the living area on the ground floor. There were two rooms off the corridor. Coaster crept through the doorway of the larger room to find Meshach awake, watching his every move. The stench that preceded Coaster was so pungent that it had aroused Meshach from his sleep. When he heard steps outside his bedchamber, he was instantly alert.

Coaster growled in satisfaction when he saw Meshach was aware of his presence. He intended that this would be fun and it would only be fun if Meshach knew in advance the pain that he was to endure. Coaster was undecided where to start the delicious torture he had planned . . . at his feet or, perhaps, his eyes. A spray of hot vapor spewed from his mouth exacerbating the awful smell that now filled the room. As fast as a flash of lightning, he threw his right hand at Meshach's throat while his left aimed for his eyes. The thrust was vicious and fast, but instead of connecting with his victim both arms collided with a force-field that not only stopped their forward progress but simultaneously locked on, yanked upwards and flipped him completely over to land in a heap back at the doorway.

Meshach hadn't moved. As Coaster recovered and rose to his feet, he snarled, "You're a dead man."

This time he sprang as though an arrow shot from a tightly wound bow to impale his body on Meshach and let the sheer force of the collision break his ribs and whatever else might be in harm's way. Again . . . he hit what felt like a thick stone, the four-feet thick kind used to build the sky-touching ziggurat. He felt his arms and legs pinned as though shackled down. He was spread-eagled and crushed against nothing, but suspended in air, easily an arm's length above Meshach's body.

Meshach spoke softly, "I know you, Coaster, and your powers. Now, you know the power of my God and His angels. Be careful, Coaster, whom you serve."

Coaster was thrown backwards, hitting the wall with such a force he lost consciousness. When he came to, Meshach was standing above him. He reached down and offered his hand to help him up. Terrified that he had more than met his match, Coaster ignored the hand and scurried along the floor to the doorway down the corridor and to the ground below. The sooner he got out of there, the better.

~

Meshach knocked on Daniel's door at dawn to tell him what had happened during the night. Three hours later, they requested an audience with Amel-Marduk. The Crown Prince was so incensed with the audacity of the attack that he immediately wanted to storm the Temple of Marduk with his troops. Reminding Amel that the conspiracy was bigger than just Coaster, Daniel saw this as an opportunity to further draw out Antiosyss's intentions as well as to issue a strong warning that this plot needed to end. He suggested they summon the high priest to the palace that afternoon.

Unaware of Coaster's early morning attempt on Meshach's life, Antiosyss walked into the palace for the meeting with Babylon's top leaders. The thought even crossed his mind that they could be bringing him into their confidence which would give him a significant leg up on Neriglissar.

Rather than bring him to the throne room where public meetings were conducted, the servants escorted Antiosyss into the private quarters the King used when he lived in this palace. Waiting for him were the Crown Prince and Daniel. He bowed in deference to the man who occupied the throne and simply nodded at Daniel. They remained seated, not offering him a chair.

"We want to talk about what happened last night," started Amel.

Antiosyss was immediately on his guard, "Last night? I don't know what happened last night."

"We suspect that you do." snapped Amel. "It's just fortunate that the attack failed. I want to know how you think you can be this brazen! You're only alive right now thanks to Daniel's intervention."

Completely confused by this turn of events, Antiosyss could only sputter, "What attack? What happened? I don't know what you are talking about."

"If I may, my Lord," spoke Daniel addressing Amel. The Prince nodded his assent and Daniel turned to address Antiosyss, "Early this morning, Coaster entered Meshach's house and attempted to kill him. Thanks to God on high, he failed."

"I know nothing about this," interrupted Antiosyss. "Surely, you don't think I put him up to this?"

"The thought occurred to us," replied Amel. "We are not unaware of your plans to weaken my authority and challenge Daniel's governorship. But never did I think it would rise to this level. I dismissed it all as palace grumbling, not insurrection."

"Sire, please . . . you must believe me. I knew nothing about this. Coaster is a difficult priest . . . he has powers that make him think he can act on his own. I did not know anything about this!"

"It's been rumored that you and Neriglissar have designs on the throne itself," said Daniel.

Both fearful at being revealed and angry that Daniel could so freely accuse him, Antiosyss faced Daniel and retorted, "I have never wanted to bend to your authority . . . everyone knows that. The god you worship is not my god. He is not the Babylonian god whom this kingdom holds high. Yes, I admit to you and to you, my Lord," he continued as he turned to Amel, "that as the high priest of the Temple of Marduk I believe I should have a higher place in this empire's ruling authority than a . . . a . . . a Jew! That is all I ask. I want to serve the King and you, my Prince. I want to make the power of Marduk available to you. I am a channel for that. Nothing else. I have no other aspirations."

Antiosyss stood silent, hopeful they believed that he had not dispatched Coaster. The thought of Coaster pricked another nerve. He thought this wild man—thing, or whatever he was—had come close to ruining everything they had planned. He had to be removed.

"I want you to deliver Coaster to the palace guards before night fall," ordered Amel. "The guards can easily occupy the temple and find him. But I think it is your responsibility as the high priest to bring him to us. He is no longer welcome in this city or this kingdom."

Amel-Marduk rose and dismissed Antiosyss with a wave of his hand, "Now leave."

The meeting was over. Antiosyss bowed and retreated from the room. As he hurried back to the temple, his mind was racing. He had to find Neriglissar to tell him what happened but, more importantly, to warn him that they needed to back off things for a while. Of course, he had to locate Coaster immediately and somehow get him to leave the city. This would be a problem, he mused, as Coaster was clearly beyond his control. Yet, if Coaster remained in Babylon, Antiosyss knew that his plans would be jeopardized.

~

Antiosyss nervously paced back and forth, too tense to simply sit. He and Neriglissar were in his preparation room inside the heart of the Temple of Marduk. They could hear the drums and chanting of the priests in the assembly room where the idol of Marduk hovered over the sacrificial altar. But right now, temple ritual was not on his mind. He had just finished telling Neriglissar about his meeting with the Crown Prince and Coaster's attack on Meshach. "I cannot believe he would act so stupidly or without talking to us," he concluded.

"Coaster is . . . well, let's just say, he's not of this world and clearly not understandable to us," said Neriglissar who was comfortably seated. "You're right that he needs to be removed."

"We've searched the entire temple and cannot find him. I don't think he's here, but then he could be on the roof or have even wormed himself into one of the stones. As you said, he is not of our world. He could be anywhere, even within our hearing, and we wouldn't know it."

"He could have left the city," surmised Neriglissar. "It sounds like he more than met his match. If and when we see him, we've got to act forcefully. He must no longer be associated with the temple as it will only draw undue attention to us."

Antiosyss dropped heavily into a chair with a sigh, "Let's hope he is gone. If we see him, we'll call on every spirit and demon we can to get rid of him."

He shifted uneasily in his chair and continued, "What I don't know is how we continue. Daniel is always one step ahead of us. Now that we've been openly rebuked and warned, we need to be very careful . . . perhaps, take a hiatus."

Neriglissar leaned forward and grabbed Antiosyss's arm, "My friend, don't run scared. To stop now when we have so much working in our favor is to give them the victory. You have been able to curry great favor with the leading men of Babylon. They fear you! And I have well over half of the empire's army— the Imperial Guard—aligned behind me. No, now is when we press hard . . . if nothing else, to let Daniel know we will not be intimidated."

"You make sense. But there's a leak somewhere which undermines our advantage of surprise. We've got to find it and stop it."

"Agreed," affirmed Neriglissar who rose to take his leave. He turned back to Antiosyss before opening the door and quietly spoke, "I've had an idea in the back of my mind. I think it's time to share it with you. It might uncover the informant we seek as well as discredit Daniel's ability to govern." He walked back to Antiosyss to look down at him.

"You've always wanted your own canal . . . a direct waterway from the Euphrates River into the temple grounds." He smiled and looked at Antiosyss questioningly.

"Why . . . ah . . . yes, I guess I have," responded Antiosyss nervously. "What does that have to do with—"

"As I recall," Neriglissar cut him off, "you also wanted to connect the temple to the ziggurat with an underground tunnel so you and your priests could go back and forth . . . creating a bit of magic for the public by your sudden, unexpected appearances in ceremonies. Am I right?"

Not knowing where this was going, Antiosyss swallowed the lump that was growing in his throat and simply nodded.

"I'm thinking you should have that canal . . . a canal that brings water directly into the temple grounds creating beautiful ponds and fountains." He paused and smiled knowingly at Antiosyss, "That same canal should be diverted underground into two arms feeding into the ziggurat and into the bowels of the temple itself."

Neriglissar bent low, his face directly in Antiosyss's face . . . smirking, "Underground to give you the tunnel you seek between your two religious palaces."

Neriglissar straightened up and stepped away from the priest. As he seated himself to let Antiosyss absorb this new thought, he quipped, "You know, if we do this . . . you'd be the only one with a private waterway from the river. Not even the King has one."

That's an interesting thought reflected Antiosyss. The inherent power he would reap from this accoutrement alone would hasten his quest for ultimate dominance in the kingdom. He started to smile, tight-lipped at first, but then broadening to consume his face. Could Neriglissar play so easily into his plans to take control of Babylon?

He shook his head, the smile quickly disappearing from his face.

"Yes, but Abednego's strict policies on delivery and conservation will prevent us from diverting any water from the river. He would never authorize it."

"So . . . let's just build it without him knowing it. What's he going to do then?"

"He'll see the construction. We can't keep it from him."

"Maybe we can," mused Neriglissar. "In the process, let's plant a few misleading stories to see if we can discover our leak. Two birds with one stone would make a nice hunt."

The two men sat in silence for a few moments, assimilating all they had discussed. In one short hour they had put a seeming catastrophe behind them and crafted a bold, new move going forward. They smiled in unison as the recognition of what they had just accomplished hit them. Neriglissar rose to bid Antiosyss goodbye and left the temple. Both buzzed with anticipation of what next lay before them.

~

The summer settled upon Babylon with all its constricting heat. Construction at the central market slowed and the city itself shifted into a leisurely pace. It was not a time of wars or of commerce. The fields were tended to as needed, but for the most part the land was left to flourish in the sun. Rymen made sure there was plenty of shade in Nebuchadnezzar's pasture. He had added two new fenced areas of rich grass where the evening breezes blew unabated. It was probably the most pleasant place in the city to be, and Amel went there often.

Summer was the busiest season for the Temple of Marduk. Worshipers enjoyed the coolness of the stone interior. Antiosyss was back in full command of temple rituals and sacrifices, the centerpiece of Babylonian society.

Like Antiosyss, Neriglissar was busier than normal. He decided that the most opportune time to build the diversionary canal from the river into the temple grounds was during the worst season of the year for construction. He was intent on concealing the project from the governing authorities, particularly Abednego. He recruited a select group of workman from the central market project which was on summer hiatus. They were appreciative of the double wages he paid them and readily swore an oath to secrecy concerning the project.

Rather than beginning at dawn, the work day for the canal began after sunset. The men worked very quietly, taking twice as long as normal to do each task. They were careful to leave no noticeable signs of construction near the site. During the day, their work was masked by plantings. When he saw that he wasn't going to complete the project by fall at the rate he was going, Neriglissar enlarged his crews. Progress improved overnight and the canal began to take shape.

In their continuing quest to unearth the informant, Antiosyss and Neriglissar by turns leaked misinformation looking to see which falsehood made it to Daniel and the royal palace. They zeroed in on the people they heretofore most trusted, particularly their servants. It finally occurred to them that servants were privy to all their conservations and they could well be the source that led to Daniel.

In a matter of weeks, Amel-Marduk accused Neriglissar of disloyalty on several occasions. Once, it had been leaked and, subsequently, the Crown Prince had been told, that Neriglissar had been stirring up the third battalion of the Imperial Guards to oppose Amel's claim to the throne during the illness of Nebuchadnezzar. Neriglissar easily deflected the charge by bringing before the Crown Prince the commanders of the battalion who, in fact, credited him for their renewed allegiance to the throne and the empire.

Another time, Neriglissar threw out the lie that he was conspiring with Zocor to merge the palace guards with the battalions of the Imperial Guard which he commanded so that he would gain armed control of the palace. The charge was so loudly refuted by Zocor that by contrast it painted Neriglissar as a wrongfully charged and innocent man.

The ruses worked. Each time, he was able to ascertain that the channel of information flowed from his household servants to servants in the other palaces of the royal family. Usually, servants talked to servants and it ended there. Gossip rarely rose to their master's attention nor to those outside the palaces. In this case, however, there seemed to be a breach in protocol. As Neriglissar dug deeper, he discovered the probable culprit was Dorcas, a servant in Amel-Marduk's palace. Dorcas had been easily identified because of her close relationship to Amel.

Pleased finally to have discovered the leak, Neriglissar called Antiosyss to his palace one night for dinner to share the news. Following a sumptuous meal and more than enough wine, Neriglissar dismissed the servants to leave the two men alone in the dining room.

"How is the canal project proceeding?" asked Neriglissar, carefully looking around to ensure there were no servants hovering in the doorways.

"Good," replied Antiosyss, "and it's picking up some momentum thanks to the new men you added. But that's not why you invited me to dinner."

Neriglissar laughed, "What I really want to tell you is that I've found our leak. As you suggested, it was through the palace servants. The end of the line seems to be a Jewish servant who enjoys a closer than normal relationship with Amel-Marduk. Her name is Dorcas, not that it matters much."

"How interesting," smiled Antiosyss.

"She needs to be removed . . . eliminated," continued Neriglissar. "That's going to be difficult given she's part of the Crown Prince's household. You know that in spite of our efforts to keep things private, something is going to fall on the ears of those that surround us. We need to be rid of her."

"Let me talk to Narseniah about this," Antiosyss replied. "I suspect she might have an idea, woman-to-woman so to speak." At that both men laughed

~

As the summer reached its zenith and the afternoon heat its most oppressive, Amel found himself spending more and more time in the latter part of the days visiting his father in his well hidden and protected pasture. Their relationship had become close—much closer than when Nebuchadnezzar was in full control of his faculties. Amel now sat on the grass inside the fence watching him graze or sleep. What had once seemed bizarre was now taken for granted. Amel had mentioned these welcome breathers in his daily schedule to Daniel and encouraged him to join him sometime.

It had been a tiring day, both from the heat and the city's business. Amel had been tied up with his duties and then his mentorship on governance under Daniel into the evening. When he finally left the palace to visit his father, the sun had begun to drop into the horizon. Today he especially looked forward to relaxing with Nebuchadnezzar in the cool evening breezes.

He drew near to the main pasture and let himself in the gate. Nebuchadnezzar was not in sight so he walked down to where the adjoining pasture had been built with the large shade trees where his father often rested. He could not be found. Something was amiss.

"He's gone!" Amel said out loud to himself. He began running along the fences to see if there was a break. Within seconds he spotted a couple of broken boards on the other side of the pasture. He hurtled through the break and began running into the open meadow searching for his father. The palace guards who were assigned to the King ran towards Amel to find out what was wrong.

"My Lord, what's happened?" asked the first to reach the Crown Prince.

"He's gone!" shouted Amel. Whirling around to gesture at the pastures, he yelled, "We have to find the King. Take a couple of men and search every street or alley that lead out of this meadow. I'm going to the barns to see if he might be there. Tell the other guards to fan out in a large circle from the pasture. Search every possible trail or street where he could have gone."

He raced back to the barn shouting for Rymen. It was empty inside and all seemed in order. As he emerged into the sunlight, Rymen met him.

"What's wrong, Sire?" questioned Rymen.

"The King is gone . . . disappeared!" replied Amel.

Visibly shaken by this news because it was always his greatest fear that something bad would happen to the King on his watch, Rymen leaned on the fence to catch his breath before speaking. "He can't have gone far. I'll bring every herder I have in for the evening to search. We'll find him, Sire."

The search continued throughout the night. Zocor and Rymen limited the men they employed for the task to those they felt were most trustworthy and could maintain the secret of Nebuchadnezzar's condition. Amel concurred as they could not unleash the Imperial Guard upon the city to search door by door.

That would only let the cat out of the bag and provide fodder for his enemies. They had to keep this under wraps.

Completely exhausted the next morning, Amel agreed to return to his palace to get a few hours of sleep while Daniel took charge of the search. When he returned in the late afternoon, the King had yet to be found. Night again turned into day as the search entered its second day. Palace guards were now moving throughout the city looking for him trying not to call attention to themselves; the King's herdsmen were totally out of place as they, too, searched the city. It was no longer possible to quell the speculation that began to rise.

Catching wind of a story that the prize bull in the King's herd had escaped and smelling an opportunity, Neriglissar told everyone he met that it was just another example of ineptness in the empire under Daniel's governance. As he told the story each time, it grew in hyperbole to where he began to suggest that Daniel had, in fact, instructed the herdsmen to leave gates unlocked and broken fences unfixed as he refused to spend any more money on these endless repairs.

Amel was no longer thinking clearly. He had lost sleep and was deeply concerned over his father's disappearance. At the afternoon's regularly scheduled Governing Council meeting, his mind incessantly wandered until he lost control of the proceedings. Neriglissar maintained that Daniel wasn't paying attention to the affairs of the kingdom. If the Governor couldn't be trusted to maintain the integrity of the King's palace and barns, how could they trust him with the management of the empire? As insipid as this argument was, Daniel's enemies—by now, the majority of the Council—rode this figurative horse to its death. Clearly, Daniel was incompetent. Amel was uninterested in defending Daniel which only added fuel to the fire.

"Enough," said Amel. "Obviously there are questions about security and caretaking that we must examine. I've heard your charges. Maybe we have a serious problem facing us; maybe we don't. I need to think about all that has been said and get some rest. We'll resolve it tomorrow. Your charge is serious enough for the entire Governing Council to take action and not just the inner circle of advisors."

He dismissed the group, remaining seated on the throne. All he knew was that his father was gone and very vulnerable. They had to find him soon. The problem was that no one had any idea of where to search next. At this point, he could be persuaded to believe anything, even that Daniel was, indeed, incompetent and therefore singularly responsible for the escape of his father.

Daniel remained behind the others. Once they had left the room, he approached Amel and said, "Sire, this has become like a wildfire . . . out of control! The truth is clouded. None of them know what is really happening. That they can make the escape of a bull equal to the import of empire governance is . . . well, it's ridiculous!"

Amel lifted his head and stared blankly at Daniel and spoke without feeling, "Daniel, you have let me down. I don't know what happened, but Rymen directly reported to you. My father has disappeared, and I believe you are ultimately responsible."

Stunned that Amel could even suggest he was derelict, Daniel stood speechless.

"Go. I need to think," Amel ordered. "Leave me alone."

Dumbfounded that Amel had bought into Neriglissar's argument, Daniel backed away and withdrew from the throne room. He felt as isolated as he had ever been in the service of the King.

Chapter Six
ATTACK
569 BC

Amel-Marduk wasn't happy with himself or with much of anything. He was fearful and frustrated that he couldn't find his father and angry that Daniel's usually well-managed fabric that enveloped the affairs of the kingdom had torn badly. If I can't trust him, who can I trust, he questioned. His exhaustion exacerbated his emotional turmoil causing no small disturbance within his servant staff. Finally, his head servant Maximillan had stepped in to urge early retirement for the evening. Sleep was what he needed most, and even Amel had begun to realize this. He quit fighting it and let himself fall into bed.

The grey light of pre-dawn outlined the walls of Amel's bed chamber. The whistling of the songbirds welcoming the new day had roused Amel from sleep. His eyes followed the dim light to the opening of the window where he saw the initial rays of the sun signaling morning had begun. As he rose and dressed, his mind reviewed the activities of the previous day. The distance that the night's sleep had given him from yesterday's meeting of the Governing Council enabled him to see how ridiculous the charges were against Daniel. He chuckled to himself to think that he had taken Neriglissar's arguments seriously.

Word quickly spread among the servants that Amel was back to his normal self. Breakfast was served with unusual enthusiasm and energy, the fruits especially prepared and arranged in appetizing fashion. As he was preparing to leave for the royal palace, Dorcas approached him in the foyer.

"My Lord, may I have a word with you?" she asked.

"Of course," he smiled at her. She was always the center of calm and reason, one of the few people on earth he could completely trust because of her loyalty to him.

"I heard about the accusations that were made against Daniel in the Governing Council yesterday. I know Daniel's character and his heart. He would never let his guard down at any time, especially with the King. Please, Sire, you must not believe the lies that were told you. They all hate him, and, because he is your chief advisor, you as well. You must trust Daniel."

"Dorcas, you've been a valuable help to me . . . making me aware of those who want my throne. Perhaps now it is time for me to deceive them by pretending I no longer fully trust Daniel. Let's see how they take that bone and chew it."

He laughed gently, patted her cheek, and walked to exit his palace. Relieved that he was not going to take action against Daniel, she ran after him and caught him at the entry: "Will Daniel know your plan? I mean. . . I . . . I don't want to see him hurt . . . he can help."

Amel turned to her, "Oh, he'll know. He can see through me. But why don't you tell him as well. Just make sure no one overhears you." He started down the steps as Dorcas fled out the alley hoping to reach Daniel before he left his house for the palace.

~

Rymen ran like the young man he was not from the King's barns and into the royal palace, breathing heavily, his heart pounding. He did not stop at the entry but headed straight for the throne room. Finding it empty, he headed for the public wing which housed Daniel's offices brushing off assistance offered by the palace guards. There was always a beehive of activity in the Governor's offices . . . people stating their case to adjutants willing to listen, people waiting to be seen, and people lined up at the door to Daniel's private office hoping to speak with him.

He hurtled through them all, bursting into Daniel's chamber. "We found him! He's safe," he blurted out.

Daniel and Amel had been deep in conversation with a group of men. All looked up at Rymen's sudden outburst. Then it dawned on Amel what he was saying. With a wide grin, he raced for Rymen's side grabbing his arms in joy, "He's okay? You have him protected?"

Completely spent, Rymen could only nod his head vigorously as he leaned on the wall to remain upright. Not wanting their secret out, Daniel herded his visitors out the door, apologizing that an emergency had come. Once they were gone, he joined Amel and Rymen who had yet to regain his breath.

"The King is safe?" asked Daniel.

"Yes, Sire," Rymen barely got out. "He's in the barns. He is not hurt."

"Where did you find him?" asked Amel.

They brought Rymen over to a chair where they seated him and drew up two other chairs next to him. At first, he refused to sit in deference to Amel's authority, but he was so drained of energy he finally yielded.

"He must have made it through all the streets of Babylon unseen because they found him outside the city among the royal herd," gasped Rymen in between breaths. "I can't believe he got that far without being seen!"

"Thank God he's safe," prayed Daniel under his breath.

"You brought him back to the barn by the palace?" queried Amel.

"Yes, once my herdsmen spotted him they took him back here. They were careful to shield him from any onlookers."

"And the fence is fixed? Reinforced?" asked Daniel.

"Yes, sire. I made sure everything is double strong and the gates double locked," replied Rymen.

"I want to go see him," said Amel as he rose to leave.

"My Lord," cautioned Daniel, "we should not call attention to this. Rymen has him safely in the barn. Let's finish our business for the day and then adjourn."

"You're right as always," agreed Amel. "No sense making this food for speculation. Rymen, go back and let him out into his pasture . . . and stay with him the rest of the day. Watch him carefully in case you missed any injury. I'll be there later this afternoon."

"Yes, my Prince," replied Rymen, finally breathing closer to normal. He rose and bowed low, exiting the room.

~

Amel looked around the room at the Governing Council. He had called them together hastily by messenger. To a man, they were terribly curious as to the meeting's agenda. At their last meeting, Neriglissar had led a vicious attack on Daniel's credibility and trustworthiness. Perhaps today the axe was coming down and a new Governor would be named. They sat in great expectancy, but none dared to speak before the Crown Prince revealed the occasion of this gathering.

"I am happy to report to you that that what was lost has been found and returned," began Amel-Marduk.

The murmuring was thick in the room. The councilors could not help but speculate among themselves what this might mean. Amel simply sat quietly and watched the room, particularly Neriglissar and Antiosyss. Quickly, they felt his cold eyes and quieted.

Amel continued: "At our last meeting, our Governor's ability to continue serving the kingdom was questioined. I have had time to consider these charges and to review the incident calmly now that all is back in order. Neriglissar raised valid concerns I could not ignore. At the same time, under Daniel's leadership, we recovered our loss." He paused, letting speculation of his decision grow in the room.

"I have decided Daniel shall remain as Governor, however, he no longer has my complete confidence. I will review all of his actions with my inner circle of advisors as well as this Governing Council. I am sorry that it has come to this, but until that trust is restored this is how we will govern."

He turned to look at Daniel who remaining stone-faced simply nodded in assent. He tried his best to look duly chastised.

This time the murmuring erupted into a loud buzz in the room. They had not seen a major shift in power like this since Nebuchadnezzar first elevated Daniel to leadership thirty-five years ago.

Neriglissar's voice broke through the clamor, "Sire, you have made a wise decision which I gladly support."

"Hear, hear!"

"So be it."

The chorus of endorsement rose in volume and filled the chamber. Everyone was pleased. Daniel had been put in his place. The object of their envy no longer enjoyed the independence of his authority of the past.

~

Later that afternoon, Amel and Daniel sat in the shade watching Nebuchadnezzar graze. He seemed content and peaceful after his foray into the herd where by all rights he should have been hurt by the young bulls and protective new mothering cows. They were pleased that their ploy had worked, and that they were now on the offense toying with those who had viciously conspired to take them down.

Likewise, Neriglissar and Antiosyss sat inside the coolness of the Temple of Marduk reliving the day. They were pleased that Amel had lost some confidence in Daniel but unhappy that he had not removed him completely from his powerful position. The battle was still on, but now they had an advantage they did not have before: they could leverage the open rift to drive the Crown Prince and Daniel further apart until their relationship completely snapped.

"We still need to eliminate this Dorcas. Without her gone, we can never be sure we are acting in secrecy," said Neriglissar. "Once we gain the element of complete surprise, I don't see that it will be that difficult to widen the breach between the Crown Prince and Daniel."

"I have been working on an idea I think you'll like," countered Antiosyss. "I agree with you that Dorcas needs to go. The key to that has been right in front of us all this time. We have simply missed it."

"What's that?" asked Neriglissar, mildly curious about the next idea Antiosyss would throw him.

"She is very close to the Prince," replied Antiosyss. "We just need to get someone closer." Neriglissar looked at him questioningly and extended his arms to suggest he continue.

"Narseniah can turn the heart and enflame the lust of any man on earth," Antiosyss continued. "We need to enlist her now while Daniel has fallen out of favor with the Crown Prince. There is a void there that probably runs deeper than just politics. I suspect underneath it all is the loneliness of a man seeking to be satisfied once he allows his inner desires to be released. I don't believe Dorcas is the woman to do this. I know Narseniah can be."

"So how does that get rid of Dorcas? It seems to me that just puts us on the inside of the palace, " said Neriglissar. He added quickly, "Don't get me wrong. That in itself is good, but we will still have our leak to contend with."

"Once Narseniah has turned Amel's head with her charms, it will be an easy matter for her to convince him to remove Dorcas. Think about it! Who would you rather have: the most beautiful, sensual woman on earth in your bed or Dorcas as a servant in your house?"

Neriglissar sat there, letting this new plan take root in his mind. He smiled broadly and then began to laugh. "What a perfect idea! The time is right to prey on his senses. He's vulnerable, and we must attack." He got up from his chair and paced the room, thinking of the possibilities. He turned to Antiosyss, "Will she do it?"

Antiosyss laughed loudly, "Do you know who you are talking about? She hates Daniel and the Prince as much as we! This woman who is inhabited by the demons of Marduk...who has no fear of either the human or spirit world? Yes, my friend, she not only will seduce the Crown Prince but she is happy to do it."

~

For the next few weeks, Daniel and Amel played their roles as adversaries to the hilt, increasingly seeming to grow out of sorts with each other. Amel appeared to challenge most decisions Daniel made, forever bringing in the Governing Council to review his actions much to their delight. Members of the Council grew emboldened to assail Daniel's character . . . first with little white lies, then with blatant untruths. They no longer feared royal retribution.

All of this bode well for Neriglissar's and Antiosyss's temple canal project. Any other rumor in the city paled by comparison with the drama unfolding at court. Their crews were working with more abandon, not concerned about covering their tracks as before. The project had to be completed before they lost their labor to the restart of the central market project.

Narseniah readily agreed to the scheme concocted by her father but was concerned about penetrating Amel's palace guards to access his chambers at night. Neriglissar reminded her that the growing discord between Daniel and the Crown Prince would make it easier to approach Amel on the pretext of sharing conspiracy information regarding Daniel's activities. He assured her that Amel's mistrust of Daniel would pique his curiosity. "No one wants to miss any information concerning an adversary," he told her. Furthermore, given that she was Antiosyss's daughter and a key player in the Temple of Marduk, the Crown Prince would easily believe that she was privy to concealed information.

It occurred to Neriglissar that he could kill two birds with one stone. He needed to delay work on the central market so he could maintain the labor force on the canal. If he could create the perception that Daniel opposed restarting the central market construction which was Amel's pet project, he could drive another wedge between the Prince and the Governor. This would only increase the antagonism between the two men and drive the issue into the hands of the Governing Council where he could easily fan the flames of debate for days and weeks thus delaying restart of construction.

It was time for Narseniah to work her magic. Antiosyss told her he had overheard Daniel colluding with Polynices to gain his vote to oppose restart of construction on the central market. They did not tell Narseniah this was a complete fabrication as Neriglissar and Antiosyss felt she would perform better if she believed it to be true. Moreover, it had enough hint of authenticity for her to ease by the guards and even get the Prince's attention. Most important, this lie had a real chance to disrupt planned construction.

Rather than attempt to enter the Crown Prince's palace surreptitiously, Narseniah boldly entered the palace grounds through the main entrance on Procession Way. She had dressed in her most beautiful robes which, when parted, revealed a bare midriff and lots of leg. She knew her assets and used them well. Inside the gate, two palace guards stopped her asking what business she had and with whom. Since they recognized her from her temple rituals, they let her pass.

She made her way around the royal grounds and quickly walked to the Crown Prince's palace where she again was stopped by two guards. This time, she let her robes open a bit revealing parts of the most beautiful woman's body either had ever seen. Then she informed them that she had word of a plot against the Prince which she needed to share with him immediately. Combined with her well known persona throughout Babylon, this was enough to enable her to continue into the private quarters.

Narseniah leaned into one of the guards and asked, "Is the Crown Prince alone or are there servants in his quarters?

"No. He has retired for the night," replied the guard.

This bode well for her. She entered his sitting room and found it empty, the lanterns extinguished. She moved on to the bedchamber and hesitated at the entrance. Amel was lying on his bed drawing some designs for the market by the light of a bedside lamp. The scintillating scent of her perfume preceded her presence into his room, causing him to glance at the doorway. Seeing her standing there, he rolled over to a sitting position never taking his eyes off her.

"What are you doing here?" he asked suspiciously.

"My Prince, I have heard tonight of a conspiracy I could not wait until morning to tell you. Please, may I come in?"

Amel gestured for her to enter, pointing to a chair along the wall.

"How did you get past the guards?"

Putting on her most innocent face, she answered, "I told them I had important information to share with you that concerned your well-being. I guess they all knew me from the temple so they allowed me to pass." She remained standing.

"What is it you need to tell me?"

Narseniah proceeded to recite what she had been told by Neriglissar. Wanting to add fuel to the fire, she invented a few other lies assailing Daniel's character and intentions. She hated the man and wanted to destroy him. Amel didn't interrupt her once. He was curious what his enemies had concocted to pit him against Daniel. This story topped them all. And the story-teller was the best he had enjoyed thus far.

She had let her robes slide open revealing more than a little of her naked body beneath. Amel caught his breath at her beauty. He was beginning to recall the ceremony at the temple when, naked on the altar, she had invoked Marduk to enter her. He was beginning to lose his train of thought. He suddenly realized that she had finished and they were facing each other in silence.

"You are a beautiful woman," he mumbled more to himself than to her.

Narseniah smiled and slowly let her robes slide off her body to stand before him, "Do you really think so?"

The years of being without his wife and suppressing any thought of being with a woman collided with the stunning, sensual woman standing before him. He could obviously have her. She wanted him as well. It was all too much for him. He reached his arms out to her. She walked slowly toward him.

"My Lord!"

The shout at the doorway broke through the clouded world into which he had entered like a spike driven into a timber. His head swiveled from Narseniah to see Dorcas and Maximillan at the door, startled by what they had come upon.

"How did you get in here?" angrily asked Dorcas who moved from the door directly to Narseniah, picking up her robes and throwing them at her.

"Sire, are you all right?" questioned Maximillan who had come to Amel's side. Suspended between the dream world Narseniah offered him and the reality now present in the room, he struggled for words but couldn't answer.

"My Lord, are you all right? Should I get the physicians?" asked Maximillan

Dorcas had helped Narseniah dress and hustled her out the door. She guessed what had taken place, and she was furious that the Crown Prince had been taken advantage of and played for a fool.

Narseniah turned to speak to Amel, but was shut down by Dorcas who commanded, "Don't you even dare speak to him. We heard you had maneuvered your way past the guards. They should be punished for letting you through." Over her shoulder, she spoke to Amel, "I'm showing her out of the palace, Sire. This is no place or time to have a meeting." And then back to

Narseniah, coldly, "If you have business with our Prince, you see him at the royal palace during the day. Now, good night."

Amel finally came to his senses, whispering under his breath, "She is the most beautiful woman I have ever seen."

Maximillan simply nodded. They didn't move. Finally . . . "Can I bring you a drink . . . some food . . . anything?"

Amel smiled and lay back in bed: "No. Just put the lamp out. I'd like to go to sleep now."

~

Building the new central market was not just a matter of demolition and construction of the buildings. More challenging were the re-design of streets that provided farmers and vendors easy access to their sales stalls and the logistics of accommodating their parked wagons and teams of oxen not to mention the carts of market customers which further jammed the passage ways. With construction on the market about to begin, these plans had moved to a high priority for Daniel and Amel.

The morning was half-gone and things were getting nowhere. It was obvious that Amel was not focusing on the task. Deciding to take a break, Daniel stood up and stretched, saying, "Let's get a little distance from this for a few minutes. Perhaps we all need to walk around . . . maybe get a refreshment. We need to freshen our thinking." He turned to the Crown Prince and asked, "Is that all right with you, Sire?"

"An excellent idea, Daniel," responded Amel who was only thinking of how he could entice Narseniah back to his palace that evening without his servants getting wind of it.

"I could use a break," concurred Meshach whose job was the oversight of the kingdom's roads and streets.

"Why don't you get a little fresh air," said Daniel. "I'd like to speak with the Crown Prince about some other matters in the interim."

When Meshak and his aides had exited, Daniel turned to Amel and asked "Are you feeling all right? You seem disengaged today and that's not normal since this entire project is of your making."

"I'm fine," smiled Amel. "I just have some other things on my mind. Maybe we should dispense with this for today. We can pick this back up tomorrow."

"That's no problem," replied Daniel. "In fact, if you want to cancel the Governing Council's meeting this afternoon, we can do that too. There is nothing urgent on the agenda." He paused and smiled peevishly at Amel, "Unless you want to question any of my decisions this week."

Amel laughed. "Maybe we should stop this ruse. The members of the Council are beginning to think they have my confidence. They are like children. If we give them enough rope, they will begin to think they are actually running the kingdom."

Before Daniel could reply, there was a commotion at the door and Nebuzaradan, Supreme Commander of the Imperial Guard stormed in. His face, already hardened from years of battle, was grimmer than they had ever seen it.

"My Lord, we have been attacked," he blurted out as soon as he set foot in the room. "The Egyptians have crossed our borders and are advancing with a large force in the southwest province. I just received the news from one of my soldiers who was dispatched to Babylon as soon as my commander for that area verified this was a full-on attack and not just another border skirmish."

Snapped out of his vapid haze, Amel immediately took control and began snapping orders, "Bring your top commanders and a full set of maps to my chambers. I want everyone there as soon as possible. Daniel, I want you to join us. I want a complete report on this so have the man who was sent to us in attendance as well. We need to form our battle plan."

Amel was already exiting Daniel's chambers, Nebuzaradan in close pursuit. Daniel called for one of his aides to gather everything up they had been working on. The central market project was on hold indefinitely.

~

The members of the Governing Council ambled into the palace's spacious throne room, speculating as to what might happen in the continuing power struggle between Daniel and Neriglissar. Their meetings had become good theater. While the opposing factions had broken off into sub groups plotting strategy, those who were neutral stood silently waiting for the Crown Prince to arrive. Usually, everyone was in place by the appointed hour. Today, however, noticeably absent were Daniel, Nebuzaradan, and Neriglissar exacerbating the anticipation of interesting theatrics.

The palace guards banged their spears on the stone floor announcing the arrival of the Crown Prince who swept into the room followed by the three men who had been missing and a retinue of top commanders of the Imperial Guard. Their demeanor instantly stilled the cacophony that always preceded Council meetings. Amel-Marduk stepped onto the throne as the others flanked him on both sides. No one was seated. The silence was overwhelming.

"The empire has been attacked," Amel declared in a strong, steely voice. "Egypt has pierced our border with at least three battalions and is over-running the southwest province. We have reports there are more forces behind the first wave of attack. This seems to be more than just a skirmish. It is a serious threat to Babylon. We must deal with it immediately."

The shock of this news registered on every face in the room. All of the in-fighting and routine jockeying for power fell away at the prospect of war.

"We received this news this morning," Amel announced. "Follow-up reports have been trickling in as messengers arrive from the front lines. I have been discussing our options with Nebuzaradan and his commanders. Right now, we know we must dispatch no less than six divisions. Fortunately, the Imperial Guard is always ready to move at a moment's notice. We have sent orders to mobilize one division of troops from both the central and northwest sectors to the battle area. They are in a position to reinforce our border troops more quickly than the divisions we will dispatch from Babylon."

"Neriglissar and Rabmag will leave tonight with one division each. We all know Neriglissar's leadership in battle is second to none. He will be joined by the commanders you see standing before you, all quite capable men," said Amel as he gestured to acknowledge the soldiers standing on either side of the throne.

"Nebuzaradan and I will depart tomorrow with two more divisions. We understand that the Egyptian Pharaoh may be with the second wave of soldiers they plan to send into battle."

He paused and smiled, "I intend to personally stand on his body while holding his head in my right hand and watch his defeated troops rush headlong back to Memphis. No one shall ever threaten our empire and live to see another day!"

With that the silence in the room was broken. Cheers broke out spontaneously. Those closest to the military leaders grasped their arms in a show of solidarity while others embraced whoever was next to them or lifted their arms into the air in victory. All the bickering of internal politics ceased in favor of a long forgotten patriotic zeal. An exuberant spirit foreshadowing a Babylonian victory had replaced the shock of invasion.

Amel-Marduk let the emotional surge go on for a bit, pleased to see unity in his Governing Council. He quickly checked the faces of the most powerful in the room to ensure all were in accord. To his relief, there was not a frown or dispassionate look. If nothing else, the Egyptian attack solidified Babylon in its resolve to protect the empire. He finally lifted his hands signaling for quiet. Soon the room settled down; everyone wanted to hear further plans.

"Are there any questions or concerns?" asked Amel.

"We are in good hands with you and Nebuzaradan in command," responded Mysonus who usually served as the chief spokesman for the court's wise men and assorted courtiers. "May you have a swift and overwhelming victory."

"Yes, yes," echoed the other members.

A tall man with an exceptional stately bearing stepped forward seeking to address Amel and the Governing Council. Although without title or official position in the King's court, Mister, a magician and wise man favored by Nebuchadnezzar, enjoyed a commanding presence among the leadership of Babylon. He was to be taken seriously.

"Sire, who will be in charge of the city and the kingdom's domestic affairs in your absence?"

The room changed character in an instant. Nationalistic fervor was replaced by longstanding factional suspicions. While no one wanted their shared camaraderie to dissipate, it was a question on everyone's mind. Now that it had been hurled to the forefront, they looked expectantly at Amel for the answer.

Without missing a beat Amel looked Mister in the eyes and answered, "Daniel was the Governor appointed by my father, King Nebuchadnezzar, and he shall remain Governor. There is no more loyal servant to this kingdom or to the King than him. We have had a few issues, I grant you that. Nevertheless, I have found all charges against him lacking. They have been nothing of substance and, in fact, are frivolous accusations."

Amel paused and looked slowly around the room, catching the eyes of most everyone to ensure they knew he was deadly serious. He continued, "Daniel is in charge. Daniel is my Governor and therefore your Governor as he has been for many years." He suddenly raised his right fist into the air and shouted "Victory to Babylon!"

The Imperial Guard commanders instantly responded "Victory to Babylon" with their fists in the air. Amel smiled and then shouted even louder to the entire chamber, "Victory to Babylon!"

This time every man thrust his fist into the air and echoed "Victory to Babylon."

Not wanting to give any opportunity for further dissent, the Crown Prince descended the throne, gathered his commanders, and exited. In a loud voice, Daniel bid them farewell, "May your victory be swift and sure. We send you into battle united in spirit."

"Hear, hear," echoed the Council members.

"Gentlemen," said Daniel as he took his seat, "we have a few issues to deal with today. Please take your seats and our afternoon session will get started."

~

The sun had not yet broken over the horizon. In the grey of early dawn, thousands of fiery Arabian horses were prancing and mulling about as their riders made every effort to keep them calm to save their energy. Tens of thousands of foot-soldiers were forming ranks. The main division of the imperial Gujard stood, shoulder to shoulder as far as Procession Way stretched. Every soldier was outfitted in full armor and carrying at least two weapons. Babylon was going to war.

Nebuzaradan was astride his steed at the front of the column at the bottom of the steps of the royal palace and command center of the Babylonian empire. With him were his key staff, all generals and, more importantly, successful war strategists. The absence of chariots was notable since many of the command staff preferred them to riding horseback when embarking on a long journey as was ahead of them that day. However, the Crown Prince preferred to ride horseback and so protocol dictated the chariots be left at home.

Daniel and Dorcas exited the palace with Amel-Marduk dressed in the full battle regalia of the King of Babylon. The view down Procession Way past the looming Temple of Marduk was breath-taking. There was no finer show of the power of Babylon than the thousands of well-armed soldiers massed before them. A smile crossed Amel's otherwise stern face as he reflected on the advantage he had in the upcoming battle. Who would dare to take on this powerful force?

"My Lord," shouted Nebuzaradan from below, "the Guard is ready to march."

"May Egypt rue the day they crossed our border," Amel shouted back. "A moment."

He turned to Daniel as they grasped right arms in friendship: "Maintain the affairs of the kingdom as though you were the king. I have complete trust in you. Watch over my father. If you're right, he will be back on the throne in due time and we will all have to answer to him. I, for one, intend to bring back a victory for him."

Daniel bowed his head before Amel, gripping his arm even tighter, "May God go with you and may God guide my actions. I pray for a short and victorious campaign."

Amel took Dorcas's hands in his and looked deep into her eyes, "You have been so loyal and faithful to me over the years. I leave with a glad heart knowing the affairs of my house are in good hands."

Attempting to respond but finding herself overcome with emotion at thinking she might never see him again should he get killed in battle, she simply stood speechless, the tears streaming out of her eyes like glistening waterfalls down her cheeks. Her heart raced, I want to grab you and hold you but I can't. You are the Crown Prince and I am but a simple servant in your household.

Amel abruptly turned and proceeded down the steps to his waiting troops. He vaulted into the saddle and said to Nebuzaradan, "Let's go." The Imperial Guard Commander held his hand high, and in a sweeping motion brought it down to point forward.

One simple command, "Forward!" put the war machine of one-hundred thousand seasoned troops in motion.

~

Things had gone well in the days after Amel and the Imperial Guard had left for the south and west sectors. With Neriglissar also gone to war, tensions seemed to ease in Daniel's office and he could get on with the work of ensuring a smooth running nation and capital city. One thing was beginning to concern him, however. The royal treasury was dwindling as a result of Nebuchadnezzar and Amel's quest to make Babylon a city unequaled in the known world. It was not serious at this point, but for once Daniel was forced set priorities. Together with Meshach and Abednego, he had to carefully plot a timetable for road and waterway construction.

Daniel hoped the afternoon meeting of the Governing Council would take his mind off these important but mundane issues. It was the first meeting of this group since the Crown Prince had left for battle. The meeting chamber was full when he arrived and took his place beside the King's throne.

As he sat, he smiled at the room, "Welcome to the regular meeting of the Governing Council. It's too soon to expect some word from our front lines, so I have none. Our agenda is rather light today which may give us some time to discuss and reflect on policy or, if you prefer, to adjourn early and retreat to our homes."

Before he could get to the first item on the agenda, Beltekasmer stood and walked with unusual dignity and bearing to the open oval in the center of the room from where he could address all the members at a closer distance.

"I am gravely concerned about the state of our kingdom given this new war with Egypt because we do not have a sitting King. Where is King Nebuchadnezzar? Why haven't we seen him in over three years? Is he really sick or have you simply killed him?

The room exploded in every direction as the thought of Nebuchadnezzar lying dead at the hands of Daniel was the height of treason and tyranny. All were talking at once as the various factions began to speculate.

"That's preposterous!" shouted Daniel. "You know the Crown Prince, the Queen and all members of the royal family have been caring for the King. They would never be part of the plot you are suggesting."

"Does he know what is happening?" demanded Beltekasmer. "Does he know Egypt has attacked? Are you even talking to him, or is he so ill he cannot function? And if that is the case, then I say that we do not have a sitting King and we as a nation are in trouble!"

Seeing an opportunity to intensify the fray, Antiosyss leaped to his feet, "If he is so ill, why haven't I been called in to heal him? I have the power of Marduk which is greater than all else in this world, and you have not used me. I think Beltekasmer has finally brought into the open what all of us have been afraid to say."

"Quiet!"

The command was as sharp as it was short. The room hushed and all strained to see from where it came.

"I have seen the King and he is in very good hands. He is ill but I feel he will regain his strength at some time, and so he is still my lord and ruler."

Polynices had risen slowly to speak. As the wealthiest patron of the court and leading merchant in the city, his words carried no small weight, "Our King has full confidence in the Crown Prince as interim ruler, and he has full confidence in Daniel. I must warn you, if you challenge either man you are challenging the King himself."

Nobody said anything for a full minute. Finally Beltekasmer regained his composure and with a deferential bow to Poynices said, "If you have seen our King and he is resting as you say, I withdraw my charge. But we, the wise men of the court, have not been called upon for insights, advice, and guidance as in the past under King Nebuchadnezzar. We should like to think that we still have value in the kingdom." Turning directly to Daniel, he continued, "You, Governor, must not continue to disregard us."

"The same is true for us—the priests of Marduk," shouted Antiosyss. "Marduk is the god of Babylon and it is through us that his powers can be harnessed. We were here long before you and your Jewish God were brought to Babylon, and we will be here long after you and your kind are gone."

"Let us not disrespect the Governor who was chosen by the King himself," cautioned Nolter, a well-respected merchant, who had also risen to join Polynices. "What you both say is true. But listen to Polynices who says the King lives and is still our ruler. Our allegiance must be to him and thus to his surrogate," Nolter nodded towards Daniel.

Crossing to speak directly to Daniel, Nolter bowed slightly, "Sire, the traditions of Babylon cannot be easily broken and changed. The astrologers, magicians and enchanters have long played an important role in the royal court as has the priesthood. Let us invite their input as together we govern this great kingdom. We must be united as our nation goes to war."

There was a lull in the chamber as the four men returned to their seats. It was Daniel's move. Everyone waited expectantly. Daniel's eyes moved slowly around the room penetrating the heart of every Council member. He closed his eyes and looked upward in prayer. When he reopened his eyes, they were bold and determined, reflecting a man at peace with himself.

"This discourse has been good," he began. "I appreciate and well understand the frustrations Beltekasmer and Antiosyss laid forth today. It is true. I have not sought your council. But as Nolter has so wisely spoken, we must be united during this time of uncertainty."

Daniel rose from his chair and stood directly before the throne. Pointing at the empty throne behind him, his voice bold and commanding, Daniel declared, "I represent the King whose throne this is. He had tasked me to govern this kingdom long before he was struck ill, and he continues to do so today. I shall not waver from this responsibility."

He directed his eyes to Beltekasmer, "I shall more actively encourage your ideas and counsel, Beltekasmer, as the wisdom you and your colleagues bring to the court provides a different insight than mine. It is to be valued."

Gesturing to Nolter and Polynices, he continued, "The merchants of our land certainly have the pulse of the people. You know that I have always and will continue to value your counsel. The input of Nebuzaradan and our military leaders has never been less than excellent and the guidance I receive from the members of the royal family clarifies decisions." Sweeping his arms to take in the room, Daniel exclaimed, "We lead this country together for our King."

He paused. Locking eyes with Antiosyss, Daniel spoke in a soft but ice cold voice: "All of you know that I do not acknowledge Marduk nor subscribe any validity to him and his priests. In all good conscience, I can never do this nor will I. I answer only to the one true God." Another pause.

"Having said that, I recognize the deep-rooted tradition that the Temple of Marduk plays in our culture, and so I will cooperatively make every effort to work with you, Antiosyss, and your priesthood as you advise me on anything other than religious affairs. I will not call you in to exercise powers to heal the King but I will ask for your input on such affairs prioritizing the building and repair of our city's infrastructure."

He nodded at Zocor who instantly set the palace guards in motion to open the large doors of the throne room.

"Thank you for your counsel. This Governing Council is dismissed."

With that Daniel briskly exited the room towards the Governor's Office on the other side of the palace. The normal buzz that concluded council meetings was absent. Each man was left to sort out for himself what next would happen.

~

More spacious than most in the ambling souk or old central market area, Nolter's shop was a favorite for Babylonians. There was never a lull in foot traffic. Sales grew year after year. The day thus far had gone well. Nolter had managed to secure some beautiful cloth at a low price which he, in turn, was offering at a bargain to his customers. Toward the end of the day, he was totaling his receipts and counting his money in a little cubicle separated from the store by a curtain of strung beads when one of his clerks interrupted him.

"Sir, there is a man seeking to talk with you. He looks like a priest from the Temple."

Before Nolter could respond, Antiosyss swept through the strands of beads into the cramped space. "Nolter, we need to talk. Things are not going well. I need your help."

Startled by the intrusion, Nolter instinctively began sweeping the piles of counted coins into the cash box. Somewhat put out by Antiosyss' surprise appearance, he snapped, "It is getting near the end of the business day and I have much to do. You should have given me advance notice that you wished to meet."

"I apologize, but I wanted to speak with you apart from the Governing Council and the others." Antiosyss looked around the cubicle that only housed one chair and continued, "Is there some place we can talk that is private? Your customers and clerks should not hear what I want to tell you."

Locking the cash box in its hiding place, Nolter stood and brushed by Antiosyss through the curtain into the shop area saying, "Come with me. We'll go to my storeroom. It's not very pleasant but there is room to sit, have some tea, and talk."

Antiosyss followed him out of the shop where Nolter turned into a little alley and opened a door into a room full of goods yet to be placed in his shop for sale. The room smelled musty and was dark. Nolter lit a small lamp on a table around which stood three stools. "Please, sit down. My helpers will bring us some tea."

Dropping onto one of the wooden stools, Antiosyss waited to speak until Nolter had found his seat. "I'll get right to the point." He looked out the open door to make sure no one would overhear their conversation. "The Governing Council for the most part is very unhappy with Daniel's governance. He doesn't listen to us . . . he always acts on his own and with the war waging no one is comfortable with this. You know the wise men and most of the military have joined the priesthood to oppose his cavalier style. Now, a majority of the merchants are disenchanted as well."

Antiosyss paused to let it all sink in. Nolter listened impassively, not revealing any emotion one way or the other. Antiosyss continued, "We need you to join us. You are among the most prominent merchants. All who are unwilling to take a stand will do so once they see whom you support."

One of Nolter's clerks entered the door with a pot of tea and two cups which he placed on the table. Antiosyss stopped speaking while tea was poured. When the man had left the storeroom, he picked up his glass, took a sip, and leaned in to Nolter speaking in almost a whisper.

"Nolter, I know Daniel let you make your payment to the King's treasury late this year. I can only assume there was good motivation." He paused. "Look, let's not be coy. I know—for that matter, many of us know—that you must have put a pretty good bribe on the table."

"I did no such thing!" snarled Nolter, rising from his stool.

"Calm down," cooed Antiosyss. "Sit down. I'm just telling you what we all think. This story is going to become public very soon. If you corroborate it and accuse Daniel of taking the bribe, you'd make a lot of friends in high places, not to mention you'd be off the hook for any illegality."

Nolter slowly sat back on the stool, his mind racing through all the options he could take. It would be a lot easier on him if he participated in this lie, but it would be like putting a knife in Daniel's back for no wrongdoing but only to help at a time Nolter was short of money. He looked at Antiosyss, his eyes heavy and sad, and said, "I cannot lie when Daniel did so much to help me. He is a good man . . . an honest governor. He . . . I . . . did nothing wrong."

"You're making a bad mistake. When this story comes out, you will get hurt. I want to protect you, but you need to help me in return."

Nolter shook his head slowly, "I cannot hurt Daniel who helped me. I'm sorry."

Antiosyss rose and stepped to the doorway, then stopped. "I'm not done with this. You know I have powerful forces I can call upon to make things happen. I do not want to see you hurt. Think about this carefully. We shall talk again." With that he exited.

~

The ceremony was in full swing by the time Nolter arrived at the temple. He rarely attended religious events other than the major feasts and festivals, but he had received a note from Antiosyss asking specifically that he be present tonight. The drumming and incantations of the priests inside reverberated into the outside air down to Procession Way. As Nolter climbed the steps leading to the Temple's entry, his heart beat faster anticipating what Antiosyss might have in store.

He reached the large doors at the top of the steps and pulled them open. Inside was a swarm of people. While most were on their knees bowing to the image of Marduk hanging on the opposite wall, others were wildly dancing in the aisles and along the walls chanting in a language he did not understand. The large assembly room magnified the cacophony to the point where it was impossible to think clearly. On the altar under the Marduk statue were two naked women writhing in contortions.

Suddenly priests began leaping into the air reaching heights no mortal could hope to attain. Twenty . . . thirty feet . . . even higher, they soared over the crowd kneeling in homage to Marduk. One came directly at him from the side, knocking Nolter to the floor. As the priest passed by, Nolter heard him shout, "On your knees! Do not anger Marduk."

He bent over, his face to the ground. He wanted to see what was taking place but did not dare lift his head for fear of being struck again. And then . . . he felt an intense heat before he heard the "WHOOSH." The air evaporated from the room leaving only a vacuum. As he struggled to breathe, Nolter lifted his eyes towards the altar to find it fully ablaze. The flames leapt above the image of Marduk to skip on the ceiling of the room. The two women continued to dance. Antiosyss materialized at the top of the flames and slowly descended to the burning altar as the flames receded. It was almost as though he was being lowered by the fire as no other visible support could be seen.

The altar burned fiercely, the flames surrounding Antiosyss and his two female priestesses. He lifted his arms into the air, shouting, "Marduk reigns! Marduk be praised! All hail Marduk." Each phrase was echoed by those prostrate on the floor.

And then it all stopped. The fire went out; the women disappeared. Antiosyss stepped off the altar and made his way through the people still prostrate on the floor to stand before Nolter who had lifted his head, watching in total awe.

"Come with me," Antiosyss said. "Get up and follow me."

He turned and walked back the way he had come, Nolter closely behind. He opened a door behind the altar and entered, holding it open for Nolter to join him. They walked in silence through the corridors until they reached a heavily decorated door in gold and silver which Antiosyss opened, gesturing for Nolter to enter.

"Very few people see this room," said Antiosyss as he removed the ceremonial robes and religious ornaments he used for the ceremony. "This is the high priest's preparation room. Please . . . sit down as I take this off."

Nolter had not yet spoken. His eyes were wide, taking in the symbols and images of Marduk that surrounded them. There was a heavy, frightful air about the room that was oppressive. He could not think clearly. He was too frightened by awesome powers that swirled around him. Moreover, it was difficult to breathe as the stench of incense overwhelmed him. He was up against the gods themselves.

"I wanted you to see who and what you are opposing by your unwillingness to accuse Daniel of demanding payment from you in exchange for delaying your treasury payment. Don't take this lightly," Antiosyss said as he looked at Nolter sternly.

"I . . . I . . ." stammered Nolter. He was too frightened to speak.

Antiosyss suddenly relaxed and smiled, walking over to sit by Nolter. He put his arm around his shoulder and in an uncharacteristic warm voice said, "Nolter, I don't want you to get hurt. You cannot fight Marduk or me, his emissary. His powers are too great as you witnessed tonight. You will only be destroyed. So . . . will you join us in defeating Daniel? Will you make the accusation at the next Governing Council?"

Nolter opened his mouth to speak but could not get his vocal cords to work. He tried again. He looked at Antiosyss, his eyes still full of fear, then nodded his head in agreement.

"Good," said Antiosyss. "This is all good."

~

The buzz in the room was louder than usual as members of the Governing Council huddled in groups preparing their strategies in anticipation of a contentious meeting. After the last

Council meeting, it was common knowledge that Antiosyss intended to challenge Daniel that afternoon. The sides were drawn. As the reality of a revolt came close, the men were forced to examine the consequences of their alliances upon Amel's return from war or even the King's recovery from his illness. The wrong vote cast today might well solidify their fate for years to come.

Daniel entered the chamber and each one drifted to his regular seat. The room became eerily quiet. He presented the afternoon's agenda which included the normal discussion items concerning streets, water distribution, agriculture, and various citizenry grievances. He noted there was no news from the war front and informed them at the conclusion of the meeting he intended to give some time for general policy discussion as the members desired.

They waded their way through several hours of routine governance affairs. Finally, the agenda was exhausted. Daniel looked around the room, asking, "Does anyone wish to bring anything else up for discussion?"

Antiosyss got up from his seat and answered, "I do."

"Very well, you have the floor," replied Daniel.

Walking into the center oval of the room, Antiosyss talked as he walked, ensuring that he made eye contact with every single member of the Council.

"Some information has come to my attention which I think demands the careful examination of this Council. I had long suspected this indiscretion in the Governor's Office, but only received reliable proof of it last night. Our Governor, Daniel, solicited and received a bribe from a member of this body in exchange for delaying payment he owed to the treasury."

The temperature dropped twenty degrees in the room. No one moved.

"These are serious charges," calmly said Daniel. "Where is your proof?"

Antiosyss walked to Nolter's seat and placed his hand on his shoulder. "This is my proof. Nolter will confirm that you offered to delay his payment for quite some time in exchange for a significant bribe."

The silence broke as everyone began talking at once.

Not flinching, Daniel said in an even voice," Nolter, do you wish to speak? Do you verify Antiosyss' charge?"

Antiosyss lifted Nolter to his feet whispering to him to tell his story. Nolter could not look at Daniel but hung his head as he uttered his lie.

"It is true. Daniel told me I could be several months late in payment, provided I gave him a sum equal to one-half of what I owed. I didn't want to do this, but I had no other choice. I didn't have all the money at the time."

"That is not true," said Daniel. "Why are you lying, Nolter? What have I done to hurt you?"

"I must go," murmured Nolter, "I need to leave." He bolted from the room.

"I call for a vote of no confidence in our Governor," said Antiosyss turning to survey the entire room. "I demand a vote right now.   We cannot be led by a man lacking in basic integrity."

"This is a ridiculous accusation," Shadrach said leaping to his feet. "All of us in this room have had many years watching Daniel govern the kingdom. Never has he wavered in his honesty and adherence to truth."

"Antiosyss! We know you have been trying to unseat Daniel for some time," shouted Meshach. "Your lies will not work in this Council."

Seeing his opportunity to put the final nail in Daniel's coffin, Antiosyss ignored Meshach and stepped towards Daniel, his arm outstretched and his index finger jabbing the air, "Did you or did you not allow Nolter to make a late payment on his last bill to the treasury?"

Looking straight back at him, Daniel replied, "I did."

Before he could go on, Antiosyss turned to the assembly and with a satisfied smile on his face said, "There it is. Proof. Even Daniel admits wrong doing."

"There was no wrong doing," chided Daniel, now growing impatient with Antiosyss's innuendo and half-truths. "Nolter did not have the money to pay and so I gave him an extension. There is nothing wrong with that."

"For how many others have you done this?" shot back Antiosyss.

"No one. I have never needed to," answered Daniel.

"Because there was no bribe offered?"

"You are perverting a simple act and . . ."

Antiosyss laughed derisively, cutting Daniel off in mid-sentence, "Your words cannot undo an unlawful deed. We are not naïve about how these things work."

The members of the Council whispered among themselves, quite astonished that Daniel for once appeared to be caught in a scheme not becoming to the kingdom's Governor. And then Antiosyss dropped the sword again.

"I put to a vote of this Governing Council that Daniel be declared unfit to continue in his role of Governor and that an interim triumvirate of Beltekasmer, myself and Marduk-Sum-Lisir assume his duties immediately." The chattering in the room began to subside.

Antiosyss shouted, "I demand a vote right now!"

No one spoke, no one moved. It was as though the entire Governing Council was frozen in place. While some members were quite pleased by this turn of events and had long wanted to be rid of Daniel, most were stunned by the accusation and seeming truth of the charges. Fearing the King's wrath if they did the wrong thing, many feared making this monumental move so suddenly.

"Well?" smirked Antiosyss as he slowly turned to look every member in the eye.

Mysonus rose, silencing Antiosyss, "It would be extremely unwise for this Council to take such an action on the basis of your charge and Nolter's admission. Daniel has conducted himself with the utmost integrity during his tenure. I, for one, find it difficult to comprehend—let alone believe—the accusation you make. We need to discuss this . . . ask questions . . . find out the reasons behind each action in this story you glibly throw out to us."

"Oh-h-h-h . . . this is not difficult to understand, honorable Mysonus," retorted Antiosyss. "But perhaps you are getting too old to grasp the simple details. I think standing is exhausting you." Antiosyss snapped his fingers to release a visible electric charge that collided with Mysounus's body, knocking him momentarily senseless and making him fall into his chair.

Beltekasmer was on his feet instantly and with his ceremonial rod in his hand pointed at Antiosyss unleashed a more potent bolt that knocked Antiosyss off his feet to the floor.

"There's more than one of us that can do that," he snapped. "I caution you to never exercise your powers on us again. We may sometimes disagree with each other, but as a group, we magicians and wise men are one. Did you forget that your powers may pale by comparison to ours?"

The tension in the room had escalated. Antiosyss lay on the floor in a semi-conscious state. The entire group of wise men and magicians were now standing, glaring at those in the room as though to dare them to make a move.

Mysonus broke the silence, "I think there is no need for a vote today. We have heard terrible things. We need to go away and ponder all this before we act."

Daniel stood and spoke in a quiet voice, "Your advice is as wise as always, Mysonus. We must sort out truth from falsehood, and we will do so in the quiet of our own homes. This Council is dismissed."

Chapter Seven
WAR
569 – 568 BC

It had been three months since Amel-Marduk left Babylon and the comforts of his palace for the battlefront in the southwest sector of the kingdom. To the surprise of the Imperial Guard, they found the Egyptians to be much tougher and more disciplined warriors than they had experienced a few years prior. Moreover, the continually changing tactics of the enemy which kept Nebuzaradan's forces off balance suggested that they were up against a well thought out war strategy seldom seen in the battles they had waged during Nebuchadnezzar's reign.

Two battle fronts were clearly developing: one on the southern and one on the western border. It was still too early to determine where the main thrust of the Egyptian invaders would come. Nebuzaradan had called for a strategy meeting with Amel and his five division commanders. He also sent for Neriglissar who traveled through the night from where his division had camped near Raphia to join. The seven men gathered around the makeshift table on which were various maps that stood in the center of the tent that served as their command center.

Using a beautifully forged knife that had been given to him by the King as a reward for his many victories, Nebuzaradan pointed to a site on the southern border where Egyptian troops were reported to be massing.

"Our scouts tell us the Egyptians have almost forty thousand troops on the hills surrounding Zoar and they continue to mass. This could be the location of their primary attack."

Neriglissar countered, "But they have to come down off the hills into the valley below to take the city advancing up the next ridge to move into our land. Why would they risk a major offensive from such a defenseless position?"

"That's what I can't figure out," answered Nebuzaradan. "It's not good strategy, but why are they building up troops at that point?"

"It's obvious they hope to deceive us," sneered Neriglissar. "I am certain that they are going to come at us from the west through Raphia and then up through Gaza. It's much closer for them to send in troop replacements and to support their soldiers because it is on a direct line from Memphis." He stabbed the map with his finger on the southern end of the Dead Sea. "I can't believe they are thinking of making a major attack through Zoar. The sheer logistics of marching troops and horses, to say nothing of the water and food needed to cross the desert, makes this unsustainable for them!"

Amel had been listening to the arguments on both sides of the issue. He was carefully studying the maps. He could see the Egyptians might take a path across the hills bridging the valley of Zoar if they could divert the Babylonians' attention. This was not as cut and dry as Neriglissar made it out to be. At the same time, the possibility of his own theory being right was weak given that the maps could not be trusted, particularly with respect to the terrain.

"You make a lot of sense, Neriglissar," said Amel, "but at this point we need to protect ourselves on both fronts. I can't see concentrating our troops in any one direction until the enemy's plans become clearer to us."

Making every attempt to control his disdain for the Crown Prince for thinking the Egyptians would even consider a major attack from the south, Neriglissar spoke slowly and with barely concealed condescension, "I am willing to stake my career on this. Believe me, they will be attacking from the west, and they will come in wave after wave after wave until they swamp us if the majority of our troops are not there to stop them."

"I'm not ready to leave the southern border undefended and assume the major attack is coming from the west . . . not when they have so many troops massed near Zoar," said Amel. "We cannot afford to be wrong . . . especially when we still don't know their plans."

Nebuzaradan, ever thoughtful and having been through many battles where obvious enemy moves turned out to be deceptions, weighed in, "Neriglissar, since you feel so strongly about the attack coming from the west, move all the battalions in your division to that front. Show them some strength on our part. And position yourself to withstand a full assault for at least two days. That will give us time to re-deploy our other divisions to back you up should you prove to be right. Rabmag, you move your division and camp between here and Raphia. I want you to be able to move quickly to support Neriglissar if necessary. At the same time, I want you to be able to move back to us if the assault comes at Zoar."

"I'm comfortable with this strategy for the moment," commented Amel. "Let's be ready at either front but not tip our hand. Let them move first."

"I hope you're not making a mistake," quipped Neriglissar. "My soldiers are good and they will fight to the death, but thousands cannot hold back tens of thousands."

"Does that mean you would like another division to hold the western border?" asked Nebuzaradan.

"Not at all," laughed Neriglissar. "I prefer to be at the center of the attack. I know it's coming there. I intend to hold them, if not stop them, while I wait for the rest of you to join me." He saluted his colleagues and left the tent to rejoin his troops.

~

Amel-Marduk and Nebuzaradan stood motionless on a hill overlooking the Egyptian forces which were growing in number on the southern border by Zoar. Without taking his eyes off the action below, Amel said, "It appears this is where they intend to break through."

"On the surface, it does," answered Nebuzaradan. "They could be bluffing, but why would they send so many troops here?"

An aide hurried up the hill to Nebuzaradan, "Sir," he called out breathlessly, "a messenger has just come from the western front. The Egyptians have struck and are breaking through that border."

The two leaders turned as one and ran down the hill, leaped on their horses and rode quickly back to their command center where they found the soldier who had been sent by Neriglissar. He was exhausted but starting to eat the food that had been brought him. When he saw the two leaders enter the tent, he struggled to his feet and saluted.

"Sit down . . . keep eating as you speak. You've ridden a long ways," said Amel.

Refusing to sit in the presence of the Crown Prince, the soldier began to deliver his message, "Commander Neriglissar sent me to tell you that the enemy has finally attacked. They broke through our front lines last night. They must have had more troops in the region than we first suspected because the waves of new forces kept coming and coming, driving our ranks further back with each charge. Commander Neriglissar finally had the advance battalions withdraw to the defensive perimeter that he set up around Raphia where he hopes to stop the invaders."

"Have Commander Rabmag's forces joined your troops yet?" asked Nebuzaradan.

"They're probably there today. I know Commander Neriglissar sent word to them to come as quickly as they could. That messenger went out the same time that I left to come here."

"Thank you for getting here quickly," said Amel to the soldier. "My men will take you to a tent where you can continue eating and get some rest." He gestured to an aide to escort the man out of the command center.

Nebuzaradan was busily studying the map on the table, "They finally made their move. Good. Neriglissar called this one right. Given the logistics, it makes sense for them to go through the western border."

"They're going to need reinforcements," observed Amel, his eyes now glued to the map as well. "If the main attack is underway, two divisions will not keep them from over-running Raphia. Rashad needs to take one of our divisions to assist them immediately."

"But what if the Egyptians attack us here?" asked Nebuzaradan. "Are they just waiting for us to deplete our forces by diverting them to Raphia? If this is their strategy, they are going to come across the border with a vengeance because we won't have sufficient troops to hold back what we just saw massed in the valley."

"It may be exactly their plan," answered Amel. "We won't know until we make our move. But one thing I know is that Neriglissar needs help and he needs it fast. Until we know what they plan to do here, Rashad needs to join him. That will give him enough strength to protect Raphia, defeat the enemy there and drive them back to Memphis. As for us, we can call on Babsaris' division which is nearby. We'll have two full divisions remaining which with our advantage of the hills should hold the Egyptians at bay."

Nebuzaradan nodded in agreement. They had their plan.

~

Back in Babylon, the Governing Council refused to let surface a vote to unseat Daniel. It was one thing that Antiosyss' ruse was so thinly veiled that few failed to see through it. It was quite another to tamper with what was in place and was working. No one felt compelled to risk suffering the humiliation the high priest had endured. At the same time, Daniel's credibility was tarnished. He had become the object of increasing skepticism.

Daniel recognized that he needed to build support among the Council members. He became more collegial in asking for their advice as he sought greater transparency in his governance. All in all, the domestic affairs of the empire seemed to be moving forward.

Antiosyss was down but he wasn't out. Never had he endured such public humiliation, even under the reign of Nebuchadnezzar. Anger consumed him and only exacerbated his desire to overthrow Daniel. He decided to resort to the strategy with which he had had the most success: a no holds barred assault on the libidos of his enemies.

He summoned Narseniah. She found him waiting for her in the high priest's room in the temple. It was late in the evening. The streets were quiet, and the last ceremony of the evening was long over. He heard a knock on the door and quickly crossed over to let his daughter in.

"You didn't fare well at the Council today," she said as she ambled over to sprawl on a divan next to a table, helping herself to with some sweets and fruit.

"That's in the past," snapped Antiosyss, displeased that this is how their conversation would begin. "What has happened is good. Daniel is weakened for the first time. No one looks at him the same way. His integrity is now in question. It is time to make our next move."

Narseniah laughed as she popped a grape into her mouth, "You're serious about continuing the fight? You didn't look so good yourself, you know."

"I said that's in the past," he growled. Antiosyss moved to sit in the chair across from the divan where he could talk directly to Narseniah: "What we're up against is bigger than either one of us. We need to work together." He smiled as warmly as he could and patted her hand. "One thing worked well for us in the past and we need to go back to it only do it better." His face grew smug as he thought about it. She looked at him quizzically.

"You are the most sensual woman on earth. Sometimes I even forget you are my daughter when I watch you in the temple ceremonies. I want you to use your sexual charm like never before on those closest to Daniel in governing the kingdom. I suspect they are not as strong as him to withstand you. It's obvious that you would have had Amel following you like a lost puppy if Dorcas hadn't stumbled onto you that night. You are the best weapon we have: your sex going up against their lusts. It works. We know that."

Narseniah smiled coyly back at him, nodded her head and said, "It's not just about sex. It's all about how you enflame them until they're out of control."

"I totally agree. You have no equal," Antiosyss smiled, nodding his head in agreement. "That's why I'm asking you to do this."

"Who do you have in mind?"

Antiosyss rose and began to pace across the room as he spoke. "We have three targets: Shadrach, Meshach, and Abednego. They are the only men that Daniel relies on and in whom he confides. If we—you—can get even one to succumb to your advances, we'll pierce the underbelly of Daniel himself!"

He stopped his pacing and looked at her, "Those three would never want their purity or integrity questioned. They take so much pride in these . . . these meaningless qualities. It defines their character. If we can make that crumble, there's not much left for them on which to rest their credibility as state administrators. I suspect they will go to any lengths to avoid public scrutiny . . . even to the point of accusing Daniel of some illicit behavior should that be the price we ask them to pay for our silence."

"This will not be easy," cautioned Narseniah. "These men are not built of the same stuff as everyone else."

"You're right. That's why their fall from grace will cause much upheaval," replied Antiosyss. He walked to her and stood challengingly before her.

"Are you up to it, or is this too much, even for you?"

Narseniah laughed as she spoke: "I know your game, father," she said with added emphasis on the last word. "We both know I have no equal, and certainly no better." She stood up, brushed her robes into place, then, wiped the smile off her face, "So who is it going to be?" she hissed.

"I think Meshach. He has his hands full right now with the roads and seems to be near exhaustion. Yes," said Antiosyss clapping his hands in delight as he walked to the door to let Narseniah out. "Yes, Meshach should suit our purposes nicely."

Narseniah put her finger to her lips then placed it on Antiosyss' lips as she walked by him through the open door. Without looking back she cheerfully said, again emphasizing the last word, "Goodnight . . . father."

~

Things were different now mused Narseniah as she and her brother, Antiobud, climbed the steps to the royal palace on their way to visit Meshach. This was the first time Antiosyss enlisted his son in his plot to discredit Daniel and his chief aides to gain the most powerful position in the empire next to the King. Serving as the Shangu, the temple administrator who oversaw the support system of the temple, Antiobud had rarely been involved in Antiosyss' political affairs. It was curious that their father now felt he could be helpful in what appeared to be an all out assault on the ruling powers. Nevertheless, she reasoned, Antiobud was somewhat of an unknown and therefore might throw Meshach and the others off balance in their favor.

They entered the Palace and made their way to Meshach's administrative quarters in the Governor's offices. Her eyes darted everywhere; she did not want to be seen by Daniel or any of his household staff who might be in the palace . . . not after that dreadful night when he had thrown her out of his house. They made it without incident and were immediately ushered into Meshach's private room whose walls were filled with maps of the city and even of all the outer provinces marking the road system that Meshach oversaw. They were quite complex, obviously requiring a keen mind to manage. When Narseniah saw the intricate detail, she had momentary doubts that their ploy was going to work. Maybe we underestimated Meshach, she thought.

"Please sit down," Meshach gestured to the chairs surrounding his table. "I understand you have some concern about where all the roads come together onto Procession Way at the Temple of Marduk."

"Yes sir," answered Antiobud who was to take the lead in the discussion leaving Narseniah free to set the trap—the real reason for their visit.

"With new roads leading to the new central market, several of the streets that feed into Procession Way have had to be moved. The result is a confluence of too many people, carts, and animals. Everything simply comes to a stop during most of the day. We need to find some solution to this. It poses a huge problem for those wishing to participate in our ceremonies in the temple."

Placing a large map of the city's interior on the table before them, Meshach bent over to examine it. He traced his finger along Procession Way in front of the temple.

"Hmmmm," he murmured. "I see what you are talking about. But I think we looked at this several months ago and have since drawn up plans to alleviate the congestion."

Meshach looked out the open door of his room and shouted, "Luxor! Please come in here."

One of Meshach's aides quickly entered the room, "Yes sir?"

"Didn't we note that we have too many streets converging onto Procession Way near the Temple?"

"Yes we did," answered Luxor. "But we also solved it. We are just finishing up the new drawings right now. We will be starting construction within a week or so."

"Take Antiobud and show him what you've drawn. He has every right to be concerned. I want him to see how we have solved it." Turning to Antiobud, Meshach continued, "Please give us any suggestions that you see as you look at these drawings. This is the time to make adjustments."

"Come with me," said Luxor.

The two men exited the room leaving Meshach and Narseniah alone. This was a perfect time to make her move. With her back to the open entry, she stood and leaned towards Meshach as though to examine the map before them. She moved her hand ever so slightly across her abdomen causing her top garment to separate revealing her ample naked breasts. Without missing a beat, she pointed to the temple on the map and said, "I was thinking that we could close this road and divert those using it to these three side streets. What do you think?"

Meshach did not respond. After all, he was a man. To see one of the most beautiful women in the empire standing half-naked in front of him had literally taken his breath away. His eyes wantonly fixed on her breasts. Narseniah smiled, knowing he was hooked. It was time to spring the trap.

Leaning further towards him, she whispered, "Would you like to see more? I would love to show you more."

Meshach swallowed hard, almost choking on his saliva. He was struck dumb. He shook his head, both hoping this temptation would go away and that it would not.

"I will visit you at your home this evening," Narseniah purred. Straightening up, she pulled her garment covering herself, turned and left the room.

For the rest of the afternoon, Meshach tried his best to shake the mental picture indelibly etched on his mind. He even went into Daniel's office and without divulging what had happened asked him to pray to remove temptation from his life. While relief was momentary, as soon as he returned to his own quarters Narseniah's nakedness loomed larger than life. He reluctantly admitted to himself that he very much wanted to see her again that evening.

~

What Meshach thought was his secret was not. One of the servants tending to chores in his quarters had accidently witnessed the entire scene. Meshach's face told the whole story. His complexion turned scarlet as he broke into a cold sweat. This was the perfect grist for the servants' gossip mill. Within a few hours, the episode had made it to Laconius, Daniel's chief aide. Laconius, in turn, felt compelled to share it with Daniel. Thinking back to earlier that afternoon when Meshach had suddenly entered his office asking him to pray with and for him, Daniel put the pieces together.

Although it was the end of the day and the palace was empty of visitors, Daniel hurried through the halls hoping to find that Meshach had not yet left. He saw Meshach sitting at his table holding his head in his hands, a blank stare on his face.

"Meshach," he softly spoke as he entered the room. "We must talk."

Startled by Daniel's intrusion into his daydream, Meshach looked up then stood, "What? Wha—oh, please come in Daniel. I'm sorry, I was deep in thought and didn't hear you arrive."

Daniel gently replied, "Please sit down, Meshach. I know what happened today."

An involuntary shudder shot through Meshach, hoping beyond hope that Daniel did not know about Narsenish's visit.

"I heard about Narseniah's coming to see you today. It's not the first time she has tried something like this. You are not alone in falling under her spell."

"I—I—nothing happened!" blurted out Meshach.

"I believe you," said Daniel. "But I also know this isn't the end of it. If I know her, she will attempt to see you privately and then . . . well, I don't want to see you entrapped by such evil. Nothing good will come of it."

"I know, I know," answered Meshach. "That's why I came to you this afternoon asking you to pray with me. I felt good during my time with you, but as soon as I returned to my quarters I could not get rid of the image of her standing exposed in front of me. Daniel, I was consumed by lust and have been all afternoon!"

"Did she ask to see you again?" questioned Daniel.

"Yes. She is coming to my house this evening, she said." Meshach got down on his knees before Daniel, grabbing his hands. "I don't want this to happen to me. You have to help me. Help me . . . drive her image out of my mind. I know she is evil."

Daniel lifted Meshach up. "I know you are innocent. We will figure this out and get through it." He turned to leave, and then faced Meshach, "Antiosyss is once again sending the foxes into the hen house, or so he thinks. He is determined to discredit us. We must not let this happen, and with God's help, we shall not. We are up against evil forces, Meshach. We cannot give them an inch." His voice hardened, "And we will not."

~

A hooded and cloaked figure hurried along the deserted streets into the neighborhood where many Babylonian officials resided. The sun had set over an hour ago, and households were preparing to retire for the evening. It wasn't common to see anyone on the street at this hour, but then this area of the city being what it was—a gathering of governing bureaucrats—did more often than not have its share of late night messengers and emissaries dipping in and out of clandestine assignations. Narseniah attracted no special attention and soon arrived at Meshach's front door.

She had barely lifted the brass knocker when the door opened and a servant invited her to enter. He asked her to wait and went to inform Meshach of her arrival. Wanting to start up where she left off with Meshach earlier in the afternoon, she was glad for the opportunity to remove her cloak and hood and re-arrange her robes to present her most alluring self. She quickly checked her reflection in the mirrors hanging on the walls and was pleased with what she saw. How do you resist such a sensual presence and beautiful body she thought . . . then laughed silently as she flashed on the scores of men who had fallen like ripe fruit in her wake. At the last moment, she removed a beautiful scarf from her shoulders so that the transparent blouse left nothing to the imagination.

"My master will see you now," said the servant who had silently returned catching her off guard. "Please follow me."

He ushered her down a corridor to a large receiving room. As she reached the entry, she put on her most demurring smile hoping to swamp him with her raw sexuality. "Meshach," she purred, "I have so looked forward to. . . ."

She stopped mid-sentence. Never in her wildest dreams did she expect to see Daniel waiting for her in Meshach's house. Yet, there he was . . . standing beside Meshach who despite being quite uncomfortable in the situation stood stone-faced to greet her.

"Have you no shame?" spat Daniel walking directly to her. "You tried this with the Crown Prince in my home, and now you attempt to seduce one of my trusted officials in his house. You are a disgusting sight to me! You are evil incarnate."

Struggling to regain her composure, Narseniah instinctively retorted, "You aren't supposed to be here!" Then finding her courage returning, she pressed the fight forward, "Why are you here? Are you Meshach's protector like you think you're the royal family's guard dog? You are the one who is disgusting."

Whirling on Meshach, she snorted derisively, "Can't you take care of yourself? Don't you have a mind of your own, or does this man tell you what to think and do?"

"Narseniah," he answered, "stop it. I asked Daniel to be here because I did not think I could resist you on my own. Maybe I cannot take care of myself."

"Get out!" commanded Daniel gesturing towards the doorway.

"We could have had such a good time," she smiled at Meshach. "Too bad you're not yet of age to make your own decisions." Then facing Daniel, she snapped, "I pity you. The pleasures of life have always eluded you."

Angry but getting control of himself, Daniel stepped to the doorway and turned to Narseniah, "I ask that you leave . . . now. You are not welcome here."

Glancing at Meshach, Narseniah arched a questioning eyebrow.

"Please go," Meshach said. "This was all wrong from the beginning. I fault myself for wanting to see you again. I'm sorry. This can never be. Now . . . please go."

Realizing that the game was over, Narseniah looked from one man to the other then quickly exited the room. Never did she expect to fail tonight. Putting on her cloak and covering her head, she stepped onto the street. Antiosyss needs to come up with a different strategy because this one is going nowhere, she mused. Daniel's cocoon engulfs his key people. It would take a frontal assault to bring him down, not nipping at his heels as she found out forcefully tonight.

~

"Were you ever wrong!" shouted Narseniah as she stormed into her father's private quarters unannounced and startling him out of his sleep. "It was a set up! For me! I was set up! It was supposed to be the other way around. I was setting up Meshach. What a laugh. They played me like a naïve kitten."

Antiosyss pulled himself up to a sitting position and rubbed his eyes. He was completely caught off guard by his daughter's abrupt intrusion.

"Why are you here? What are you talking about?" he asked.

Narseniah's rant could not be calmed. Daniel had played her for a fool for the second time, and she was furious. "I hate the man! I absolutely hate the man!" she screamed.

"Hate who?" asked Antiosyss, finally standing and sufficiently awake to recognize the extent of her anger.

"Daniel," she replied. "He stops us in our tracks every time we think we have a new strategy how to discredit or unseat him."

Walking to her, Antiosyss placed his hands on her shoulders trying to calm her. "Tell me what happened. I didn't think you were planning to see Daniel tonight."

"I wasn't," she screamed at him.

Shrugging off his hands, Narseniah paced about the room slamming her fist on tables and kicking anything in her way. "I went to Meshach's house as I had arranged with him this afternoon. His servant was obviously expecting me. He ushered me into the receiving room. Who did I see but Daniel standing there beside Meshach."

"How did he know what you were up to?" asked Antosyss, his attention now alert and focused on Narseniah. "I mean, how did he know? Who let him in on your plans?"

"Obviously, Meshach," retorted Narseniah. "They were waiting for me. Like a spider's web...I fell right into it."

"He knew you were coming?"

"Yes, he knew I was coming," screeched Narseniah just inches from her father's face. "I hate him. I cannot tell you how much I hate him. I want to destroy him!"

Antiosyss was unprepared for the intensity of her fury and hatred. He instinctively stepped backwards to deflect the energy of her emotions which were overwhelming her.

"Your plan is a failure!" she continued screaming at him. "Forget ever trying to topple Daniel through a back door. It will not work! The man knows what you're up to before you are able to make a move. I counted on you, and even you failed me. He is too smart for you."

Antiosyss remained silent, hoping that by letting her vent she would eventually calm down.

Narseniah stepped to him, pointing her finger in his face and snarled through clenched teeth, "I will kill that man. I will destroy him. I've been made a fool twice; never a third time. If you're not man enough to take him on directly, then I will."

She began to tremble, all her emotion spent.   Antiosyss
saw her start to swoon and caught her, placing her on a divan to
sit by him.   He knew he had to do things differently if he was
going to win this power struggle with Daniel.   He rubbed her
shoulders and in the most father-like tone he could muster spoke,
"We will prevail. Do not worry.   We will take him on directly as
you suggest. We will seize the first opportunity that comes our
way."

~

What they presumed to be a straightforward mission to
drive the invading Egyptian forces back into their own land
turned out to be one of the most difficult wars the Imperial Guard
had ever waged. Their opponents did nothing they expected, and
everything they never imagined would happen. Logic suggested
the primary frontal assault would come from the west. This path
provided the most direct route from Memphis to the war front for
both supplies and fresh troops. Furthermore, by building up
massive troop strength here, the Egyptians did everything to
indicate this would be the win or lose battleground. At the same
time, they directed enormous resources to the southern border
which left the Babylonians in a quandary, guessing from where
the main attack was to come.

The initial attack came at the western border. Just before
dawn, the Egyptians were on the move. Wave after wave of
ground troops enhanced by thousands of cavalry drove the
Babylonians back in short order. By the end of the second day,
Neriglissar's battalions had retreated so far that they were just
outside the city of Raphia. All the residents had packed up and
were making their way to Gaza as reinforcements were quick-
stepping in the other direction to augment the forces digging in at
Raphia. Neriglissar had requested more help, and Commander
Rabmg immediately mobilized his entire division to the west.
The Babylonian troops were not in place to withstand the hordes

of enemy soldiers confronting them, however, so the Egyptians continued to prevail.

~

Two days later, the Egyptians poured across the southern border relentlessly slamming tens of thousands of troops against the greatly diminished Babylonian troops, crushing them like grapes in a well-engineered wine press. Just as Amel-Marduk had posited, a good portion of the Egyptians had crossed the mountains to Zoar where they set up an ambush slaughtering the Babylonians as they retreated from the enemy's overpowering frontal attack. Albeit they were a well trained army, panic began to settle into the Babylonian ranks as there seemed to be no direction for them to turn to avoid the enemy.

At his command post, Nebuzaradan received report after report of his battalions being over-run and surrounded by a cagey, unpredictable enemy. In a quick strategy session, he agreed that Amel should take all the cavalry he could muster around Zoar and then ride hard down the mountains to sneak up on the Egyptians' unprotected flank. Meanwhile, the remaining Babylonian forces would retreat to the hills surrounding Zoar in the north. By digging in on the high ground, he hoped to gain an advantage to buy time for Babsaris' reinforcements to join them.

For over a week, the fighting waged fierce as the Egyptians continued to press forward, albeit slowed in their advance. Thousands of soldiers lay dead . . . strewn on the mountains and hills. Worst of all, the Crown Prince seemed to have disappeared into a void. He and his troops had vanished.

~

It was a pleasant day, a breeze gently blowing and not all that hot. If ever there was a day to be grateful to be alive and at peace with life, this was it. The Governing Council was working together for once, and the rumblings of dissension were unusually quiet. Things are running smoothly in Babylon mused Daniel looking out his window, but we haven't heard from the war front in several weeks. Then, as to quiet himself and regain perspective, he realized if there were problems they would have sent a messenger. No news was probably good news.

So much for self-reflection. Daniel rose from the comfortable chair he enjoyed by the open window in his private quarters in the royal palace and walked into the outer room to face the next set of the kingdom's problems. What was a small concern months ago had now become more serious. The royal treasury was running low—too low—given the enormous drain by the current war effort. He had no choice but to mandate restrictive controls on expenditures demanded by the city's infrastructure burdens, and he needed to get a firm grip on where things stood with the war. Both of these then had to be balanced against the taxes assessed the merchants and growers.

He gathered some documents and prepared to leave for a meeting in a larger room in the palace. There a group of officials awaited him when a very dusty and ragged-looking soldier burst into the offices.

"Governor," he saluted, stopping in mid-stride to rest on a column. "I've been sent from Commander Nebuzaradan. I have been riding for almost two weeks without rest as they ordered me to make haste."

Daniel grabbed the man's arm and helped him to a chair, at the same time asking others to bring some water and fruit. The comfort of the chair was so overwhelming that the messenger momentarily nodded off, his eyes closed and his muscles relaxing.

"He needs nourishment," said Daniel.

Daniel offered him a cluster of grapes which he greedily devoured followed by a full goblet of nectar. He took a pear from the bowl of fruit placed in front of him and ate it quickly. As he started on a peach, the beginnings of energy started to surge into his being and he attempted to stand once again as was required in the presence of his superiors.

"Please stay seated," said Daniel. "Eat. You need to gain some sustenance. You can talk as you eat and drink."

The exhausted soldier gratefully nodded. "I have to give you my report," he stammered. "The Imperial Guard has suffered huge losses and a major defeat in the south. When the Egyptians finally engaged on that front, they poured through the border . . . there was no end to their troops. We could not hold them. I don't think the other division sent to support us ever made it."

He reached for another goblet and drank heavily. In telling his story, he had forgotten to breathe and he was now drinking in air as well. He wiped his mouth and forced himself to continue. "The Crown Prince is missing. As our troops retreated and the commanders re-grouped, the Crown Prince did not join their ranks. The last time anyone reported seeing him he was engaged in battle at the very spear-head of the enemy's assault across our borders. And then, he disappeared."

He fell back into the chair, gasping for air.

Suddenly he shot upright in his chair and grabbed Daniel's robe, "Sire, I did not want to tell you this. I've been a soldier in the Imperial Guard for twenty-two years but I've never seen us so decimated as this. I don't know if we can withstand the Egyptians this time." And with that he fainted to the ground.

~

The call went out to the Governing Council to convene in an emergency session. Meanwhile, Daniel ordered those in the room who had overheard the report to keep silent until he had a plan in place. The last thing he needed was a city in fear as rumors grew unabated.

Knowing that he needed to improve and speed up communications to and from the war front, Daniel directed that a relay system of messengers and horses be put in place. There were to be fresh horses and men stationed every fifty miles or so from Babylon to the war front so messages could be transmitted quickly without exhausting both men and animals.

As members of the Council were notified and made their way to the palace, Daniel met privately with Zocor, Shadrach, Meshach, and Abednego to assess the situation. The last thing he wanted to do was to face the Governing Council without the constructs of a well-thought out plan in place. He needed to act. There was no time for policy discussion and debate as the fate of the nation hung in the balance. The Egyptians seemed to have the upper hand, the Imperial Guard was in retreat, and the interim King could well be dead. He had immediately sent messengers to the war front for a more complete assessment of the situation but it would take three to four weeks for them to get there and back, even with the fastest horses. He could not wait that long. He needed to act today if this city and the rest of the empire were to withstand an impending assault.

"Gentlemen, thank you for coming so quickly," began Daniel once the last member had entered the room. He then proceeded to tell the assembly what the messenger had told him. The questions tumbled out in a volcanic eruption, the fear quite palpable in the room. Of course, most of the questions could not be answered due to lack of information which further unsettled everyone. Finally, Daniel finished conveying to them all the details he had gleaned from the messenger, and the questions ceased. The uncertainty they faced was fully grasped and the room grew cold as ice.

"Governor," finally spoke Beltekasmer. "Do you have a plan?"

Daniel rose from his customary chair next to the throne and stepped into the center of the room before he spoke. He pointed to each man as he mentioned his name, "Zocor, Shadrach, Meshach, and Abednego met with me as you were being summoned for this meeting. We need more information and have dispatched messengers to the war front. However, it may take at least a month to get answers."

He began to pace slowly, facing his audience directly as he spoke, "We all acknowledge that this is not a time for debate. Plans must be put in place today and the truth be told our citizens or Babylon will disintegrate into chaos." He paused before continuing, "Our city may be under attack in just a few months. We don't know what is happening but we must prepare for the worst."

A few grunts of approval greeted this assessment from around the room.

"I am taking some steps immediately. We will begin rationing our food supplies, restricting the amount that can be sold to any single person or household. We cannot exhaust our grains and other non-perishable food stuffs. Shadrach will be issuing rules and conditions later today by which all citizens will abide. There will be no exceptions. Moreover, by tomorrow we will establish storage areas throughout the city where we can store and hold food as it is shipped into the city from the growers.

"Secondly, price controls will be established to protect our citizens from unscrupulous dealers who will try to take advantage of this crisis for their own gain. Anyone caught selling food for more than the established prices will be guilty of a criminal offense and dealt with severely."

The murmurs of approval began to give way to dissension as the merchants in the Council saw an abrupt stop to the kingdom's commerce and their livelihood. Leandrus, the largest grower in the empire stood, inquiring, "How long is this going to go on? You realize that what you are going to do will bring great harm to those of us who make our living by competitive commerce?"

"Yes, I do," replied Daniel not giving an inch, then repeating the question rhetorically, "How long will this go on? Who knows at this time? Until we get word back from the front and learn the status of our troops, this will go on indefinitely."

"Third, I am putting a curfew into effect in the city at sunset. No one is to be on the streets for whatever reason after dark. Zocor will have patrols throughout the city. Anyone not in his house between sunset and sunrise will be jailed. There will be no exceptions.

"Fourth, all road, waterway, and building construction will cease. All laborers instead will be assigned to those craftsmen making armor and weaponry so that production will increase. Our troops are away which leaves the defense of this city to us. We must be equipped to meet the enemy."

Mysonus who had been unusually quiet stood to his feet, "Now you are going too far! If you stop construction on the roads, we won't even be able to mobilize those left in the city to stop any invasion."

He was joined by Antiosyss who saw an opening to challenge Daniel, "He's right! The congestion around the temple is unacceptable. Better you pick up the pace of the work rather than to slow or stop it. But more to the point, right now we need to call on the powers of Marduk to save our kingdom. The temple is the source of our salvation and the citizens of this city need to have unobstructed access as they seek his protection. Marduk empowered the King to build this great empire. He will likewise protect it."

"Marduk has never been of any consequence to Babylon," retorted Daniel. "He is a piece of art created by a craftsman. What can this . . . this . . . this piece of metal do to help us?"

Antiosyss ran screaming at Daniel, his very authority challenged, "You dare to desecrate the power and godhead of Marduk! You should be sacrificed on his altar."

He pummeled Daniel with his fists and would have knocked him to the ground if cooler heads had not stepped in. Daniel instinctively drew back from him. Antiosyss' wild eyes and anger made everyone realize they had to be careful what they said and how they handled this volatile situation. Slowly gathering his wits about him, Antiosyss backed away . . . still angry but now under control.

"I did not mean to hurt you, Antiosyss, nor offend you," said Daniel. Then in a louder voice to the entire assembly he added, "If you find comfort in praying to Marduk, do so. But the construction must cease as we must be focused on our defense."

"Let's get back to the roads," thundered Leandrus. "If we don't have unobstructed roadways we might as well close up the city." All the merchants who saw this as another impediment to their business joined him. If people could not travel the streets freely and with ease, very little commerce would be take place.

Refusing to address their objections, Daniel patiently waited until everyone had spoken. The room grew silent once again.

He continued, "Fifth, every male fourteen years and older will be conscripted into the palace guards, trained and assigned a specific function in the defense of Babylon. No one will be exempted."

"Hear, hear," came scattered approval. They needed soldiers so this met no opposition.

"Finally . . . and I know this will not be well received but it is absolutely necessary . . . the war coupled with our construction efforts has drained the royal treasury. We cannot embark on an additional initiative—that is to produce armor and weapons—without adding to our coffers. As of today, taxes on all sales of goods and services will be doubled until we are on the other side of this crisis."

"Double?" shouted Leandrus. "Have you lost your mind? You tell us we cannot sell more than what is rationed and for no more or less than a specific price . . . you curtail the hours that people can go the market with a curfew, that is, if they can even get to the market through the unfinished construction clutter in the streets . . . and now you want to double our taxes. I for one say no. You are going too far!"

Everyone jumped into the fray talking at once. There were as many defenders of Daniel's plan as there were opponents. Soon verbal battles escalated into wrestling matches and fisticuffs. The usual decorum of the empire's leading government body had been shredded to pieces. It was every man for himself . . . exactly the chaos Daniel was trying to prevent from swamping the city when news got out about the Imperial Guard's defeat and the missing Crown Prince. Here it was . . . rampant in front of him in the very place where leadership should prevail.

Daniel made his way through the melee to the throne and stood where only royalty was to stand. He rapped a stick on the gold throne and shouted above the din hoping to bring order to the anarchy that prevailed.

"Order! There must be order!" No one heard him; no one cared.

He signaled Zocor to put in place the plan he had hoped they would not have to use. The palace guards slammed the heavy doors of the chamber shut while others filtered through the room breaking up fights. Since the palace guards outnumbered the members of the Governing Council two to one, they could not be easily dismissed. The craziness of the moment subsided as fast it happened.

When order was restored, Daniel chided them, "I trust you will exercise better leadership as you leave this chamber and go into the city. If the anger, fear and self-interest that you just demonstrated were to ignite in our streets, we have no more hope . . . certainly not against a strong enemy invasion."

He surveyed the room which, now chastised, had grown silent. "This Council is adjourned." He stepped off the platform to the floor, walking briskly out the large central doors which opened for him.

On his way out he commanded, "Zocor, empty the palace of all but the royal family and those assigned to my office. As for the rest of you, let's be the leaders we think we are, and work to save Babylon and the empire."

~

Nebuzaradan's strategy eventually halted the Egyptian sweep into Babylonian territory. The fighting was intense and the losses were great on both sides. These were disciplined armies who fought to the death rather than admit defeat. By the twelfth day of battle, the two armies had come to a standstill in the south. The only problem was that Amel had not been heard from, and Nebuzaradan did not know if he had successfully made it around Zoar or if he had been intercepted and destroyed. He opted to give the Crown Prince the benefit of the doubt. He waited two more days before ordering an offensive attack designed to press the Egyptians backwards into Amel's waiting spears.

On the morning of the fifteenth day since the Crown Prince's departure, Nebuzaradan was up early, eagerly awaiting word that Amel was in position. As the day wore on and no word was forthcoming, he noticed that the enemy was using the stalemate to once again build up their troops presumably for another full out attack. He had to do something. He gathered the commanders of the two major divisions hunkered down in this region and laid out the battle plan for them. Whether Amel was in place or not, he had to take the offensive and attack.

Long before dawn, the Imperial Guard began to move quietly into position. They were within less than a hundred feet of the Egyptian front lines when Nebuzaradan sounded the battle call. The combination of surprise and the darkness enabled the Babylonian troops to take the advantage and put the Egyptians into retreat. It wasn't until midday that Egyptian commanders were able to regroup their forces and initiate a counter-attack.

~

Over the past two weeks, Amel-Marduk's battle had more to do with the terrain than with enemy troops. With his cavalry numbering over one-thousand men and horses, forging new trails up, down and around the mountains forced unexpected delays. There was a continuous search for water simply to keep the animals and men alive. What he thought would take three or four days turned out to be fifteen.

Amel had no idea what was happening on the primary battle front. He hoped he would not be too late for their strategy to work. All he could do was to press forward knowing Nebuzaradan would wait as long as possible to give him time to get into position. At some point, however, Amel knew Nebuzaradan needed to act to quell the continued Egyptian attack—whether or not Amel was in place.

As they rounded the last hill, the Crown Prince's forces saw before them the two armies in violent battle and immediately swept down on the Egyptian forces from the rear. No thought had been given to an attack from this direction by the enemy, and so the pickings were easy. The kill ratio was easily ten per man as the mounted Guard decimated the Egyptians on their rear flank. As their colleagues were being killed behind them and in front of them, the Egyptians formed a central phalanx and started a slow retreat away from Zoar back to the border. For the moment, the Imperial Guard had taken the upper hand.

Likewise, on the western front, it wasn't until many days of battle that Neriglissar was finally able to maintain his position rather than retreat. As Rabmag's troops augmented those already in the throes of war, the Imperial Guard began to regain its morale and strength. By day eleven, they had gone from being the defeated to being the aggressor. They began to make small advances against the Egyptians, sending them into retreat. Over the next two weeks, the Imperial Guard slowly clawed its way back to Raphia, pushing the enemy up against its own border.

Eight months since they had left Babylon and three weeks since the enemy attacked, Nebuzaradan finally had all his commanders accounted for and assembled at his command post to plan their next move. There was no more question of where the attack was going to come from and no more waiting for the enemy to make a move. He was in control of the war and henceforth he would dictate all moves. They had the Egyptians on the run. He needed to send this news to Daniel and the Governing Council. A messenger was dispatched that morning.

Chapter Eight
INSURRECTION
568-567 BC

The sun was midway up its arch in the sky welcoming another beautiful winter day in Babylon. The birds were still singing their early morning song in the trees. A recent rain kept the grasses green in the King's pasture providing plentiful grazing for the prize horses and cattle Nebuchadnezzar enjoyed from his boyhood. There was a peaceful calm in the air that belied the war and imminent disaster facing Babylon. The man who should have been most uneasy was curled up asleep under one of the large trees scattered around the pasture he had now called home for almost four years.

Marduk-Sum-Lisir had risen that morning with a growing apprehension about what lay in store for the empire his father had built and whose benefits he enjoyed as a member of the royal household. Although he had never been the warrior that his brother was, he harbored thoughts of being on the war front more from guilt that he wasn't actively protecting the kingdom than from a desire to engage in combat. Three years younger than Amel, Marduk-Sum-Lisir had no desire for power or to rule. He was perfectly content to pursue his creative instincts which had driven him to be quite an accomplished artist. It was his flair and insights that enabled both Nebuchadnezzar and Amel-Marduk to build structures of uncanny beauty. All he wanted to do was build out Babylon to fulfill the visions continually bursting from his brain and heart.

Following breakfast with his mother, Queen Amytis, he did what he did every morning and went to his studio on the roof of the palace to work. He had never had an interest in women

and thus never married. He was the only child of
Nebuchadnezzar and Amytis who remained in the King's palace,
something for which Amytis was grateful as it was he who kept
her company.

By habit, he entered the studio and immediately crossed
the room thru the doors that led onto the rooftop patio from
where he could see the entire city. The beauty of the morning
was not lost on him, but in the forefront of his mind was the war
with Egypt of which he was not a part. If they defeat us, he
thought, what happens to us? Will we all be killed? Where will
we end up? In Memphis?

He walked to the north side which looked down onto the
King's barn and special pastures...special because they were
inside the city where land was extremely valuable and special
because they housed the elite stock. That was in normal times.
Today, and for the past four years, this was where his father was
also kept. How sad and bizarre, he reflected. Will he ever regain
his sanity? He suddenly was filled with a compulsion to go visit
Nebuchadnezzar . . . if for nothing more than to simply spend a
few moments with his father. Maybe he will understand me. He
knows the answers to some of these questions that plague me.

Marduk-Sum-Lisir abruptly headed down the stairs to the
public reception area and then down the long back steps which
opened onto the walkway leading to the barn. Listening to the
birds singing and looking at the lush pastures in front of him, he
began to sink into the warmth of the morning and joy of a new
day. He reached the fence of the pasture that adjoined where his
father was kept and hopped over it, opting to walk through the
thick grass and take the short cut rather than walk around. He
was glad he did as just the feel of the velvet-like grass on the tops
of his bare feet cocooned in his sandals felt refreshing. The
burden of his earlier concerns was beginning to slide from him,
more so the closer he got to his father.

Then the terror struck!

He heard the pounding of hooves just before he whirled
around. His body flew through the air and landed like a heavy

sack of grain fifteen feet from where he had been standing. As he regained consciousness, he looked up to see the bull charging him again as he lay on the ground. He couldn't move to get out of the way. All he could do was brace himself for the impact.

Again . . . blackness.

Nebuchadnezzar had been napping under his favorite tree in the adjoining pasture when he heard the angry snort of the bull penned next to him and saw him charge Marduk-Sum-Lisir. At first, he was amused by the sight . . . a young bull feeling ornery and playing in the field. When what he hit did not get up and fight back, however, Nebuchadnezzar got up from the ground and trotted over to the fence to see what was really happening. As he did, he saw the young bull back up and prepare to attack the immobile object again. For some unknown reason, he realized that this was not another animal but a human being. The bull ran full bore ramming the limp body head on, this time his horn tearing a large gash in the man's leg. The King instinctively knew he had to stop this slaughter.

He kicked the top two fence boards out with his feet, then leaped over the remaining fence rails into the next pasture. He knew he had to get to the man on the ground as fast as possible to prevent the next goring which the angry bull was lining up to do. He reached the body on the ground and turned to face the bull that was ready to make his run. As he did, Nebuchadnezzar leaped to his feet, his arms held high above his head, and ran toward the attacker bellowing. It was not what the young bull expected. He pulled up short and veered to the right to get out of Nebuchadnezzar's way. The King dropped to all fours as he and the bull faced off, each threatening the other stamping the ground and exchanging loud snorts. Nebuchadnezzar was now angry and of no mind to stand aside to this upstart. The bull's instincts told him to back off. After a few more snorts, he lowered his head and turned to walk towards the other end of his pasture.

Marduk-Sum-Lisir struggled through the gray clouds of his mind and carefully opened his eyes to assess the damage. He felt like he had been run over by one of the large stones used in building the ziggurat. There was a large pool of blood around the lower half of his body which concerned him but he could not turn to see where it was coming from. He looked to see where the bull was and saw his father standing ten feet away looking at him with curiosity. Had he stopped the attack? What happened?

"Father," he moaned, "I can't move. Help me. Please . . . help me. I'm bleeding badly."

Nebuchadnezzar looked at him quizzically. He was not sure who this creature was but there was some familiarity to the voice and even the way he looked. He knew he had to help it get out of the pasture before it was attacked again so he shuffled towards the prone body and began to roll it with his head towards the fence. Marduk-Sum-Lisir screamed in pain, then, blacked out. Nebuchadnezzar was startled but continued to push the body with his head as he stood on all fours. Three more rolls and he reached the fence where he was able to push the body under the lowest fence rail into his pasture. The King then turned and galloped back to the broken spot in the fence and climbed back into his own domain. He ran to Marduk-Sum-Lisir's limp body and for the first time saw the open wound in his thigh where he had been gored by the young bull's horn. It was an open mass of flesh, nerves and exposed bone. Again, instinct kicked in. He knew he had to get help or the life would drain out of the being he just saved.

Never one to be agitated or cause a ruckus in the years he had been in this pasture, Nebuchadnezzar now ran towards the barn, leaping and bellowing at the top of his voice hoping to attract the attention of the King's herdsmen. One of the men inside the barn mucking out the stalls finally came out to check on all the commotion. When he saw it was the King throwing a tantrum, he yelled back into the barn for Rymen to come quickly.

As Rymen surfaced and ran towards the pasture, Nebuchadnezzar turned and ran back to where Marduk-Sum-Lisir lay. Rymen straddled the fence and ran after Nebuchadnezzar, hoping to calm him down. He saw the King stop at the far fence line and for the first time saw a body lying on the ground.

"Come quickly," he yelled to his helper who stood by the fence watching. "And get the others. We have an injured man on the ground."

He picked up his speed as he raced to where Nebuchadnezzar was standing, looking anxiously at the body on the ground, sniffing it and nudging it in hopes it would get up. Rymen could only see the massive wound, which was now a combination of dirt, grass, bits of flesh and blood. He knelt down and gently turned the man's torso so he could lie on his back and breathe easier. He was not ready for what he saw.

"Marduk-Sum-Lisir," he whispered. "The King's son! What are you doing here?"

He rose to his knees, turned back to the barn and screamed as loud as he could, "Come as fast as you can! It is the King's son. We must get him to the palace at once."

~

Daniel hurriedly walked out of his office and down the long corridor to the grand marble staircase that led outside. He walked briskly towards the King's residential palace on the river. He had been summoned by the Queen to hear the prognosis of the physicians attending Marduk-Sum-Lisir the past two weeks since the attack. He was very concerned for the prince's life as he had been slipping in and out of consciousness, his body refusing to stabilize.

At the same time, the threat of an impending Egyptian invasion had been alleviated. The messenger from the war front who reached him yesterday reported that the Babylonian Imperial Guard had finally halted the enemy's charge through the borders on both the western and southern fronts. There was still no word on whether they had pushed the Egyptians back into their own territory or, for that matter, if they were even continuing to hold their own. Daniel, however, felt at peace that the city was once again safe and that Amel was no longer missing. Now his focus was on restoring Marduk-Sum-Lisir to health.

At the top of the stairs he was greeted by Amytis. She had obviously not had a good night's sleep in many days. The strain and tension of possibly losing her second son showed clearly on her tired face.

"How is he?" questioned Daniel.

"I haven't seen him yet this morning," replied Amytis. "Last night when I left him, he was still unconscious . . . moaning about needing to talk to his father . . . something about what would happen if we were captured by the Egyptians."

Daniel smiled at her and assuredly said, "Well, at least we don't have to worry about that any longer." He proceeded to tell her about the messenger from the front lines informing them that their troops had halted the Egyptian advance. "It looks like our forces may now gain the upper hand and turn the tables on our attackers."

"That's wonderful news, Daniel," said Amytis. "If his fever would subside and my son could come out of his netherworld, this might be the very news to calm his spirit."

"So what do the physicians say?"

"That's why we're here. They informed me that they wanted to meet with me in my son's room only a half hour ago, and that it might be wise to bring you into this as well as you are the ruling leader of the kingdom in the absence of the Crown Prince and indisposition of the King." Amytis paused as a tear trickled down her cheek. She grabbed Daniel's arm, "I'm afraid of what they're going to tell us. Thank you for being here."

The head servant of the royal household who had just come from Marduk-Sum-Lisir's quarters approached and with a smile said, "My Queen, they are ready to see you." Nodding respectfully to Daniel he continued, "Governor, please come with us."

They walked down the tapestry-emblazoned hall and entered Marduk-Sum-Lisir's receiving room. There they found more servants and physicians' aides attending to the prince. The door to his bedroom was open and they went directly in.

"Hello mother."

It was more a whisper than a spoken greeting. Neither Amytis nor Daniel was prepared to see Marduk-Sum-Lisir propped up in bed and fully conscious. He was being fed by one of his servants. The badly gored leg was elevated and heavily bandaged.

Amytis rushed to gather him into her arms, laughing and sobbing at the same time, "You're awake!" She leaned back to look at his face which now boasted a broad smile, then hugged him even harder. "Thank the gods, you are alive and well. I was so worried . . . so frightened. Your father's illness . . . Amel off to war . . . and then your terrible accident . . . it was all too much to take!"

"It's good to see you, mother. I can't remember much of what has happened. I feel like I've been swimming for days in a rushing river . . . sometimes able to breathe, then going back underwater and into darkness. I'm tired, but I think the swim is over." Relief flooded his face and he began to weep, knowing he was safe and with his family.

The others in the room melted into the background, allowing mother and son to have their time. To see a terrible fight between life and death give way to this joyful reunion struck everyone squarely in their hearts. Finally Amytis pulled slowly away from her son and rose to gesture towards Daniel, "The Governor has also come to see you."

Daniel quickly approached the bed and dropped to one knee taking Marduk-Sum-Lisir's hand in his. "My Prince, this is a happy day for all of us. May God continue to heal and bless you."

"Thank you for coming, Daniel," whispered Marduk-Sum-Lisir. He leaned forward, "I have to tell you . . . I was so overwhelmed with anxiety at the thought of the Egyptians conquering our kingdom . . . it's why I went to see my father. I had to talk to him."

"The invasion has been stopped," replied Daniel. "A messenger from the battle front came yesterday with news that the enemy's forward progress has been stopped by the Imperial

Guard. I believe you need not have worries about that any longer."

"That is good news," said Marduk-Sum-Lisir leaning back into his pillows. Turning to his mother he continued, "We can use good news . . . a lot of it . . . right now."

At that point, the lead physician attending the prince approached the Queen bowing low before her, "Your Highness, we called you and the Governor here today to report on the prince's condition and recovery. Praise the gods he is alive and will live a healthy life; however, the bull's horn did a lot of damage to his leg. It severed the muscles and ligaments and, I am afraid, will result in a leg no longer able to function."

"Are you saying that he will be lame? That he will not have use of his leg for the rest of his life?" asked Amytis.

"Yes, my Lady, he will need assistance walking for the rest of his life," answered the physician. "But good health will be his, and he has full and normal use of all his other limbs not to mention his mind."

Amytis was stunned. She feared the worst but the thought of Marduk-Sum-Lisir being a cripple had never occurred to her. She wavered slightly. Daniel moved closer to her, holding her by her arm for support.

"It's not as bad as it sounds, mother," said Marduk-Sum-Lisir, his voice coming back a little stronger. "Look, I'm alive. I can think and create. It could have been a lot worse."

Amytis began to weep. She went back to the bed and sat by her son, holding his hands in both of hers. "You are so, so right, son. When they asked us to meet here an hour ago, I feared for your life. To see you smiling...alive! Well, we can deal with this." Turning to the physicians on the other side of the bed, she said, "Thank you for giving me back my son."

~

It didn't take long for the news to reach Beltekasmer's ears. He was the dominant figure in the circle of wise men that counseled the King. They were now denigrated to a secondary position in the Governing Council under Daniel's governorship. Beltekasmer had long been looking for some opening that would let him challenge Daniel's authority and this seemed the perfect opportunity. Kept well informed by the attending physicians since the day the accident happened, he felt he should strike while the iron was hot. Although Marduk-Sum-Lisir had only regained full consciousness that morning, Beltekasmer decided not to wait but to sow the seeds of doubt and mistrust within Marduk-Sum-Lisir while the sting of learning he was lame for life still smarted.

He arrived at the prince's quarters unannounced and uninvited. It did not matter. His presence in the palace was as predictable as the furniture and furnishings and as comforting. The prince's servants seated him in the receiving room and then made sure the prince was awake and could receive him. They re-appeared a few moments later and ushered Beltekasmer into the bedroom where Marduk-Sum-Lisir had been sketching on a vellum board.

"My Prince, it is good to see you well after such a terrible accident," gushed Beltekasmer as he dropped to one knee in royal obeisance.

"Stand. Please stand, and thank you for coming to see me" replied Marduk-Sum-Lisir, continuing to draw. "To what do I owe this visit? In all the years I have been in the palace, I can't remember a time when you and I had a private conversation." He laughed, "This is historic!"

"Sire, I stand guilty as charged. Your father overshadowed everything and everyone else when he was well. Then . . . well, the transition to Daniel's governorship and your brother's leadership left us a bit unbalanced," he hemmed and hawed. "But that's no excuse. I have often wanted to visit with you as you have brought such a great aesthetic to our city in the buildings and projects undertaken by the King and the Crown Prince. We knew it was you—the artist—responsible for the beauty we all enjoy."

Marduk-Sum-Lisir smiled and set his drawing materials down. This sat well with him. It was good to know that the people of Babylon knew who the artistic force was in the palace. "That's very nice of you to say, but I know you are here for a specific purpose. Speak."

"Sire, all of us in the Governing Council have had grave concerns about Daniel's leadership for a long time. He does not seek the advice and counsel of men who have served your father, the King, for as many years as he is alive. He dismisses our culture and religion, choosing to follow a god that is foreign to us and, in fact, the god of a kingdom we long ago destroyed. And lately he is usurping the collective authority of the Council to dictate laws as though he were the king. Sire, I am here on behalf of the wise men and all the court who have served the King loyally to express our concern that the Governor is not wisely attending to the affairs of the King and the kingdom."

"Beltekasmer, you are a wise and loyal man. I respect your loyalty to my father. At the same time, my father appointed Daniel Governor of the land which has also been upheld by my brother who rules in my father's stead. I hear your concerns. What is it you want me to do?"

Beltekasmer shifted nervously on his feet and then approached the bed on the side of the injured leg. "I—we—don't have a specific request, sir. What we're—I'm—trying to do is just make you aware of gaps in Daniel's oversight. We think he has become a little bit drunk with power and thus has become lax in administering the King's affairs."

Gaining some confidence, Beltekasmer moved closer and pointed to the prince's injured leg, "Take your situation, for example. It was irresponsible to leave such a dangerous animal loose in a pasture within the confines of the city. This animal belongs in the pastures outside the city where he has the freedom necessary to his instincts and fiery spirit. Certainly, responsibility may be put on the chief herdsman, but he was only acting within the policies proscribed by the Governor."

His voice growing louder and more accusatory, Beltekasmer exclaimed, "An injury to a member of the royal family within the palace grounds is cause enough to question the integrity and ability of Daniel!"

Marduk-Sum-Lisir's face hardened. He did not know whether Daniel was a good Governor or not, but perhaps Beltekasmer had a point. He had no desire to get into the squabble that Beltekasmer wished him to enter, but he could not refuse to consider the information that was presented to him.

"I hear you, Beltekasmer. There is nothing I can do at the moment. But I am willing to be watchful from now on and see if I see what you claim to see."

"That is all we ask, Sire."

"Well, I will do that."

"May I report back to my colleagues that you harbor our concerns and now will be more attentive than in the past?"

"I didn't exactly say that," responded Marduk-Sum-Lisir. Then with a wave of his hand to dismiss Beltekasmer he added, "I will be watching . . . especially if the war shifts again and the Egyptians successfully penetrate our defenses."

"Thank you, Sire. I shall so inform the Governing Council of your concerns," Beltekasmer said graciously, bowing low and leaving the room.

~

The Governing Council filled the throne room well before the meeting time. Word had leaked that a second messenger from the war front had arrived. The question on everyone's mind was whether an invasion was imminent or the enemy had been turned back? Due to the severity of the situation, most Council members had brought their aides with them to hear for themselves the discussion. They pressed against the walls of the chamber quietly talking in small groups as their superiors sat in the only available chairs, talking amongst themselves. The room was unusually hot and tepid with the body heat of so many conspiring to overwhelm the gentle breezes blowing through the open windows.

Contrary to his normal punctuality, Daniel entered the room well after the appointed meeting time. He hurried to his Governor's chair and he remained standing, apologizing for his tardiness and immediately reported the news that had come from Nebuzaradan and Amel-Marduk. When the Council members heard that the Egyptian attack had been repulsed, relief broke out in the room and much of the mounting tension began to fade. There was a roar of delight and approval as Daniel reported that the Babylonians had stopped the Egyptian invasion and turned the tables on the enemy. The Babylonian forces were now on the offense, driving the Egyptians back across the borders. After weeks of fearing an enemy attack on the capital city itself, to hear that the momentum had shifted in favor of the empire brought smiles to everyone's face.

The more Daniel shared what he had learned, the more the council hurled questions at him from all sectors of the chamber. Had the Crown Prince been found? How many soldiers had been killed? Which commanders had survived? Which territories did the Egyptians presently occupy? Could the Imperial Guard hold their position? What was the ultimate objective of Egypt? When will it all end? Everyone seemed to talk at once, but eventually all questions were answered and the room quieted into a post-climatic lull.

Sensing the time was right, Beltekasmer stood and asked Daniel if he could speak. He began graciously, "This is wonderful news, Governor. I thank you for sharing all that you know with us. The only question remaining in my mind is does this lift the onerous sanctions you unilaterally imposed on our kingdom without our counsel or consent?"

"What do you mean?" snapped Daniel, somewhat caught off guard by Beltekasmer's hostility in the midst of their celebration.

Beltekasmer burrowed in relentlessly, his anger building as he spoke, "Are you finished playing King? When do you plan to return to your role as Governor?"

"You know I never had anything but the safety and good of Babylon in mind. We were on the brink of being invaded! All that mattered was that we took measures to protect ourselves. As to . . ."

"Rationing food and imposing an evening curfew is one thing," Beltekasmer cut him off in mid sentence. "Implementing price controls and arbitrarily halting our road, waterway and building construction went beyond your authority. And then . . . doubling monies to be paid to the royal treasury! Governor, you not only exceeded your authority, you violated the trust placed in you by the King and this Council. Your ego exceeded your office!"

The tension released by the good news of the war's changing momentum flooded back into the Council chamber. Along with it came all the backlog of consternation, bickering and anger that had ruled this body for months.

Always looking for an opening to pierce Daniel's leadership, Antiosyss leaped to his feet in accord, "Hear, hear! You dismissed our counsel summarily and acted outside the purview of your office. Beltekasmer is right!"

The muttering of the malcontents started at once as others in the assembly too afraid to speak out directly began to support the accusations against Daniel. As astute as Daniel was about human nature, he was not ready for this. He thought the news of the Imperial Guard's victories would bring everyone together in unity. He sat down, not knowing how to respond.

"Members of this esteemed Council," thundered Beltekasmer as he pushed ahead. "I just learned that the King's second son—the next crown prince should Amel-Marduk lose his life in battle—recently suffered a catastrophic accident which nearly took his life. He was gored by a bull recklessly penned in the King's pasture and barn which lies next to this very palace. Thanks to the protection of our god, Marduk, his life was spared.

But hear this, my colleagues, I want you to know that he will be crippled for the rest of his life. He has no function in his right leg."

The assembly rustled nervously, many vocalizing their surprise at this news. The questions began at once as Council members inquired as to Marduk-Sim-Lisir's health. Beltekasmer waved them off with his hands, continuing in a louder voice.

"He will regain his health but he will never walk again without assistance. And all this need not have happened if the leadership of this great nation had not been so reckless and careless in caring for the royal family."

He pointed at Daniel with his arm outstretched, "You, sir, were not paying attention to the King's barns and to proper security. You should have clearly set forth policies for the King's herdsmen prohibiting the enclosure of such dangerous beasts inside the city. These animals belong on the King's pastures outside the walls. Not here . . . on the palace grounds."

Daniel started to speak but was cut off by the chorus of "yeas" that erupted throughout the room. Beltekasmer had only warmed up to the climax of his attack which he delivered as he stepped into the open oval to eyeball everyone assembled.

"I visited with the Prince last evening." He paused for effect. As he had hoped, his direct access to the prince threw Daniel off balance and, on the other hand, increased his stature and gravitas with the Council. "I told him that all of us in the Governing Council have grave concerns about Daniel's leadership . . . that he does not seek the advice and counsel of men who have served the King for many years . . . that he dismisses our culture and religion and chooses to follow a god that is foreign to us.

"I told him that the Governor is usurping the collective authority of the Council to dictate laws as though he were the King," Beltekasmer's voice rose in volume to almost a shout as he neared the end of his indictment. "He agreed that there may well be cause to question the integrity and ability of Daniel, and he asked me to report back to you that he harbors our concerns."

"That's a blatant lie!" shouted Daniel, his voice matching the volume of Beltekasmer. "I, too, spent time with Marduk-Sum-Lisir yesterday and even in the days before. He is in good spirits. His concern is only that the war which is going in our favor may yet turn to favor the Egyptians—not the petty nonsense that you are bringing up. He and the Queen have complete confidence in my governorship."

Empowered by his own voice and finally regaining his composure, Daniel stepped off his podium and approached Beltekasmer in the oval. He had taken the offense and the Council knew it. Most importantly, Beltekasmer knew it.

"What you bring up is utter stupidity in this time of national security and war. To question why the Governor of this empire is not concerned about livestock policies and the management of the King's barn when our troops are putting their lives on the line and dying for us on our borders is not only ridiculous . . . it is acting without honor to those defending our land."

Daniel jabbed his finger into Beltekasmer's chest with more than a little force, "I always respected you as a wise man, a valued counselor to the King. It is difficult for me to see you now denigrate yourself in the assembly of your colleagues. Your charges are outlandish! Beyond decency!"

He turned and walked among the Council members, looking at each one intently and questioningly as he continued, "Do you really take these charges seriously? Do you really think I am usurping the King's power? Do you think the war is now over because our troops repelled the invasion and that we can pretend we are safe? Are you ready to celebrate a victory that has not yet been won?"

No one could sustain his glance. All eyes were focused on the floor as each man wrestled with the scolding delivered by Daniel, No one able to deny that it was justified. Beltekasmer faded from the center oval and backed out the doors exiting the chamber. Antiosyss sat back down, all wind gone out of his sails.

Moving towards his regular seat in the throne room, his hands thoughtfully clasped behind his back, Daniel said, "What started as a gathering of joy and good news has deteriorated into a childish display of petulance. I am sad for us. There is still a war going on—one that needs our full support and attention. When you are ready to re-assemble as the leaders of this kingdom and exercise the wisdom God has given you, we will re-convene. Right now, this Council is dismissed."

The room emptied . . . silently . . . quickly.

~

Now that there was no longer a threat of imminent invasion to the capital, Daniel knew he had to relax the emergency policies he had put in place to shore up Babylon's defenses. The first to go was the evening curfew. While few people really cared that much about this restriction as most people retired to bed early, its mere existence was an irritant that gave the citizenry something about which to grumble. Wanting the merchants and growers back on his side, he next lifted the price controls on commodities and relaxed rationing of food. All this sent a positive message to the people throughout the city signaling that the crisis was over and they could get back to their normal routines.

More than a few messengers had come from the war front requesting more armament and weaponry as the battles took their toll on both men and equipment. Hence, Daniel opted to keep in place the doubling of payment to the royal treasury from goods and services traded in the marketplace. Labor was badly needed in the shops constructing weaponry and armor so he also maintained his policy that the moratorium on infrastructure construction be sustained.

As he worked through these policies with his most trusted aides, certain concerns came to light suggesting it might be difficult to stay the course, especially on the construction moratorium. The old central market had been demolished to make way for the building of the new one, the Crown Prince's special project which he had personally supervised prior to the war. With the old market gone and the new one not yet built, the business life of Babylon was in disarray and getting worse each day.

Shadrach, his administrator in charge of agriculture, reported that the slow place they faced in getting their foodstuffs to market increasingly frustrated the growers. Inadequate facilities caused further delays in selling to the general public. This, in turn, impacted the traffic on the roads leading to the central market where wagons filled with produce often stood grid-locked unable to move forward, back up or turn around. It was one thing to deal with logistical problems for a day or two, but since construction on the new market had halted for close to two months the situation had become untenable. Shadrach pleaded the case that the emphasis on weapon manufacturing needed to be balanced with the exigencies of daily living. The moratorium was causing more harm than good.

Reluctantly, Daniel knew he had to either lift or violate his own decree and get the new central market built. The importance of this issue drew more and more people in the various governing offices into the discussion. As much as Daniel wanted these discussions and plans kept confidential, it was impossible to contain them to the palace.

~

Narseniah ran up the steps of the temple, eager to find Antiosyss. Her hatred for Daniel had only intensified since he had ambushed her at Meshach's house. At the same time, she had kept a low profile, knowing she was marked by the administration. The news she bore tonight would be of interest to her father and could possibly be instrumental in taking Daniel down. She relished the thought of his losing the governorship.

She entered the temple and found her way to the high priest's preparation room where she knew she would find her father. Without bothering to announce herself, she opened the door and walked in. Antiosyss was enjoying a bowl of fruit and cup of wine with a man she recognized as a key aide to Neriglissar. He had remained in Babylon to take care of Neriglissar's property and affairs rather than accompany him to the battle front.

"Have you lost the decency to knock before entering?" quipped Antiosyss as he bent forward to take the cup of wine resting on the large engraved table by which they sat.

"Please, father. Don't be a bore," she replied, "I thought you might like to hear what I just heard from Synthora who heard it directly from one of the people working in Meshach's office." Turning to leave, she coyly said over her shoulder, "But I see you're busy. I can wait until your visitor has left."

"Well, you've interrupted us so speak up. Tell me your news. I have no secrets from Neriglissar's house," Antiosyss chuckled, slapping the back of his guest who joined him in conspiratorial hilarity.

"Apparently the standstill in the construction of the central market due to Daniel's moratorium on building has created more problems than he figured. Everyone is angry. The growers can't sell their foodstuffs fast enough. The merchants can't accommodate the buying public...they have no place to set up shop since the market has been closed. And . . . the people feel wronged. There is plenty of food, but no place and means to sell it!"

"So what?" snapped Antiosyss, "we've seen this coming the past few weeks. This isn't news."

Narseniah moved to the table and sat down directly across from her father. She smiled as she bent forward to speak, "But this is."

She paused to get her father's undivided attention. Before he could retort, she continued, "Daniel intends to restart construction on the central market in the next week, even though he will keep in place a moratorium on all other construction. He's going to defy his own edict and hope no one cares."

Antiosyss smiled as he popped another handful of grapes into his mouth, the juice dribbling down his cheek. He started to nod as he thought about the conundrum Daniel was entering. This could be quite interesting . . . this move could come back to bite Daniel rather badly if the Governor's detractors could orchestrate it as a corruption scandal.

He looked at his guest with a smirk, "This could be very good for us." They both laughed . . . the laughter that comes easily from men on the verge of drunkenness.

He leaned across the table and patted Narseniah fondly on the cheek, "This is good news, Narseniah . . . very good news. It seems that except for planting a few well-placed rumors all we need to do is sit back and let Daniel hang himself on this move. I don't see how he can keep this from erupting in his face once that large crew begins work. I want to see him justify that single project while everything else in this city sits dormant."

While his guest chuckled at this good fortune, Antiosyss' smile without warning morphed into a frown. The impact of Daniel's decision on his own destiny suddenly dawned on him. He slammed his fist on the table and stood.

"What's wrong?" asked Narseniah, also rising.

"We must get the canal project moving much faster," he snapped at Neriglissar's aide. "If Daniel is going to restart the market project next week, we better use the time between now and then to put more laborers on our project and get this done. Once the market restarts, it will suck every good worker away from us and the canal will sit unfinished! We've got to move immediately and work night and day."

"But if we get too aggressive, word will get out that we are in violation of Daniel's decree," retorted his guest. "If we work during the day, there is no way our secret can be maintained!"

"We have no choice," spit Antiosyss. "We may have five or six days at best before we lose our workers. If we bring more men in to help, and we work day and night, we can finish the canal into the temple grounds. If we are found out, no one will care because they will be too busy with the market. We have to take the chance!"

"You're right about losing our labor force, but...the risk is too great!" said Neriglissar's aide who was now standing as well.

Antiosyss turned to him, his face directly in his and hissed, "If you're too afraid to do this, I'll take over the project. I know your boss wouldn't have a doubt about what to do given the circumstances." He paused and smirked, then continued, "I'll let him know how you felt."

Turning abruptly, Antiosyss headed for the door to put things in motion. "Wait!" bellowed his guest. "I didn't say I wouldn't do it." He stepped towards Antiosyss who was at the door.

"You're a damned priest! You don't know how to supervise a construction crew. This is my project. You pay for the men and I'll get the canal finished in five days."

~

On making his regular round of the streets and waterways of Babylon to note needed repairs, Synossus decided to end the day near the Temple of Marduk where he could participate in the evening ceremony. It had been weeks since he had gone to temple, and his luck was suffering for it. Perhaps a reconnection with the spirit world was what he needed to get his life back on track. His day had been routine . . . the normal wear and tear on the city's infrastructure but nothing major about which to be alarmed. Since new construction had come to a halt, he was just trying to fill his time by keeping a close watch on damages so they could be addressed before they became major concerns. Because of his diligence, his supervisor—Abednego—gave him a free hand, something he valued highly.

Synossus stopped at a neighborhood tavern for a beer and some local gossip. There was some buzz about an influx of many new laborers near the temple. He thought he should check this out since he wasn't aware of any construction work there. He finished his drink and trudged along in the heat of the late afternoon to the main entrance of the temple off Procession Way. It was worse than hot; for some reason, the humidity seemed unusually high. He couldn't help but stand and admire the mile length of the grand avenue with its gold lions that Amel-Marduk had built. Nothing like it in the world, he mused. It's good to be a Babylonian.

He noticed by the sun's position in the western sky that he had some time before the evening rite began. He decided to walk around the large temple to see if there was anything to the rumblings he had heard about an abundance of laborers in the area. He had walked two lengths of the building to no avail and had turned the corner to walk along the back. He had heard several years ago that this spot was where the temple's high priest wanted to build a canal diverting water from the Euphrates River into the temple grounds. It's too bad this project never happened, he thought. A waterway here could be quite beautiful. Better than the clutter of palm branches, sheaves of straw and all the litter that seemed to stretch across the backside of the Temple and into the horizon to his left.

He let his mind drift off . . . visioning what a waterway with all the lush vegetation along both sides would look like. Then . . . an unexpected movement of the clutter caught his eye. He focused on the spot only thirty or forty feet away. Suddenly, the fallen palm branches and clutter began to move creating an opening in the debris. Four men surfaced from below, struggling to haul up a large bag which they then emptied to the side. It was dirt and rocks. As quickly as they surfaced, they disappeared. That is curious, Synossus thought. Since the opening had not been closed back up, he cautiously walked to it and looked down below.

At that point, he saw another group of men dragging a similar bag to hoist up and empty as those before had done. Not wanting to be seen, he ducked behind a large flowering bush next to the temple and watched. The men he saw climbed up the ladder to the level where he was hiding, pushed and pulled the bag up with them and emptied it as before. This time, a couple of them picked up a few branches to lay on the fresh dirt as well as scattered some straw over it so it blended in with the long expanse of clutter people had become used to seeing.

He had to get down inside this opening and see what was going on. He waited, in case another group of men came up with more dirt up. Sure enough, the process was repeated and repeated . . . well over twenty times during the time he spent in hiding. The sun was sinking into the horizon and night was falling quickly. Realizing this was no small project he had stumbled onto, Synossus determined he had to see for himself what they were working on. Because it was getting dark, he reasoned that they could be through for the day and that this might be his most opportune time to drop down underground to investigate. He crept noiselessly to the opening and slowly let himself down the ladder into the darkness below.

But it wasn't all dark. As his eyes adjusted to the dim light, he saw lamps burning in the distance giving the tunnel a warm glow. He picked his way towards the light, always seeking a rock or some indentation against which he could hide should another group of workers come by. As he closed in on the light ahead, he saw a large number of men digging out the earth and filling the bags with dirt that he had seen hoisted upwards. He could not believe his eyes. This was a major construction project -- a covert operation directly violating the moratorium the Governor had put in place. Abednego needed to see this. First, Synossus needed to get out without being caught. Slowly he backtracked to the opening through which he had come. Once outside on the street, all thoughts of participating in the temple ceremony were gone. He needed to report to his superior what he had seen.

He ran back to the front of the temple and down Procession Way. It was getting quite dark so he had to slow down to avoid hitting others on the street or even the lions that dotted the avenue. It occurred to Synossus that the palace was a good half-mile away. Moreover, the administrative offices would probably be empty by this time as everyone would have returned to their homes for the night. To bother Abednego during his evening meal could end badly, especially if he knew about this project and it was authorized. And so Synossus pulled up to a stop, opting to go home himself for the evening. This could wait until the morning when he went to work.

~

"There's where I saw them bringing up the dirt, sir," pointed Synossus. "There's a lot more of it this morning than what I saw last night."

Abednego brushed by his aide and crossed to the opening to peer below. Because of the sun's glare, it was all dark below. The only way for him to get a look at what was going on was to drop down into the hole. As he prepared to climb down the ladder that was propped exiting the opening, he heard voices approaching below and promptly stepped away from the hole. In only seconds, two burly laborers came crawling up the ladder with ropes suspended below. Abednego and Synossus were somewhat hidden in the debris that cluttered the site. The men began tugging on the ropes and soon a large burlap bag rose out of the opening pushed by a couple of other workers making their way up the ladder. With a concerted heave, the bag came out of the ground and emptied itself of the dirt it was carrying.

"What are you doing?" Abednego stepped forward, surprising the four men.

"What does it look like?" retorted one of them. "Carrying out the dirt."

"I can see that," returned Abednego who had now come close to them to where they could see his clothing distinguishing him as an official of some sort. "I want to know what is going on down there. What are you working on?"

One of the men pulled the spokesman for their group away from Abednego whispering, "I don't think we ought to say anything more. Jonedab needs to talk with him."

"Who is this Jonedab?" demanded Abednego. Something was clearly going on that shouldn't be, as was evident by their caginess.

"He's the construction supervisor," replied the workman. He turned to one of his co-workers who had started back down the ladder underground, "Go get Jonedab and tell him to come here quickly."

It was clear that the workers did not want Abednego to go below ground; one of them stood on the ladder while the other two blocked Abednego's access to it. It was only a matter of a few minutes before the ladder began to move sending the man on it above ground. From below came the construction super, squinting his eyes as they adjusted to the sun. He finally made out the figures of Abednego and Synossus, then, pulled himself fully out of the opening.

"Who are you?" he walked directly into Abednego's face.

"I think the question is, who are you and what are you doing?" replied Abednego.

"I don't have to answer to you," said Jonedab. He nodded towards the temple looming above them, "I answer to Antiosyss and the royal family."

"You may have some sort of relationship with the high priest and the temple, but I can guarantee that you are not working at the behest of the royal family," Abednego said with authority. "You see, I do work for the Governor and the King, and thus the royal family. My name is Abednego and I am the Administrator of Water in the city and the empire."

Jonedab took a step back, startled by this disclosure. "Ah . . . well, sire. . . I think you need to talk to Commander Neriglissar and Antiosyss who employ us. I don't . . ."

"This site is shut down as of now!" snapped Abednego. "I want you and your workmen gone from here within the hour. Meanwhile, I am going below to take a look for myself to see what you are up to. And I suspect it's no good."

Synossus slid over to Abednego's side, pointing up the walkway where Antiosyss and a small entourage of his priests were hurrying towards them, "Sir, look."

"Good," said Abednego, smiling at Jonedab. "I guess we can take care of this right now."

By now, several dozens of men filled the debris-laden area around the opening where they stood. They had come up the ladder and from other areas of the construction site when the word got out that there was trouble. Antiosyss and his people added to the crowd . . . an angry crowd hearing that their work was being terminated.

As Antiosyss neared them, Abednego looked him directly in the eyes and quietly but with a searing intensity said, "I might have known you would defy the law. You have fought Daniel at every turn and done your best to have him unseated since the Crown Prince went to war. Have you no shame?"

"I've been told you want to shut this construction site down," Antiosyss sneered at him. "You have no right to do this!"

"I have every right to do this," replied Abednego. "Whatever you are building, you know there is a moratorium on construction in the city. As an administrator in the Governor's Office, it is my duty to see this decree is obeyed."

The two men stood in silence, staring each other down. Finally, Antiosyss smiled and moved to Abednego to take his arm and walk him away from the crowd which had gathered around them.

"Let's get some space . . . let's talk . . . just you and me."

After they were well clear of being heard, Antiosyss stopped and said,"We are both on the Governing Council. We both want what is best for Babylon. I think you'll agree with me that this project is important."

"I still don't know what it is," replied Abednego unsmiling and refusing to be sucked into the artificial camaraderie Antiosyss was attempting to generate.

Antiosyss patted him on the shoulder as though they were friends, "You know that many of us have been proposing for years a canal waterway from the river directly to the temple. Besides, the temple needs access to water for our many ceremonies and rites . . . something we presently don't have."

"I . . ." Abednego began to respond.

Antiosyss cut him off, "Neriglissar and I approached the Crown Prince a while back—long before the Egyptians attacked—asking him to move this up on his priority list to which, I must gratefully say, he agreed. But he had to lead the Imperial Guard to war before he had the opportunity to put it in motion. So we moved forward with it, knowing we had his support."

"If this is true, I would have been the first to know this as Administrator of Water," coldly replied Abednego.

"I guess he didn't bother to tell you. I'm sorry for that."

"You know," said Abednego, "he had all the laborers that could be mustered working on the central market before he left. That was his priority! To take workers away from that would slow it down. I know he wanted that project completed as fast as possible."

Antiosyss smiled condescendingly, "Abednego, our project did not take anything away from the market. All of our workers worked after hours on the canal waterway and were paid separately. We had no intention to endanger the market."

"So why didn't you stop when Daniel put the moratorium on construction in place?"

"We felt he had no right to do that . . . to supersede the Crown Prince's wishes and directive to complete the market and all necessary infrastructure work."

"Well, you were wrong. Amel-Marduk put Daniel in charge of the kingdom during his absence giving him the full powers and authority of the throne."

The niceness faded from Antiosyss who saw this was going nowhere. His voice changed to threateningly icy, "It would be in your personal best interest to back away as though you've never seen this site today."

Abednego abruptly turned and walked back to the growing crowd of workers. Antiosyss had to run to keep up with him asking, "What are you doing?"

"I'm shutting down this project," snapped Abednego.

Antiosyss slowed, then stopped, He shouted after him, "We'll see who wins this battle at the Governing Council."

~

The last echoes of daylight were quickly being absorbed by the fast approaching darkness of night. In the tent that served as the Babylonian command center, a lantern had been lit and suspended over the maps scattered on the table that dominated the enclosure. The side flaps had been pinned back to allow the evening breezes to rush through. Nebuzaradan stood straight at one end of the table, his arms folded across his chest. He was studying the man hovered over the map pinpointing the position of the Imperial Guard troops.

"My Lord, we have finally gained the upper hand," smiled Nebuzaradan. "We completely surround the enemy on both the western and southern fronts and are in an excellent position to not only push them back but push their borders back as well. They are demoralized and seem without a plan, whether it is to attack or retreat."

Amel-Marduk looked up at him and slowly straightened up to stand. His back hurt from being bent over the maps for so long. He placed both hands behind his back just above the hips and rocked back and forth, hoping to relieve some of the muscle tightness.

"You've led our troops well in this war, Nebuzaradan. I am grateful for your command."

"Thank you, sir." The Supreme Commander of the Imperial Guard was pleased to receive this praise from the Crown Prince. Nebuchadnezzar was not given to praise, he mused. It's good when the King—or in this case, the Crown Prince—recognizes professionalism.

"Sire, I've asked Neriglissar, and the other division commanders to join us tonight to strategize our next moves," said Nebuzaradan. "When morning dawns, we should be moving forcefully while we have the upper hand."

"Agreed," replied Amel. He stretched and bent down once again to examine the maps. "It looks like we're only a few days from pushing the Egyptians back across their border. Maybe we can wrap this up within the week and think of going home."

"That's one option," nodded Nebuzaradan.

Neither man spoke for a few minutes. Amel remained focused on the map while Nebuzaradan waited for the right moment to advance his plan. Suddenly the Crown Prince looked up at him, realizing he hadn't finished his thought, "What's your option?"

"My Lord, I cannot recall when we have been in such a strong position to attack and our enemy has had such a vast absence of leadership." He paused to make the point.

"Go on," said Amel, again standing upright to relieve the tension in his back.

Nebuzaradan walked around the table across from the Crown Prince and with his dagger began to describe troop movements across the mountains and into the Egyptian desert. "This is the time to attack and drive them all the way back to Memphis. We have never had an opportunity to add to our territory so effortlessly as right now. In fact, I think we can completely annihilate Egypt and extend our empire."

"Hear, hear!" came a loud voice from the entry to the tent. Bursting into the light still dressed in full battle armor, Neriglissar grabbed one of the tankards of beer proffered by a servant and strode to the table to join the other two.

"Egypt is ours to take. My men have captured several of their officers . . . it's all the same story. They have not had any communications or directives from their superiors in several days. All decision making is at the lowest platoon level. When they see our troops breathing down their necks every day, their decision is to retreat. They're running back to Memphis as fast as they can. The only thing to slow us down is our own lack of energy."

"There are consequences to taking over another country," quietly said Amel as he backed away from the table and sat heavily in a chair. "I don't wish to go there when we have no need to. The Egyptians are defeated. They have learned a good lesson. Right now, they respect us. Why make them hate us?"

Neriglissar banged the table with his hand loudly and said "They started this whole thing. I say we finish it."

He turned to Nebuzaradan. "I don't know why you called us together tonight, but I say we go for a full attack and total decimation of Egypt. To back away from our advantage makes no sense."

By now, the other division commanders had filtered into the command center and were picking up on the conversation. To a man, they were of a mind to take the offensive and march all the way to the Egyptian capital to claim total victory. Not only were they righting the wrong of being attacked by Egypt, but each man had been itching for a good fight for years during the long peace that Babylon had enjoyed. Making war is what they did. Now that they were back in the throes of action, they had no desire to stop. Adding Egypt to the empire would greatly strengthen the Babylon kingdom as well as enhance their individual positions.

Amel let the conversation go on, trying to sort through their reasoning to see if he could discern a valid argument to justify an invasion beyond their borders. If our country was threatened, yes, it would make sense to invade to eliminate the threat he mused. But he wasn't hearing that tonight. The argument was nothing more than we are in a power position to annihilate the Egyptians and so invasion is a reasonable action. Not good enough, he thought.

"We are of the same mind," summed up Neriglissar. "Let's prepare our attack plan."

"I think not," said Amel. "We have enjoyed years of peace during which we have built a wonderful capital city and secure borders. The day we go back to the hunt to conquer new territories and broaden our empire is the day we will find enemies threatening us on all sides of our kingdom."

"It already happened to us," sneered Neriglissar. "Why are we out in this miserable country? Because we were attacked!"

"And we successfully defended ourselves," retorted Amel. "All our neighbors have watched and they have noted our strength. No one is going to try this again. Not any time soon."

"Right," snapped Neriglissar. "All are in fear of us. It's the right time to push forward . . . when everyone sees what happens to them if they so much as challenge our right to our territories."

"I do not intend to give rise to any more enemies at this time," said Amel as he stood and walked to stand with Nebuzaradan. "Not with my father ill . . . not when we don't need to take the risk."

Amel walked around the table slowly, the others backing to the sides of the tent to give him space. As he walked, he talked, "I thank you for your outstanding service in this war. Every one of you has led with integrity. You have not asked your men to do anything you have not done and did not demonstrate on the battlefield daily. Our kingdom is indebted to you and honors you for your service."

He stopped, then turned around in a full circle to look at every man in the eyes before continuing. He smiled at them in appreciation, yet maintained a distant sternness demanded of his position. Right now, in this tent on this war front, he was their King.

He came back to Nebuzaradan, addressing him as though no one else were in the tent, "We are not invading Egypt. Prepare your plans to drive the enemy out of our territory and re-seal our borders. Once that's done, plan our return home."

"Yes, Sire," saluted Nebuzaradan. He knew better than to argue as Amel had made up his mind.

Amel turned back to the battle-scarred division commanders around the table and said kindly, "Please prepare your plans. I'll be back in an hour to review them." With that he briskly walked out of the tent into the darkness.

~

When the doors swung open to the throne room which since the King's illness also served as the Governing Council chambers, those waiting to enter were startled to see Daniel already in place on his Governor's chair. Beside him sat Shadrach, Meshach and Abednego; the sternness of their demeanor suggested trouble. This was not Daniel's style. He never entered the room until all the members were present and the Council was ready to tend to business.

Slowly the room filled. Even Marduk-Sum-Lisir was present, specifically requested by Daniel to join them today. Polynices was one of the last to arrive, accompanied by Antiosyss. Daniel made a mental note of this. He knew these two men rarely saw eye to eye on any matter. For them to come to the Governing Council together suggested some sort of collusion. Could they be aligned after all the fights between them? As startled as they were to see Daniel and his close advisors precede them into the room, Daniel was equally surprised to see them engaged in an intense conversation entering together. Polynices nodded at Daniel and approached him to engage in small talk. Antiosyss sneered and simply went to his chair to take his seat.

Daniel signaled Zocor who loudly stamped the butt of his spear on the floor three quick times and called out, "The Governing Council is now in session."

The room quieted more quickly than normal. All present sensed a tension in the air.

Daniel spoke first: "I am pleased to report to you that the war with the Egyptians has taken a decidedly good turn in our favor. A messenger arrived from the front just this morning to report that our troops have taken the upper hand and are now poised to drive the enemy back across the borders into their own land. The Crown Prince and the Imperial Guard will be returning to Babylon within a few months."

Spontaneous cheering broke out in the room. The tension that pervaded the room had been dissipated and relief flooded the chamber. Council members slapped each other on the back in joy and shamelessly hugged as the good news of victory settled on them. This was a day they had all hoped would happen and for which they had been waiting.

Daniel stood, holding his hands in the air to ask for quiet. The council members slowly came back to order although they did not want to stop celebrating. Once he had everyone's attention, Daniel lowered his arms and continued, "That is the good news. I regret that I must now turn to some bad news."

He stepped off the platform on which his chair sat and walked crossed the room to stop in front of Antiosyss. In a loud, commanding voice he asked, "Antiosyss, why have you disobeyed my decree that all construction must stop?"

Never thinking in a million years that he would be called out so publicly for continuing construction on the canal project, Antiosyss was speechless. He tried to maintain eye contact with Daniel but finally drew his eyes away, then looked from side to side for allies who would come to his defense. The silence was painful as the council members watched the high priest humiliated before them.

Daniel abruptly turned away from him and now spoke to the entire assembly, "Two months ago, I called for a moratorium on all construction, asking that our workers be used in our armament and weapons foundries to supply our troops on the front lines. Everyone cooperated . . . that is, except for this man." He pointed at Antiosyss whose face reddened as he struggled to regain his composure and sense of right.

"Two nights ago, Abednego discovered a major construction site behind the temple. There, large numbers of laborers have been employed surreptitiously building a canal diverting water from the Euphrates River directly to the Temple of Marduk. They knew they were violating the law because they covered their construction site with palm branches, debris and shrubbery to avoid being seen. At first they worked only by cover of night, and we completely overlooked them. In the past week, they began to work days as well, and grew smug thinking they were safe from detection. And then they became careless. Rather than continue the laborious process of carrying freshly dug up dirt unseen through their underground tunnels, they took the easy alternative and simply spread it off to the side where they were digging. I thank God that Abednego saw this and was able to intervene to stop this flagrant illegal work."

"Daniel, I cannot remain quiet," said Polynices who stood up across the room, his anger rising to a boiling temperature. "I appreciate that this work may have not been exactly according to your decree, but this is a very important project for the temple. I applaud Antiosyss for having the courage to re-kindle this project that brings glory and honor to our god Marduk. It is a good thing."

The mumblings in the room and the nodding of assent by most indicated that there was great sympathy for the project in spite of its violation of Daniel's decree.

Leandrus, the major grower in the Babylon valley chimed in, "It is a good thing! Your decree was arbitrary and—we see today by our victory on the battle front—unnecessary. I say let them continue. No harm done."

Sensing a groundswell in his favor, Antiosyss decided his best defense was an aggressive offense. He leaped to his feet, shook his finger at Daniel and shouted, "We are tired of your arrogance . . . of your assuming that you have a royal authority over us! Everything that you have put in place to limit our freedoms has been done for no purpose other than to control everything we do. It is time for this to stop!"

"Hear, hear."

"It's too much."

"Govern the land but do not pretend to rule it."

"How dare you demand more payment to the royal treasury?"

The clamor of support grew loudly from those present in the room. Obviously, many of them felt Daniel had taken things too far with his edicts.

Caught up in the moment, Antiosyss left his chair and strode to the King's throne where he stepped up onto the royal podium and stood where only the King stood. He lifted his hands for quiet and shouted, "I think Daniel may be suffering from some affliction. I say he is no longer competent to serve as our Governor. He needs a rest. It is obvious he no longer can think clearly. And I say that Meshach and Abednego are no longer capable of being in charge of our roads and waterways. They do not have the public's interest in their decisions. Surely, when the smoke of incompetence this great comes to light, there are fires of corruption burning underneath. This whole administration must not stand!"

Beginning to see that he was on the wrong side of the debate, Daniel scanned the room quickly looking for support . His eyes settled on Nolter who did not want to enter the debate but felt compelled to stand for what was right. At the very least, he had to neutralize the insanity that was unfolding in the room.

Nolter rose heavily to his feet, his face fixed in a frown, "Colleagues," he began in a somewhat subdued voice. No one seemed to hear him, so he spoke a little louder, "Colleagues, may I speak to the issue?"

Those around him sat back in their chairs, surprised that the merchant would stick his neck out to take a public position on such a volatile issue. They hushed the room so he could be heard.

"Colleagues, we've just received good news from the war front. And yet we argue and fight among ourselves over issues that are not life and death matters. I have heard the opposing positions, and I, for one, still believe in the rule of appointed authority." He swallowed hard, not altogether confident in what he was saying or doing, standing up to those who always enjoyed a higher profile than he.

Nolter knew he couldn't stop now, and so he plunged ahead, speaking even louder, "Antiosyss, you have no right to stand where you are now standing. You talk about Daniel usurping the King's authority! Look at yourself!! You stand where none but the King should stand. Do you now claim to also have royal approval? I think not. Shame on you, Antiosyss."

Heads bobbed up and down as the Council recognized the audacity of Antiosyss. But no one dared to speak. Feeling totally vulnerable, Antiosyss stepped off the podium to the floor and returned to his seat. The momentum he once had was now gone. The room was completely neutralized, the cloud of combat totally dissipated. They sat in silence.

Mysonus, who had remained uncharacteristically silent throughout the waging debate, finally spoke, "Many accusations have been hurled today. Too many! I suggest we adjourn the Council, retire to our own homes and offices, and consider all that has been said today. We are not a barbarian empire. We live by laws and by appointed authority. Most importantly, let us relish the victory of our great army and leaders. We have much to celebrate. It makes no sense to let dissension take this from us."

He rose from his chair and walked out of the assembly room followed by the other wise men and magicians of the court and then the others. Knowing he had overstepped his boundary, Antiosyss anxiously found Polynices and a few of his cohorts seeking comfort in numbers. As there was nothing left to say, they quietly walked out of the room. Shadrach, Meshach and Abednego started for the exit softly speaking among themselves, surprised by how the meeting had spun out of control and then suddenly evaporated. They paused at the door, looking back on Daniel who was the lone figure remaining in the room, still seated on his chair.

"Daniel, can we do anything for you?" asked Shadrach.

He looked at them with a sad smile spreading across his face, "No, but thank you. I let my anger at Antiosyss' disobedience get the best of me today. I was not governing; I was looking to get even."

He rose and walked toward them, "All is well. God did not let it collapse on us. We just have to earn back our right to govern by the justness of our actions. I will be so glad to have the Crown Prince back."

~

As Antiosyss walked back to the Temple, he remained frustrated that he was not able to topple Daniel from his position at the Council meeting. His son, Antiobud, accompanied him. He had brought him to Council as he thought he was going to finally be granted the leadership he sought and he wanted his son to be present for the experience. He did not expect Daniel to come at him so brazenly and quickly, and so he was momentarily put off balance to which he attributed his lack of victory today.

"I despise the man," he muttered through clenched teeth as they quickly walked down Procession Way.

"It wasn't that bad," countered Antiobud. "Most of the council members shared your anger and were more than ready to get rid of Daniel. You had defeated him until Nolter stepped in to calm things."

"I don't know what it is about the man. He always seems to counter every move I make and come out on top. His luck can't run on forever!"

They walked in silence for several minutes, each reflecting back on the meeting and pondering all that happened. While Antiosyss was reliving his anger, Antiobud had taken hold of an idea that might be their answer.

"You said something this afternoon that made a lot of heads nod in agreement with you," said Antiobud.

Antiosyss looked at him, "And what was that?"

"You said you thought Daniel may be suffering from some affliction and that he may no longer be competent to serve as Governor . . . that he no longer can think clearly.'"

"I was mad. I just made that up."

"I think it may be the best argument you have ever come up with to challenge his decisions and methods," said Antiobud. "A lot of important people on that Governing Council will agree with you when you suggest he may be a bit touched in the head and lacks the competence to hold his position as Governor. Or, if they don't agree, they will be glad to take up the argument as a means of getting rid of him."

"I don't know if we can use that as the basis of a successful campaign to dump Daniel."

Antiobud grabbed Antiosyss by the arm and turned him to face him. They had stopped dead center in Procession Way.

"It's brilliant. It answers why Daniel suddenly began rationing food, instituted price controls, implemented a curfew, halted construction and then doubled what everyone has to pay into the royal treasury. Why would any official do all this when our army was defeating the enemy and there was no danger to any of us here in Babylon?!"

"But for a moment there was a danger of invasion."

"That's easily forgotten now," countered Antiobud. "Everyone's been wondering why these stringent regulations were put into effect. It made no sense to them! If we tell them the reason was that Daniel has lost his mental faculties . . . well, that's something they could believe."

"Maybe you have something," said Antiosyss beginning to grasp the full power of this argument and how it could play with people.

Antiobud smiled at him, pleased he could help his father and contribute to the plot that had now been going on for almost four years. He was determined to make this succeed. He patted his father on the back and they continued walking back to the Temple. He could not help grinning ear to ear.

"We're going to make this one stick," he said gleefully.

~

Within days, Antiobud had visited with the entire membership of the Governing Council, leading merchants in the city, the various priesthoods of the many temples in Babylon, and the intellectual thinkers who were the opinion makers of the region. From sunrise to dusk, he was a whirlwind in motion, often managing to see as many as a dozen people per day.

Over the past few years he had observed that Antiosyss' hard line opposition to Daniel did not play well with the majority of people. Daniel was a man of extraordinary gifts and wisdom, and to continually dismiss him as incompetent or disloyal to the King had no traction. The leading echelon of Babylon might not have always favored his decisions, but they respected his leadership skills and governance.

Antiobud took a different stance. He always initiated his conversations by commending the years of peace and prosperity Babylon enjoyed due to Daniel's governorship. For most people with whom he talked, he gave credit where credit was due which had the effect of instantly creating a common bond between them. They had no axe to grind with Daniel; they simply wanted fair and just leadership. By agreeing on this issue he was granted unstated permission to discuss other ideas on which they might also find agreement. Of course, for those feeling threatened by Daniel or who hated his policies, he took the opposite tack and commiserated. In either case, his first move was to befriend before he attempted to persuade.

Whether he was talking with a Governing Council member, the wise men of the palace, the philosophers holding forth in the square or the farmers bringing produce into the market every day, Antiobud was a compelling force. At the right time, he asked questions that had the effect of raising doubt in everyone's mind. These were questions to which there were no clear cut answers; they merely suggested a weakness or hinted at a failing that could wreak disaster.

Do you think that the constant stress Daniel is under is taking its toll on him? Don't you think he's carrying more responsibility than any one person can bear? How is it possible that his judgment can remain unclouded with all the decisions he must make daily? I'm sure the lack of sleep is wearing him down, aren't you?

Once the seeds of doubt were planted, Antiobud let them grow. Like a gardener, he tended to them, re-visiting everyone to pick up the conversation where he had left off. It was not long before he was able to give life to the rumor that due to exhaustion Daniel had suffered a mental collapse and should take leave from his governorship. It even reached the point where many felt Daniel should be incarcerated for his own protection.

Strangely, Daniel's camp was shielded from Antiobud's chicanery and was oblivious to the dangerous web he was spinning. Raising publicly the issue of Daniel's mental competence was to invite charges of treason since he was the King's viceroy. Shadrach, Meshach and Abednego were outside the loop; even those with whom they worked regularly feared bringing it up to them. By praising Daniel for his years of good leadership, Antiobud had been able to create a rumor and doubt not construed as malicious on his part. He was perceived as acting for the good of the kingdom and its citizens, and so, there was no need to defend the Governor or to counter the shared belief growing in the minds of the citizenry that Daniel needed relief.

The more Antiobud stirred the pot, the more the leadership of the Governing Council began to talk among themselves. The wildfire had been set, and it was now spreading out of control. Beltekasmer, the dominant wise man in the court, finally took the issue public and demanded a meeting of the Governing Council be convened.

~

Daniel remained in his office until an aide reported that all members of the Governing Council were seated. He had heard wisps of a rumor that was running rampant in the city suggesting that he was touched in the head causing more than a few people to question his ability to continue to oversee the empire. When he thought back a week before to the last Council meeting where he had lost control of the assembly, he, too, had to admit that maybe he had lost his edge. Today's meeting was not something he looked forward to.

He gathered himself and walked out of his office down the large stately halls of the royal palace to the King's throne room where everyone sat waiting. When he entered the room, he noticed that the normal buzz of multiple conversations was absent. The quiet was overwhelming. He nodded at those with whom he caught eye contact on his way to his seat. Once there, he opted to stand rather than sit in an attempt to maintain his authority.

The meeting was his to open. He began on a high note, "I am pleased to report to you that the first two divisions of the Imperial Guard are on their way back to Babylon having won a decisive victory over the Egyptians. I expect them here within four to six weeks."

Normally there would have been cheering from this group and affirmation of victory. Not today. No one spoke; no one moved.

"Well, Beltekasmer," Daniel gestured to him, "you wished for us to meet today. I will turn the floor over to you."

Beltekasmer rose and with great deliberation surveyed the room with his piercing eyes. As he did so, he moved into the center oval to take command. Daniel remained standing at his chair, unflinching in his authority.

"Many of us have recently become concerned that the governance of this kingdom is coming unraveled," he began, ignoring Daniel and speaking directly to the members of the Council. "I've been privy to many conversations with a good majority of you in this room as well as with other city leaders and the leading thinkers of our day. To a man, it would seem, there is serious concern that judgment may be flawed and the King's will not necessarily carried out in the affairs of Babylon."

"Are you saying that I am no longer fit to serve as Governor of this land?" interrupted Daniel who was making every attempt to control his anger by this flagrant accusation. Beltekasmer remained standing with his back to Daniel.

"Look at me!" Daniel demanded.

As Beltekasmer turned to face Daniel, Nolter stood and said, "Daniel, many of us are concerned about the great stress you have been under. That's all. We want what is best for you and the kingdom."

"Yes, we are saying that you are not fit to govern Babylon," shouted Antiosyss.

"And you are?" snapped Abednego right back. "You who have no compunction about violating official decrees, who is willing to lie to further your own interests, and who is deceitful beyond imagination?"

"I know what's best for our country and am not afraid to stand for it when senseless decrees and arbitrary regulations hinder our ability to help ourselves," retorted Antiosyss.

"Daniel, may I speak?" asked Mysonus who had come forward to join Beltekasmer in the center oval.

Daniel nodded, gesturing to him to take the floor. He knew this was a man of great wisdom and integrity who might be able to calm the tensions encircling the room.

"Colleagues, some very serious doubts have been in the air the past few days concerning Daniel and the decisions and actions he has taken since the war with Egypt began. In all fairness, these must be balanced with the decades that Daniel has served as our Governor, and I might add, with the full approval and blessing of our King Nebuchadnezzar. Daniel has been a capable leader . . . one of integrity, fairness, and loyalty to the King. That he has come under undue stress in recent months is understandable. No one can serve at the pace demanded of him by the many problems confronting the Babylonian empire without some fracture in his governance."

"Excuse me," shouted Meshach who was now also standing. "Are you agreeing that Daniel's leadership is frayed and beginning to fail?

Mysonus smiled at Meshach, "No. Not frayed, but beginning to tire. He is still our Governor, however, and we must be loyal to him. What we must do is help him. We must shore up his office and take more responsibility for decisions which he can easily delegate to us."

"Not good enough," said Antiosyss. "It's time he steps down, or we force him to step down."

"Is that what you want?" questioned Polynices. "Do we have the authority to overthrow the King and act to unseat his appointed Governor?"

Quiet followed this question. All the bickering had come to a halt. They were struck by the reality that what they were demanding was to deny the King's authority.

Beltekasmer held up his hands to ask for silence. Daniel, Mysonus, and he were the only ones standing. He spoke, "I believe I speak for the majority of this Council. I hereby ask that we vote by raised hands to remove Daniel from the governorship for a period of thirty days so that he may rest and regain his mental and emotional faculties. During this period, I recommend that the governorship be shared by Mysonus, Antiosyss, and Marduk-Sum-Lisir."

All eyes looked at Daniel to see his reaction. Rather than weaken himself by a defense, he looked at all them kindly and said, "My friends . . . my colleagues. You know the authority granted to me by the King. You know how I have ruled. You know my integrity and my dedication to this kingdom." He smiled and focused directly on Antiosyss, "And you know who has continually spoken against me and who has challenged me at every juncture."

Again taking in the full room, he quietly said, "Please . . . take your vote."

The room fell into an icy silence once again. No one wanted to ask for the vote; no one wanted to be the first to call for insurrection.

Beltekasmer started to speak, "I will . . ." but he was unable to continue due to a tightness in his throat. He cleared his throat loudly, than began again, "I call for the vote. Those who believe Daniel should step down as Governor please raise your hands."

Slowly the hands went up, reluctantly at first, but then more quickly as it seemed a majority was agreeing to the motion.

Beltekasmer smiled as he counted the votes, savoring his victory. But then, as he neared the end of the count, his face visibly sagged in defeat. He was one vote shy of a majority. He had taken a stand against Daniel and he had publicly lost. That this could be interpreted by the King and the Crown Prince as treasonous to the throne itself frightened him. Turning pale, he collapsed into his chair.

Mysonus, who had voted against the motion turned to Daniel, "My Lord, you have retained your Governorship, albeit it was not ours to take from you. What is your pleasure for this Council?" He sat down, leaving Daniel the only one standing in the room.

Exhausted from the tension he had endured since the meeting began, Daniel softly spoke, "You are still my friends and my colleagues. We have bridged a large divide this afternoon. Now we must go forward with the leadership entrusted to us and prepare to welcome our troops home."

His voice grew in volume as he regained his moral strength and renewed authority.

"There is no other business for us to discuss. This Council is adjourned until the return of the Imperial Guard and the Crown Prince."

Chapter Nine
ASSASSINATION
567 BC

It was a glorious day! The sun bounced off the gold lions
that flanked Procession Way producing a festive light show on
the spectacular palaces, temples and large monuments that made
this boulevard the centerpiece of Babylon. The population of the
entire city seemed to fill not only the central avenue but all the
side streets as well. Colorful pennants carried by many fluttered
in the air adding to the expectant sense of celebration. Vendors
were doing a landslide business selling sweets and drinks from
their carts. Babylon was still the victor and dominant force in the
known world!

As the first wave of troops led by Neriglissar and his
commanders on their prancing horses rounded the corner at the
southern wall of the city and began their victory parade down
Procession Way, the crowd exploded into enthusiastic screams
and applause.   They were not going to be denied a celebration of
victory. Neriglissar wallowed in the accolades that only grew in
volume and intensity as he made his way up the one mile avenue
towards the royal palace. His pride welled up as he thought to
himself, these people would make me king if given half a chance.

Battalion by battalion of the Imperial Guard smartly
marched to the shouts of the viewing crowd. Each one was led
by its commanders on horseback, the horses kicking and snorting
responding to the excitement in the air. The footsoldiers waved
and smiled, broadly enjoying their welcome home. Within
minutes, the length of Procession Way was a mass of troops and
horses flowing by the Temple of Marduk to the royal palace and

thrilling hundreds of thousands of people lining both sides of the street.

Daniel waited with the Governing Council members on the steps of the royal palace for Neriglissar and his troops to reach them. It was a grand day for Babylon. The excitement of the swarming crowds crushed in along Procession Way was contagious. Even Daniel felt a tingling up his spine as he took in the sheer spectacle of thousands of troops marching towards him surrounded by a rainbow of colors in the applauding masses.

When Neriglissar arrived at the foot of the palace steps, he dismounted smartly while his senior commanders remained on their horses. The entire procession had come to a halt, and the crowd quieted. Neriglissar energetically climbed the steps to the waiting dignitaries where he grasped their arms in greeting. The members of the Governing Council fawned on him like suckling puppies. When he reached Daniel, he stopped and merely stared at him.

"You and your colleagues have given Babylon a monumental victory," Daniel said, breaking the ice between them. "I congratulate you and welcome you home." He stepped towards him, extending his arm in greeting.

Hesitating at first, Neriglissar finally grasped Daniel's arm for a short, perfunctory greeting. He immediately turned away from him to face the throng below and threw his hands into the air as he shouted, "My victory is Babylon's victory! We are invincible!"

A roar went up from the soldiers and welcoming civilians in response, gathering steam and volume as it swept the mile length of Procession Way. Then the chant began: "Neriglissar, Neriglissar!" It was quickly picked up by the members of the Governing Council who were caught up in the moment. Only Daniel, Shadrach, Meshach, and Abednego remained silent as they watched Neriglissar swell with pride at the wild reception he was accorded. We have created a monster mused Daniel to himself, knowing that the challenges to his authority were going to escalate. I hope Amel-Marduk returns sooner than later.

~

There had been a party to end all parties at Neriglissar's palace that evening to celebrate the victory over the Egyptians. Since he was the sole division commander returning to the city, he enjoyed the victor's crown and was given full credit for winning the war by the leading citizens. Not only were his various lieutenants, captains and generals in attendance but every leader and politician of any importance joined the celebration. Princess Kassaya, his wife, held court as his queen and relished every moment of the awe and respect accorded them by those in attendance. For all practical purposes, they were the reigning royalty of Babylon that evening, and they played it fully.

As the guests left his palace, Neriglissar sought out Antiosyss and asked him to stay behind. Finally, the partygoers made their way to the door and bid the victorious couple good night. Antiosyss stood at the side of the entry with Antiobud, his son.

Neriglissar turned to them and said, "A grand evening wasn't it?"

Nodding affirmatively, Antiosyss replied, "Very good . . . but it could be grander."

"What do you mean?" challenged Neriglissar.

"I'd like to put forth an idea."

Neriglissar shrugged, "Why not. I'm not tired. Come, let's go into the sitting room."

Antiosyss quickly replied, "I'd like to do that but I would also like Antiobud to join us. He is proving to be very helpful to our cause." Antiosyss then proceeded to tell Neriglissar how Antiobud had almost destroyed Daniel by spreading the rumor that he was mentally unbalanced and should be given a leave from his duties. Neriglissar grinned, gladly agreeing to include him in their conversation.

Once they had settled into the comfort of the large cushioned chairs and had been brought fresh drinks, Antiosyss quipped, "You were the King today."

Neriglissar smiled, "A hero's welcome. I enjoyed it immensely."

Suddenly Antiosyss sat up straight, an idea forming in his head. "You could make it happen, you know."

"What are you talking about? What do you mean?" replied Neriglissar as he took a sip of the wine he so missed while on the battlefield.

"What if the Crown Prince never returned to Babylon?"

"But he's already on his way. He will probably be in Babylon with Nebuzaradan in ten days."

Antiosyss stood and crossed to the doorway to ensure no servant or household staff was eavesdropping. "Let's say something happens to him on the way back here. An accident . . . an unexpected attack against which there is no defense."

He now had Neriglissar's full attention. He sat up straight, looking directly at Antiosysss and then at Antiobud. "Do you have a plan?"

It was time for Antiobud to join the conversation. He remained relaxed in his chair as he spoke. "If Amel-Marduk is prevented from entering the city, you have no competition. You will have the interim power until such time that the King recovers . . . if he ever does." He paused to let that thought sink in, and continued, "We need to see that Amel-Marduk doesn't return."

"And how are you going to do that?" asked Neriglissar.

Antiobud sat up straight, now his eyes locked on those of Neriglissar, "Assassination."

The word just sat there . . . hanging eerily in the air. Neriglissar stopped breathing. The idea was novel . . . risky at best. The other two men kept their gaze on him waiting for his response.

Neriglissar finally said, "Assassination?" He took a deep breath and asked, "How?"

Antiosyss answered, "On the road home . . . when he is most vulnerable and unprotected by his personal guards . . . like when he needs to relieve himself or has become separated from the others."

Warming to the idea, Neriglissar asked, "Who? Who is going to do this? It can't be any of us, and we can't even hint at this idea to anyone else or it will result in our demise."

Antiobud leaned forward and said, "Coaster."

Neriglissar turned to him asking, "Coaster?"

"Yes, do you remember the half-demon half-man we had at the temple who tried to kill Meshach a year or so ago? We had to send him out of town into exile because Daniel was determined to find him and put him to death?"

"Yes, I remember that incident," replied Neriglissar. "He's a crazy, independent spirit. It would be difficult to control him, would it not? I mean, if he makes a mistake and was caught, who knows what he would say or do."

"He can do it," calmly said Antiobud. "I have him under control. Moreover, he wants to do it. He hates Daniel almost as much as Narseniah. He will do anything to get at him, and he'll be careful. I'll see to that."

All three men sat in silence, pondering the idea. It was an audacious move that could bring them all down as easily as it could elevate Neriglissar and, by association, the other two men as well.

Neriglissar broke the silence, "We need to act fast. This has to happen in the next few days at the very latest. I will find out where Amel and his divisions are . . . how close they are to arriving in Babylon. Then . . . you set Coaster loose."

Antiosyss raised his goblet to toast the decision. The three drank heavily, then, started to laugh, the tension broken.

~

The road never seemed to end for Dorcas. She was eager to see Amel-Maraduk after ten months of separation. The minute she heard the war was over she began visiting Daniel's offices every day to find out when the Crown Prince would return to Babylon. She thought it unconscionable that Neriglissar was the first commander to enter the city with his troops and take all the glory for the victory. This was Amel's right, as Crown Prince. It was wrong that the triumphal welcome was taken from him. If anyone should have stayed behind to ensure the wounded were taken care of and that border lines were re-established, it should have been Neriglissar or one of the other division commanders.

When Dorcas finally got word through a messenger that Amel, Nabuzaradan, and the remaining Imperial Guard had begun their journey home, she convinced Maximillan to take one of Amel's chariots and drive out to meet them. She was emphatic that Amel be given advance notice of all the attempts to discredit and unseat Daniel. He was returning to a labyrinth of plots and counter-plots that could not only shake his confidence in Daniel but also undermine his own authority. She wanted him to be intellectually armed as he entered the fray.

"Will we reach them today?" she asked Maximillan who was driving the chariot.

"I hope so, but . . . maybe he didn't leave at the time we were told. A problem could have come up that required he stay another day or two," answered Maximillan.

It was approaching noon of their fourth day on the road, and every rut and bump in the road that hit the spring-less chariot was exacerbated ten-fold. These vehicles were for men of war, not for women who never left the palace.

Seeing the look of discomfort on her face, Maximillan pulled over at a tiny village. He told her the horses needed to be watered so she would not object to the rest stop. She had been determined to reach Amel as fast as possible, not caring about her own comfort. Maximillan, however, knew it was time to have a break and some food and water for themselves. Dorcas stepped down from the chariot and found a bench in a shaded shop while Maximillan tended to the horses. The local villagers rushed to meet Dorcas' and Maximillan's every need. They saw by the finery of the chariot and its markings that it was from the royal stables.

They were on the road again in less than an hour. Peering into the blazing sun all day took its toll. By mid-afternoon, it was hard to look ahead at the road alone stare into the horizon to catch sight of the approaching troops. More than a few times, Dorcas had to shut her eyes to rest them. She hated doing this as it took her focus off her objective. Meanwhile, Maximillan stoically guided the two horses into the raging rays of the sun.

"This may be them," shouted Maximillan as he shook her arm to startle her out of her momentary lapse into sleep.

"Where?" asked Dorcas as she rose from the padded, cushioned seat specially built for the Crown Prince. She shielded her aching eyes with her hand and looked as far and as hard as she could muster given the fatigue that she felt. Then suddenly, "I see them. It looks like a large cloud of dust. It's got to be them."

"It's them, all right," agreed Maximillan who had now put the horses into a brisk trot to shorten the time it would take to reach the oncoming soldiers.

Within less than an hour they were close enough to make out the individual colors and identities of those at the front of the column of marching troops which seemed to extend for miles into the horizon. They spotted Amel-Marduk riding point in the center with Nebuzaradan at his left. Five minutes later, they pulled the horses to a stop in the center of the road forcing the oncoming entourage to stop.

"My Lord," called out Maximillan. "We are grateful to see you well. The entire city of Babylon joyously welcomes you back in victory."

Perplexed to see his servants here, a good four or five days' journey from Babylon, Amel sat astride his horse at first just staring at them, then nudged his horse to approach them while telling Nebuzaradan and the others to halt. He rode up to them and stopped directly by the side of the chariot.

"What are you two doing here?" he asked rather severely.

Dorcas's joy at seeing him after missing him so long evaporated. Had she over-stepped her bounds by coming here? She was suddenly flooded with insecurities. She had no right to chase after the future King of Babylon like this. What did she think she was doing?!

Maximillan spoke first, "Master, we have news of things that have taken place in Babylon that we feel you should know before you enter the city. In our opinion," he nodded to Dorcas and for himself, "very troubling things."

"Really?" snorted Amel, a bit derisively. "And they concern me?"

"Yes, my Prince, but much more Daniel. In your absence, there have been many attempts to remove him by the Governing Council."

Now they had his attention. Amel straightened in his saddle and moved a step closer to where he was almost directly in their faces. "Turn your chariot around and I'll join you."

He motioned one of his aides to come take his horse as he dismounted and hopped into the chariot to sit by Dorcas while Maximillan moved the horses forward at a brisk walk.

"Tell Nebuzaradan to keep the Guard moving behind us. We'll camp for the night in two hours." The aide saluted smartly and returned to Nebuzaradan leading Amel's horse behind his own.

"So what is so important that the two of you had to drive four days in this sun to meet me?" he asked. "I'm glad to see both of you . . . you look well. But this is highly unusual, you must admit."

With that, Dorcas opened the floodgates reviewing the last ten months of political intrigue in the capital city as Daniel's enemies relentlessly worked to bring him down. First, the accusation that Daniel allowed Nolter to delay his payments to the royal treasury in exchange for a substantial bribe. Then, Narseniah's attempt to compromise Meshach which was narrowly avoided when Daniel became privy to the plan and drove her out of Meshach's house. Next, news that the Egyptians had driven the Imperial Guard back and were invading the Babylonian empire.

Dorcas explained how, in an effort to shore up defenses, Daniel had issued edicts rationing food, implementing price controls and a curfew, halted construction on roads, waterways, and buildings so more workers could be used to fabricate armor and armaments. She added that Daniel had levied increased payments by all merchants and growers to the royal treasury.

"That must have been well received," sarcastically commented Amel with a smile.

"It was almost his undoing," replied Maximillan. "With those moves, he had a majority of the Governing Council against him.

"But the worst was yet to come," said Dorcas. She told Amel how his brother, Marduk-Sum-Lisir had been seriously injured by a bull in the King's pasture and how Beltekasmer used this to challenge Daniel's competence in the oversight of the King's affairs.

"The charges were such nonsense that Daniel was able to dismiss them without incident from the other members of the Governing Council."

"But doubt was raised," interjected Amel. "I know how that works. Beltekasmer is not a stupid man."

Dorcas continued, revealing how Antiosyss violated Daniel's construction moratorium, secretly contining to build the waterway from the Euphrates to the Temple of Marduk at night, then brazenly adding more laborers to his project and working during the day when he got wind that Daniel was planning to restart construction on the central market.

"Meshach discovered what Antiosyss was doing and reported it to Daniel, who confronted Antiosyss at the Governing Council meeting."

"I would have liked to have been there," smiled Amel.

"It was terrible," Maximillan spoke without answering his smile. "Polynices joined with Antiosyss in supporting the waterway to the temple saying it was a much needed project for the good of the city! Then things got out of hand. Antiosyss accused Daniel of no longer being competent to govern the kingdom!"

"That's ridiculous," snapped Amel. "No one could believe that!"

"They can if they want to," countered Dorcas.

"Unfortunately, Antiobud began to spread the rumor in the city that Daniel was, indeed, 'touched' in the head and no longer capable of governing," continued Maximillan. "It was not long before this idea swept through the leading citizenry of Babylon."

"Beltekasmer called for an emergency meeting of the Governing Council. There, he and Antiosyss directly challenged Daniel's competency," interjected Dorcas. "They blamed it on the great stress he was under to sound like they were looking after his good. Before he could counter, they called for a vote of the members to ask Daniel to step down for a period of time until he regained his senses."

"Did they vote?" asked Amel, all ears now as he had no idea how close to treason things were slipping in the capital.

"Yes," replied Maximillan. "The motion failed by one vote."

"One vote?" exclaimed Amel. "Daniel's position has never been weaker!"

"That's why we felt it was important to meet you before you reached Babylon and were confronted with Antiosyss' lies and the anger of the Council," said Maximillan as he turned to look at Amel. "Daniel is barely holding things together at this point."

They rode in silence for several minutes as Amel processed all this information. Finally he looked at both of them, then spoke, "Here's what I want you to do. We are going to camp shortly. The men are tired from many days of marching and they have a week more to go to get home. I'm going to let my horse get some food and rest. Before the sun rises, I will depart for Babylon with only my personal guard. I intend to arrive there the night after tomorrow, when no one will see me enter. We will deal with the Governing Council and all these pretenders to the throne the following morning. You two can either travel with the troops or strike out on your own to return to the city tomorrow morning after breakfast."

"Be careful, Sire," pleaded Dorcas.

Amel smiled at her as he took her hand, "You were both courageous to come find me to tell me all that is going on." He looked her deep in her eyes, piercing into her very soul, "You are treasured in my heart."

He stood up and ordered Maximillan, "Stop the horses. I'm returning to lead my troops. I don't want any concerns or rumors to begin tonight so we'll just say you came to talk with me about matters pertaining to my household which needed my attention."

Maximillan brought the chariot to a halt. Amel jumped off and motioned to his aide to bring his horse. Once in the saddle, he waved at Dorcas and Maximillan and returned to ride with Neubzaradan, motioning them to fall into line behind him.

"Everything all right, Sire?" asked Nebuzaradan.

"Fine. Just some issues with my family that can be easily taken care of," answered Amel. Then he turned to Nebuzaradan with a terse smile, "When we camp tonight, I want to speak with you—privately—about our return to the city."

"Yes, sir," replied Nebuzaradan.

They rode on in silence. Amel had more than a few things to ponder.

~

Coaster had been watching the returning troops from a distance for one day. He was far enough from the road not to draw their attention. Dusk was fast approaching and it was apparent that the soldiers were tired and hungry. He knew there was a spring an hour up the road where a little village had sprung up, and surmised that the Imperial Guard would camp there for the night. By getting there ahead of the troops, he would be able to get the lay of the land as well as fit in with the villagers to avoid scrutiny. He got up from the small hill where he was lying to observe the marching units below. In seconds, he was running at full speed out of sight of the army using his supernatural strength to arrive at the village long before the advance guard arrived.

Campfires dotted the landscape for almost half a mile in concentric circles around the village and its spring. It had been a spectacular sunset; the brilliant orange and yellow rays reflecting off the sandy soil had brought a peace and calm to the military encampment. The war was well behind them. The men thought of returning home to their families and the good life of Babylon. Supper had been good and plentiful. Nebuzaradan always ensured his men were well fed to face the rigors of battle. Conversation was light-hearted and quiet as many had already retired for the night exhausted after four weeks on the road.

Amel-Marduk was sitting by the fire in front of his tent when Nebuzaradan walked up. He had been lost in his thoughts as his eyes absorbed the flaming cinders . . . so lost that he didn't hear the first salutation of his chief commander.

"My Lord, you wished to speak with me?" asked Nebuzaradan a second time.

Realizing he was being summoned, Amel shook his head to clear his mind and looked up to see Nebuzaradan standing ten feet in front of him. He quickly rose and grabbed Nebuzaradan by the arm to usher him into his tent.

"Are the men taken care of?" he asked. Amel, too, had as a priority the wellbeing of all who served in the Imperial Guard. He knew they were the protectors of the empire, and he never took them for granted.

"Yes, Sire," replied Nebuzaradan. "Many are already sleeping, hoping to get a good start tomorrow as they head home."

"Good," laughed Amel as he gestured for Nebuzaradan to take a seat while he closed the entry flap to his tent to give them privacy. He settled into a chair across from his commander. Leaning forward and in a very quiet voice, he began, "You know that I trust you with my life. You have never failed my father or me in any battle. I respect and admire your loyalty, and that is why I am telling you tonight what we are facing in Babylon when we return."

Nebuzaradan nodded and listened without interruption as Amel revealed all that he had heard from Dorcas and Maximillan. As the story unfolded, he became angrier and angrier. When Amel had finished, he exploded, "While you and I were risking our lives and those of our men on the battle front, these ingrates who have never been tested for their mettle in battle gossip and preen for power! It's despicable! Despicable...and treasonous!"

"Now that we know what they are up to, we can deal with those who would seek the throne," quietly answered Amel, touching his forefinger to his lips to caution Nebuzaradan to speak softly. "Unfortunately, that includes Neriglissar whom, I am sure, enjoyed a hero's welcome upon his return to Babylon ahead of us. If I knew what I know now, I would never have sent his division ahead."

Nebuzaradan who had stood during his explosion sat back down. Amel leaned forward and whispered, "Here's my plan. I am going leave camp several hours before sunrise, taking only my personal guard. If we ride hard, we should reach Babylon at nightfall in two days. I will have Daniel call for a Governing Council meeting the next morning before anyone knows I am back in the city."

Nebuzaradan smiled, liking the plan. The two men then settled into a strategy session focused on how they would maneuver over the next week to cull the pretenders to the throne and restore order to a government teetering on the brink of chaos. It did not take these two leaders long to finalize their plan. They had faced many challenges from arrogant opponents over the years. To react without thoughtful planning was to feed into the opposition's strength. Better to counter attack with surprise moves that kept their enemies off balance.

Nebuzaaradan left the tent less than an hour after arriving. Knowing he had to be up in four hours, the Crown Prince laid down to rest. Sleep came on him in moments. He was exhausted.

~

He waited for a good two hours after the last of the troops were asleep in their tents. Sentries had been posted around the perimeter of the outer circle of tents, but the security was casual at best since the war was over and there was no expectation of attack. In fact, most of those on guard duty nodded off. Coaster, already inside the village, had free rein to move undetected about the encampment.

Coaster was counting on the element of surprise, assuming Amel-Marduk would be resting on his laurels from his victory over the Egyptians. The Prince's guard would no doubt be down. Moreover, Coaster knew all the returning troops were exhausted from their march home; sleep was their most welcome companion. Tonight was an excellent time to kill the Crown Prince. With Amel gone, Daniel would be easily toppled, offering unhindered access to the throne for Neriglissar and Antiosyss. He smiled at the thought that he would once again be granted free range in Babylon to enjoy a high position in the hierarchy of the Temple of Marduk.

Identifying the Crown Prince's tent was easy. The division commanders together with Nebuzaradan and Amel-Marduk occupied a camp within a camp at the center of the sprawl of troops. Their flags and beautifully decorated tents made them easy to spot. Coaster's main concern was passing undetected through the Prince's personal guards who surrounded his tent. Yet, when he crept within twenty yards of the "command complex," he noticed there was only a handful of guards and all of them half asleep. The one sentry posted at the entry to Amel's tent who dutifully stood for the first hour of his shift had sunk to the ground by the campfire and was vacantly staring into the mesmerizing flames, his primary responsibility all but forgotten.

Coaster quietly made his way to Amel's tent. He was well hidden in the shadows of the new moon night. Edging to the front of the tent, he lifted the flap noiselessly and slipped inside, standing for a full minute to let his eyes adjust to the darkness. Soon he was able to make out the Crown Prince sleeping against the back of the tent on blankets that covered the ground. Taking a wickedly spiraled dagger from his tunic, he stepped gingerly towards the prone body. It was now or never! There would probably be only one chance at doing this and he wanted to ensure the first thrust would kill. He plunged the blade downward into the body with his entire weight.

Without warning, Coaster was slammed by a club crashing down on his back narrowly missing his skull. As he was thrown over, he saw Amel raising his sword high in the air seeking to sever his head. Fire and smoke spewed from Coaster's mouth as the demons took over defending themselves. It was enough of a diversion to startle Amel who missed his target, his sword only superficially cutting Coaster's arm.

By now, the two men were standing, facing each other in a match they both knew had to end in the death of one or the other. Coaster screamed and lunged at Amel, his fingernails extending like the claws of a raptor. Amel dodged but was cut on his forehead which started to bleed profusely. He, too, screamed at the top of his voice.

"Guards! Into the tent!"

The entry flap to the tent flew open as several of the Crown Prince's personal guards entered with their weapons in hand. Coaster knew he only had one more chance to finish Amel because the odds against him were multiplying by the second. He feinted left, then, whirled to his right knocking over the first guard in the tent while grabbing his sword. In one continuous motion he swung hard at Amel who managed to hit the ground escaping the over-passing weapon. Without missing a beat, Coaster brought his sword up high and plunged it downward to disembowel Amel. Reacting on instinct that this would be Coaster's next move, Amel executed a backwards summersault to land three feet away from where Coaster's sword now stuck deep into the ground. Amel propelled his entire body head first into Coaster's side to knock him to the ground. Realizing the fight had been lost, Coaster scrambled on his hands and knees under the tent flap against which he had been thrown. He had to get out before the entire Imperial Guard was on him.

As he emerged from the tent, pushing the flap up with his super-human strength, his last sight was the razor sharp point of the spear that caught him straight in his face, crumpling him to the ground. Instantly, five other spears and swords were thrust into his body by the gathering guards to make sure he was dead. As much as the demons inside him struggled to avoid death, there was no escape. His body viciously convulsed, heaving itself well over a man's height into the air as the super-natural sought a way out. In the end, he collapsed to the ground in his own blood and a sickeningly smelling, noxious, yellow liquid that poured from his body's orifices. The guards drew back at the disgusting sight and smell.

Amel exited his tent and came around to the back to ensure Coaster had been killed. The smell staggered him. Then he began to see something he had never before seen in his life. The yellow liquid had begun to eat away at the flesh, disintegrating it quickly to reveal the skeleton beneath. Who or what had attacked him? This was no ordinary man, he thought, as he covered his nose and looked at the ooze that had once been a living, breathing human . . . or so he had thought.

"My Lord," shouted Nebuzaradan who, wakened by the commotion, had come to check on the Crown Prince. Seeing Amel's face completely bloodied, he grabbed his arms to stabilize him and said, "Your head has been cut. We must clean it immediately and stop the bleeding."

Turning to one of the soldiers standing in awe of the disintegration of what had once been Coaster, he yelled, "Snap out of it. Get the physician immediately. The rest of you gather up that mess and dispose of it well out of camp. Bury it."

The two men slowly walked back to the front of the tent to sit by the fire that still burned bright. Nebuzaradan handed Amel a cloth to wipe his face.

"I'm really fine," Amel said. "The cut is superficial. It looks a lot worse than it is."

"Who was that?" asked Nebuzaradan.

"I don't know," replied Amel. He thought for a moment as he mopped his face. "Something more than human."

They sat in silence, each caught up in his own thoughts. Nebuzaradan wondered how an assassin could so easily penetrate his security forces. We were sloppy . . . off edge. Praise the gods the Crown Prince lived to see another day. Meanwhile, Amel started to put the pieces together. The move to overthrow Daniel, his and the King's appointed governor . . . the continual tension with Neriglissar . . . the disregard of the law by Antiosyss . . . and now the attack by someone quite possibly of the supernatural world.

"I am leaving right now," he suddenly blurted out. "As soon as my wound is bandaged, I'm off to Babylon."

"Do you want me to come with you?" asked Nebuzardan. "It seems like we are up against powerful forces and it may be a good time to couple our strength."

"I didn't think so before this last incident, but . . . yes . . . I'd like you to come with me."

Nebuzaradan rose. "I'll get the men ready."

~

The royal palace resonated with excitement at the Crown Prince's return from war. Word that Amel was back in Babylon only began to filter out in the early morning hours but, within a short time, had cascaded through both the ranks of palace officials and servants. It felt good to have a King back, albeit an interim King. Everyone was eager to hear Amel's battle stories.

Amel had entered the city well after dusk and immediately went to Daniel's house for a first-hand report of the Governing Council's actions. Once he had verified all that Dorcas and Maximillan had told him, Amel told Daniel to convene the Council in the morning. He was counting on the element of surprise at his sudden return to get the jump on those seeking to unseat Daniel. Daniel had sent out couriers to the members at sunrise, requesting their presence.

As was his custom, Daniel waited until the appointed hour to enter the throne room. The mood was festive. It was as though the bitterness of the previous meeting had been swept away to be replaced by celebratory unity at the return of the Crown Prince and his Supreme Commander. The room was full of smiles and laughter. Daniel noted that even Antiosyss, Neriglissar and Beltekasmer were enjoying the moment, engaged in cordial conversations with Mysonus and Nolter. Curious how special events and occasions create strange bedfellows, he mused. This was going to be an interesting day.

Daniel was cheerily greeted by everyone as he walked to his seat. He spotted Nebuzaradan, surrounded by members of the Council querying him on the war and congratulating him. Walking over to him, Daniel leaned through the group and patted him on the shoulder with a "Well done, Commander, well done."

Nebuzaradan immediately pushed through the men to grab Daniel's arm in greeting, "Thank you Governor. Your words mean a lot to me. It is good to be back."

When Daniel reached his chair, he looked at Zocor standing at the entry doors. The joviality continued for a few more minutes until Zocor signaled Daniel that the Prince had arrived. Daniel held his hands up to quiet the Council. Moments later, Amel burst into the room. It made no difference that his face was stern and his movements brusque. As one, the Council leaped to its feet in shouts of accolades and applause, greeting their returning hero. They were proud of Babylonia's victory over a very tough enemy and they hailed the leadership of the Crown Prince who put himself in harm's way on the battlefield when he could have easily remained home in the city.

Amel stood by the throne, accepting the platitudes and praise showered upon him by the city's leading elders. When he had had enough, he stepped onto the throne, ready to conduct business. However, the shouting merely intensified. When he finally sat on the throne of his father, King Nebuchadnezzar, his officials vicariously gloried in his victory. The euphoria grew until it finally had no further place to go at which time Amel clapped his hands for quiet.

"I commend to you, Nebuzaradan, the greatest general in the world today," he said in a loud voice. "We share in this victory over the Egyptians."

The shouting and clapping began again, this time accompanied by feet stomping as the Governing Council showered its appreciation on the Supreme Commander of the Imperial Guard. Nebuzaradan nodded his head in acknowledgment, a smile filling his face. Amel let the accolades go on for half a minute then raised his hands for quiet. The energy had peaked and was now ebbing out of the room. Members took their seats in anticipation of hearing exploits of valor and bravery.

Not wanting anyone in the room to miss his words, Amel waited until all rustling stopped and silence prevailed. Then, he waited again . . . an uncomfortable silence that gave rise to individual introspection fostering self-doubt and guilt. Yet, no one moved or made a sound. The Crown Prince was signaling his intent. It behooved everyone to be invisible for the moment.

"An attempt was made on my life three nights ago," Amel spoke quietly.

The room awakened. "No," "Who would dare?" "Why?" and a host of other questions came forth in mumbles from the Governing Council members who were quite astonished by this news.

The Crown Prince raised his hand to quiet them. He stared directly at Antiosyss and Neriglissar.

"One of your priests, Antiosyss, whom we had expelled from Babylon, entered my tent in the middle of the night and stabbed what he thought was my body. How did he know we would be returning on that road at that time?"

His eyes pierced those of Neriglissar, finally causing him to lower his gaze, "Why did he want to kill me after peace had been restored to our empire?"

Again, Amel let silence prevail in the room, deliberately forcing everyone to squirm, if not physically, then mentally. He rose to his feet and looked directly into the eyes of each man as he surveyed the room.

"I have been away almost one year. I left this kingdom in the good hands of Daniel, as did my father. Yet, I return to find this Governing Council a den of vipers . . . snakes spewing poison as you struggle for power, disregarding the governor my father, the King, put in place and whom I entrusted with power.

"You—Nolter—a merchant of integrity in all the years I have known you. How could you collude with Antiosyss to charge Daniel with bribery?!

"The bumbling attempt to seduce Meshach . . . violating the edicts that Daniel put in place when he—and we—thought our land was being invaded by the Egyptians! That was you again, wasn't it Antiosyss? You felt it was your right to ignore the moratorium on construction and continue to build your waterway. In fact, you knew it was unlawful so you did your work at night! It is curious, isn't it, that so many of these attempts to challenge Daniel's authority originated with you.

"Polynices . . . I believed you were better than to support Antiosyss' flagrant disobedience of a lawful edict."

He stepped down to the open oval in the center of the room and walked to stand in front of Beltekasmer. Pointing at him, he whispered, "Wise man? You pretend to be a wise man in my father's court and don't have the wisdom to follow the protocol set forth by me or my father."

Beltekasmer shrank back at the vociferous nature of the Prince's attack. Amel burrowed in further, "How dare you question Daniel's capacity to govern? How dare you call for a vote of this Council to unseat him?"

He whirled around, eyes blazing, taking in everyone in the room. Shaking his finger at them, he shouted, "You are all guilty of insubordination. This Council has no authority. You were only advisory to me and by extension to the Governor."

He turned back to Beltekasmer pointing, "Where did you ever get the idea that you held the authority to dictate the way this kingdom is ruled?"

He took a breath, then spit out, "You should all be put to death!"

No one spoke or, for that matter, dared to lift their eyes from staring down at the floor in front of them. Amel had spent his fury and was now pacing in the center oval determining his next move.

Cutting through the silence, Neriglissar rose and spoke gently, "My Prince, you know I was with you on the battle front until just several days ago. Upon my return, I had the opportunity to talk with many members of this body. They have only sought the good will of the throne and this empire. They had cause to be concerned about Daniel's competence, particularly when a laxness in palace affairs resulted in serious injury to your brother, Prince Marduk-Sum-Lisir. They meant no harm, and certainly no challenge to your authority."

Polynices joined in, "My Lord, we know we are only advisors. When Daniel ceased to seek our input and took full control of the kingdom into his own hands upon hearing that invasion by the Egyptians was imminent, it was of great concern to us. Rather than invite the collective thinking of the best minds in Babylon, he began to make new laws, many of which hurt the commerce and infrastructure of this city. And so we obviously questioned his behavior."

Gathering courage from those who had spoken to counter Amel's charges, Beltekasmer slowly rose to speak, "Crown

Prince, I am duly chastened by your remarks. Yet, I cannot forget that Daniel engaged in corrupt behavior by accepting bribes and favored only his closest associates. I was only looking after your interests, my Lord, and those of the King."

Having heard enough falsehoods and lies, Mysonus angrily stood to challenge Beltekasmer, "That is nothing but a lie and you know it!" Turning to Amel, he continued, "This Council acted in a cavalier manner, Sire. We were wrong. We were fearful . . . afraid this city would be over-run by the enemy. And we reacted with our hearts, not our minds. It is no excuse, but it is a reason."

"Enough!" shouted Amel. "I have heard all I want to hear. The truth of the matter is that you are incapable of advising. How can you save a kingdom when all you are interested in is your own greed and self-advancement?"

He strode to the entry doors and turned to glare at them, "Daniel may have short-comings. He is only a man. Nonetheless, he is still my Governor. As for this Council, it is hereby disbanded and no longer exists."

As he walked through the doors, the air seemed completely sucked out of the room leaving nothing but a vacuum. Nebuzaradan moved to stand by Daniel. They watched in silence as the room emptied. Only Neriglissar had the courage to approach them.

"This will come back to bite him . . . and you, too, Daniel."

He turned and left, his head held high, undefeated.

~

Daniel was deeply troubled the rest of the day. He left the throne room, uneasy that Amel had acted so decisively and impulsively without leaving any room for Council members to save face. If governing this huge kingdom had been tough before, he knew he was now going to face active opposition on many fronts. If the anger of these men ever amalgamated, it would be very difficult to maintain the royal palace's authority.

Shadrach, Meshach and Abednego were waiting for him in his offices with Mysonus and Polynices. They expressed grave concern over what had just taken place and pleaded with Daniel to reason with the Crown Prince to restore the Governing Council or enact some measure that would bring the city's leaders back into the fold. While they were well aware that Nebuzaradan controlled the Imperial Guard and was loyal to Amel and King Nebuchadnezzar, they also knew the esteem in which Neriglissar was held by the troops. If the discontented Council members enlisted him, a divided kingdom was a reality.

At the end of the day, Daniel stepped onto the veranda of the royal palace to think. The stunning beauty of Procession Way failed to lift him that evening; rather, it depressed him as he thought of a city divided and this boulevard fielding a nightmare of brother attacking brother. He had to be successful in his mission to restore calm in the leadership circle. He needed to talk to the Crown Prince right away.

~

He was admitted to Amel's palace by Dorcas who received word that he was coming. She had heard what happened as the information pipeline among servants in the palace grounds was incredibly fast and accurate. She brought him to Amel's private sitting room where the Crown Prince waved Daniel to a chair. Daniel was glad to see the Prince relaxed. This would make it easier to review the morning's explosive meeting and determine a strategy to bring things back together.

"So what brings you to come see me tonight?" asked Amel, totally oblivious of the repercussions and fallout from the day. "I thought we had enough of talking to each other last night," he chuckled.

Daniel was caught off guard. Rather than sensing trouble, Amel seemed to feel that order was restored and all was well. How do I begin, wondered Daniel.

"It's good to have you back in Babylon," answered Daniel.

"You don't know how good it is to be home . . . to be clean . . . sleep on a real bed, and," he smiled broadly, "have a beer."

He gestured to the chair facing him, "Sit down."

Daniel nodded and sat in the chair Amel had designated. "My Lord, I am quite concerned about what took place this morning."

Immediately Amel's face clouded over. "There should be no concern. Things were restored to order," he quipped.

"You had every right to be angry. Things did get perilously close to the brink with the Council's relentless challenge to my authority. I thank you for backing me with your full support."

"Good," snapped Amel. "They needed to learn their place."

Daniel hesitated before speaking, carefully choosing his words. "Sire, I am only concerned about where we go from here. I am seeking your guidance and direction. As you know, the canal project diverting a waterway to the Temple of Marduk is again under construction. This has diverted many workers from the central market reconstruction. Where should our priorities lie?"

"The market is, of course, most important. It feeds to the very heartbeat of commerce in Babylon."

"At the same time," countered Daniel, "we cannot ignore the temple canal project. It is very close to completion. If you concur, I'd like to keep a smaller crew on that and shift most of our men to the market. It would ease tensions with Antiosyss and the priesthood . . . probably even Neriglissar."

Amel slowly nodded. He was savvy enough to see what Daniel was getting at.

"That's a reasonable plan. Just make sure the market gets back on schedule quickly."

Pleased to see that Amel seemed aware that relationships needed to be restored with members of the Governing Council, Daniel pushed forward, "I'd like to continue to bring the Governing Council into our deliberations."

Amel abruptly turned to glare at him.

Daniel felt the tension of the morning's explosion returning; nevertheless, he plowed on, "There are some good men on the Council who have been of enormous help to me. Mysonus, Leandrus, Nebuzaradan, even Polynices! There are others. I value their advice and opinions as we craft policies."

Amel's shoulders relaxed as he slowly nodded in agreement, "What you say is right. These are good men and have good minds."

"Even those who oppose me have value," hastily continued Daniel. "I ask you to re-consider the abandonment of this governing mechanism. I think it can work for us now that you are back from the war and present in Babylon. We need these men on our side, not against us."

"They're nothing but trouble-makers! All of them," snapped Amel. "Why should we let them into our tent? All they will do is soil it . . . and you in the process."

"I believe it is important to include Antiosyss in our deliberations. He enjoys a tremendous power base in this city. The vast population of Babylon considers him next in importance to you and the King because of his grip on the priesthood. Better to bring him in than to fence him out."

"Perhaps," replied Amel. "I am very fond of his daughter. I would like to get to know her more. Nevertheless, never take your eyes off him. And watch out for the collusion between him and Neriglissar. They are cunning—and dangerous—to both of us."

Daniel cringed at the mention of Narseniah. She was undoubtedly the most dangerous person in Babylon to the safety of the Crown Prince. Although he had not seen her since he threw her out of Meshach's house several months ago, he knew she was in league with Antiosyss and probably Neriglissar.

"Sir," began Daniel, then clearing his throat nervously continued, "during your absence one of my most trusted officials was almost undone by Narseniah of whom you speak. She attempted to seduce him in the hope of compromising his integrity, and, therefore, mine as well. I had to expel her from the palace and all official gatherings. It may not be wise to have any further relationship with her."

"Governor, you will not tell me whom I can and cannot see," sternly retorted Amel. "I have been listening to your logic and was even beginning to re-consider bringing the Council back together again in spite of their insubordination. Maybe, I thought, maybe Daniel is on the right track. But don't you ever tell me not to see a woman who has nothing to do with the affairs of government."

"She's dangerous, Sire. She has powers greater than human. You don't know her."

"Enough," belted out Amel who had risen and had walked to the doorway. "I will do as I please. As regards bringing the Council back together, I refuse to do so. You almost persuaded me, but I think the power I have given you may be going to your head. When you start telling me what to do, the cart is definitely before the ox."

He pointed to the doorway. "You may leave. I've heard enough. Don't make me do something we will both regret. Now . . . get out."

Daniel mutely nodded and left the room. As he stood outside in the dusk, he felt he had failed as never before in his life. How do I hold this kingdom together when I am an island surrounded by contentious gathering storms!?

~

The servants sensed a tension in the palace counter to what they expected upon a victorious hero's return. For the most part, they avoided the Prince who seemed to be angry and lost in himself. Battle weary, they surmised. Dorcas was not content to accept this. Throughout the day she attempted to see if she could get anything for Amel. She was the only one he did not snap at, but even she could not shake him out of his bad humor. He did enjoy the moments when she was in his presence but they evaporated as soon as she left.

The breech with Daniel left an emptiness in his heart. Yet, he was angered that Daniel should tell him to stay away from Narseniah. She was probably trouble, he readily acknowledged, but he was never able to shake the magnificent beauty of her face and sensuousness of her naked body—even during all those months at the war front. He wanted her. His lust was all-consuming, and now that the war was over he determined he would fulfill his desires.

In the late afternoon, Amel sent a messenger to the Temple of Marduk requesting that Narseniah come to his palace that night. He did not want Dorcas or any other servants to thwart his assignation so, well after the household staff had retired for the night, he arranged for his personal guard to escort her through a little used entrance to his palace. Once his plan was in motion, his anticipation of the consummation of his lust made time move endlessly slow. He tried working on his building projects but spent most of the time pacing the floor. As the sun began to set in the west, he went out on the roof patio to take in the brilliantly lit skies, relishing the thought that she would soon be with him.

Amel was still on the roof when he heard his guards bring Narseniah to his private quarters. The darkness of the night brought a cooling breeze that refreshed the entire palace. He entered his bed chamber and then walked from there to his private sitting room where he found Narseniah standing with two of his guards. She was more gorgeous than he had imagined.

"You may go," he said to the guards who saluted smartly and exited. He took her hand and led her to the center of the

1

room. As she stood, he backed away never taking his eyes off her.

Silently he walked around her, absorbing her beauty. Narseniah enjoyed his naked lust and fed it further by slowly loosening the belt that held her robe together resulting in a plunging neckline revealing most of her plentiful breasts. When he had come full circle and saw what she had unveiled for him, he pulled her body to him hungrily, kissing her open-mouthed. Her eager response told him all he needed to know. He lifted her in his arms and brought her to his bed where he gently lay her down and proceeded to undress her. Their bodies soon dissolved into a frenzy of lust and passion lasting into the early hours of the morning.

His energy was completely dissipated. He could barely get his breath as he rolled off her onto his back. His eyes were half-closed, everything dizzily spinning. They had yet to speak a word to each other. He felt her hand gently brushing his hair and gliding over his face, chest and arms. He had never felt so peaceful . . . so completely relaxed. Within minutes, he was fast asleep, the cares of yesterday forgotten.

~

"Agh-h-h," was the only sound he could make, as he gasped for air.

"Agh-h-h!"

Awakening from a deep sleep, Amel-Marduk realized someone was trying to strangle him. His wind pipe was constricted to the point he could not get any air into his lungs. Suddenly he realized that someone had wrapped a corded belt around his throat and was pulling it tightly from behind. He sensed he was about to lose consciousness if he did not act quickly. Employing every ounce of strength remaining in his body, he jerked his head forward, tucking it into his stomach while kicking out with his legs to flip over. The pressure on his throat loosened. He grabbed the belt and jerked it away as he rolled to an upright position.

He looked up to see Narseniah, still naked, lunging at him with his dagger she had taken from the table where he had laid it for the evening. As hard as he tried to avoid her, he still did not have his full breath back leaving him unable to move quickly. The knife plunged into his left arm to the bone. The pain was instant and intense. Before he could react, she had pulled it out and managed to stick it in his upper chest near his shoulder. This time, he threw her across the room as the adrenalin coursed through his body in self defense. But he was at the end of his rope. Bleeding profusely and barely conscious, he sat crumpled on the floor desperately trying not to black out by using the wall to support his back. She stood up looking at him and laughed, the evilness of the sound echoed from the very pit of hell.

She cackled, "Coaster couldn't do the job, but I did."

Amel fought with every reserve he had to avoid slipping into unconsciousness. Narseniah seemed to be drawing away from him, but he had to get some answers.

"Why?" he whispered. "We could have had the world together. Why this?"

Realizing that Amel was no longer a danger to her and was, in fact, dying, she casually walked to the pitcher that sat on a table near the bed and poured water into the accompanying bowl. Washing her hands and face as well as cleaning off Amel's blood that had smeared her body, she dried herself and dressed.

"Why?" she repeated his question, then hissed, "Because stronger people than you deserve to rule Babylon . . . real men who will put to death that despicable Jewish Governor and allow our gods and traditions to reign."

Two of Amel's personal guards dismissed for the evening but overhearing the ruckus burst into the room. The look on their faces was sheer horror as they saw the Crown Prince lying seemingly dead in a pool of blood in one corner and Narseniah in another, untouched and without injury.

"What happened?" the first one in the room bellowed.

Without missing a beat, Narseniah pointed out the other door, sobbing, "It was awful! Two of them—I don't know who they were—entered the room as we lay sleeping. I woke when I felt the Prince's body jerk. They were choking him, and then they stabbed him as he fought back. It took both of them to take him down. I was able to sneak away as they beat him in that corner."

By now the senior guard had reach Amel. He felt for a pulse and was relieved when he found one. "He's still alive," he said. He ripped bands of cloth from the sheet on the bed and began bandaging the wounds to stop the flow of blood. "You go after them," he instructed the other guard. "Wake all the palace guards. Have them search every room and find these bastards! We don't want these villains free to do this again. Once I get the bleeding to stop, I'll send for the King's physician. The Crown Prince has been hurt badly."

As the second guard ran out of the room in search of the perpetrators, Narseniah slid out the door into the sitting room and then quietly through the palace to the front entry where she quickly disappeared into the night's enveloping darkness. If the Crown Prince survived her attack, she had to flee as quickly as possible.

Chapter Ten
ISOLATION
567 BC

The day was overcast. The sky was hazy and a rare rise in humidity left one sticky and tired. Amel-Marduk, frustrated by an apathy that consumed him whether he was dealing with the affairs of the kingdom or designing new buildings, decided this morning that he needed to talk with his father. Perhaps in some miraculous way Nebuchadnezzar would discern his troubling spirit and be of some comfort to him.

It had been two months since the attempt on his life. His wounds had healed well. The loss of blood, however, had taken a toll on him. It was not until a few days ago that he felt his full energy return and he was physically fit to resume his normal activities. He had not expected to run into the wall of apathy that blunted his progress. As hard as he tried to create and develop new ideas, he was often overwhelmed by listlessness that left him drained.

He walked down the path from the palace to the King's barn with hope in his heart at seeing his father. He spotted Nebuchadnezzar lying under a large, shady tree at the far end of his pasture. Smiling at the sense of freedom his father now enjoyed in his carefree existence, Amel wished for the same. He crawled over the fence and walked across the large grassy expanse to sit on the ground across from the King.

The past five years had been hard on Nebuchadnezzar's body. To the stranger, he appeared to be an odd, unknown animal and certainly not human. His hair and facial hair now reached below his waist. This, combined with an unsightly growth of body hair, made him look more like an orangutan than anything else. His nails, fingers and toes, were so long that they curled to form talon-like claws. As much as they tried to bathe him, he preferred rolling in the dirt to give him protection from the flies and heat of the day. He was not the sort of domestic beast that attracted people.

After several minutes of watching his father sleep peacefully, Amel softly spoke: "Father, I don't know if you can understand me, but I need to talk to you."

Nebuchadnezzar stirred in his sleep, Amel's voice faintly heard in the background. He opened his eyes to see his son sitting across from him, then, slowly brought his head up to look at him.

"A lot has happened in the kingdom since you were afflicted by your illness. And a lot has happened to me . . . not all of it good. It has all become too hard to understand and it's sapping my spirit. So . . . I've come to talk . . . to get some advice from you if you can understand me."

Amel-Marduk's head dropped to his chest as the tears began to flow. His shoulders shook as he sobbed uncontrollably: "Forgive me, father. I don't mean to be so weak. You despise weakness . . . I'm sorry." He lifted his head and looked at Nebuchadnezzar, "Help me."

Nebuchadnezzar stretched his arms and then his legs, then squirmed over to Amel. He sat leaning against him, back to back. There had never been any bodily contact before between the two men. The suddenness of it caused Amel to tense, but soon his father's body heat, coupled with the rhythm of his breathing, brought a sense of peacefulness and relaxation throughout Amel's body. There was something about father and son, sitting back to back after many years of no physical contact that spurred him on.

For well over an hour, Amel recounted all that had happened, not leaving anything out. When he told about Antiosyss's attempts to challenge Daniel and his own right to the throne . . . about Neriglissar's insubordinate behavior . . . and, finally, about Coaster's and Narseniah's attempts on his life, he could feel Nebuchadnezzar's back growing taut as though he was understanding. The same was true when he recounted his battles with the Egyptians and his conquests. The King seemed to relax and enjoy the fights and victories as war had been so central to his early years.

In between the stories, Nebuchadnezzar would grunt and make a few animal-like sounds. For the most part, the conversation was completely one-sided, but his father's body language—albeit minimal—encouraged Amel to believe there had been some communication.

His stories told, Amel sat in silence simply feeling the up and down movements of his father's breathing against his back.

"I have never felt so isolated," said Amel. "I'm the interim ruler of the most powerful kingdom in the world, and, yet, I feel completely alone with no friends . . . no one I can trust. What's wrong with me?" He buried his face in his hands.

Slowly he realized that there was no longer any pressure against his back. Then something nudged him on his side, first gently then more vigorously. He raised his head and turned to see that his father was now standing on his four limbs, pushing his head against his shoulder as to tell him to stand up. Amel watched this behavior with awe, beginning to suspect that his father had grasped some of what he had told him. Nebuchadnezzar's pushing became harder. It was evident that he wanted Amel to stand up, and so he did.

The King moved behind him and began to push against his legs and buttocks as though to make him walk. Amel was mesmerized by his father's attempts to communicate something to him . . . what, he still did not know! Almost knocked over by Nebuchadnezzar's pushing, Amel took a step forward. Before he could stop and look back, he felt his body shoved harder by his father as though telling him to continue walking. Now he got it. His father wanted him to walk, and so he did. When they reached the end of the pasture and came to stop against the fence, Amel saw that they had turned a corner and were facing the royal palace. The pushing had stopped.

Without warning, Nebuchadnezzar raised his body to stand on his legs and let out a thunderous yell, "Argh-h-h-h!" Not once, but four times as his head bobbed up and down as though he were nodding towards the palace.

Amel looked from Nebuchadnezzar to the palace, then back again to Nebuchadnezzar. What was his father telling him? He gingerly lifted his hands to brush away the hair from Nebuchadnezzar's eyes to look deeply into them. In an instant, he knew that his father was telling him, "I trust you. Get control of yourself and be the King I know you can be."

As abruptly as he had stood, Nebuchadnezzar dropped to all fours and trotted back to the tree under which Amel had first found him. His mission was completed. Amel followed his father with his eyes, smiling in spite of the few tears that trickled down his cheek. He heard me, he reasoned. And he told me to get back on my feet . . . act before they act on me. The old man was still the warrior . . . and still the King.

~

"We have to stop this!" shouted Beltekasmer as he pounded the table around which they sat.

Neriglissar chuckled and responded, "You were warned . . . you just were too fearful to do something about it."

"There's nothing funny about this," snapped Beltekasmer. "This kingdom has been hanging in the balance for well over a year. Our financial position has deteriorated. While our enemies have been kept at bay, they know we are tired and weakened. And our King lies ill while his son gives the reins of the empire to a Jew! No, there's nothing funny about any of this."

They were sitting on the rooftop porch of Neriglissar's palace in the early evening. Beltekasmer had asked Neriglissar for a meeting earlier in the day. What was supposed to be a conversation between the two men had now multiplied to a lively discussion among six dissidents—all of them leading citizens in the city. Neriglissar had asked Antiosyss to join them. He, in turn, brought his son Antiobud. Beltekasmer brought Polynices and Econor, another wealthy merchant, with him. At the table were representatives of the military, the priesthood, the palace wise men and the merchants.

"There is no more Governing Council," said Polynices. "At least, that offered a forum for us to express our views, if nothing more than to temper decisions that impact all of us. Now we don't even have that."

There was a lull in the conversation as each man reflected on this reality. Breaking the silence, Neriglissar suddenly stood and looked at each man around the table, "Are you ready to do something about this?" He stared hard at them, one by one. "Are you finally ready to take action?"

Beltekasmer slowly responded, "What are you suggesting? What action?"

Neriglissar began strolling around the room as he talked, "Our plan must be two-fold. First, we get rid of Daniel. Second, we neutralize Amel-Marduk . . . force him to move aside or, if need be, kill him."

Their anger and clamor for change had just taken a turn down the very dangerous road of murder. Each man realized what was now being asked of him. If word of this meeting ever leaked out or their plan failed in any part, it meant certain and immediate death for each of them.

"I'm in," said Antiosyss.

"So am I," quickly added Antiobud.

The three of them looked expectantly at the other three men. Beltekasmer breathed heavily then spoke, "This is very dangerous ground we are treading . . . but on the face of things it must be trod. I am fearful that our coalition is insufficient to turn the tide for our success."

Neriglissar was ready for this, "Suppose we gain the support of the Queen and the Crown Prince's brothers? Nebudaren does whatever his mother tells him and Marduk-Sum-Lisir doesn't really care anymore what happens. If the palace was divided with the majority of the royal family in league with us, would that give you confidence?

"How are you going to do that?" Beltekasmer asked incredulously.

"If I made it happen, would you then stand up like a man and join us?" growled Neriglissar.

"Yes, I would join you," whispered Polynices. "We have to get our commerce moving again or there will be bad ruptures in the fabric of Babylon."

"And I," chimed in Econor.

"Beltekasmer?" asked Neriglissar. "You're the only one left to hear from."

Beltekasmer did not like being pushed into a corner, but he knew he had brought it upon himself. With the power of the royal family aligned with them, he felt less likely that the charge of murder in addition to treason would color their cabal. As he reflected on it, he concluded that they really did have a chance at correcting the problem which began with Daniel.

He nodded his head, "If you get the Queen and the princes to join us, I will do my part to have the palace wise men unite with us. Count me in."

~

The trick was to arrange a meeting with the Queen and the two princes, Marduk-Sum-Lisir and Nebudaren, without catching the attention of the Crown Prince. There were few secrets in the palace compound, given that all the servants and governing officials were constantly moving among the various palaces. Neriglissar had given this a lot of thought and came to the conclusion that his wife, Princess Kassaya, was the key to convening this meeting without raising suspicion. He had her first set up a dinner with Marduk-Sum-Lisir. They agreed that it would be best to gather at the King's residential palace on the Euphrates River because Marduk-Sum-Lisir still found it difficult

to get around. It was to be nothing more than a family affair—
just mother and three siblings less Amel-Marduk. Once they
were in the palace, Neriglissar reasoned that it would be a simple
matter of asking the Queen to join them.

It took several days to bring it all together. They enjoyed
a delicious meal of lamb, an abundance of vegetables and rice
and were now taking pleasure in an assortment of fruits and
sweets generously served by the household staff. At the last
minute, Kassaya had gone to her mother's quarters in the palace
to ask her to join the siblings. The Queen was pleased to see all
of them in one place which was a rarity, and immediately asked
why Amel was not present. Kassaya explained that he was busy
with an affair of state.

It was time to get down to business. Neriglissar
dismissed the servants and asked the palace guards to keep
everyone out of hearing distance of the dining room. When the
room was secure, he began.

"It has been good to be together tonight, has it not?"

Heads nodded in agreement accompanied with murmurs
of assent. Everyone felt well fed and well loved.

Neriglissar continued, "I regret that Amel-Marduk could
not be with us tonight, but in a way that is a good thing. You see,
I really wanted to speak with you about our brother because I
have serious concerns that he is not being advised well. I am not
the only one with this concern. Three evenings ago, one of the
leading wise men from the court came to ask me what can be
done to stop the dangerous course that Amel is pursuing at
Daniel's behest. Not only the wise men are concerned; this man
was joined by our city's leading merchants who are gravely
troubled about the kingdom's finances and slump in our
commerce. Many of the Imperial Guard are divided as well,
fearing we will not be fit to face another attack on our borders
should it come. And, of course, you know that the priesthood has
long opposed Daniel for refusing to accept our traditions and
gods."

He stopped to see if anyone wanted to counter him or question where he was headed.

"Your father-in-law, the King, trusted Daniel implicitly," said Amytis. "What's changed?"

"You are right, Queen Mother. Something did change. Two or three months ago, just when Amel returned home from the war with Egypt, he lost his temper in a Governing Council meeting. He didn't want to hear opposing voices, even though the Council had nearly voted to put a new governing team in place of Daniel because of their loss of confidence in him. Instead, Daniel had so blinded him and his judgment that he abruptly disbanded the Council. I'm sure each of you has heard about this. You probably didn't see it as a major concern because you think your brother is in charge. But he is not! No more are advice and input invited from the leading citizens of Babylon. The affairs of our empire are entirely in the hands of one man: Daniel. Frankly, I suspect he is deliberately leading Babylon into chaos, fulfilling the Jewish prophecy that he and his people will leave our city to return to Israel."

He had their attention . . . even the Queen's. It was time to put the question to them.

"A growing consortium of city leaders has asked me to ask you for your support to save our kingdom . . . to protect the kingdom so that when the King is well once again he will have his empire totally intact, as it was when he took ill. The support of the royal family will carry much weight with Amel. We must convince him to ask Daniel to step down and to reconvene the Governing Council as a decision-making body to govern this nation with him. We will only be successful if we join together to guide the affairs of Babylon."

He had said his piece. It was time to let the family respond.

"I will not let this kingdom slide out of the hands of King Nebuchadnezzar," sternly said the Queen. "We must do whatever it takes to help Amel avoid this. If it means asking Daniel to step aside, then we must so act."

Marduk-Sum-Lisir nodded his head in agreement, "I know what our brother is up against with Daniel. He is stubborn, opinionated and has no interest in hearing from others, but I didn't think he was doing all that badly. I mean, I can take him or leave him, but I will go along with the majority. We need to at least warn Amel and help him."

"What about you, Nebudaren?" asked Neriglissar. It really didn't matter what Nebudaren thought as he was rather slow-witted and never took a role in the affairs of the kingdom. Although he was in his mid-forties, his mind had never grown beyond that of a ten-year-old. He was harmless, but sadly never gained favor with his father who thought he was a mistake from birth.

Nebudaren looked up at Neriglissar with a wide smile and said, "I will do whatever my family says."

Breathing a sigh of relief, Neriglissar pressed on. "Tomorrow I think you, my Queen, and all of us should gather together at the end of the day, just like we did tonight, with Amel. You can make the case why Daniel needs to step down and why Amel should avail himself of his advisors on the Governing Council. I think it will be best if I am not involved as I suspect Amel sees me as too closely aligned to the Council members."

"Agreed," said the Queen. "I shall send a note to Amel first thing in the morning."

Pleased that they had united as one to take positive action, the talk drifted back to their children and the latest art works and musical performances they had recently enjoyed. Business as usual in the royal household mused Neriglissar. He could not help but smile broadly as he reflected on what happened tonight. I thought I could get them on my side if I pitched it as benefitting Amel. They really do not care too much about how the kingdom works which plays well for me. When I finally take control, it will seem like a normal sequence of events.

~

Amytis had taken full control. When she heard there was the possibility of her husband's kingdom unraveling, she knew she had to do all that she could to snap Amel out of his slump to rule with wisdom rather than emotion. She had noticed the difference in her son since he returned from the war. He had simply lost interest in much of anything and could not focus for any length of time on a single project. He no longer seemed to have energy, and there was a new anger in his attitude she had never seen before. He spent most of his time isolated in his palace, and was seldom seen in the public royal palace which was the heartbeat of Babylon.

Whereas her husband ruled with complete authority, Amel had been more interested in designing and building the city, leaving all state affairs in the hands of Daniel. Under Nebuchadnezzar, Daniel had governed faultlessly. She reasoned that perhaps her son's lack of interest in governance gave Daniel unwarranted freedom to pursue selfish interests. She had to get Amel to once again take responsibility for Babylon. If that meant regularly bringing in the dissenting advice of others, so be it.

It was a simple affair... just an intimate dinner of the immediate royal family. Amel could not remember when he had last sat down to a meal with only his parents, two brothers and sister. As he walked from his palace to the King's palace, he smiled at the remembrance of years long ago when as a child he enjoyed sharing dinner with his siblings. Mother was always present as well, but usually his father was off to war or on some adventure that prevented him from being present.

Amytis greeted her son warmly as he entered her spacious receiving room. There he found his brothers playing a simple board game much to the delight of Nebudaren, who seldom saw them. Kassaya arrived right behind him. Amel was rather touched by the warmth of everyone's greetings. The burdens that had been plaguing him lightened and he began to sink into the inviting cocoon of his childhood memories. The siblings recounted story upon story of how they had played tricks on one another in their early years, and reminisced of the rare times that their father paid them attention and rough-housed with them. At one point, Amel closed his eyes and tried to visualize Nebuchadnezzar in the room. All he could picture was his father lying in the pasture, dirty, hairy and oblivious to humanity.

The meal was delicious. Amytis had her servants prepare every favorite food of her four children and brought out the finest wine from the King's cabinet. The more they ate and drank, the greater the gaiety at the table. It was going well, she thought.

Dessert was the Queen's speciality. Over the years, her family and courtiers close to the royal family had come to know that a meal in the palace was always crowned by a magnificent sweet dish—never the same and always savory. Tonight, she had prepared with her kitchen servants a creamy pudding filled with exotic fruits and topped with sweet cream from the King's elite herd of dairy cattle.

"A toast to our mother and Queen," said Amel as he rose, extending his goblet. "You are unsurpassed for your meals, grace and dignity. May you live forever!"

Amel was joined by an echo of agreement from his brothers and sister. Amel looked at them with genuine feeling. The pressures of the empire's politics and finances were far removed.

When they had finished eating, Amytis asked them to retire to her sitting room where they could talk more comfortably. There, she said she had something to say to them before they went their separate ways that night. They willingly settled into the large, comfortable chairs and sofas that decoratively accented her private den never open to other than family members.

Amytis leaned forward and began, "Amel, I don't quite know how to start this. I—we—are very concerned about something that we must discuss with you. I do not want you to be alarmed in any way. I just want you—all of us—to consider all possibilities."

The hairs on the back of his neck stood upright as Amel sensed a tension rising in the room. While everyone was still smiling, muscles turned taut as though readying themselves for a struggle. He decided to keep quiet and let Amytis speak her piece.

"Amel, you're a good ruler . . . the perfect match for your father to shepherd the kingdom during his terrible illness. You have proven you are the warrior he is by your overwhelming defeat of the Egyptians. Praise be to Marduk, you protected our borders and restored the supremacy of the Babylonian empire. Your father would be very proud."

Amel smiled at her, nodding his head in agreement. He knew this was the buildup but could not see what was coming next. He spoke softly, "I saw him this afternoon."

Amytis leaned over to put her hand on Amel's arm in motherly affection, "Son, some bad things are happening in the kingdom. You are privy to more than we, but nothing is a secret in this building. We know what has taken place with the Governing Council and we know the loss of confidence in Daniel by almost every leading voice in the city."

Amel tightened, pushing his back against the chair. A scowl came over his face that did not go unnoticed by the rest of the family. But they had no recourse. Kassaya decided to jump in to assist her mother. Amytis had opened the door and they had to push on.

"Amel . . . my brother," said Kassaya who had risen and moved to stand on the other side of the Crown Prince. "We are really frightened that Daniel is no longer governing our kingdom for the pleasure of our father...and you. He has distanced himself from everyone to the point where they are becoming your enemies as well because of your loyalty to him. Even the Imperial Guard is starting to question their allegiances."

"This is nothing but trash talk you're hearing from your husband," snapped Amel, his anger beginning to rise. "The army would never question my authority."

"It's not just them," rejoined Amytis. "I know the wise men who have advised your father for many years fear Daniel has lost his way . . . that his wisdom has dimmed."

"Our city's commerce is deteriorating! We see it around us. The concerns of the merchants and growers reach even us," said Kassaya. "And now the temple has taken up the issue. Antiosyss and the priesthood are calling for Daniel's dismissal."

Amel exploded out of his chair. He had heard enough.

"You think I don't know this is going on!" he shouted. "Everyone seems to have lost their minds since the war. You're not telling me anything I don't know."

Amytis stood and cautiously approached him, placing both hands on his arm.

"We want you to dismiss Daniel as Governor," she said in a voice almost inaudible, "for your own good and to protect the kingdom for your father. If even for a month or two, he needs to step aside and you need to re-assert yourself."

"Bring the Governing Council back together," pleaded Kassaya who also had risen and was at Amel's side. "Make your opponents your friends. We do not need a divided kingdom. We will lose everything!"

"Daniel is the most honest man in Babylon," retorted Amel. "But right now, I trust no one. And after what I have heard tonight, not even you." He had backed away and was taking in all of them with his eyes.

"Funny I should say that," a wry grin—almost a grimace—on his face. "A couple of days ago when I talked with father about these things, he seemed to understand me. I could see in his eyes that he trusted me to be the king he knew I could be. Yet, none of you—my flesh and blood—do."

The anger was overtaking him, and he knew it but he did not feel like stopping it. If he was to be an island in this chaotic sea, that was fine with him. He would re-assert himself . . . he would take control. But not on their terms.

"The Governing Council no longer exists," he said to them through tightly pursed lips. "Whether or not Daniel stays in place, I don't know at the moment. One thing is certain; he does not act without my concurrence."

Amel abruptly stepped to the doorway and went through the Queen's receiving room to open the door into the vestibule. "Guards!" he shouted. "Bring Zocor to me immediately."

As the guards scrambled, he slowly walked back across the outer receiving room and re-entered the Queen's private sitting room. His mother sat slumped in her chair, defeated. Kassaya had gone to stand by her and his brothers remained silent, afraid to move or otherwise call attention to themselves.

"Yes, Sire," said Zocor who appeared at the outer door. "You called for me?"

"I want the palace grounds shut down immediately as of right now. No one from the public will be allowed to enter without my personal approval starting tonight. You are to let only my family members come and go as they wish."

"What about the wise men and the court's advisors?" asked Zocor. "And Daniel and his key officials?"

"No one," said Amel, his voice growing louder. "No one without my personal approval. Is that understood?"

"Yes, sir," saluted Zocor.

"Kassaya, I think you should return to your home," ordered Amel. "Mother, the meal was excellent. I wish it had all stopped with that. I, too, am returning to my palace. I shall be back in the morning." Then a wisp of a smile crossed his face as he added, "We'll see who is in charge of Babylon."

Amel turned and briskly walked out of the Queen's quarters followed by Zocor. Kassaya quickly followed. Amytis began to sob, her remaining sons frozen in place and powerless to offer any comfort.

~

He had been spending more and more time on the rooftop terrace off his bed chamber. Here he was isolated . . . an escape from all who demanded his attention . . . free from the decision making process he once enjoyed but which now had grown onerous. His favorite time of the day was nightfall when the breezes picked up and the heat of the sun diminished. Looking out over Babylon and its many beautiful buildings, Amel-Marduk took solace in the city his father and he had built.

Amel sat on the raised ledge that protected those on the terrace from accidentally slipping off the roof. He felt almost like a kid again as he sat with his legs hung over the side chancing the danger of falling sixty feet below to the street. It felt good . . . to be young again.

He drifted off into the inner recesses of his mind— something he did often up here. I wish my father would snap out of whatever has twisted his mind and take back the throne. Daniel said it might be another year or two as best he could discern from that terrifying dream that prophesied my father's dementia. Amel reflected further on the possibility of another two years of the current disorder. I don't know if the kingdom can withstand the pressures of all who would be king for that long. If it were not for Daniel, this would have come to a head a long time ago. I would probably have faced a mutiny in Babylon when I was at the war front. That could have been disastrous! Now, everyone has lost confidence in Daniel or wants to get rid of him. He even irritates me. So what do I do? Throw him out and take control of the kingdom myself? He shook his head, I don't want to deal with all the minutia of government . . . it bores me.

Swinging his legs back over to the terrace, he stood up and looked at the Temple of Marduk. And I don't want to listen to the whining of Antiosyss and the complaining of Beltekasmer, let alone face the relentless insurrection of Neriglissar.

Do I just kill them? At least then I wouldn't have to deal with them any longer. He smiled grimly, then shook his head again as he paced. That would really exacerbate things, would it not? I might not survive that if I was not careful.

Lost in his thoughts, Amel unknowingly retreated further and further inward. As he paced the vast expanse of the terrace, his world began to close in on him. He did not hear the knocking at the doorway to his private rooms even as it increased in volume and intensity. When Dorcas suddenly appeared in his line of sight, he was so startled, he involuntarily flinched and instinctively moved behind a pillar to take cover. She stood motionless in the entry to his bed chamber, watching him intently.

It began to register in his mind that it was only Dorcas. He had no reason to be apprehensive in spite of the fact that he had no warning of her entry. Stepping out from behind the decorative column, he collected his thoughts and made the leap back into the real world which he inhabited.

"You surprised me," he spoke gently. "What do you want, Dorcas?"

"I am truly sorry, my Lord," she replied. "We were knocking at the outer doorway and when we didn't hear any response I feared something bad might have happened. And so . . . I came in to make sure you were all right."

"Dorcas, Dorcas," Amel laughed, "What would I do without you? You are the last person in Babylon who I can probably trust. Not to worry . . . I'm glad you came."

The Crown Prince beckoned her to join him on the terrace where there was a grouping of chairs. A full moon was rising in the southeastern sky and the light it cast on the rooftops of the many tall buildings in Babylon made the city look like a field of diamonds. He sat in an over-stuffed, pillowed chair and motioned for her to do the same next to him. Dorcas remained standing. As a servant, her lot was not to assume any familiarity with members of the royal family.

"Come on, Dorcas," said Amel patting the chair next to him, "sit down." He turned to her and smiled, "I order you to sit down."

She could no longer refuse so she sat on the edge of the seat cushion in such a way as to allow her to promptly rise if asked for anything.

Amel pulled her back into the chair laughing, "Would you just relax and enjoy the evening. You're not on duty any longer tonight."

They sat in silence taking in the grandeur of the view before them. Slowly, Dorcas began to relax into the soft pillows. She had to admit to herself, it was a fantastic sight and the Prince seemed to be at ease rather than angry with her for coming unannounced into his bed chamber.

"I meant it when I said you're probably the last person in Babylon I can trust," said Amel as he looked out at the sky. Turning to her, he continued, "Can I? Do I really have your full confidence?"

She didn't answer at first, then looked at him. Her eyes were full and free of guile. He could see that. "You are the beginning and the end of my world, Sire," she said. "I have never had anything except what you have given me. When you went to war, you trusted me to care for your palace. It's no different now."

He reached over and grasped her hand, squeezing it before letting it go. "Of course, I knew the answer to the question before I asked it. Thank you, Dorcas. You have been such a mainstay of my household. I have to count on you going forward to be a mainstay of my life as well."

She nodded her head in affirmation, afraid to say anything for fear of crying. It was obvious that he was hurting. She hated to see him like this. They looked back out at the moon and its various reflected shapes on the buildings. A bond had been formed. No words were necessary to cement it.

"My mother, sister and brothers invited me to a family gathering this evening. They told me listen to those who are in high places . . . whom they think know best how things should work. They asked me to re-convene the Governing Council and throw Daniel out."

Dorcas shuddered and inaudibly gasped, "No, not Daniel."

"Did you say something?" asked Amel turning to look at her. He was momentarily caught by surprise at how the moon illuminated her beautiful face and perfectly shaped cheeks and neck. Why had he never taken this woman seriously before as a partner and helpmate?

She replied, "I just said 'not Daniel'." She moved her chair to face him more directly, their knees almost touching. "You said tonight that I may be the last person in Babylon whom you can trust. I know in the depth of my heart that you can also trust Daniel. His integrity has no end, and he loves your father, the King, and, by extension, you and your family."

Suddenly uncomfortable at being so direct with her master, Dorcas turned her head away and started to rise.

"No, don't get up," Amel said as he restrained her. "You speak truthfully. I know this in the bottom of my heart." He then poured out to her all that had been going on since his return from the war including Daniel's warning about avoiding Narseniah and her attempt to kill him. He struggled for words as he looked at her, "I was so stupid. Why didn't I listen to his advice? But, no, I only wanted to please myself."

As Amel looked at Dorcas, for the first time he took stock of her innocent beauty. It began to dawn on him that she was as beautiful on the inside as on the outside. Suddenly, he wanted to apologize to her, "I'm sorry, Dorcas, for that stupid, stupid night. Please forgive me."

She understood what he meant and teared up. She reached out and grabbed his hand, unable to speak. They held each other's hand tightly as he went on to tell her about the family dinner and how he felt completely isolated from everyone close. He told her how he had shut down the royal palace, even denying Daniel entrance to his own offices.

When he had finished, they again sat in silence. Minutes went by. Each focused on their own thoughts. It was good to have this strong bond between each other, but both knew there was more trouble on the horizon. What to do? That was the question they needed to answer.

Dorcas inched closer to take Amel's other hand in hers. She held both hands tightly, then lifted them to underneath

Amel's chin so she could turn his head to look at her. He forced a smile which she returned.

"Talk to Daniel," she pleaded. "I am convinced that he is as loyal to you as I am. Talk to him. I know you both have to gain each other's confidence back. It starts by honestly talking to each other."

He nodded slowly, biting his lower lip as the enormity of the kingdom settled on his shoulders. He could not run away from this, that he knew. Maybe he needed to re-consider who his true friends were.

~

The royal palace and grounds remained a fortress isolated within the city. True to his promise, Amel-Marduk shut out all but the essential administrators to conduct the affairs of the kingdom. He did, however, have the good sense to open up communications with Daniel and bring him and his key managers back into their offices. People with complaints, questions or ideas had nowhere to go. If there had not been an underground in place where issues could find their way to Daniel, Shadrach, Meshach, and Abednego for resolution the kingdom would have fallen into rebellion. The Crown Prince, however, saw no one and participated in no meetings. He had grabbed the reins of his authority with a vengeance, all the more disturbing those formerly in the Governing Council.

It was not long before the movement to unseat Daniel segued into an effort to overthrow the Crown Prince. This delighted Neriglissar and Antiosyss. They re-doubled their efforts to sow seeds of doubt in the minds of their former Governing Council colleagues, and quite openly went about recruiting others to join their insurrection. Amel remained oblivious to this as a result of his self-imposed isolation. Daniel, on the other hand, was more active than ever. He publicly managed the affairs of the empire through his offices and secretly kept his eye on things through the underground network that had sprung up. More of his meetings took place outside the palace than inside. He labored to handle everything without raising the ire of Amel. If the Crown Prince knew Daniel had, in effect, re-opened the doors of government to the public he would once again shut him out and, for certain, Babylon would implode.

Beltekasmer arranged a meeting in his home in the evening hours with Daniel, sensing a willingness on his part to work with the prominent leaders of the city. This, of course, was contrary to the Prince's edicts. There was no love lost between these two men as they had gone head to head in the waning days of the Governing Council. Yet, each respected the wisdom and gravitas of the other. Daniel hoped to find out new information about the coalition he knew was working to overthrow the Crown Prince.

Beltekasmer got right to the point. No sooner had Daniel settled into a chair in his spacious home and was offered a refreshing mint drink than the self-declared leader of the court's wise men apprised him of the dissent fomenting in the city since the day the Crown Prince had dissolved the Governing Council. Daniel was aware it, but he was surprised that discontent with the Crown Prince was growing. He had no idea that a majority of Imperial Guard division commanders had secretly swung their allegiances to Neriglissar nor that Antiosyss had intimidated virtually every major grower and merchant trading in the central market to fall in step with him. It seemed that very few men were still courageous or independent enough to stay neutral. This was most disturbing. The issue was no longer about loyalty to the King and his heirs; rather, it was about joining or not joining the revolt.

Daniel was shaken. When Beltekasmer finally broached the subject, asking him to join their coalition behind Neriglissar, he was speechless. He never thought he would hear this proposition put to him so directly and without shame or fear. Beltekasmer strengthened his case by claiming Neriglissar had a right to the throne by virtue of his marriage to Kassaya, Nebuchadnezzar's daughter.

"It makes so much sense," he gripped Daniel's arm, concluding, "We seek to honor the hierarchy of Nebuchadnezzar's line. When he recovers from his illness, he will have his empire back stronger than ever! Neriglissar has sworn to hand it over at that time. But if we don't act now, Babylon's days are numbered."

Ashen-faced and almost without energy to put one foot in front of the other, Daniel left Beltekasmer to walk home. It wasn't far, but tonight it seemed like a thousand miles. He had remained non-committal to Beltekasmer since he needed to keep the lines of communication open with him to gain further information about the rising rebellion. His heart was heavy. The potential devastation of this impending crisis overwhelmed him.

He walked quietly with deliberation, using each step to think how he might save the empire he had been charged to maintain by Nebuchadnezzar, and, for that matter, God. Running short of solutions, he did what he always did when confronted with an impossible situation. He prayed, "Oh, God Almighty, grant me wisdom. This is beyond me, and I need help." All he could do was repeat these words over and over. He did not know what else to say. The situation was getting out of hand and he needed direction fast.

As he walked heavily up the steps to his house, a plan began to take shape in his mind. He could waste no time, and although the hour was late, he called for his chariot. Accompanied by a small guard of four men, he quietly made his way down the streets of Babylon.

~

The captain of the guard came to see who was seeking entry to the Supreme Commander's headquarters in the middle of the night. He recognized Daniel immediately. According him the respect his office deserved, he asked Daniel what he needed. Daniel told him that it was urgent he see Nebuzaradan immediately. The captain took him into the Supreme

Commander's receiving room while he went to waken Nebuzaradan.

Nebuzaradan had not slept well that night. It was almost with relief that he heard his name called at the door of his bed chamber. Throwing on a robe, he stepped into the light of the torch-lit hallway. The captain who had admitted entrance to Daniel stood anxiously before his Commander.

"What going on?" asked Nebuzaradan of the captain. "You didn't wake me up without good reason, I presume."

"Yes, sir. Sorry, sir," sputtered the captain who pointed towards the receiving room doors. "The Governor wishes to see you."

Startled to be paid a visit by Daniel in the middle of the night, Nebuzaradan made his way to his receiving room. This is no good, he thought. Something very bad is afoot.

He walked into the room and greeted Daniel, "Governor, it is always good to see you but what are you doing here at this hour?"

"I am sorry to bother you, but it cannot wait," said Daniel looking intently into Nebuzaradan's eyes.

Nebuzaradan nodded his head slowly then asked, "Something serious has happened or you would not be here. Tell me."

"I am going to take you through all that has happened since the war ended and the Crown Prince returned to Babylon," said Daniel. "You know much of it already, but it is important that you hear it all because the kingdom is in danger tonight."

And so he proceeded to bring Nebuzaradan up to date on the political machinations, plots and sub-plots, and mounting insurrection. He left nothing out, especially emphasizing Neriglissar's latest efforts to win the trust of the Imperial Guard commanders. An hour later, he finished the story.

"What does the Crown Prince say about all this?" asked Nebuzaradan.

"He has no idea most of this is going on!" exclaimed Daniel. "I have had to deal with people without his knowing. He will not hear what I or anyone else has to say. The final straw for me was when Beltekasmer had the audacity to ask me tonight to join them in overthrowing the Prince. I was shocked that it had gone this far. They did not hesitate to bring me in on their plans."

"They must be stopped," said Nebuzaradan, his military mind fully engaged and planning the next steps.

"That's why I came tonight," replied Daniel. "I need you and your forces to protect Amel-Marduk. He is the rightful heir to the throne. To usurp his authority is to dismiss the King himself!"

Nebuzaradan rose, his shoulders firm and his face never more somber: "His father is my King, and in his absence, the Crown Prince is my King. You have my full allegiance."

~

They made their way silently to the palace grounds. There, Nebuzaradan ordered a full battalion of the Imperial Guard to surround Amel-Marduk's palace, securing the building. The two men made their way up the steps and asked the sentry guards to announce their presence.

Unable to sleep for several weeks since he had withdrawn to his palace, Amel had retired for the evening to his favorite spot on the rooftop terrace. He was more than a little surprised when Maximillan entered to tell him he had visitors in the outer chambers. He hurried down the stairs to the public areas below to greet Daniel and the commander of his forces, asking the servants to bring some fruit and drinks.

"Thank you for seeing us so early in the morning and without warning," said Daniel. "We would not have come if we did not think it terribly important."

"I assume that is the case," replied Amel.

"After what I heard from Daniel, Sire, I felt compelled to see you without delay," echoed Nebuzaradan.

Amel raised his eyebrows at this, looking from Nebuzaradan to Daniel and then back again. "Tell me, what is going on."

"You are in grave danger, my Lord," Nebuzaradan responded quickly. "There are rebellious forces growing in number who seek to overthrow you."

"I'm quite aware of Neriglissar's ambitions and his alliance with Antiosyss," retorted the Crown Prince, "but he has been posturing for years . . . ever since my father took ill. As to the rest of them, they are so splintered that I don't take them seriously."

"Sire," spoke Daniel for the first time. "Since you dissolved the Governing Council, things have changed. The loss of power made for strange bedfellows. There are now many factions supporting Neriglissar."

Daniel was unable to stifle the yawn that bubbled up from inside. "May we sit? I'd like to tell you the whole story that led up to a meeting I was asked to attend with Beltekasmer earlier this evening. For the first time, I was aware of the seriousness of this situation. For your protection, I felt I had no choice but to bring Nebuzaradan into my confidence."

Amel gestured to the chairs in a corner of the room, dropping into one himself. Daniel began to recount all that had happened since the day the Crown Prince had dissolved the Governing Council. He revealed the establishment of the underground network he had established to contain the boiling emotions and anger of those who felt dispossessed. Amel reacted angrily during Daniel's discourse, but Daniel refused to be dissuaded and relentlessly pressed on. The more he revealed how the insurrection had been cobbled together, the fewer objections Amel raised and the more intently he began to listen.

"When Beltekasmer asked me to become part of the conspiracy to put Neriglissar on the throne, I was shaken to the core," concluded Daniel. "Until then, I had no idea how rapidly the factions had come together or how dangerously potent the revolt had become."

The three men sat silently, their minds turning over the events of the past few months and the danger that imminently faced them. Each was grappling for a way to neutralize the insurrection and the conspirators. Minutes ticked by. Too tied up in knots to sit still, Amel stood and paced the room . . . thinking . . . his emotions changing from apprehension to disgust to anger that those under his authority would have the audacity to challenge him.

"My Lord," Daniel slowly and reluctantly spoke. "May I suggest we use the element of surprise to take the teeth out of our enemy's jaws?"

Amel stopped pacing to look at Daniel, "And what is that?"

Lifting his head to look Amel-Marduk in the eyes, Daniel replied, "Re-convene the Governing Council. Do it tomorrow morning, unexpectedly."

"You are asking me to humiliate myself in front of these people," sputtered Amel. "I can't possibly do such a thing and gain strength."

"It's a good strategy, Sire," said Nebuzaradan. "This is the last thing any of them expects. In battle, nothing works as well as the unexpected attack."

"Then what?" asked Amel. "We convene the Council, and then what? What do we talk about? Do I dissemble before them and apologize for my behavior? Come on, men, a King doesn't do this!" He had returned to his chair and sank wearily into it.

Daniel spoke slowly and with confidence: "When the members of the Council arrive tomorrow, they will see a strong Imperial Guard presence on the palace grounds It will intimidate them. More importantly, it will signal that the Imperial Guard serves at your pleasure and stands ready to defend against anyone foolish enough to challenge you."

"But you have told me Neriglissar has a majority of the Imperial Guard loyal to him," said Amel. "How is this going to shift that locus of power?"

"Neriglissar answers to Nebuzaradan, the Supreme Commander of the Imperial Guard," retorted Daniel. "For that matter, so do all the division commanders. Do you think well-trained soldiers who have served in battle after battle for decades under this man will dare to go against him? Not on your life!"

"It will work," said Nebuzaradan. "Surprise plus strength . . . it is a successful strategy."

The Crown Prince nodded his head but remained silent. The other two men had said their piece; they now waited to see what the Prince would do. They watched him anxiously. A smile started to take shape on his face as he thought about the various personalities who made up the Council and how they would react to this move.

"I like it," he said, looking at them with a grin that had too long been absent from his face. "I'll reconvene the Governing Council, re-establish regular meetings seeking their advice and counsel, but rule with authority like my father. They need to know they can make suggestions but it is my province to make the decisions."

Both Daniel and Nebuzaradan smiled at the energy they saw flowing back into the interim King who had for so long been defeated in isolation.

"Daniel, see that the palace is open for business as usual tomorrow morning and thereafter. You have my full confidence. Nebuzardan, you have served my father well for many years. Your continued service is noble. Your loyalty to this family and throne shall never be forgotten."

Amel-Maraduk and his two guests rose. He walked to the outer doorway to usher them out. As they passed by, he gripped their arms in support and said, "Go to your homes. Get some rest. We need to be fully alert for tomorrow." Then he disappeared into his private quarters.

Daniel patted Nebuzaradan on the back as they exited the palace, "Thank you for coming with me. I believe we have the son of Nebuchadnezzar back on the throne."

~

Sleep eluded Nebuzaradan as he lay in bed reflecting on all that was stirring in the winds of Babylon. He sensed rather than heard someone at the entry to his house. He swung his legs onto the floor and yawned. He was not able to sleep anyway so he got up to see what it could be. He nearly collided with the guards in the hallway who had also heard the gentle knocking.

"Go back to your posts," he told them. "I'm wide awake. I will see who this is."

He opened the door and was stunned to see Antiosyss standing outside. His mouth could not even fashion a greeting. The cunning high priest walked right by him into the foyer.

"We have to talk. Right now," he said as he brushed by him. "It cannot wait until the morning. I want to know why you have swarmed the palace grounds with the Imperial Guard?"

"What are you talking about?" asked Nebuzaradan incredulously.

"I know everything," snapped Antiosyss. "You think you can throw a battalion around the palace in secret after spending two hours with the Crown Prince?" He laughed, "No, my friend, I have eyes and ears everywhere."

"What do you want?" asked Nebuzaradan, on his guard.

"Let's say I want your cooperation," cynically offered Antiosyss. "Can we have this conversation in a room rather than in the hall?"

Nebuzaradan shrugged and ambled into his large living room where he took a seat in the corner away from the entry. Antiosyss followed and sat beside him.

"I know that you and Daniel and the Crown Prince are up to something. My guess is that you intend to unfold it tomorrow. I don't know what you've heard, but you need to know that members of the Governing Council are unanimously agreed that the kingdom can no longer endure the rule of Amel-Marduk. He's indecisive and weak, and has isolated himself from everyone. He has so offended your own division commanders that they have pledged their support to Neriglissar—as well as the merchants, the wise men of the court, the growers and the priesthood. We feel Neriglissar has a right to the throne by virtue of his marriage to the King's daughter."

"That's treasonous!"

"Call it what you may, it's the way things stand tonight," quipped Antiosyss.

"So what do you want of me?" asked Nebuzaradan.

"We want you to join us. Stop whatever the three of you were putting together earlier in the evening and come to our side," forcefully pleaded Antiosyss. "You would remain Supreme Commander of the Imperial Guard. Nothing would change for you except you would be operating from a position of strength rather than weakness."

"I cannot do that," replied the Commander standing. "My allegiances do not bend like a willow in the wind. Think of what you are asking me!"

Antiosyss stared hard at Nebuzaradan, then rose and moved to stop inches from his face. If he was going to bring the Commander to his side, he needed to do something extraordinary. He sensed that Nebuzaradan might be swayed by the super-natural, so he opened himself to the demonic. As the transformation began, his eyes turned yellow . . . his breath emitting an unbearable sulfur stench. His body gave off an evil aura that was frightening, even to a seasoned soldier like Nebuzaradan. He flinched but stood his ground.

"You will suffer if you refuse to join us! The consequences will be severe. I know you're not afraid of death, but do you want to lose your manhood and become a walking dead man? You will be struck with an incurable illness within the month," hissed Antiosyss. He recognized that he had guessed right. The fear in Nebuzaradan's eyes was palpable.

He raised his hand and touched his forefinger to Nebuzaradan's chest, "Don't treat me lightly. I have access to powers you know not."

Antiosyss's finger burned like molten metal. Nebuzaradan jumped backwards at his touch. He recognized that this was a man and a force that could do damage. At the same time, he could not be disloyal to his King and to his son. If he had to die to maintain his integrity, the gods must so will it.

"I cannot oppose my King," whispered Nebuzaradan. "Do what you have to do, but I cannot and will not be unfaithful to the house of Nebuchadnezzar after all these years." He touched his chest where Antiosyss's finger had been. Blood was already oozing through his light robe.

Realizing he may have pushed things too far too soon, Antiosyss changed character abruptly, returning to his normal humanity. A genuine empathy filled his eyes and a gentleness seemed to overcome his being. Nebuzaradan watched in amazement at the chameleon nature of his shift, ready for the next threat.

"I should not have said that," soothed Antiosyss. "I didn't mean to be that harsh . . . come on that strong. Please forgive me."

Nebuzaradan did not respond. He felt he had been hurled into a stone wall by a catapult and no longer had any working senses in his body.

"Babylon needs you, Commander," spoke Antiosyss gently. "We are a nation in some chaos. We count on your military leadership. I did not intend to threaten you or drive you away from our coalition. I know you don't believe we have the good of the empire in mind. All I ask is that you observe things for the next week. See for yourself how unstable the Crown Prince has become, and then we will talk again."

This was too much . . . too much to comprehend! Nebuzaradan struggled for clarity in spite of the swirling confusion that overwhelmed him. What was Antiosyss doing to him? What was he to believe? The man was crazy! No, evil! Dangerously evil!

He stood completely still, unmoving . . . not blinking . . . certainly unable to talk.

Antiosyss extended his arm to grip in friendship. When Nebuzaradan did not respond in like fashion, he stepped to his side and gave him a gentle pat on the back.

"I spoke in haste tonight. All I ask is that you watch everything that goes on in the palace under Amel-Marduk's rule. For my part, I pledge to you that I will do all I can to keep things calm this week. Neriglissar would like to act but I will hold him at bay. The same for the rest of them. I will keep the lid on the boiling pot so you can see for yourself why we must act."

Antiosyss tipped his head to say good night, and rapidly left the house.

Nebuzaradan remained standing as though glued to the floor. He could not summon the strength to move his legs. The prospect of an incurable illness had not been an idle threat. He knew he was a serious obstacle to their cabal's rebellion. Antiosyss had strange and mysterious powers not possessed by other men. Nebuzaradan had no doubt that he would deliver on his promise, if needed.

"Whew," he exhaled deeply. He finally took a step, then listlessly trudged up to his bedchamber. Things are worse than Daniel knows, he thought. At least we bought some time tonight. Antiosyss said he would give us a week.

~

No one slept well. Both Daniel and Amel-Marduk were up at dawn, eager to see what the day would bring. The first order of business was to dispatch messengers to the homes of every member of the Governing Council notifying them that the Crown Prince wished to reconvene the Council. A meeting was scheduled for early afternoon.

Antiosyss had wakened Neriglissar in the early morning hours after leaving Nebuzaradan, to tell him that he was unable to strike a deal with the Supreme Commander to join their revolt. The high priest was confident, however, that Nebuzaradan would remain neutral. He had the sense that the general had taken his threat of a curse seriously and therefore was prepared to observe before chosing sides. Neriglissar, on the other hand, was apprehensive. He was unsure what Nebuzaradan would do at the Governing Council meeting.

Fear pervaded the throne room as the members entered quietly and took their seats. The usual chit-chat that preceded these meetings was absent. To a man, they were uncertain what was going to happen. The last time they had met, the Crown Prince had accused them of insubordination and thrown them out of the palace. Had he had a change of heart or was he bringing them together to deliver a final death blow?

When everyone was present and accounted for, Daniel took his seat. The Crown Prince entered shortly thereafter and promptly got down to business.

"We have—each of us—undergone severe pressures in the past few months as we struggled to recover from a war and restore our commerce back to good health. I know you have had your issues with Daniel, but he is still the Governor of the land. It is time to end your various power plays. "

Amel paused to look directly at Neriglissar and Antiosyss before continuing.

"A few of you think you have the loyalty of our army, and it gives you the courage to dance on the edge of treason." He held their eyes by sheer force, and then spoke softly, his lips tensing, "I will not tolerate this. Babylon's Imperial Guard has always been, is today, and will be loyal to the King. But don't take my word for it," he sneered, "listen to their Commander."

Nebuzaradan walked directly to stand before Amel and the King's throne, "My Prince, your armed forces have secured the palace grounds in response to rumors of a mutiny." Bowing low before the Crown Prince, he added in a strong voice, "We stand ready to serve at your will and pleasure."

Neriglissar was both startled and furious, but controlled his outward expression. He had just been overpowered. He knew this strong public display of loyalty to the Crown Prince meant he could no longer use the army as a tool to garner support from other sectors.

He whispered cynically under his breath to Antiosyss at his side, "This is no neutral observer."

Antiosyss scanned the room, trying to make eye contact with Beltekasmer, Polynices, Marduk-Sum-Lissir and all those he had worked hard to recruit over months to support his faction. No one looked at him. They focused on Nebuzaradan and the Prince. He would have to change strategies immediately if he hoped to remain atop the power structure of Babylon in the days ahead.

He leaned in to Neriglissar, "Keep your temper under control. We haven't lost this one yet."

With the momentum shifted his way, Amel-Marduk forged ahead to take the reins of leadership. He stepped onto the podium supporting the King's throne. Daniel and Nebuzaradan flanked him on either side.

Speaking slowly and with the full authority of his position, he said, "My father was a strong ruler. He did not suffer fools lightly. Most of you in this room know that. Nebuchadnezzar, however, valued the collective wisdom of leaders from all walks of life. In a moment of anger, I lost sight of that. Henceforth, this Council will be reconvened and meet regularly as before. I remind you of only one thing. You are advisors. You are not decision makers. Therefore do not try to be decision makers. Do not assume power you do not have. I will make the decisions of this kingdom. Those decisions I don't wish to deal with, Daniel will make."

Neriglissar sat through the rest of the meeting with a half-smile on his face that never changed. He was livid on the inside, appearing calm on the outside. The chemicals in his body were at war. It was not long before he became nauseous and sought to leave. Antiosyss held him rigidly in place, keeping him there to the bitter end.

~

One by one, those who had opposed Daniel on the Governing Council realized that they were still on the wrong side of power. Just when they were hopeful that the politics were shifting in their favor, it all had stopped abruptly. Not only was Daniel back in charge but they had been rudely reminded that they were advisors only, not decision makers.

Starker, a powerful broker of Babylonian exports, sought out Polynices and other merchants to complain. With Daniel back in power the kickbacks they were beginning once again to enjoy would cease. His freedom to trade at will would have to give way to official trading channels dictated by Daniel. Before the evening meal, this group had found Antiosyss in the Temple of Marduk and demanded of him a new strategy to remove Daniel. Tempers reached the boiling point. They felt they had been played as simple pawns—advisors, he called them—by the Crown Prince.

Antiosyss urged them to remain calm, promising them that he and Neriglissar had a plan. The worst thing that could happen, he maintained, would be for the Council members to oppose the Crown Prince openly before they were ready to act. He exuded confidence, telling them only that one piece had yet to be put in place but that it would be soon. Albeit disgruntled, the merchants agreed to wait.

No sooner had they left than Beltekasmer with some of the court's wise men appeared at his door expressing their frustration that Antiosyss did not challenge the Crown Prince that day. They felt they had been dismissed as bystanders, subservient to Daniel. Beltekasmer emphasized that even members of the royal family had concerns about Amel-Marduk. Like the merchants, the wise men and magicians of the court longed for their power back. Since Nebuchadnezzar had fallen ill, they felt they had been treated as second-rate appendages in the palace. They were not going to tolerate such treatment any longer!

Antiosyss spent the entire evening soothing ill tempers and hurt feelings, encouraging all of them to be patient. He and

Neriglissar had things well in hand, he said. They were just days away from bringing the Prince around to their way of thinking and restoring a shared governance with the Council. That the two of them had no such thing in mind was beside the point. Politics demanded that they keep things simple; lies were the currency of the hour. Their strategy was to keep tempers under control by promising everyone an equal seat on the throne.

The following morning, a priest from the temple made his way to the Crown Prince's palace, carrying a message from Antiosyss asking for a private meeting. Amel's first instinct was to throw the messenger out. Why should he meet with Antiosyss? He was the acting King. But on second thought, he realized that he needed to tread carefully to appease those who could be persuaded to support him. Word had already come back to him via Daniel of the disgruntled Governing Council members. He had made an unfortunate choice to so strongly exclude them from the decision making process. He had to know what Neriglissar was up to and there was no better source than Antiosyss. So, he agreed to see him. The meeting was set for late afternoon in Amel-Marduk's palace.

~

Amel did not wish to show any deference to the high priest whom he genuinely disliked. He waited for him in the public receiving room of his palace. He did not want the man in his private quarters. He had just returned from a strenuous day working closely with Daniel on efforts to restore a robust commerce within the kingdom which included opening new trade channels with other nations. The war with Egypt had seriously depleted the royal treasury. Restoring Babylon's wealth and resources was a top priority.

Maximillan appeared at the doorway with Antiosyss, "The high priest, my Lord."

Antiosyss stepped forward and bowed low, wanting to do everything to make this meeting go his way, "My Prince, thank you for agreeing to see me on such short notice."

"Come in," motioned Amel, "please sit. Maximillan, please bring us some refreshment."

"Of course, sir," bowed Maximillan, hastily slipping out of the room.

Getting directly to the point, Amel curtly asked, "What do you want to see me about? I don't presume this is a social visit."

"Yes, sir . . . ah, no, sir," stammered Antiosyss not ready to dive into the issue that fast. "I mean . . . well, you must know there were a lot of unhappy people after that meeting yesterday."

"So? My job isn't to make people happy, is it?"

"No. Sir. It's just that I think I can be helpful to you . . . do what I can to keep a lid on the anger and frustrations of certain city leaders so that they work with you rather than against you."

Amel looked at him in mock amazement, "Do you presume to tell me that any of these so-called city leaders have any right to stand up to me? That I need their support? Have you forgotten that this is the kingdom of Nebuchadnezzar and that I am his first son?!"

This was not going as well as Antiosyss had planned. Better to cut to the quick of the issue than to prolong the prologue, he reasoned.

"My Prince, you are indeed the interim King and the rightful heir. I know that and I swear allegiance to you. But you must know that there are certain powerful people who would have your throne . . . who challenge your right."

"I know of whom you speak," said Amel.

"I believe I can help persuade others to distance themselves from these pretenders to the throne and thus support you. But we need to work together to give them the idea that you want their input in the affairs of the empire . . . that you respect them. Right now, they feel you are acting in isolation whether or not you convene the Governing Council."

"I will ask again, what do you want?"

Antiosyss sat on the edge of his chair, leaning in to Amel as he spoke, "I ask you to make finishing the canal to the temple a top priority. I want the canal completed before starting the central market. The canal is important to the efficiency of the temple. Most of all, your making the canal a priority signals to the people the high regard you have for Marduk and his priests."

"You mean that your star will rise in their sight?" snapped Amel.

Antiosyss simply nodded.

"So I have your pledge that you will be my advocate with the dissident members of the Council . . . that you will neutralize them in my favor?"

"Yes," smiled Antiosyss.

"Not good enough," snapped Amel. "What I want is to know everything that my brother-in-law is planning long before he acts. Understood?"

Antiosyss suddenly felt a cold sweat come over his body. The pretender had been identified. Apparently Amel was well aware of the close alliance that he had with Neriglissar. Now he had to convince the Crown Prince that his loyalties lay with him. Never one to sidestep a lie when it was to his gain, Antiosyss nodded his head vigorously, "Of course."

Amel stood up. "I think we have an agreement."

Antiosyss rose as well and attempted to seal their deal with a clasping of arms but Amel had already left the room. The high priest walked into the entry hall just as Maximillan rounded the corner with a tray of two goblets and a pitcher. He smiled at him, "We're finished Maximillan. I'm on my way out."

As he walked back to the temple, Antiosyss knew things had to slow down. He had to let the Prince think that he was acting in good faith and doing his part to encourage cooperation among all parties. And he had to keep Neriglissar from acting. He could not afford to report false information to the Prince and maintain his confidence. Indeed, Neriglissar had to be careful. For the meantime, he was willing to leave Nebuzaradan alone as well. Nothing must tip their hand until all was in place and there was no room for failure.

Chapter Eleven
TRAPPED!
566 BC

Surprisingly, Babylon was rather peaceful for the next
nine months. Antiosyss kept a tight lid on Neriglissar and the
various factions that had called for Daniel's ouster only a year
before. The Governing Council met every two weeks and Daniel
and Amel-Marduk employed it to their advantage to advise them
on the affairs of state. The members began to feel good about
themselves once again as their voices were sought and respected
in the governance of the kingdom. No one wanted to stand out as
a malcontent, so advice was offered without prejudice and self-
dealing, and neither the Crown Prince nor Daniel had need to go
against the grain of their recommendations. Advice was
promptly acted upon and follow-up reports brought back to the
Council. For once in more than a year, communications flowed
seamlessly.

Things were running as smoothly as they had before
Nebuchadnezzar took ill. Nebuzaradan had a tense month
waiting for Antiosyss to force him to choose a side, but the
ultimatum never came, so he eased back into his normal routine
of running the Imperial Guard. Within a few months, he had all
but forgotten the high priest's threat. Moreover, Neriglissar was
taking care of business managing his division. All hint of
insubordination was gone.

Daniel and Amel-Marduk governed well as a team. They
were of a mind to never allow a cloud of mistrust or doubt to
come between them. They met regularly to review decisions and
Council meetings and kept each other apprised of rumors and
conversations pertinent to the key leaders of the city. In spite of

the growing good will and cooperation of the Governing Council, both men knew dissent still rumbled in the trenches. They kept a careful eye on the ringleaders, always careful to note who was meeting with whom. It was only a matter of time before the next strike took place . . . and they well knew that one could be fatal.

It was almost six and one-half years since people had last seen Nebuchadnezzar; yet he remained a dynamic presence in the known world at that time. Feared and respected, the King was not a warrior to be dismissed because of a sick bed. Lesser men had come roaring back after long periods of recovery much to the dismay of their enemies. While the kingdom had become accustomed to Nebuchadnezzar's absence from the royal palace, the questions and suppositions remained. Why hadn't the King recovered by now? What could incapacitate him for so long? Was he ever returning to the throne? Why didn't the Crown Prince just take over?

Amel-Marduk regularly had spent time with his father until he left for the Egyptian War. During the past two years, however, he saw Nebuchadnezzar only once until that fateful day when his father challenged him to snap out of his isolation and take control of the throne. From then on, he made it a point to visit the King at the royal barn and pastures at least once a week. Amel did all the talking while Nebuchadnezzar peacefully napped under a shade tree. The conversation was one-sided, but the time together seemed to quiet the souls of both men in quite different ways.

The noise of the city had quieted in the late afternoon. Markets were closing, stores wrapping up their day's business, and people headed home for the evening. The Crown Prince looked forward to seeing his father. Walking down the path from the back of the palace, Amel saw Nebuchadnezzar resting in his favorite spot on the far side of the pasture. He smiled, glad that his father could enjoy such peace, yet sad that this warrior king who knew no defeat in battle had been relegated to the life of an unthinking bull. Fate had played a cruel trick on the King . . . or, he reflected suddenly . . . was it the act of a God he didn't know . . . Daniel's God?

He reached the lush grass that spilled from the pasture outside of the fence. He was going to enjoy the grass between his toes as he prepared to run over to his father. Slipping off his sandals and, feeling especially spry and fit, he grabbed the top rail and swung over the five-foot barrier. The instant he landed, a piercing pain ran up his leg. It was so painful that he hung onto the fence, afraid he would faint if he did not. Picking his foot up, he saw he had impaled his heel on a wicked looking thorn that felt as though it had run all the way up to his knee. The pain gave way to dizziness. He had to sit before he fell.

"Guards," he called out, knowing Zocor never let him go anywhere on the grounds without at least two of the most trusted palace guards watching him. But his voice had no volume. He tried once again, "Guards! I'm hurt. I need your help."

With that he sank onto the pasture grass, grabbing his foot to wrestle with the thorn. He pulled at it, but it refused to budge. It felt like a piece of hot iron that had sat over a coal furnace. Was no one there to help him?!?

He tried one more time, "Help! I need help!"

Tears flooded his eyes from the intensity of the pain. And then . . . he fainted.

~

Daniel had rushed over to the Queen's quarters as soon as he received word of Amel-Marduk's injury. When he arrived, he found Amytis in the center of a beehive of activity . . . physicians, their assistants and the household servants running in every direction. Amel lay on the large bed in delirium, babbling and drifting from stories of green pastures and flower-filled fields to empire related policy discussions with the prize cattle and horses in his father's barn. Sweat was pouring down his face. He twisted uncomfortably, swatting at imaginary flies, sometimes attempting to sit so that he could reach to grab something.

Not wanting to interfere, Daniel remained in the background unnoticed. The King's lead physician with whom he had talked a number of times over the past six years concerning Nebuchadnezzar's condition had taken Amytis by the arm and was backing her away from the bed. As he did so, he ordered the other attending healers to tend to various tasks while he talked to the Queen.

Looking up, he caught Daniel's gaze and a look of relief flooded his face. With a little more urgency, he pulled Amytis towards where Daniel was standing, his eyes pleading for Daniel's help.

"My Lady, the Governor has arrived and needs to hear from us," he spoke into Amytis' ear, all the while continuing to move her away from Amel.

Amytis turned around to see Daniel, then immediately rushed to embrace him. Until now, she had contained her emotions as she tended to Amel. When the guards first carried him to the palace and called for her, she froze upon seeing his inert form. Was he dead? Then she heard him moan. She had leapt into action, directing them to carry the Prince to her bedroom and ordering the servants to fetch the royal physicians. She wanted both to scream and cry when she saw his foot which had swollen to three times its normal size. It was her role to maintain discipline so that no time was wasted in cleaning the wound and making Amel as comfortable as possible. But now, she clung to Daniel sobbing.

Daniel wrapped his arms around her, providing what comfort he could. His eyes trailed from the Queen's heaving body to the face of the King's physician, silently asking what was his prognosis.

"The Crown Prince stepped on a very poisonous thorn down by the royal barn," he said softly as he leaned close to speak into Daniel's ear. "It pierced his heel and went deep into the foot. He must have jumped onto it for it to go in so far."

"Do you have an antidote?" asked Daniel.

The Roar of the Lions

"We do . . . for a thorn that superficially grazes the skin," the healer replied. "But we have a twofold problem right now. One, this went in so deep that the poison has infected the muscles, tendons, and blood simultaneously possibly weakening the effect of the antidote. Secondly, the shock to his system is so potent that it has completely dis-oriented him. He is in a delirious state. We have to bring his temperature down and bring him back to consciousness. At the same time, we need to cut into the foot and make sure we scrape out any remnant of poison. My fear is that doing the latter will exacerbate the delirium."

The deep sobs had stopped and Amytis rested, exhausted against Daniel. He patted her back, then held her at arm's length, "My Lady, you may well have saved your son's life by your fast action. It is not often that a mother is a nurse first. Now you must let the doctors do their work. Your's is done for the moment."

Amytis turned to look back at the bed where Amel still laid heaving and twisting in pain, calling out for help. It was difficult to take in. She turned back to address the royal physician, "Will he live? Can you help him?"

"My Queen," he replied, "he has suffered a very deep and serious wound. We are using, and will continue to use, all that medicine has to offer to heal him."

Holding her shoulders firmly as she stood in front of him, both looking at the Crown Prince in great pain, Daniel asked, "May I do something that may appear unusual to you?"

Amytis nodded her head, "If it will help, do anything."

"I'd like to pray to God to ask for a miraculous healing."

Expecting him to let go of her and move towards the bed to perform a ceremonial rite as would the priests of Marduk, the Queen moved aside.

Instead, lifting his eyes upward, Daniel began to pray right where he was standing, "God of all ages . . . God of the heavens and the earth . . . God of all gods, I ask for your healing mercies on our Prince. Guide the physicians as they remove the poison and offer him healing potions. May their hands be your hands as they minister to his body. And, God, I pray for a peace to descend on this room and palace. May all of us sense your presence and release our tensions and anxieties. I thank you, God, for hearing me and for allowing me to approach you in this time of need."

Several seconds passed. Amytis and the doctor finally looked at each other and then at Daniel whose face was still upwards, his eyes closed.

"That's it?" asked Amytis. "You just stand there and pray? No ceremony? You didn't even touch Amel!"

Daniel simply smiled as he looked into her eyes, "That's all we need to do. It's now in God's hands."

Amytis looked at him questioningly. She wanted something more. At the same time, she felt more at peace than at any time since the guards had rushed the Crown Prince to the palace. In fact, there seemed to be a quieter atmosphere in the room. Everyone was tending to their tasks like a well-trained army in battle, but without the attending clamor.

"Look," said the King's physician who had watched Daniel with no little cynicism as he prayed. He pointed to Amel lying still on the bed. "The Prince seems to be resting more comfortably. I think his fever has broken." He stepped to the bed to verify what his eyes were telling him.

"Thank you, Daniel," whispered Amytis. "Whatever you did and to whomever you prayed . . . it seems to be working."

~

For the next several days, Amel-Marduk drifted in and out of consciousness, his fever coming and going. The palace medical staff attended to him around the clock. The wound was well cleaned and poultices applied every six hours. The lead physician tried every herb and combination of ingredients he dared to stabilize the Crown Prince. Thus far, nothing seemed to work. The peace that had pervaded the bedroom the day Daniel had been summoned and prayed was still present albeit Amel's condition had not changed that much for the better.

Daniel sat in his office mulling over in his mind all that had transpired in the preceding week. A regular Governing Council meeting was scheduled for today, and he did not think it wise to postpone it. They had successfully kept the Prince's injury under wraps but it was time to let the city's leaders know that they now had an incapacitated King and Crown Prince. Was there no end to the threats to Nebuchadnezzar's throne? I don't know how much more I can take, spoke Daniel silently to God.

The men had gathered. It was time to begin the meeting. Daniel picked up his papers and walked down the long hallway leading to the King's rooms where the large throne room served as the Council's meeting place. Since all was going well in the kingdom, everyone appeared in a good mood and ready to enjoy what promised to be an amiable meeting.

Daniel called the group to order and decided to address the most serious issue right up front. He reviewed for them Amel's injury that occurred six days ago. He took them through the ups and downs the Crown Prince had endured since then. While the vast majority was shocked by the news, the conspirators could not help but share knowing glances with each other. Timing was everything, and it looked like an unforeseen opportunity had fallen into their laps.

"So what happens now?" asked Neriglissar when Daniel had concluded.

"What do you mean, what happens now?" asked Daniel in return. "Things are proceeding smoothly throughout the nation. We are not at war nor have the prospects of war, and our planning has scheduled the next several projects. The canal to the Temple of Marduk is nearing completion, and the labor force for the central market project has been substantially increased."

"How will Babylon be governed if both the King and the Crown Prince are unable to fulfill their responsibilities?" asked Beltekasmer. "By the way, Governor, we should have been informed about the Prince's condition the day he was injured. As the wise men and magicians of the palace, we do enjoy certain magical powers that could have been brought into play."

"The same goes for me," hastily interjected Antiosyss. "While you may not worship the god of the Babylonians, do not underestimate the power of Marduk."

"I ask again, how will Babylon be governed?" repeated Beltekasmer.

Daniel knew this was coming. There was only one way to deal with it and that was head on, come what may.

"As Governor of Babylon, I will continue to administer the affairs of the kingdom and report to the Crown Prince. Everything remains the same."

"Oh, no, it does not," declared Neriglissar shaking his fist at Daniel. "You have no one to report to. Both our leaders are seriously ill. No authority has been granted to you to be a power of one."

"Hear, hear" chimed in voices from around the room.

"But Daniel is the Governor. He has the authority by virtue of his appointment," the other side retorted.

Daniel stepped into the center oval to speak. He waited until the grumbling had stopped and they were ready to listen to him. "I would not be King. I did not seek to be Governor. Once appointed, however, it was my duty to serve the King and, then, the Crown Prince. I seek your cooperation as we work our way through these difficult days. I value your advice."

"That is how you have always seen us! We give advice, but you rule," Neriglissar cursed as he hurled his accusation at Daniel.

"That is the way the kingdom has always been run," snapped Daniel, his eyes boring through Neriglissar and into his brain. "That is the King's way. I have never seen anyone in this room challenge him."

The room quieted. Daniel had just thrown out the prospect that to think otherwise could be construed as treason. Nebuchadnezzar's charisma still ruled, no matter he had been out of sight for close to seven years.

"I serve the King and his heir," continued Daniel. "Quarrel all you may with the protocol established for governance, but until I hear differently from the King, I will rule by it. You will do well to accept this as well."

The opposition duly chastised, silence prevailed. Then, as if to show he had no intention of backing down, Daniel looked at the Captain of the palace guards and the Supreme Commander of the Imperial Guard and ordered, "Zocor and Nebuzaradan, we have things to discuss. Come to my offices."

He turned and walked briskly to the door, the two military leaders trailing.

"Bastard!" snapped Neriglissar under his breath to Antiosyss. "He has no right to be the authority of Babylon. I am not going to take this."

"Later," quipped Antiosyss, "we'll talk about this later. Right now, keep your composure. The Council must see that Daniel cannot excite you."

By now, those who had long opposed Daniel had congregated around the two men, spilling their anger and frustration at the sudden turn of events. Even Council members who had always favored Daniel looked in their direction to get some signal of what was to come.

"Friends," Neriglissar said to a few he knew could be persuaded to listen to him, "this is a sad day for Babylon. Our great King is ill and our Crown Prince who led us to victory against Egypt is disabled. And we are left with a Jew to rule us."

A chord of dissent was immediately touched. There was no one in the room who did not sense this. More importantly, there was no one who was not inflamed by this stark reality bluntly thrown at them.

"He's right," shouted Beltekasmer. "Do we want to be ruled by a Jew? We captured him and brought him back to Babylon just forty years ago, and now he thinks he is our ruler!"

Everyone talked at once. Tempers were ignited, and the flames of hatred and racism burned brightly. Neriglissar took in the uproar with pleasure. Finally, he had turned people's minds to support his rebellion toppling the throne.

"Men," Neriglissar shouted. He stepped onto the platform bearing the King's throne, the highest point in the room. "Men, listen to me." They stopped talking and turned to listen to him. "We have a problem, do you agree?"

A chorus of voices answered him, "Yes!" "Yes, a Jewish problem!" "We must stop Daniel."

"We will fix this. But we must do it carefully." Neriglissar sounded so sincere even Antiosyss wondered where he was going next.

"I will discuss this with Zocor and Nebuzaradan. I am sure they will agree with us that our empire could be in danger. I will also make it a point to talk to each of you to hear your wishes. A plan will come together . . . a plan we jointly create. All I ask of you right now is more time. Do I have your approval?"

Everyone thundered their approval. Neriglissar had taken center stage and was better positioned than ever before to fulfill his dream of leading Babylon.

~

They could not fail this time. Antiosyss felt good about the previous day's Council meeting and the way diverse personalities rallied together under the anti-Jewish banner that Neriglissar had raised. Too often, however, he had seen rock solid efforts like this come undone at the last minute. They were up against a formidable enemy in Daniel and could take nothing for granted. Better, he thought, to over-populate our arsenal with weapons than to come up short in the heat of the battle.

When Antiosyss heard of Amel-Marduk's injury and delirious state, he was at first pleased. With Amel indisposed, their frontal assault on Daniel would have less resistance. As he thought about the situation, it occurred to him that this created a new opportunity to co-opt the royal family in their efforts to unseat Daniel. If he could work his way into the good graces of the Queen—and especially if he could use Marduk's supernatural powers to heal the Crown Prince—they would be indebted to him forever. When life is at stake, nothing else matters!

A jumble of thoughts and possibilities rumbled through his mind as he made his way along Procession Way to the palace. He usually enjoyed the gold lions flanking the great boulevard, but that day they blurred as he focused on the task ahead. He hoped Amytis would see him so that he could propose a plan which once again would open up the royal palace to him.

Antiosyss was ushered into the Queen's receiving hall. Unbeknownst to him, the Queen was glad to hear he was in the palace. While she appreciated Daniel's genuine concern for her son and his efforts to call upon his God to intervene for Amel's life, she was also a product of the religion of Marduk. At this point, she wanted to use all entreaties to the supernatural world. Certainly, the high priest of the Temple of Marduk had to be high on the list of miracle workers.

No sooner had Antiosyss entered her chambers than the Queen appeared. As he stooped to bow, she grabbed his arms, pulling him to stand as she spoke, "I appreciate your coming to see us, Antiosyss. I suppose you have heard about Amel at the Governing Council meeting."

Antiosyss nodded, "Yes, my Lady. We had no idea the Prince was suffering and was so ill until Daniel told us. I would have been here sooner, of course, had I known."

"He's very sick," whispered Amytis through tears that were involuntarily coursing down her cheeks. "It has been over a week and he continues to gain and lose consciousness. The physicians are doing their best, but he needs more powerful help."

"That is why I came," warmly said Antiosyss. "There is a woman in the temple with healing powers. She is possessed by Marduk himself. When allowed to work through her, Marduk has done things far beyond our understanding."

"Yes, yes, that is exactly what my son needs to get up off his sick bed," pleaded Amytis.

"I will be glad to bring her here, if you wish," answered Antiosyss. "Her name is Marlee. Be forewarned; she is unlike anyone or anything you have ever seen. What she does may frighten you. Once Marduk starts to manifest himself through her there is no stopping without risk of death . . . to someone."

"I cannot be any more frightened than I am now," said Amytis. "I am on the verge of losing my first-born child. If there's a chance she can heal him, I will take it."

This was going far better than he could ever hope for, the high priest thought. Whether or not Marlee could do anything for Amel, made no difference. What counted is that Antiosyss appear helpful. In fact, if the Crown Prince were to die, that would eliminate a major problem.

"This is fantastic!" he mumbled to himself. "I have been given the opportunity to rule Babylon if I keep my wits about me and maneuver through this carefully."

In spite of wanting to smile at his good fortune, Antiosyss made every effort to suppress his glee and maintain a serious but gentle expression on his face. He took the Queen's hands in his, bowing slightly, "I will take my leave, my Lady. I will return tonight after dark with Marlee."

"Yes, please do come back tonight," begged Amytis. "We've no time to spare."

~

Antiosyss nearly ran back to the temple to put things into motion. He had convinced himself that the better alternative was to ensure that the Crown Prince did not recover.

He immediately sought out Marlee and together they concocted a plan that would take Amel's life. Marlee felt it could happen quite naturally using the demonic powers of Marduk. She had no concern that this alone would bring a quick death.

But to be safe, she agreed to force a poison, disguised as a healing potion, down Amel's throat.

Dorcas and Maximillan met Antiosyss and Marlee at the King's palace. The two servants had been brought there to care for their master. Ever since she had been told Antiosyss and Marlee were coming, Dorcas could not shake her suspicion that something sinister was afoot. She was determined not to let them out of her sight while they were in the King's palace so she had waited by the door once night had settled in.

Not recognizing Dorcas, Antiosyss and Marlee dismissed her as just another household servant. When they arrived at the Queen's quarters, they brushed by her, entering unannounced, and made their way to the bedroom where Amel lay. Amytis was seated on the bed, wiping the Prince's brow. Two physicians stood on the other side quietly talking.

"My Queen," announced Antiosyss, "may I present Marlee, healer of thousands and—tonight—of the Crown Prince."

Amytis rose and went to them, taking their hands in hers even as they bowed. Her eyes were full of hope, "Thank you for coming. He's resting more comfortably right now than he has for most of the day. Whatever you can do, please . . . we are indebted to you."

Marlee approached the bed and bent to touch Amel's forehead. He was hot. Dorcas had made her way to the other side of the bed and reached out to bathe his face with a cool towel.

"Don't touch him," snapped Marlee. "From this point, no one touches him other than me." Her gaze settled on the two physicians and then moved to Maximillan who was standing a few feet from them. "If we are to let Marduk and his spirits bring healing to the Prince, you must keep away from the bed."

Dorcas shuddered, instinctively knowing she was in the presence of evil. She refused to move; she did not want to leave Amel unprotected.

"Listen to what she says, Dorcas," said the Queen. "We are putting Amel into her hands tonight. I want you to back away."

Marlee glared at everyone with the knowing look of newly granted authority. Nothing further was said as those in the room shrank back against the walls. With unfettered access to the bed, Marlee began to withdraw from her bag a variety of ceremonial items. She placed a gold snake on the pillow directly facing Amel's head followed by six grotesque idols around his body. Next, she carefully encircled the Prince with a gold chain. She then lit a dozen bowls of incense affixed to the chain's links. When all seemed to be in order, she asked that the lamps in the room be extinguished. Other than a candle placed on a small table at the foot of the bed, the room had gone eerily dark.

Dorcas was struggling to control her emotions. The darkening of the room seemed evil-inspired. Then, she smelled the acrid incense. Marlee had placed several pots around the room emitting a very thick, greenish smoke. Her eyes stung and lungs ached from inhaling the pollutant. Marlee, on the other hand, seemed to thrive, gathering energy the smokier and darker the room became.

The healer stood at the head of the bed, softly incanting a ritual in a singsong voice. As she lifted her arms in the air, her voice grew louder. What started out as intelligible become gibberish or, at best, a language unknown to the others in the room. Marlee slowly circled the bed, punctuating her singsong ritual with shouts and leaps. It was obvious that she had been transported to another state of being. As she whirled and danced, no one wanted to risk being touched by her. They withdrew to the far corners of the room, watching in awe.

Amel began to moan, then, started thrashing about in the bed. Marlee responded by gathering strength in her voice and frenzy in her dance. She was twirling and writhing, her body distended in bizarre and unnatural configurations. Suddenly, she leaped high in the air directly over Amel lying on the bed. The onlookers gasped as one. Rather than collapse on him, she seemed to float in the air, levitating as she positioned her body to mimic his. Slowly, she descended onto the Prince to engulf him. At the touch of her body pressed against his, Amel's eyes shot wide open and he screamed.

"No, not this!"

Dorcas could not stand still any longer. She rushed to the bed to hold Amel but Marlee singlehandedly tossed her against the wall. Dorcas fell in heap, seriously dazed by the ferocity of the throw. Marlee began to roll on the bed holding Amel tightly. As hard as he tried to escape her stranglehold, she laughed and squeezed tighter. He could no longer breathe. His body went limp as he lost consciousness.

Marlee finally let go of his body, then rolled off him and the bed to stand looking down at him. She snapped her fingers at Antiosyss who quickly came to her side, offering her an elegant, small vase. Without looking at him, she took the vase, bent forward to raise Amel's head with her right hand, and brought the vase to his lips with her left.

"The nectar of Marduk," she spoke in an otherworldly voice that sent chills up the backs of the onlookers in the room. "This is the gift of life. If it is Marduk's will for the Prince to live, this will renew his body."

She lifted his head to enable him to take the liquid. At that instant, Dorcas dived across the room from where she had fallen, her arms outstretched, focused on destroying the vase. She hit the vase dead on, sending it flying against the opposite wall. In the process, she knocked Marlee to the floor and ended up on top of her. Antiosyss was livid. He grabbed Dorcas by one arm and jerked her off Marlee who was now exhausted and devoid of the spirits which had invaded her body. She lay moaning on the floor, unable to move. Antiosyss dropped to his knees to revive the healer.

Dorcas scrambled to get back to the bed where Amel lay unconscious, holding him gently and whispering, "Dear God, breathe your life back into him . . . don't let him slip away. Your power is almighty. Defeat the evil we have seen here tonight. Grant our Prince your mercy."

Dorcas glared at Antiosyss and Marlee who were still on the floor. They recognized that the tables had turned. Dorcas had taken Marlee's place. With all the authority she could muster, Dorcas commanded, "Get out! Take all this . . . these evil things, and get out!"

Antiosyss helped Marlee up. He opened his mouth to speak to Dorcas, but thought better of it. Holding Marlee, he exited the room. No one else moved. It was as though they were frozen in time. They watched in fascination as Dorcas simultaneously prayed to her God and spoke lovingly to Amel, gently holding and rocking him.

"Why did you stop her?" Amytis asked in a barely audible voice. She was still impaled on the wall, her composure not yet secure enough for her to move.

Without looking at her, Dorcas simply buried her head in Amel's hair and replied, "She was going to kill him."

"Have you lost your mind?" cried Amytis who finally had strength enough to hesitantly walk towards the bed. "She was about to give him the nectar of Marduk. It could have saved his life!"

"No," Dorcas shook her head vigorously. "No, it is poison. He could not have survived that potion in his weakened state."

"My Lady," said Maximillan stepping forward to pick up the vase from the floor. He looked inside, then holding the vase out to Amytis continued, "You know my loyalty to your son has been unquestioned for many years. On the risk that I may no longer be accorded your favor, I must say that I believe Dorcas may be right. With your permission, we will test the little liquid that is left in the vase on an animal."

Thoroughly confused and her energy spent, Amytis no longer knew what to believe. It was a dream gone bad. For that matter, was she even awake? She slipped slowly down to the floor to sit with her knees drawn up to her chin and nodded her approval. Her eyes had not left Dorcas and Amel who looked as though they were one body. The woman cares for him, she thought. May he live.

Thunk.

The Queen fainted, hitting the floor hard.

~

Neriglissar waited impatiently at the Temple of Marduk for Antiosyss and Marlee to return. He was pleased that fate had worked to his advantage, but now he was eager to hear how the assassination attempt went. It was one thing to talk and plan; it was another to be successful.

He sat in the high priest's private room listening to the din of temple ceremonies in the assembly hall. A servant in the priesthood entered to offer him another goblet of wine which he gladly accepted. He leaned back in his chair, his mind moving forward to plan how they would announce Amel-Marduk's death to the Governing Council and the public at large. His thoughts then turned to his appointment as the logical heir to the interim throne. In seconds, he was planning the death of Nebuchadnezzar. Once he ascended to kingship he knew he had to act quickly to thwart the plans of others who aspired to the seat of power.

The door flew open jarring him out of his thoughts. Antiosyss stormed in, a scowl on his face. He grabbed the goblet extended to him, and drained it in one gulp, then threw it hard across the room against the stone wall.

Neriglissar was wide awake, "What happened? Is he dead?"

"No!" snapped Antiosyss.

"What happened?"

Antiosyss was suddenly extremely tired. His body sagged. He sank heavily into a chair next to Neriglissar. He sat staring at the wall covering, an embroidered scene of writhing snakes in the center of which a giant snake stood on its tail...Marduk! He shook his head and thought, Marduk failed us tonight.

Neriglissar kept pressing. He wanted to hear the entire story, blow by blow. When Antiosyss had finished, Neriglissar stood, his face contorted in anger.

"You were stopped by a servant girl?" he sneered. "You should have killed her on the spot. I thought between you, Marlee and Marduk nothing could stop you."

"She acted so fast," said Antiosyss. "We didn't see her until she had slapped the vase out of Marlee's hands. By then . . . what can I say . . . all the power had left Marlee. She just lay there in a heap . . . useless . . . used up. We had to leave."

"You mean to say, you failed," Neriglissar said with all the derision he could muster. "You failed! It's time we quit dabbling with the spirit world and regroup to the real world of power and strength that we know." He walked back to his chair and sat, sulking.

Antiosyss looked over at the hardened warrior then spoke softly, "There is one thing we may be able to do."

"What's that?" snapped Neriglissar.

"Bring Nebuzaradan to our side."

"And how are you going to do that? He is completely loyal to Amel-Marduk and Nebuchadnezzar," retorted Neriglissar.

"But not necessarily to Daniel."

"Explain."

A slight smile crossed Antiosyss's face as he looked at his visitor, "Do you remember when he sided with Daniel to place a battalion of the Imperial Guard on the palace grounds to protect the Crown Prince almost a year ago? I visited him that same night to seek his alliance in our opposition of Daniel. I warned him that if he continued to oppose us, I would call upon Marduk to inflict on him a life-threatening illness. I said it in half-jest, but he took it very seriously. I could see my threat made him anxious."

"He's a believer in the spirit world?" dubiously asked Neriglissar. "He's a warrior, not a philosopher."

"I think he's fearful of the gods," answered Antiosyss. "He believes in the power of the supernatural world and would prefer not to chance an encounter with it."

Neriglissar hunched forward and grabbed Antiosyss' arm with a grip that hurt, "If you can intimidate him into crossing over, do it! Do it now! With him on our side, we would have the entire Imperial Guard and military might at our disposal. Nothing could stop us!"

Antiosyss's felt like he had lost the blood supply to his arm. He tried to release Neriglissar's grip but failed, "Let go of my arm. You're hurting me!"

Not realizing what he had done, Neriglissar released his hand, allowing Antiosyss to jerk his arm away. Antiosyss rubbed his arm to get the circulation going again. The division commander glared into the high priest's eyes and threatened, "That pain is nothing compared to what you will feel if you fail me again."

They sat in silence, staring each other down. Like two cocks preparing for a fight, they took stock of each other, each one doing his best to intimidate the other. Finally . . . Antiosyss blinked, "Shall we visit him together?"

"No, you see him alone. You started it, you finish it."

Antiosyss did not move. He processed this strategy without comment. Neriglissar stood to leave.

"I think we might fare better if we bring a delegation of several to meet with him . . . to convey the sense that many of us are concerned and have the best interests of the kingdom at heart," the priest spoke slowly for effect. "Remember, we did not take the Crown Prince out. So the argument should once again be focused on the need for Babylonian leadership rather than Jewish leadership."

Neriglissar paused at the doorway, stopped by this thought. He smiled as he turned to look at Antiosyss, "You may be right. Nebuzaradan is an honorable man. If he can be persuaded that the kingdom is best protected for his King by putting new leadership in place, I think he will make the move to our side." As he walked out of the room he said, "Let's talk more tomorrow."

Antiosyss sighed heavily and sprawled in his chair. He had no energy left to move.

~

It had been two weeks since Amel-Marduk stepped on the poisonous thorn. He was still moving in and out of consciousness, battling raging fevers. Dorcas rarely left his side, religiously ensuring that all the directives of the physicians were carefully fulfilled. When he did open his eyes and have moments of lucidity, she quietly talked to him to assure him that the kingdom was running smoothly and all was well. She was his window to the outside world and she refused to let him see anything that was unsettling.

Daniel visited daily but usually found Amel in delirium and unable to communicate. This was starting to take its toll on everyone. At first upbeat and positive about his recovery, Dorcas was now weighed down by the prospect that he might not live. Likewise, Maximillan had begun to have doubts about the Crown Prince's recovery. It took all the energy that he could muster to keep the Prince's palace operating in between the many hours he spent in the King's palace at Amel's bedside.

Daniel stayed current on Amel's condition from the physicians, Maximillan and Dorcas. In the first week, he was hopeful that Amel would recover, but expectations were now greatly lowered. He was particularly distressed to see Dorcas' optimism fading.

It was late in the afternoon and Daniel was meeting with Abednego to review the completion of the temple waterway canal and how the crews working on that project could be assigned to other essential river tasks necessary to keep a large city like Babylon efficiently serviced. An aide stuck his head in the doorway to ask if Daniel could be disturbed to meet with a member of the royal family's staff. Thinking this had something to do with Amel, Daniel immediately said yes, and requested that the person be shown in.

Before the aide could leave, Dorcas burst into the room, her eyes red with tears. Throwing protocol to the wind, she ran for Daniel and clung to him. She was cried out, but she needed to be held . . . to feel the comfort of another human being who cared as deeply as she did about Amel. Neither said a word. They stood, embracing each other, Dorcas receiving energy and Daniel freely giving.

After several minutes, Dorcas loosened her hold and leaned back to look at Daniel's eyes. She knew he was a man of God and had always trusted him. Finally, she found her voice, "The Crown Prince will not recover without God's intervention. Everyone has done all they can; nothing seems to work." She gripped his arms tightly, her eyes piercing his, "Please come and pray for him. There is no one who enjoys a closer relationship with almighty God than you."

Her eyes darted to Abednego who was watching her intently. "Please . . . good sir . . . ask him to do this for us . . . for the kingdom. And you, Abednego, too . . . come too. You are worthy in God's sight. I know. I have observed you day after day, and you are no different than Daniel."

Daniel patted her arms and said, "Of course, we will come. If it is God's will, the Prince will recover."

Rising to his feet and gathering the maps spread out on the table, Abednego concurred, "This can wait; the Prince cannot."

In a matter of seconds they were walking out of Daniel's office and down the grand hall towards the King's palace. Dorcas led the way, almost running in her haste to bring healing to Amel.

They entered the bedchamber where Amel lay to find Amytis soothing his feverish head with cool cloths. The Crown Prince was very hot and twisting uncomfortably, albeit unconscious. One of the palace physicians was getting ready to apply an unguent to his heel in an attempt to draw out the fever. Maximillan stood at the foot of the bed ready to do whatever it took to help his master.

Daniel smiled and bowed to Amytis, as did Abednego, then moved to stand at the head of the bed with his hands held high over Amel's face. "My Lady," he said, "with your permission, I would like to pray for Amel, to ask my God to take him in His arms and breathe healing into him."

Amytis nodded and whispered in return, "Of course . . . yes . . . he needs all the help he can get no matter where it might come from."

Knowing he was being upstaged by Daniel, the attending physician rolled his eyes, put the ointment he was about to apply aside, and left the room. Abednego moved to take his place on the other side of the bed from Amytis as Dorcas dropped to her knees in the doorway.

Lifting his eyes upward, Daniel prayed, "All powerful God of the heavens and of the earth. I commend your servant Amel-Marduk into your hands and ask for healing. We acknowledge that our efforts are futile. It is only by your power and if it pleases you that our Prince will be raised from his sick bed."

For well over thirty minutes, Daniel pleaded with God to touch Amel with good health and give him life. Abednego joined Daniel in prayer, both working in tandem to entreat God's intervention. Amytis was deeply moved to see the strong faith of Babylon's Governor and one of his senior administrators brought into play on behalf of her son. Dorcas was overcome with a new found optimism, weeping for joy. She was convinced that Amel had turned a corner and was on the path to recovery. On the other hand, Maximillan took it all in, hopeful of a miracle but not convinced.

When they had finished, Daniel took Amytis' hands into his own and said, "He is in God's hands as yours are in mine.

What God will do, we do not know. Our part is to trust and to entrust your son into His hands."

He crossed to Dorcas and lifted her off her knees, "Thank you for coming to us this afternoon. Thank you for your faith. Amel-Marduk's battle is not yet over. We must continue to entreat God's mercies and power every day. Meanwhile, continue to take good care of him."

He stepped to touch Maximillan with his hand, "You are the most faithful servant a man could want. Stay the fight. Take care of the Queen as well."

He signaled Abednego and they left the room. The three remaining in the room looked at each other for a few seconds as though to confirm something special had just taken place. But the moment had gone and they were once again thrust into the reality of seeing a man they loved, fighting for his life.

Maximillan was the first to spring into action, telling them, "I will find the doctor. I believe he wanted to apply something to his foot for the fever." Dorcas picked up a bowl of water and carried it to the bed where Amytis dipped a washcloth in it to gently wipe Amel's swollen, red face.

~

For seven days, this routine continued. Every afternoon, late in the day, Daniel and Abednego found their way to Amel's bedchamber to pray for his healing. By the second day, they had also brought Meshach and Shadrach with them. It was always the same. The Crown Prince remained delirious but with each day, in a much calmer state. Daniel took the lead, and the four men fervently implored God to hear their prayers and heal Amel. Some days, they spent over two hours in prayer refusing to acknowledge that there was no hope for Amel.

Dorcas shared their hope and waited expectantly each day for a miracle to happen. Amytis, in turn, was won over by the steadfast faith of these men. She had never seen such resolute conviction in the unknown as on the faces of these men. Even

Maximillan was beginning to think his master would recover—
not due to any outward signs but because of the men's
unshakeable belief and their refusal to take no for an answer.

On the seventh day as they convened in the bedroom
Dorcas observed that Amel seemed to be resting easier and that
his fever seemed to have subsided. Encouraged, they spread on
all sides of the bed and began praying. Each man took a turn
lifting Amel to God, and Daniel once again prayed for God's
direct intervention.

Amel-Marduk lay on his back as he had for the past three
weeks. Suddenly, his eyes opened. As he looked up all he saw
were the palms of Daniel's hands about two feet above him. He
blinked a few times, then swept the room with his eyes to find
Abednego to his right, Meshach at the foot of the bed and
Shadrach standing behind his mother seated on the bed to his left.
No one saw him as every eye was closed. To be sure he was not
dreaming, Amel brought his right hand up to his face to rub his
eyes. He was now actively listening as he heard Daniel call upon
his God to "bring healing to the Crown Prince."

His mind sprung awake: that's me! Now, he focused.
For several minutes he listened to the prayers of the four men
who refused to stop interceding on his behalf. Their persistence
and their concern for his health were overwhelming. Never had
he had anyone other than his mother show him this kind of love.
As he lay there, tears began to trickle down his cheeks, so moved
was he by their friendship without conditions.

Dorcas opened her eyes to make sure Amel was all right.
She was standing by the doorway where she always stood in the
event anyone needed her to fetch something. She could not
believe what she saw: Amel's eyes were wide open. He had
turned his head to smile at her. She involuntarily gasped then
knelt at Amel's bed to make sure what she saw was true. His
hand rose to grasp hers.

"He's conscious! His eyes are open!" she shouted,
cutting Daniel's prayer off in mid-sentence.

Disturbed by this interruption, everyone looked at the bed to see a very much alive Amel smiling at them. "Thank you," the words barely could be heard. "Thank you for your great friendship and for your God."

Daniel lowered his hands to hold Amel's head between his palms, "My Lord, can you hear me?"

"Yes, I can hear you, Daniel," he replied.

"Oh, God . . . he's well," said Dorcas kissing Amel's hand repeatedly.

"Mother," Amel said as he looked at Amytis, "It's wonderful to see your face."

Amytis fell on his body, her face buried in his chest. She could not speak. She was overcome with a sobbing that had welled deep within her heart for weeks and was now erupting.

Daniel looked at his colleagues and said, "I am so grateful that God loves us . . . that He cares for us. Thank you, God, for extending your mercy to our Prince." He was echoed by the others. They were awestruck by the miracle that had taken place, even though they fully expected it.

Maximillan had simply slid down the wall to sit on the floor as his legs could no longer hold him up. In the last few days he had begun to hope that God would heal his master. To now see him alive, alert and talking was unbelievable! Hope was one thing . . . but the fulfillment of hope was . . . well . . . it was incomprehensible. Maximillan sat motionless.

~

He had been preparing for this night with more tactical options and strategic assessment than for many of the battles he had fought over the years. The rebellion had grown in both strength and numbers as more and more members of the Governing Council joined his ranks. If he could just bridge the last gap between himself and the throne, he would realize his ambition. Tonight's meeting was critical.

These thoughts filled Neriglissar's mind as he sat in the garden with the lead servant of his palace reviewing last minute arrangements for the dinner and agenda for the evening. Satisfied everything seemed in good order, he dismissed Hezikiel, noting ironically that even he had a Jew as chief of staff of his household. What was it about these people that made them superior and so trustworthy?

He was not left with his thoughts for long when Antiosyss was shown into the garden. Neriglissar looked up and said, "Is it time already?"

"I assume you are prepared," replied Antiosyss. "If it goes well tonight, it could put everything in place."

Before Neriglissar had a chance to respond, Beltekasmer entered with a goblet of wine in hand, "You have good servants, Neriglissar, and good wine." He tipped his goblet to emphasize the point. "The evening is starting well. May it end even better."

The three men proceeded to review the evening's agenda as they strolled through the spacious grounds with their sumptuous plantings, trees, babbling brooks and waterfalls butted up against the northern wall of the city and the old original fortress. Far from the noise and fast pace of the city's commercial life, this was a retreat Neriglissar favored to center himself. The effect was the same on all who immersed themselves in the lush environment. Voices automatically lowered, anxieties lessened, and calm prevailed. It was not by accident that he had assembled them here before their guest of honor was to appear.

They had made their way to the far corner when Neriglissar saw one of his guards signal the arrival of their guest. He instructed Hezikiel to usher him into the garden. He interrupted Beltekasmer who was telling a story, "He's here."

As they turned to face the entry that led from the palace over one hundred feet away, they saw Nebuzaradan approach and walk down the steps to their level. He was a large man, tall and broad-shouldered. Even without his sword and armor, he cast an imposing figure of power and vigor. In many ways, he resembled Nebuchadnezzar which was obviously why he was the Supreme Commander of the nation's armed forces.

They quickly hastened to greet him, engaging in typical small talk concerning the social and political life of the city. The generals exchanged jokes and eased into stories from the battlefield that always entertained their civilian counterparts. Neriglissar had some chairs brought onto a grassy area where they sat drinking and laughing. In no time, they had sunk into the deeply cushioned velour that surrounded them. Four men— leading citizens of the empire—at ease . . . relaxing as equals.

By the time they were called for dinner, each man had refilled his goblet three or four times and the power of the grape was at play. They moved into the dining room of the palace where Princess Kassaya, hosting the dinner with her husband, greeted them warmly. The six-course meal was extraordinary; it was crowned with a delicious rack of lamb cooked in savory sauces brought on a giant silver platter by two servants. Between mouthfuls of the tasty dishes exquisitely prepared by the Princess's chef and carefully aged wines to complement each, the four men had bonded as brothers. It was exactly as Neriglissar had planned it.

Princess Kassaya excused herself as the men finished their meal telling them that dessert and tea would be served in the sitting room. She thanked them for being her guests and graciously welcomed them back at their earliest convenience. With reciprocal thanks and appreciation, each man bid her goodnight and followed Neriglissar into the adjoining room where large cushioned couches and chairs had been arranged by a roaring fireplace. Bowls of creamy pudding sprinkled with a variety of fruits were placed in their hands. The pudding's sweetness was so overwhelming that though they were full from such an expansive meal they wasted no time devouring the dessert. Tea was served.

"I've heard we might have some trouble again on our western border with Egypt," Neriglissar casually interjected as they relaxed after dinner.

"Not again," rejoined Beltekasmer. "I thought the last war put a stop to that."

"It would have if I had been allowed to have my say," answered Neriglissar. "We had them on the run. I pushed to invade and re-define the border in our favor but Amel didn't want to aggravate the issue." He turned to Nebuzaradan, "I know you favored pushing them back all the way to Memphis."

"Yes, on hindsight we should have," agreed Nebuzaradan.

"So what stopped you?" asked Antiosyss. "Surely the way to let our enemies know we are masters of the world is to show no mercy . . . to overwhelm them."

"The King would have taken the battle to them," nodded Nebuzaradan. "The Crown Prince is of a different mind. All I know is that I serve the King, and the Prince was King then."

"Agreed. That is our lot as military men," said Neriglissar. "However, we do have a problem that is in our face, and to ignore it any longer is to invite collapse whether from without or within. We have a King who is ill and cannot rule; now we have a Crown Prince who is at death's door and cannot rule. We are left with Daniel, a Jew, which I find abhorrent! Is this the future of Babylon? Are we a country governed by a Jew, a former slave? Where is our pride? How can we defend ourselves when we don't even rule ourselves?"

"It's time that the Babylonians take back their rightful authority," said Beltekasmer. "Nebuchadnezzar would be the first to say so."

"Who is really opposed to this idea?" asked Neriglissar. "Every member of the Governing Council is ready to act. We need to put a leadership team into power to run the affairs of this nation. People we know who are strong and will stand up to all threats."

"Nebuzaradan, are you with us on this?" asked Beltekasmer. "You know the Imperial Guard will go as you lead them."

"My loyalty remains to the King and the Crown Prince," replied Nebuzaradan. "I do not believe it is right to even think of doing something that will undo what he has put in place. And right now, Daniel is his Governor."

Antiosyss could sit still no longer. He sprang out of his chair, "The priesthood is united in our desire to unseat Daniel. We have the power of Marduk on our side. Do any of you really grasp what that means? There is no one—nothing—that can stand up to the god of our nation. We have the power of the supernatural to wield and we don't take advantage of it. What is wrong with us?"

He stepped directly in front of Nebuzardan's chair and reiterated, "What is wrong with YOU?"

Nebuzaradan was shaken by this as he knew Antiosyss was the keeper of dark powers he could easily unleash on whomever he saw standing in his way.

"I don't know what to say. I know we're caught in a funny limbo, but asking me to go against my Prince is . . . well, it's more than I can do right now."

"Do you remember, Nebuzaradan, when you and I met and I mentioned the possibility of Marduk inflicting illness if we as his priests so desire?"

Nebuzaradan nodded, uncomfortable where this might be heading.

"That may have been the King's lot . . . even the Crown Prince," quietly spoke Beltekasmer.

"What do you mean?" asked Neriglissar.

"He's likely right," said Antiosyss who was now standing in front of the fireplace facing away from them. "Who's to say that Marduk didn't bring Nebuchadnezzar to his sick bed and cause Amel's injury?" Then, as an afterthought to cast the net of fear wider, he turned to Beltekasmer, "The King had discontinued using you and your fellow wise men to advise him, right Beltekasmer? You fell from grace as well."

No one spoke. These suppositions implied the existence of serious powers that, if summoned, could incapacitate any one of them in an instant. Nebuzaradan recalled Antiosyss' threat of a year ago. He did not fear war, but the threat of the supernatural frightened him. He could not fight an enemy he could not see.

Antiosyss slowly turned to look at the three men. Silhouetted against the flames, he cast an eerie sight. He spoke in a strange sounding voice that scared Nebuzaradan even more.

"Here is where things stand. Every member of the Governing Council except Daniel and his three Jewish dogs and you, Nebuzaradan, are with us. Since we are resolved to be rid of Daniel, the four of them don't matter." He turned back to face the fire and, almost inaudibly, said, "That leaves you, Commander. With you on our side, we are unanimous and we will be victorious. We will even include you in the ruling triumvirate: you, Neriglissar and I."

Beltekasmer and Neriglissar murmured assent. Nebuzaradan refused to look anywhere but at his feet. The warm, comfortable feeling of the garden was long gone, replaced by chills that now racked his spine.

Suddenly, Antiosyss spun around and spit out a flame that reached Nebuzaradan singeing his hair. The soldier snapped upwards, his eyes fearfully fixed on Antiosyss.

"I'll ask you, Commander, are you with us? Or . . . do you wish to face a destiny already suffered by the King and the Crown Prince? I suspect when I call upon Marduk's powers, the effect on you will be more devastating."

Nebuzaradan rose and slowly backed to the doorway, never taking his eyes off Antiosyss, "You're asking me to sell my soul and I cannot do it. I know your powers . . . I have no doubt you can do as you say. But I am the King's Supreme Commander of the Imperial Guard. I cannot desert him just because I may be afraid." With that, he exited.

Antiosyss sat back in his chair, tired from the energy he had conjured up to let Nebuzaradan know they were at a serious juncture. The three men quietly stared into the flames. After what seemed like hours, Antiosyss quipped, "He'll come around. I think we've got him."

~

From the moment Amel-Marduk emerged from his delirium, Dorcas took full control of his schedule and of nursing him back to health. Maximillan stepped aside, focusing his energies on putting the Crown Prince's long-neglected palace in order. For the moment, Amel was to remain in the King's palace so Amytis could also participate in her son's recovery.

Each day Amel gained new strength and purpose. The fever left first, followed by a lessening of the aching in his joints. The swelling began to subside as the right leg and foot regained their normal form albeit the heel where the thorn had pierced him remained very sensitive. Dorcas brought an extraordinary discipline to the task of nursing Amel. She followed precisely the directives of the physicians, carefully preparing a nutrition program designed to orderly restore his physical strength. When he was not hungry and would not eat, she coaxed him into doing so. When his foot throbbed and he did not want the dressings changed, like a mother she ignored him and kept the wound clean and always treated with healing herbs.

Several weeks went by, allowing this new relationship to flower. While visitors came and went with increasing frequency, Dorcas was ever present to monitor the length of their visits by observing Amel's energy levels. Whether it was the Queen, Daniel, Rymen or Maximillan, she had no reservation telling a visitor their time was up. Respect for her rose substantially as all saw the results of her protective care evidenced in Amel's restoration to health.

She didn't affect anyone more than Amel who watched her daily as she managed his waking hours. It was as though she shared his heart and soul, the way she knew when he needed rest or nourishment. He knew she never let him tire; rather, she seemed instinctively to know the right time for everything required to foster the healing process.

Dorcas' physical beauty had never been lost on Amel, but for the first time he saw her character and inner beauty, and it was terribly attractive. She was a servant, he knew, and therefore it was inappropriate for him to have any relationship other than as her master. Yet, he had never encountered a woman like her. Even his wonderful wife who had died years ago did not have her instincts or purity of intent.

One morning Dorcas entered his room more cheerful than usual. She hummed as she drew the curtains aside, revealing a magnificent sunrise and busied herself preparing his breakfast and re-wrapping his foot. His curiosity got the better of him prompting him to ask why she was in such a good mood.

"You are to visit Daniel at the royal palace today," she smiled at him. "You have been learning to walk and it's time you surface in public. People will be pleased to see you. Besides, it will do you good to get out of here and back to work."

Not only did the excursion go well for Amel-Marduk physically but he was gratified how pleased people were to see him for the first time in several months. They were happy to see their ruler back in good health. He even spent an hour with Daniel reviewing governance matters, and, for the first time, that even felt good.

When it was time to return to his own palace, Amel did so with great relief. As he bid his mother goodbye, he hugged her and thanked her for her care and concern. It was good to know that the Queen, with whom he had not had much interaction since he married, was still the same loving mother. He was determined not to be carried home, and informed his servants and guards that he would ride horseback albeit the trip was a few hundred feet. Dorcas attempted to dissuade him, but she relented when she saw how important it was to him to return as a victor rather than as a wounded warrior.

Within a week, Amel decided to attend the Governing Council's regular meeting. In spite of the unanimous opposition to Daniel by the members, they were glad to see Amel back on his feet and in robust health. They greeted him with a standing ovation as he entered the throne room and took his place on the King's throne. Since Daniel did not want to tax the Crown

Prince's energy his first time back, the agenda was light and the issues of little consequence. It was as though all in the room felt likewise and avoided all discord. Rather, the discussion centered on Amel's accident and recovery as he recounted for them his near death experience and healing. It was not lost on Daniel that the usual tone of dissension had given way to enthusiasm at seeing the Crown Prince's return. The question was: would it stick?

Amel felt so well the next morning he spent most of the day with Daniel reviewing all that had taken place since his accident. He was concerned about the saber rattling of the Egyptians in the west, but was assured that Nebuzaradan had calmed things down by sending a division back to the border, if for no other reason than to show Babylon's strength and determination that an invasion would not be taken lightly.

Daniel told him that the temple waterway canal had been completed and that the workers on that project were ready to be re-assigned elsewhere. After a review of all the construction projects in process and the design challenges in planning, Amel felt it was time to put all their energies into completing the central market. He was prepared to take charge of the project and felt he had the energy to do so. This meant he had to return to his design table to solve problems that had arisen in the course of the work already started. Nothing made him happier as this was the work he loved most.

Departing the royal palace that afternoon, Amel said to Daniel, "You take care of governing as you are doing, and I will build Babylon the finest new market the world has ever known."

~

For a couple of months it appeared that the rebellion and dissatisfaction with Daniel had dissipated. The Governing Council met regularly to discuss policy issues and hear reports on the western border which Egyptian forces tested regularly. Since Amel had returned, the Council rarely challenged Daniel publicly. There were the normal temper flare-ups by Antiosyss and Neriglissar at something Daniel or his top three administrators had done, but these were handled quickly and without incident.

Neriglissar and Antiosyss used this time to build their cabal which by now had co-opted every leader in the city and provinces except for Nebuzaradan. Only he remained loyal to the Crown Prince and the throne and, therefore, Daniel. Since that ill-fated dinner at Neriglissar's palace, Nebuzaradan had lived in fear of what Antiosyss might have in store for him, but with each passing day he was able to put it further out of his mind.

Nebuzaradan was the key to overthrowing Daniel and, subsequently, Amel-Marduk. As Supreme Commander of the Imperial Guard, he controlled the nation's lethal arsenal. Without him, an open assault on Daniel could result in a blood bath and total failure. Neriglissar knew he had to bring his Commander around to his point of view. To that end, he spent time meeting with military leaders, merchants, priests and magicians second only to the Governing Council members on the hierarchy tier of Babylon's power elite. His message was simple and resonated well with the pride of Babylonian culture inculcated in the hearts and minds of every citizen: we can no longer tolerate that a Jew who disregards our religion and culture governs our land. Change is not an option; it is our calling.

Once Neriglissar and Antiosyss converted people to their way of thinking, it was easy to ask them to pressure Nebuzaradan to join the cause. Many of them were friends of the Commander, so they willingly leaped into the political fray to persuade him that it was his obligation as a Babylonian to take action. Day by day, he faced an onslaught of pressure to the point where he became reluctant to leave his headquarters for much of anything save the Governing Council or when summoned by the Crown Prince. This growing isolation imprisoned him in his own mind, and, once again, the threats of Antiosyss consumed him.

~

Something was wrong and Amel-Marduk knew it. He could not yet place his finger on it but the dynamics of the kingdom had changed. While he was gaining strength day by day and enjoying his fully restored relationship with Daniel, the men with whom he had enjoyed productive social and political relationships in years past now were awkwardly distant around him. Even Nolter, whom he went to visit to discuss a new idea for the central market, appeared withdrawn. In the past, the two men would have enjoyed a vibrant discussion as they looked at the pros and cons of a design; now, Nolter seemed anxious to get on to other business and politely told Amel that if that was what he wanted to build he should do it.

He fared no better with Mysonus, the spokesman for the palace wise men and courtiers. He had tried one day to visit with him over lunch at his palace in his private chambers. When he asked for a reading of the wise men regarding his father's health and recovery, Mysonus grew quiet, uncharacteristically deferring to Daniel. Amel pushed further, asking for their interpretation of the stars as to the threat Egypt was presenting on the western border. He wanted to see how they perceived Nebuzaradan's leadership but it was to no avail. Mysonus simply admitted the signs were cloudy and unclear . . . that he could not discern at this time how they would play out. This was unheard of in Nebuchadnezzar's palace. Men lost their heads for far less than this and he angrily reminded Mysonus as such.

After that incident, he stormed into Daniel's offices where Meshach, Abednego, and Shardrach were meeting with the Governor to vent his frustration.

"What is going on in this kingdom?" he yelled. "No one wants to talk with me. Everyone seems strangely cool about anything we want to do for Babylon." He looked at them, throwing his hands up in the air, "Am I the only one who feels this way?"

The three subordinates looked at Daniel, not knowing what to say, waiting for him to take the lead.

"No, you are not the only one encountering this indifference," Daniel cautiously answered.

"So when did this begin?" asked Amel. "I didn't see this when I first recovered and resumed my work. But I sure am seeing it now!"

"My Lord, please sit down. It's a long story and it's best we start when you first left for the war well over two years ago," gently said Daniel.

The conversation went on into the night as the four men candidly unfolded the story of the growing opposition to Daniel's governance and by extension to Amel's right to the throne. The men held nothing back. Things came tumbling out that Daniel had not even heard from his friends who wanted to protect him. By the time they had exhausted themselves of all incidents and inferences, it was abundantly clear to Amel that Babylon faced a bigger threat from within than without. He needed to get back to being King or risk losing the entire kingdom. A trap had been sprung, and he had unknowingly walked right into it.

~

With a new set of eyes and mindset, Amel spent the next few days watching the people and activities around him. He considered no one safe. From his servants and personal guards to merchants and wise men to the priests and commanders of the army he controlled, he observed them all through a new lens, searching for the seeds of discontent. It became very clear to him that, with one exception, the city's leadership had turned cold to his rule. Only Nebuzaradan remained loyal and, of course, Daniel, Shadrach, Meshach and Abednego.

Amel knew that to isolate himself would only exacerbate the situation, so he became more active than ever in the affairs of state, paying particular attention to the military and those driving Babylon's commerce. As he visited with the regiments and their respective commanders, he was assured that the insurrection had not infiltrated their ranks. The Imperial Guard was still loyal to the throne. However, a different attitude prevailed among the merchants and growers. Ever since the war with Egypt began, their profits had fallen. They had found it difficult to bounce back and, in fact, had been forced to lower their living standards. These developments trickled downward to the average citizen. Life had become more arduous. In hindsight, Amel could see anger and discontent silently brewing.

The more he circulated in the city, the greater his inner turmoil as he wrestled with dynamics that were completely foreign to him as a son of Nebuchadnezzar. Never in his life had he seen anyone with the temerity to challenge the authority of his father. To do so meant certain death. What was he to do? Use the palace guard to expunge those who questioned his and Daniel's authority? It was out of the question. To do so would result in a blood bath that would only make things worse and reveal the kingdom's internal weaknesses to the empire's enemies outside its borders.

It was tough for Amel to grapple with these issues and devise a strategy of how to deal quickly and effectively with them. Other than Daniel, he had no one to talk to, and even with Daniel there was an edge. He was the sitting King; Daniel was an appointed bureaucrat. A King does not reveal his insecurities and doubts to his subjects!

He found himself talking more and more to Dorcas about these things in the evenings during the dinner hour. Since the days when she took over his nursing, she had begun to dine with him and be his companion whether it was to play games together or just sit and talk. Once he had regained his health and was active, this pattern remained in place. Amel looked forward each night to the refuge of Dorcas, particularly as his awareness of the rebellion heightened. He realized that she was the one person he trusted completely and with whom he had no fear of betraying his confidences. She was much smarter and wiser than her station in life would suggest. Her insights often triggered new solutions to problems he might otherwise not have seen.

~

It had been three days since his most trusted advisors had confronted him with the truth of the brewing insurrection. Amel had finished dinner, eating as usual with Dorcas. He described his meetings that day with various merchants and farmers, and his account only verified the discontent in the city he suspected now was pervasive.

"I'm grateful Nebuzardan stands by me," he said. "Without the power of the Imperial Guard, I—the house of Nebuchadnezzar—would be exposed."

"You are his King," said Dorcas. "He's a man of integrity and fierce loyalty. He will always stand beside you."

Amel got up from the table and walked to the door leading to the hall, "It's a beautiful evening. Come with me. Let's sit outside on the roof and talk."

Dorcas pushed her chair aside and rose to join him, "Sure, if you wish."

On the roof, they stood together at the edge looking out onto the flickering lights of candles and lanterns that extended for miles.

"It's a beautiful sight," said Amel. "We have a great city that I must hold together."

"You will," she answered. "Together with Daniel, you can do great things. You are smarter than those who would overthrow you. You only have to use your intelligence and strength to bring this to an end."

Amel looked at her quizzically, "Strength? I don't see that we have much strength right now."

Dorcas smiled knowingly, "Oh yes you do. You have tens of thousands of battle-seasoned soldiers ready to defend you if called upon."

Amel nodded, looking back out on the city. Her words stuck in the forefront of his mind. Suddenly . . . it all came together.

He said, "You're right as always. I have the full power of the Imperial Guard and now I must use it." He turned to her in admiration, "I am grateful that the Guard is on my side, but I never considered using them to take the offensive. Dorcas, you are the best advisor a King could have. The Imperial Guard is my strength, and I overlooked them completely."

She nodded in affirmation. Excited by the thought of leveraging the power of the military to turn the advantage to him, Amel grinned, "I'll meet with Nebuzaradan first thing in the morning. I'm sure a plan will fall into place."

"I will take my leave now, Sire," said Dorcas. "Night is settling in. We need our rest."

"Don't leave yet," he replied. "In fact, come, sit with me." He took her arm and steered her to the couch that was on a pedestal from which they could look over the protective perimeter wall that bordered the roof, "I have something I want to tell you."

They sat and looked out at the city now bathed in the light of a rising full moon, Amel whispered, "It's almost the most beautiful thing I have ever seen."

"Yes," agreed Dorcas.

They sat in silence. Then turning to him, Dorcas poked his chest with her finger in jest and asked, "What is the most beautiful thing you have seen if this isn't it?"

Looking straight ahead, Amel replied, "You."

Dorcas froze, then, slowly turned to look forward. She was not sure how to respond or what to do. This was the first time the Prince had ever become this personal with her although, upon reflection, he had intimated on prior occasions that he felt a closeness to her. Yet, this was very direct. Her heart leapt, but her head hurt from the thousands of opposing signals strangling her brain. She felt faint and immobile.

Sensing her discomfort, Amel took her hand in his and turned to face her, "Dorcas, I know you are a servant in my household and that we occupy two worlds that are far apart and would normally never meet. I have to tell you, I have never met a woman with your purity of character . . . totally guileless . . . a woman who is so attractive to me that you consume my mind night and day. I didn't know what this feeling was for a long time because I rejected the idea of ever being in love with a woman again since my wife died. But . . . Dorcas, I think I have fallen in love with you."

He grabbed her shoulders and turned her to face him. "I love you, Dorcas." Tears began to stain her cheeks as she heard him speak, "This is no longer a master to servant relationship. That ended for me weeks ago. You're probably afraid that if you don't respond in like fashion, you'll be punished or cast out." With a renewed urgency, he pleaded, "Please don't think like that. No matter how you respond, you will always have a place in this house."

She lifted her hands to take his hands away from her shoulders. They sat facing each other, holding and kneading each other's hands and fingers. Both could no longer speak, simply letting their emotions do the talking. Afraid to make a move, Amel looked deep into her eyes and willed that she would know he truly loved her. Her tears came more easily and flowed down her face as she absorbed the depth of his passion. She had long harbored a love for him but never dared show it for the very fear he just mentioned. It was not her place to fall in love with her master. Yet . . . now . . . he had revealed his heart to her and that obstacle no longer existed.

She let go his hands and threw her arms around him to hold him tight, "I love you, I love you, but . . . I'm afraid. Can we do this? Are we allowed to do this? Your family will not permit this, Sire."

Amel chuckled, "I so very much love you, Dorcas. But don't call me sire again. I am Amel to you henceforth . . . and let me worry about my family. From what my mother has told me, she knows no finer woman or person than you. That is not a problem."

"I do love you...with my whole being."

"And I, you," responded Amel. He held her head gently and leaned in to kiss her lips for the first time. She responded with an unleashing of passion that had been bottled up inside her for several years. They became as one, lost in a love compelled by truth and beauty of character and not of physical lust. Yet, the desire was more intense. Neither had ever felt such a longing to be one. They clung to each other, neither wanting to let go . . . both whispering over and over, "I love you . . . I love you."

~

That same night the Temple of Marduk was ablaze in light as thousands of Babylonians filled both the outer courtyards and the large inner assembly hall to take part in a specially called ceremony to honor the Imperial Guard. No matter where one stood, music filled the air . . . the horns and drums setting a tempo of celebration. Amel had been invited to attend as a courtesy, but given the offer came from Antiosyss he declined, much to the delight of the high priest and Neriglissar. They didn't want him there. They had a different agenda to play out. The special guest for the evening was Nebuzaradan by virtue of his role as Supreme Commander of the army.

All the pomp and grandeur of the military were on display. The generals of regiments and their staffs dressed grandly in their ceremonial uniforms were ushered into the hall with a chorus of trumpets. They were followed by the commanders of the five primary divisions, each taking a prominent place according to their rank. Neriglissar was in fine form, adding a few extra flourishes to his ensemble. The two bountiful, emerald green ostrich feathers with a purple, rather than red, sash spanned his chest and set him apart as near royalty. Upon his entry, the murmuring throughout the hall was audible as people made note of his obvious importance.

Last to enter was Nebuzaradan who was greeted by Antiosyss and escorted to the highest place of honor at the front of the assembled worshippers. As he entered, the horns and flutes faded and the drumming increased in intensity to lead up to the beginning of the night's main event. A large, fierce-looking man, Nebuzaradan was not a figure to be ignored or overlooked. Yet, when juxtaposed to Neriglissar in his finery, it was not easy to conclude who outranked whom.

The drums rose to a frenzied pace, then, abruptly stopped. Smoke began to emerge from the oversize statue of Marduk, suspended against the back wall of the platform which housed the large golden altar. A rumbling from deep within the temple began to sound, accompanied by pulsating vibrations that made it difficult to stand upright. The evening's magic show was beginning.

Whoosh! A flame at least thirty feet long came spewing from the ceiling to light the fire pit central on the altar. At the same time, huge columns of flames erupted from flame pots placed in a semi-circle around the altar. The heat was so intense that those close to the altar were forced to shield their faces. It seemed that the temple was on fire, a blazing offering to the god Marduk.

Antiosyss in all his regalia as the high priest suddenly emerged, suspended in the air above the columns of fire in front of the image of Marduk. He appeared to float downward, the height of the fiery pillars surrounding the stage decreasing as though cushioning his descent. Upon reaching the floor, he turned to face the statue, lifted his hands and shouted in a loud voice, "Almighty Marduk, we thank you tonight for the protection of our Imperial Guard and its leaders. We thank you for making this empire strong. May we ever be worthy in your sight to not only defend our borders but to conquer other lands to add to the kingdom."

A cloud of putrid smoke blew like a strong wind from the nostrils of Marduk, accentuating Antiosyss's prayer. The assembly stirred, affected by both the stinging smoke as well as the notion of victoriously battling new enemies. The pride of nationalism played well before this crowd and he knew it.

Antiosyss turned to face the audience. At his bidding, the flames both on the altar and those coming from the semi-circle of fire pots were reduced to a glow. He moved around the altar to stand center on the lip of the raised platform and in a strong voice spoke, "Tonight we bring honor to our Imperial Guard. We especially honor the generals and commanders who keep our warriors trained and alert to fight at a moment's notice. And we invoke the power of the spirit world of Marduk to dwell in them."

The next forty-five minutes were devoted to recognizing various military leaders by bringing them up onto the altar podium before the assembly and conferring on them the power of Marduk. Each time Antiosyss tapped a general, a bright flame would erupt from his head to burn while he intoned an incantation. It was magical and arrested the full attention of the men assembled in the room.

Before he came to the five division commanders, Antiosyss looked directly into their eyes and issued a warning, "Tonight, I am channeling the great god Marduk to give you supernatural powers as you go forth in conquest. These are powers from another world . . . from the dark world where only the spirits and those who offer themselves to be used by the demons of Marduk exist. Be warned. You will have extraordinary new powers but only as you give yourselves to Marduk and his priesthood. To thwart us is to risk personal disaster and harm."

The drums began signaling the ceremony was building. As each commander came to the altar, Antiosyss asked, "Do you accept the conditions?" With each affirmative reply, the supernatural incarnation was conjured in an incredible display of fire.

Finally it was Nebuzaradan's turn. Antiosyss asked him to join him on the podium. Suspecting where this was ultimately going to lead, Nebuzaradan was reluctant to do so. At the same time, he couldn't refuse to take part in this ceremony as it would weaken him in the eyes of his men. He slowly stepped onto the platform and faced Antiosyss, who smiled evilly at him. The sight of the priest's blazing eyes that had turned yellow sent a chill up his spine. In his heart, he knew he was now being asked to cross the line . . . to join the revolt . . . to be disloyal to his King.

Antiosyss asked the ill-fated question: "Do you accept the conditions?"

The mighty warrior froze in place, not responding.

Antiosyss repeated the question, almost screaming at him.

Nebuzaradan was mute. His loyalty won out over his fear of the supernatural. He did not move.

Without taking his eyes off the Supreme Commander Antiosyss snapped his fingers. The Marduk statue belched a large cloud of smoke out of which emerged Marlee, so hideous in appearance that a universal gasp erupted in the hall.

She flew at Nebuzaradan, screaming, "Infidel! How dare you defy the god of our people . . . the god that protects us and gives our Imperial Guard its overwhelming power."

Knocking him to the ground and kneeling on his chest she screeched, "Marduk, use me to convey to this infidel your fierce power. Bring him to his senses or strike him dead. Take control of me . . . NOW!"

With that she began writhing around his inert body, her mouth foaming as she incanted in an unknown language, conjuring spirits from the netherworld. A strange orange-like haze began to settle on her and Nebuzaradan. Although unseen by those in the room, it was evident that she had been joined by a group of demons. The spectacle had turned from an infatuation with these unknown powers to a frightening horror. Even Antiosyss had distanced himself from her.

At the center of this lay Nebuzaradan, immobilized by fear and torn by his loyalties. But the fear of something inhuman was quickly taking over. He felt that he was being forced to look into the very chasm of hell. He struggled with all his might to not slide over the edge into the sulfuric fire.

As Marlee moved around him, she never lost contact with his eyes. Finally, his body convulsed; he had had enough . . . his eyes lost their strength and closed. He succumbed. She bent over to touch his face and whispered, "Now . . . are you ready?"

Exhausted, Nebuzaradan nodded, whispering, "Yes."

She leaped into the air, clapped her hands and fell in a heap at his feet. The drums stopped. The large room went silent, all eyes on Marlee and Nebuzaradan. She lifted her head and slowly rose, extending her hands to Nebuzaradan to bring him to his feet. Never taking her eyes off the Supreme Commander, she whispered to Antiosyss, "He's ready."

Antiosyss waited a few moments to make sure it was safe. He approached Nebuzaradan and in a loud voice again asked the question: "Do you accept the conditions?"

Nebuzaradan replied, sadness filling his eyes, "Yes."

His body glowed brighter than any who had gone before him. Flames burst upwards from the top of his head to the temple ceiling, sending a blast of heat into the audience.

Nebuzaradan had finally crossed the line. Neriglissar smiled. He caught Antiosyss' eyes. Both sent an unspoken victory message to each other.

Chapter Twelve
RESTORATION
565 BC

Amel stormed into Daniel's office, brusquely brushing past his assistants.

"I'm trying with all my power to rule this kingdom in a civil manner, but it's getting more difficult to do so each day!" he bellowed as he came through the door. "They think I'm only an architect and builder—not their king."

Daniel looked up from the documents he had been studying, his eyes gentle but saddened to see his leader so frustrated, "What happened?"

"I am trying to mend fences with certain people as you suggested. I asked to meet with Polynices this morning to review with him the layout of produce stalls and shops in the new market. I thought he would be a good advisor. He owns a lot of stores and land."

Daniel rose and went to the door to shut it to give them privacy. He repeated his question, "What happened?"

"He refused to meet. Begged off saying he needed to get to his holdings outside the city . . . something about a problem with his employees and wells."

Amel's eyes blazed. He slammed his fist against the wall and roared, "Can you believe it? One of my subjects refused to see me . . . his King?"

Daniel shrugged, not knowing how to respond.

Amel hit the wall again, then, slumped into the chair opposite the table covered with all the documents Daniel had been reviewing.

"I think it's time to show this city who is ruling whom. My father would never let this happen, and I'm a fool to not rule with his iron hand."

He motioned for Daniel to sit. Then he leaned forward, staring into Daniel's eyes, the tension in his body reflected in every muscle as he spoke, "I am activating the Imperial Guard. I want to place them strategically around the city to monitor the activities and meetings of the Governing Council members, especially the priesthood and the merchants. I can shut down Beltekasmer and his wise men with the palace guard. And I am replacing Neriglissar as a division commander immediately."

"Do you need to go that far?" asked Daniel. "Using this much force could signal weakness to your enemies."

"Damn it, I don't care. I will prevail in the end," shouted Amel.

"It could backfire," cautioned Daniel. He ignored the knocking on the door.

Amel collected himself and smiled at Daniel, "I have the loyalty of Nebuzaradan. He is in full command of his troops. Whatever he orders they will obey, and no one can defy the strength and might of the Guard."

The knocking at the door intensified, prompting Daniel to rise from his chair and crack it open to see who had the temerity to interrupt a meeting with the Crown Prince. He saw Laconius, his chief of staff, who urgently whispered, "May I come in? I have news you both need to hear."

Daniel opened the door wider as he inquired of Amel, "May Laconius enter, Sire? He says he has news we need to hear."

Amel motioned him to enter the room, "Come in. It better be good as I'm in no mood for much else right now."

Daniel crossed back to his chair behind the table as Laconius hesitatingly entered and closed the door behind him. "My Lord," he said to Amel as he bowed then waited to be told to continue.

"So, speak," barked Amel.

"There was a ceremony at the temple last night honoring the Imperial Guard," Laconius nervously began.

"Yes, yes . . . I know about that," Amel retorted. "I was invited to attend but declined. Antiosyss' rituals are too much nonsense for me."

Laconius remained silent, not knowing how to proceed.

"Well? Go on," said the Crown Prince.

"During the course of the night, every commander—including Nebuzaradan—pledged allegiance to Marduk and specifically to follow Antiosyss' and his priesthood's leading. By doing so they were promised extraordinary, supernatural powers against their enemies."

"Nebuzaradan too?" asked Daniel, his ire beginning to rise.

"Yes, but not of his own free will," replied Laconius. "They—he—did so under duress. He was threatened . . . bullied by Antiosyss who preyed on his deep fear of the supernatural."

"Oh, that's typical priestly drivel," snorted Amel. "I'm sure Nebuzaradan didn't succumb to that."

"I wish it were other than what I've been told, Sire," responded Laconius, who then proceeded to recount how Marlee had tormented and brought the Supreme Commander to the point of trembling submission. When he had finished, Daniel and Amel sat in silence. The consequences of Nebuzaradan's defection hung over them like a suspended sword.

The tension in the room was excruciating . . . the air had become toxic. Laconius was so intimidated that he abandoned the room without asking leave to do so. Amel and Daniel remained alone . . . the walls closing in on them.

Finally, Amel broke the silence, slowly shaking his head from side to side, "I never thought Nebuzaradan would desert me. Never . . . after all the years he fought beside my father and me."

Daniel did not reply, He was thinking ahead to tomorrow's Governing Council meeting. The full force of the rebellion would manifest itself at that time.

"He must have been frightened beyond all human reason by the demons Antiosyss conjured," softly reflected Amel. "Nothing human could scare that man. I know that. I've seen him in battle." He looked up at Daniel and continued, "We are up against strange and powerful forces aren't we?"

Daniel nodded in affirmation, "It's going to come full force tomorrow at the Council meeting."

Amel-Marduk froze at the mention of the meeting which he had forgotten. He rose to his feet, "We may be at the end of the road, Governor. I am ashamed that I could not hold my father's kingdom together for him."

"There is still one thing we can hold onto," answered Daniel.

"No, we are finished," said Amel as he opened the door to leave.

"My Lord," said Daniel with sufficient command to make Amel stop and look at him. "God told your father that he would return to rule a kingdom stronger than ever when he recovered. That means it is not yet lost."

Amel smiled at Daniel, then turned and left.

~

As he did daily after finishing his lunch, Rymen strolled to the King's barn located on the palace grounds to check on the royalty's prize horses and cattle. He had spent the morning overseeing the vast herd of several thousand cattle and horses at the royal pastures outside the gates of Babylon. But priority was always given to the prize livestock at the palace because these were the foundation of the royal breeding program.

Ryman quickly walked through the barn checking the animals stabled in their stalls. Then he made his way to the outside pastures where, suddenly, something out of the ordinary caught his eye. In the pasture where the King was being kept, he saw Nebuchadnezzar standing upright, his arms on the top rail of the fence. For the past seven years, the King never walked or stood on anything but all fours like the other livestock. To see him now standing like a person was startling. He needed to check this out and hurriedly jogged towards the King.

As he neared Nebuchadnezzar, he slowed to a walk and stopped ten feet from him. This was his lord and master and to approach any closer was to court death, The King was mumbling . . . too soft to hear intelligibly. He looked at Rymen and stopped talking, his eyes wide and questioning.

"My Lord," bowed Rymen.

Nebuchadnezzar nodded his head up and down excitedly as though recognizing something long forgotten. He looked at Rymen and said, "Come here."

When Rymen did not move, he jumped up and down and shouted, "Come here!"

Rymen carefully walked to the King to stand on the opposite side of the fence, face to face. He extended his arm to stroke his hair as he did with all the horses and cattle under his care. The King reached out to touch him. At first Rymen jerked his arm backwards. Nebuchadnezzar said, "Sorry." Then, as Rymen put his hands back on the rail, the King said, "Please . . . I don't mean to scare you."

"You're talking," Rymen looked at him astonished.

"Haven't I always talked?" replied Nebuchadnezzar.

"Not for the past seven years," answered Rymen.

"What's going on?" queried the King. "Why am I here . . . in this pasture?" He ran his hands over his arms, torso and legs and asked, "Why do I look like this? What has happened to me?"

Rymen did not know how to answer or what to say. He had never spoken to the King in his life and now he was being asked to explain something to his ruler that, if he said the wrong thing, might jeopardize his life. And so he stood speechless, just staring at the bull who was morphing back into a human being.

Nebuchadnezzar started to climb over the fence, desperate to reclaim all the time he had lost. Rymen stepped back, fearfully. The King came up to him and grasped his arm, pleading, "I need to know what has happened to me. I can see my palace, but I don't know why I'm down here in the barn area. How long have I been here?"

The questions tumbled out of his mouth as with each one more of his senses came back to him. Realizing that the King truly did not know what had happened to him nor how long he had been living as a bull, Rymen began to tell him what he knew. He admitted that he did not know what triggered the King's transformation into a bull, but he could describe all that transpired the past seven years as he cared for him. As they talked, Rymen grew as excited as Nebuchadnezzar . . . both men happy to see a return by the King to normalcy.

Abruptly, Nebuchadnezzar stepped back from Rymen and held his arms out as he carefully examined his body. He asked, "Am I completely covered in hair as I think I am?"

"Yes, my Lord," laughed Rymen. "You are most certainly hairy."

"And my fingernails! They must be a foot long," chortled the King. "It's disgusting! Tell me, Rymen, do I smell as bad as I think I do?"

"You do, Sire," chuckled Rymen.

Over the next hour as they talked and Rymen helped bring Nebuchadnezzar back to his new reality as a human being, the two men relaxed with each other and developed a kinship. Amazement and hierarchy had given way to warm laughter and camaraderie.

"Rymen," said the King. "Take me to the barn and wash me . . . maybe brush out my hair . . . cut my nails. Look, even my toenails are long and ugly. I want to clean up before I see anyone."

Within an hour, Rymen at Nebuchadnezzar's insistence had bathed the King in the stall used for this purpose for the livestock. When he washed away all the dirt, he carefully brushed the hair covering the King's body. It sloughed off in large clumps to reveal smooth skin below. With each stroke, Nebuchadnezzar grew more excited seeing his skin return to normal.

The nails were a special challenge. They had become incredibly brittle and hardened like the hooves of horses. Rymen had to resort to the large clippers he used to trim the stock's hooves. Moreover, he had to go slowly so as not to accidently rip the nails from the King's fingers and toes. It took longer to clip the King'snails than it did to wash and brush out his matted hair.

Even so, it took several hours to remove the matting of hair that came with living in seven years of filth. Nebuchadnezzar was delighted at the result. Although he only had on a kilt around his waist that hung to just above his knees, he felt totally rejuvenated and was ready to go to the palace.

"Sire, you need a tunic or a robe . . . something to cover your body," suggested Rymen.

"You're right," answered Nebuchadnezzar. "Do you have anything here I can use?"

"Take my tunic," offered Rymen as he began to remove his outer garment.

"Stop that," said the King. "I'm not taking your clothes." He looked around the barn, walking up the corridor looking into the stalls and arriving at the tack room.

"I can just use one of these blankets," he said grabbing a light horse covering hanging on the wall. He wrapped it around himself, then, stopped in his tracks. Turning to Rymen, he asked, "How long did you say I thought I was a bull and lived in the pasture?"

"Seven years, my lord."

Nebuchadnezzar froze, his eyes suddenly wild with fear . . . then slowly . . . gradually, he understood. He dropped to his knees and looked upward, "Almighty God. God of the heavens and the earth. There is no one greater, even though I at one time thought I was."

The realization that Daniel's prophecy had been fulfilled by the taking away of his humanity was overwhelming. He began to tear at first, then convulsed into deep sobs that came from the recesses of his soul. Rymen looked on in amazement, speechless and powerless to move. To see this man feared above all men on earth on his knees crying like a child was more frightening than anything he had ever encountered.

"Forgive me, God, the ruler of all things. Forgive my pride. Forgive my arrogance," Nebuchadnezzar pleaded looking upward.

A new understanding began to dawn within Nebuchadnezzar as he realized he had been transformed into a new person. He stopped speaking. His sobbing ceased and his tears dried. For a full minute he knelt in place, feeling a new, warm presence invade his being. Slowly, he rose to his feet and said, "Thank you God. Thank you for new life."

He turned to Rymen who was still on his knees to find him staring, open mouthed, at him, "Come on, I must see my family."

He turned to walk out of the barn. Realizing Rymen was not beside him, he turned to find the herdsman still grounded to the middle of the barn's central walkway. He walked back to Rymen and threw an arm around his shoulders, lifting him up.

"I know this is a bit confusing for you. If I hadn't recalled Daniel's words to me, I'd be as bewildered as you." He squeezed Rymen's shoulders, smiling broadly, "But it has all come true. I am back to where this whole thing started seven years ago. Thank God, I now know who masters who." He began walking, bringing Rymen with him, "C'mon, Rymen. You have to take me to my family."

As they walked up the hill to the King's palace, Rymen started to chuckle. He tried to stop it but it only grew into louder laughter which was infectious. Soon Nebuchadnezzar was laughing as well and he did not know why.

"What are we laughing at?" asked the King.

"The most powerful ruler of the world covered in a horse blanket and led by his herdsman to his palace," grinned Rymen. He stopped and the two men looked at each other, doubling up in laughter. Nebuchadnezzar had never felt better. It had been a long time since he had enjoyed the simple gift of laughter.

~

In the King's palace, preparations were in full stride for the evening meal. The Queen had retreated to the magnificent garden that Nebuchadnezzar had built for her on one end of the palace spanning seven stories. Whenever she needed serenity to think clearly, she lost herself in the hanging gardens. They reminded her of her childhood home in the mountains of Mede.

Earlier in the day, Amel-Marduk had visited her quite distraught. She was well aware that strong forces sought to unseat Daniel from his governorship, but she was unprepared to hear that they had now turned against her son as well. When he lay in a coma from his injury, there had been overtures and suggestions that he should be replaced because he was incapacitated, but now that he was fully recovered and had resumed the throne it was startling to hear that a mutinous coup might unfold as early as tomorrow. With Nebuchadnezzar gone, it was left to her to save her son.

She had lost herself on the bottom level where the giant trees—some six feet in diameter and reaching fifty feet into the air—made her feel her humanity. It was her favorite place to wrestle with problems. But this one was so huge that no solutions easily came. Would that Nebuchadnezzar was in his right mind she reflected. None of this would be happening.

Unbeknownst to her, her husband was at that moment approaching the palace, his senses fully recovered. Before Rymen and Nebuchadnezzar had reached the steps leading to the entry, Zocor and a contingent of palace guards met them. He had been alerted by his men who had been guarding the King. He approached Nebuchadnezzar respectfully and bowed, "It is good to see you come back to the palace, my Lord."

"I've lost seven years, Zocor," replied the King. "After all that time, it is good to see you still in control of my personal guards and the palace. All is well?"

"Yes, Sire," replied Zocor. "I am very happy to see you . . . especially at this moment."

"Well, I don't wish to stand here any longer than I have to. I want to see my wife and family."

Nebuchadnezzar turned to Rymen, his arm extended, "Thank you. You may take your leave. Thank you for your care of seven years and for helping me clean up." As Rymen began to drop to his knees to bow, Nebuchadnezzar caught him by the arm in a clasp of friendship. "I mean that," he whispered, "thank you." Abruptly turning, he hollered, "Let's go in."

They climbed the steps and entered the central courtyard of the palace. The King lengthened his stride and charged through into the foyer as servants came running from all directions. A mixture of shock, surprise and relief flooded their faces. The King was back.

"Where's the Queen?" he asked. "I want to see her."

"She is in the gardens, my Lord," stammered one of the older servants who managed the staff, not sure if he was seeing an apparition of the King or the real man.

Nebuchadnezzar strode down the central hall that led to the hanging gardens he had built on the west side of the palace overlooking the Euphrates River. A contingent of guards and servants trailed behind him. He opened the doors that led into a lush, green forest. Stopping, he turned to his entourage and commanded, "Leave us alone. Wait here."

In a matter of a few yards, he was walking on a soft dirt path covered with tree bark. On each side were flowers and well trimmed bushes . . . ahead loomed the large cypress trees that he had brought from the northern mountains. He stopped when he reached the end of this level—the fourth of seven. He suspected

Amytis was on the first level. That was her favorite place . . . among the base of the large trees that so enamored her.

"Amytis," he called into the forest below.

The Queen stopped in place as she walked. She thought she heard her name called. Even more bizarre, she thought it was the voice of her husband. She shook her head. It could not be. I'm dreaming, she thought, perhaps hoping too much for an answer.

"Amytis, where are you?" he shouted again.

This time there was no question that it was her name and that it was Nebuchadnezzar. What had happened, she thought.

"I'm down here at the base," she answered as she stepped into a small meadow which provided a break in the trees.

As much as he strained to see her, from his vantage point she was hidden by branches and vegetation. "Stay there," he shouted. "I'm coming down. I'll find you."

There was a concealed staircase on the north side of the gardens which allowed access to all levels. Nebuchadnezzar ran to it and started down. When he reached the bottom level, he ran into the large grove of trees calling for her. Suddenly, she appeared in front of him . . . as beautiful as he remembered her. They collapsed into each other's arms, holding on for dear life. Seven long years had come to an end. They just wanted to feel each other's warmth . . . breathe together . . . share the joy of life they had mistakenly taken for granted in past years.

"I'm so glad you're back," said Amytis over and over as they embraced. "I have so much to tell you. You've come back at a critical time, and only you can save the day."

"What are you talking about?" asked Nebuchadnezzar. "Everything seems to be fine. The palace looks great. Zocor tells me all is well."

"Sit down," she said as she patted the grass. They both sat, their backs against one of the large trees. It was deceptively peaceful.

Amytis began to recount all that had happened over the seven years he had been in the pastures. When she got to the war with Egypt, Nebuchadnezzar exploded in anger that Pharaoh had the audacity to penetrate their border. She eased him back down with stories of the victory brought about by the Crown Prince's bravery and strategic decisions. Then it was on to the plots to overthrow Daniel and how Neriglissar and Antiosyss had used her to convince Amel to move away from Daniel and bring his opponents into his counsel. Amel's injury was the tipping point because he was in and out of consciousness for weeks, leaving the kingdom without a reigning member of the royal family. She emphasized how this had induced every member of the Governing Council to join the cabal that was to reach its zenith tomorrow.

"I didn't know what to do . . . how to help our son," she cried. "He is totally isolated. When Nebuzaradan took the pledge to do the bidding of Antiosyss, there was no one left to stand with Amel."

"We'll see about that," snapped Nebuchadnezzar, once more the King, quickly deserting his role as husband. He abruptly stood, slamming the tree with his fist, "How dare they challenge the house of Nebuchadnezzar?"

Rising and putting her arms around him, Amytis held him until the tension in his body dissipated. She lifted her head to look at him and said, "I know it's difficult for you to not act immediately to resolve this. I ask you to stay with me tonight. Think about all that I have told you. Don't act out of anger. Be quiet . . . reflect. Then, act . . . act out of a well planned strategy."

He chuckled, "You would make a good commander. But I'm glad you are my wife instead."

Amytis took his hand in hers and started to walk to the staircase, "You need a good bath and a haircut. Let's go up to our rooms."

"No, I don't," he replied. She looked at him quizzically, holding her nose. He quickly continued, "Really, I don't. Rymen washed me off in the barn. You should have seen the dirt that came off. And the hair! I was covered in hair which he was able to brush off in clumps."

"A king doesn't wear a horse blanket," she retorted.

Nebuchadnezzar had forgotten how he had been dressed and took a good look at himself. In spite of his anger and the impetus to lop off some heads, he had to laugh at the thought of charging into battle wearing a horse blanket. His laughter grew and, as with Rymen, infected Amytis who also started laughing. Maybe the seven years he spent with no concern other than where to graze next had done him good, he mused. He could not remember laughing like tonight since his boyhood.

~

It did feel good to remove the years of dirt and grime from the pores of his skin, not to mention shaving his face and trimming his beard and hair. As he put on the garments he had not worn in seven years, Nebuchadnezzar readily saw he had lost quite a few pounds. But it was good to be in his old clothes and to feel human once again. Of course, all the while the clean-up process was going on, he had been focused on the rebellion against his son and how best to deal with it. Even getting through the delicious meal Amytis had overseen for him was a struggle as it delayed taking action against the mutineers.

As they sat at the table at the end of their meal enjoying a variety of fruits along with a tankard of beer, Nebuchadnezzar finally brought up the subject they had avoided until now. His eyes hardened into steel as he stared straight ahead seeing nothing but the faces of those who would dare oppose his family.

"I'm going to take a regiment of the Imperial Guard and deal with Antiosyss and Neriglissar tonight."

Concerned that he did not have the full story, Amytis leaned across the table to put her hand on his arm, "You know what is best in these situations, but may I urge you to talk with Daniel and Amel first? They may give you information that will help you."

Nebuchadnezzar looked at her and slowly nodded his head, "What you say is wise. I should talk with them first." He got up from the table and started to walk to the door, "I'm going to send for them. We'll discuss this right now. Tonight!"

Nebuchadnezzar called for Zocor and told him to take a small guard unit to bring Daniel to the palace and, at the same time, go to the Crown Prince's palace to walk him over. The King gave strict instructions that they remain silent about his recovery and to say only that the Queen requested their presence.

Daniel arrived within the hour and was asked to wait in the sitting room of the King's private quarters. Five minutes later, Amel-Marduk was escorted into the room.

"Why are you here?" he asked Daniel, surprised to see him so late at night.

"The Queen summoned me," replied Daniel, "as I suspect she has you."

"She must have heard some new information she wants to share before tomorrow dawns," Amel said softly.

Before Daniel could reply, the doors flew open; in walked Nebuchadnezzar. To say they were shocked was to put it mildly. The King was the last person both men expected to see. Nebuchadnezzar walked directly to Amel, grabbing him by the shoulders and asked, "How are you, my son?"

Amel was speechless. He wanted to laugh, cry, and shout all at once. Instead, he froze in place . . . stunned by the coming back to life of his father after so many years during which he thought he'd never see him again as a rational human being, let alone restored to once more rule Babylon.

Nebuchadnezzar patted him on the shoulders then turned to Daniel, proffering his arm to clasp greetings, "Daniel, I know you've been through the fires of hell retaining this kingdom for me. Thank you."

Like Amel-Marduk, Daniel stood motionless, unable to reconcile where he knew the King was—in the pasture—with whom he saw standing in front of him.

Nebuchadnezzar laughed, tickled that his re-emergence had been kept a secret and that his presence unnerved them. He thought, *if this is the effect I have on my family and those I trust, we have no fear of those who oppose us.*

He threw an arm around Amel and drew him in close to hug him. That broke the ice. In seconds all three men were excitedly talking at once, joyful to see each other. The transformation from bull back to King was nothing short of amazing, and both Amel and Daniel spent the next several minutes just getting to know Nebuchadnezzar again as a man.

Finally, Nebuchadnezzar had them sit down. He asked for a review of all that had transpired over the past seven years. He wanted to hear it all and asked them to leave nothing unsaid. It was well past midnight when they finally arrived at Nebuzaradan's defection the night before. They warned the King of the likelihood of the palace revolt they expected to unfold at the Governing Council's meeting.

"Nebuzaradan folded?" asked the King in disbelief. "He's stood by me in battle for many years. The man is not afraid of anyone!"

"I suspect Antiosyss' threat to unleash the demons of Marduk finally got to him—that, plus the threat that he would be cursed with a debilitating illness," answered Amel.

'Hard to believe," quipped Nebuchadnezzar. "I didn't realize that he subscribed to the spirit world. All I thought he understood was life and death by the sword."

"Losing him meant losing the Imperial Guard and our remaining power base," said Amel.

"We haven't lost him!" snapped the King. "I'm sending Zocor for him immediately. He will not dare to put Antiosyss above me. We will get him back in place, and then we are going to battle. I want Zocor to tell him I have recovered and am the one sending for him. He needs to be thinking about how and where to place his allegiance on his trip here to the palace."

~

Upon learning the King had recovered and was back in control of Babylon, Nebuzaradan felt both a sigh of relief and a sense of foreboding. He wondered how much the King knew of the imminent rebellion and his own acquiescence to obey the priesthood. He arrived at the palace shortly after one in the early morning hours and was hastily taken to the King's private quarters. He walked into the room and immediately fell to his knees before Nebuchadnezzar who greeted him warmly. When he saw the Crown Prince and Daniel in the room, he grew concerned that this might be the end of the road for him. He was relieved to hear the next words come out of the King's mouth.

"Nebuzaradan, we have been through too many wars and victories for me to think you are not going to continue to stand beside me to dismiss this ridiculous rebellion I've been hearing about tonight."

"Yes, Sire," replied Nebuzaradan loudly, "we stand together." He had reasoned that it was better to die in the good graces of his King than to worry about things unseen and unknown. His decision made him feel like the man he was before that awful temple ceremony he endured.

"Good," said the King, pleased that his top military commander was back on track. "Now I want your input on what Amel and Daniel and I have been discussing. We must bring the sword down quickly. No mercy!"

There was no sleep for them that night as they planned the dismantling of the rebellion and disposition of its ringleaders.

~

The air was filled with anticipation, excitement building with every minute. Never had there been a Governing Council meeting that promised all the drama of a chariot race, be-heading, and coronation wrapped up in one event! Members with their adjutants began arriving almost an hour before the scheduled meeting time in order to socialize and jockey for position in the new regime. It was both a party and a carnival, and no one wanted to miss any opportunity to get close to the presumed emerging leaders of Babylon.

Neriglissar entered the assembly room fifteen minutes early with an entourage that had grown to proportions generally accorded royalty. Princess Kassaya was at his side, not one to miss the ascendancy of her husband to the ruling throne of Babylon. Dressed in eye-catching blue and purple robes befitting a king and carrying what looked like the royal scepter, Neriglissar looked every bit the role of ruler. All he needed to complete the picture were the crown and the throne, both soon to be his.

Beltekasmer and the wise men, magicians and astrologers had re-positioned themselves next to Neriglissar as they clearly saw the axis of power shifting his way. Dismissed by Amel as men no longer in touch with the planets and the stars and unable to foretell the future, they eagerly sought an alliance with a new leader who could restore their prestige.

Moving about the room warmly greeting everyone, Antiosyss knew his power base depended upon building bridges with all factions, no matter how small or large. He was determined to be the one most Council members thought of first when they needed help. As the time neared for the meeting to convene, he found his way to the other side of Neriglissar hoping to bask in some of his reflected glory. The pretenders to the throne were loudly visible, and no less were those currying favor with them.

As was his custom, Daniel entered the chamber at the last minute, taking his position in the Governor's chair. He was accompanied by Shadrach, Meshach and Abednego. No one bothered to speak with them or seek their attention. Everyone knew they were soon to be history.

The guards stamped their spears loudly on the marble floor signaling the entrance of the Crown Prince. A new feature was added today: a trumpet fanfare. Everyone assumed it was the doing of Neriglissar's entourage and smiled broadly at this audacious slap in the face of the entering Prince.

The doors were flung open and Zocor announced in a loud voice, "the King of Babylon." Defying convention, few members stood; most remained in their seats, still in conversation with colleagues, disrespecting the throne itself.

What happened next brought the party atmosphere to an abrupt standstill. For the first time in years there was genuine fear in the hearts of everyone present. Nebuchadnezzar dressed in his royal robes, wearing his crown and carrying the royal scepter, strode into the room. He grabbed a spear from one of the attending guards and threw it into the center oval of the room where it clattered noisily and slid to rest at the feet of Neriglissar.

"Silence!" he shouted, "and get on your feet!"

The King was back. The old King was back with all his power and fearsome aura. Those who were sitting scrambled to stand; conversations stopped in mid-sentence; smiles abruptly transformed into terror. Behind him stood Amel-Marduk, dressed as fine as his father and standing tall in his shadow. To his left was Nebuzaradan, the Supreme Commander of the Imperial Guard, in his full dress uniform.

Nebuchadnezzar advanced to the center of the room and slowly looked at every face as he turned a full three hundred and sixty degrees. He glared at each member, daring them to return his glance. For what seemed like hours, he surveyed the room and his subjects. Any thought of usurping the throne had long left the building replaced by fear for their lives.

"I am well aware of all that is going on in Babylon and what each of you hoped would take place today."

He let his words hang heavily in the air.

"You deserve death! For you to act in such an irresponsible and disrespectful manner to this throne and my family is unforgiveable. I assure you, some of you will not make it alive to evening."

No sooner had he said this than soldiers of the Imperial Guard began flowing through the doors, spreading out to circle the room. There was no question of where the seat of power now lay.

Nebuchadnezzar walked to stand directly in front of Antiosyss, pushing his scepter into his chest, "You are the viper spewing poison and fanning the flames of this rebellion since its inception. You are no longer worthy to live."

"Guards! Take this miserable, disgusting excuse for divinity away. You and your priesthood will be executed before the sun goes down."

As the soldiers herded the high priest and his attending priests out of the room, those next to them attempted to move away in hopes they would not be tainted by proximity. This, in turn, set in motion the dissembling of all factions eager to point fingers at others while distancing themselves from those who might be next in line of the King's wrath.

"Quiet!" yelled Nebuchadnezzar. "Nothing you do now will spare you. You should have thought of this months . . . years ago."

He moved to stand in front of Neriglissar and stood silently glaring at him. Neriglissar knew his hours were numbered. He could not look at the King; moreover, his knees were shaking. He was afraid he might not be able to remain standing.

"You!" snarled Nebuchadnezzar, striking his son-in-law's chest with the scepter and knocking the imitation one to the floor that was in Neriglissar's hands, "You are most despicable. I trusted you to marry my daughter. I trusted you with command of a division in the Imperial Guard long before you proved yourself worthy. And what do you do? You challenge my son's right to my throne and defy me! You will also die today."

"No," screamed Princess Kassaya bursting out of the group to stand by Neriglissar. She implored her father, grabbing his hands and begging, "Not him! He's my husband . . . the father of my children and your grandchildren. Demote him, take away his command . . . do whatever, but I beg you, please don't kill a member of your own family." She fell at his feet sobbing , her arms clutching the robe around his legs.

The King was torn. He wanted Neriglissar dead . . . but he could not ignore the pleas of his daughter for whom he had always had a special fondness. He looked down at her, then back at Neriglissar, and back again at Kassaya.

"I'll deal with you later," spat Nebuchadnezzar as he shook his daughter's arms loose from his legs and stepped forward to where his face was almost touching Neriglissar, "You live today, but you are no longer in charge of anything in this kingdom."

At that, Neriglissar's knees could no longer hold out and he fell to the floor in a faint. Disgusted at his weakness, Nebuchadnezzar moved away from him to go to Beltekasmer, Mysonus and the wise men.

"You! You sided with the wrong men. I'd have you killed right now except you're not worthy of my soldiers' energies. You are full of wrong information and have brought nothing to this kingdom in all the years I have known you. No, you are not going to die. But you will no longer suckle on the teats of the royal household. I banish you to the provinces. How you will live is your problem."

Out of the corner of his eye, Nebuchadnezzar saw Polynices and the leading merchants and growers of the city. They, too, deserved punishment. He walked to where they stood as a group and said, "I thought I could count on you, Polynices. You were always the man who said the right things . . . fawned over my decisions . . . supported me. How wrong I was about you! How dare you to be part of a rebellion when everything you possessed you acquired through my good graces? And you, Leandrus . . . .even you betrayed the throne you once supported! All out of fear of what these . . . these dung might do to you. Did you never stop to think of what I might do to you for your treasonous behavior?! You disgust me."

Nebuchadnezzar walked deliberately to the entry doors where Amel-Marduk and Nebuzaradan stood facing the room.

He turned to confront the Governing Council one last time, looking at them intently, "This meeting is over. This Council is over. It will be no more." He turned to leave, then hesitated and turned back, "Some of you may be no more. Don't ever challenge this house or this throne again."

The King turned and walked out, Amel and Nebuzaradan behind him. After a few moments to collect themselves, the members of the defunct Governing Council silently followed suit. They were simply glad to be alive.

~

Nebuchadnezzar's forces swung into action immediately in accordance with the plan he, Amel and Nebuzaradan had developed through the night. Within an hour of the Governing Council's adjournment, Imperial Guards surrounded the Temple of Marduk. Nebuzaradan took an elite regiment and entered the building ordering all priests immediately to the outer courtyard. The guards stormed from room to room, ensuring no one escaped. With over one-thousand priests serving in the temple, it took some time to empty the large building.

Nebuzaradan had his eye out for one person . . . the witch who attacked and frightened him the night he was coerced to defect to Antiosyss. When he didn't see Marlee among those in the courtyard, he ordered another search of the temple. They found her hiding in a closet in the high priest's preparation room. She did not come out easily. It took four soldiers to carry her outside and stand her before the Supreme Commander. When she saw him, she cackled, her face smirking, "You'll die before sunrise if you take me out."

Without missing a beat, Nebuzaraden smacked her across the face, knocking her unconscious.

"Take her to Antiosyss," he commanded the soldiers holding her. "I want them to watch each other die."

When they were all standing in the courtyard, Nebuzaradan had them separate themselves according to their function in the temple. Those who served in religious rituals were at the apex of the priesthood hierarchy. Below them were the scribes who maintained the written documents and historical tradition of the temple. Then came the attending priests who helped dress their seniors for rituals and who prepared the logistics for ceremonies. Finally, there was a large contingent of support staff, all of them bona fide priests. With the help of one of Antiosyss' key men who had turned on him, Nebuzaradan went through each group to identify those sympathetic to the high priest.

The process was laborious but essential in order to weed out those disloyal to the King. It was late afternoon when the last group had been vetted. Of the one-thousand plus priests serving the temple, two-hundred and thirty had been identified as untrustworthy. They were immediately taken to the ziggurat adjacent to the temple.

Nebuzaradan faced those remaining, addressing them sternly, "I believe each of you standing in this courtyard is worthy of continued service in the Temple of Marduk. There will be a complete change in your leadership; you will learn of it in the next few days. I urge you henceforth to focus only on your priestly role and duties. The King will not tolerate anyone seeking to make the priesthood a political platform for the purpose of gaining power. You have your god to serve, and that is your destiny. You have no role in civic or military affairs of the kingdom.

"Lest you are ever tempted to exceed your spiritual role, you will now move next door to the base of the ziggurat facing Procession Way. There, you will witness what fate brings to those who are treasonous," he concluded.

The Imperial Guard led them to the foot of the ziggurat where they were joined by thousands of Babylonians who had been encouraged to attend a special ceremony at sunset. The area surrounding the pyramid structure was completely full of people spilling out into Procession Way, seeking a glimpse of the shrine located on the top level soaring into the orange tinted sky.

A ram's horn sounded, the note sustaining loudly for almost a full minute signifying the start of the ceremony. Drummers around the edges of the sixth level of the ziggurat—directly below where the shrine stood—began to beat their drums. Giant flaming torches were solemnly carried by soldiers and placed around the shrine to allow those standing below to see. The cadence of the drums grew faster until the musicians' arms reached the point of exhaustion. On cue, it crashed to a thunderous finale.

As a trumpet flourish sounded from a chorus of trumpeters on the fifth level, the King stepped in front of the shrine. With one collective gasp, the crowds below surged forward to see their leader who had been so long out of public view. At first there was disbelief it was he. Then, a cry pierced the evening skies from high on the ziggurat:

"Forever live King Nebuchadnezzar."

It was picked up instantly by the thousands gathered at the base of the pyramid, the surprise on their faces turning into unabashed joy at seeing Nebuchadnezzar fully recovered and standing before them.

Nebuchadnezzar held up his hands asking for silence. The crowd complied. In a loud voice amplified through a large megaphone cone specially constructed for public ceremonies by the priests, the King spoke, "I am fully restored to health and once again sit on the throne of Babylon."

The masses below roared their approval and broke into sustained applause. This outpouring of support and enthusiasm pleased Nebuchadnezzar to no end. A smile crossed his otherwise stern face and quickly disappeared. He needed to get on to the business at hand.

"I have recovered from my illness only to find treason in the streets of Babylon. A plot to overthrow my house and my son, the Crown Prince, was raging in the higher echelons of this kingdom, consuming even the Governing Council of Babylon! Central to this rebellion was Antiosyss, the high priest of this great temple, the Temple of Marduk."

Nebuchadnezzar paused to let this news sink in. No one ever challenged the priests and certainly not the high priest. He knew this was new and potentially dangerous ground he was treading because of the fear the populace had for the gods and the magical feats regularly exhibited by Antiosyss and his senior lieutenants.

"I will not let treason gain hold in Babylon. Tonight, Antiosyss and those priests disloyal to the throne will be put to death. You will witness it."

He paused and gestured to the seven-hundred plus priests remaining standing at the foot of the ziggurat, "Most of the temple's priests are honest, worthy men. You see the vast majority of them below . . . standing with you. These are worthy servants of the temple and of Marduk. They will live and continue to serve. Respect them for their allegiance to my family and to me."

A murmur of approval rose from the thousands watching the proceedings and now focused on the priests at the foot of the ziggurat. There was relief that there was not going to be a total decimation of the priesthood. This would have left no one to make supplication to the gods for good crops, good health and good life.

"I want you to look up. See the faces of treason and rebellion."

As he spoke, soldiers brought Antiosyss to kneel at the front of the shrine. Marlee was dragged out, bound in ropes, beside him. The two-hundred thirty dissident priests knelt along the ziggurat facing the crowd. They were blindfolded. Behind each priest stood a soldier.

Nebuchadnezzar's voice grew in intensity, "Soldiers of the Imperial Guard, take up your swords."

Each soldier withdrew his sword from its scabbard and held it high above his head. The two men standing on either side of Antiosyss and Marlee did likewise.

The King screamed, "Traitors to Babylon, to me, and to God...DIE!"

The swords came down in unison on two-hundred thirty-two necks. The heads neatly severed from their respective spines rolled down the ziggurat to the level below with some bouncing onto levels further down. Blood gushed everywhere. Nebuchadnezzar intended it to be a grisly sight, not soon to be forgotten by anyone who witnessed it. Nebuzaradan only had his eyes fixed on one. When he saw Marlee's head vault all the way to the third level before coming to a stop, he was vindicated.

A deathly silence fell on the masses. And then . . . the drums began a slow, dirge-like cadence as people slowly withdrew, retreating to their homes. The sun had long set and darkness hung like fog in the streets. The flaming torches on the ziggurat gave rise to an eerie setting as their rays flickered on the heads and dead bodies strewn along the front of a magnificent building reserved for religious homage to their god.

If anyone looked up at the shrine, they failed to see the King. He had left with the downward fall of the blades.

~

Never in the history of the city did news and gossip travel as fast as it did that night and into the next day. News normally took three days to travel the enormous breadth of Babylon's city limits; but word of the King's execution of the senior echelon of priests made its way to every corner of the city in less than twenty-four hours. Everyone waited to see what would transpire next.

Following the mass execution at the ziggurat, without exception every member of the Governing Council hurried to their homes, hoping to escape the King's wrath but anticipating the worst. Huddled with their families, they spent a sleepless night, not knowing what the next day might bring. A few considered fleeing the city under cover of darkness, but concluded they would be chased and arrested, probably compounding any punishment the King meted out to them. It was a long night.

Nebuchadnezzar was a man of action. He would not rest until every traitor had been exposed and punished. He called Nebuzaradan and Zocor to the palace shortly after dawn to lay out the schedule of meetings he sought to have that day with every member of the defunct Governing Council. He instructed them to send soldiers within the hour to the houses of the members to accompany them back to the spacious anteroom outside the King's throne room where they would sit until called. It was his intent to personally interrogate each one before the lunch hour. The three men remaining in the kingdom whom he still trusted would join him but only he would assess everyone's loyalty; only he would determine their sentences.

One by one, they entered what had been their Council's meeting room and approached the King seated on his throne. Nebuzaradan was seated on one side with Amel-Marduk and Daniel on the other. A full contingent of palace guards stood along the walls. As in years past, there was only one ruler in charge of the kingdom.

The King had already concluded that Antiosyss and Neriglissar were the root of the rebellion. He previously had banished the courtiers and wise men from the city, so now his intent was to determine which of the remaining members were simply caught up in the euphoria of ousting Daniel as opposed to those who actually harbored disloyalties to the Crown Prince and the royal family. For the majority, he was able to discern their intentions quickly and reprimanded them with stern warnings. In other instances where lessons needed to be taught, he assessed harsh financial penalties. By the end of the morning, only three men remained with whom he had to deal more severely.

Polynices and Nebuchadnezzar were both in their early sixties and had a long history together over the decades that Babylon had grown into a magnificent city. The King had never doubted Polynices' loyalty in the past, making it all that much more difficult for him to dispense an appropriate judgment. Polynices stood before the throne, uncertain of his fate.

"How could you defy me?" thundered Nebuchadnezzar. "You were often my confidant . . . the man I trusted most. How could you go against my son and my appointed governor?"

"I would never defy you, my King," countered Polynices. "I truly felt Daniel's ability to govern had been weakened and I sought what would be best for the kingdom."

"No!" roared Nebuchadnezzar. "You had no concern for the kingdom. You only did what you felt best positioned you in the new ruling authority. Why didn't you stand by my son? How could you be loyal to me by opposing him?"

"He was seriously injured and could not rule when needed," replied Polynices. "I wanted more than anything for him to take control of what I perceived to be a dissembling empire in the hands of Daniel."

"Well, you were dead wrong!" said the King. "The empire only appeared to be crumbling because you and all your traitorous friends wished it to fall apart."

"You were caught up in their lies!" sneered Amel-Marduk, speaking for the first time. "Daniel's integrity never wavered, unlike yours."

Ignoring the Crown Prince, Polynices kept his eyes on the King, "Sire, I beg you to consider all the years I have served you faithfully. I may have erred in my judgment this time, but that is but a speck in our long friendship."

Nebuchadnezzar stood up and pointed his finger at Polynices, "You are not my friend, and your error in judgment is fatal. Everything you own I will give to Nolter, a man more worthy of my trust than you have ever been."

"But, my King—" stammered Polynices, falling to his knees.

"Quiet!" shouted Nebuchadnezzar. "You are henceforth banished from Babylon. Take your family and go north . . . into the mountains near the Medes. I expect you to be gone by tomorrow morning."

He turned to Zocor and ordered, "Get him out of here. See that he is gone from the city no later than tomorrow."

Antiobud was ushered into the room next. As the son of Antiosyss he fully expected to be dealt with severely but hoped, that at the very least, his life would be spared. He approached the King and fell to his knees pleading, "Oh King, live forever. Do not condemn me for my father's actions. I beg for your justice."

"You will receive justice," Nebuchadnezzar quietly replied.

Relief flooded over him. He lifted his eyes to look at the King and said, "Thank you, my Lord . . . thank you."

"I know how you influenced the Governing Council . . . spreading the rumor that Daniel was mentally unbalanced . . . touched, if you will. I have heard all about your underhanded dealings on your father's behalf. Yes, you will receive justice."

Just as quickly as the warmth of relief had enveloped Antiobud, a hard chill now made its way over his body. Knowing his destiny, Antiobud began to shake uncontrollably.

"Take him out of here," commanded Nebuchadnezzar. "Behead him and bury him. No need to create any further unrest with the priesthood. Tell them he has been rightfully executed."

After Antobud had been dragged from the room, Nebuchadnezzar signaled Zocor to bring in the last Governing Council member. He had deliberately waited to decide Neriglissar's fate until he had heard from everyone else the extent of his son-in-law's involvement in the cabal that threatened his throne.

Not one to back down, Neriglissar was dressed in all the finery his rank as a senior commander in the Imperial Guard accorded. He came through the doors confident, prepared to re-join the royal family thanks to the intervention of his wife, Nebuchadnezzar's only daughter.

He approached the throne and saluted smartly, "Oh King, live forever."

A smile crossed Nebuchadnezzar's face as he beheld the arrogance and defiance of a man who would be king. In an instant, the smile became a dark frown as he spoke, each word delivered with the intensity of a hurled spear, "Finally . . . we come to the core of treason."

"No, Sire," quickly replied Neriglissar. "It was I who did everything in my power to quell Antiosyss. He was bloodthirsty. He had lost all reason in his zeal for power."

"Stop right there," ordered Nebuchadnezzar. "Do you really think I am a fool?"

"Of course not, my King and father," answered Neriglissar. "I just want you to know the truth . . . what took place behind closed doors."

"I know the truth," snapped the King. "It does not reside in you."

Turning to Nebuzaradan, Nebuchadnezzar asked, "What do you think I should do with this piece of dung?"

"Put him to death," replied Nebuzaradan without a moment's hesitation. "He defied your authority. He defied Daniel as Governor of the land. And he defied me as the Supreme Commander of the Imperial Guard. Death can be the only right and just decision."

"I agree," said the King. "It seems the only question is what kind of death . . . how to make it commensurate to the scope of his crime."

The King looked back with disgust at Neriglissar who stood still, refusing to beg for mercy in favor of dying with the dignity his office deserved.

"Daniel," the King said as he turned to his Governor, "what's your verdict?"

Daniel hesitated, then, spoke slowly and thoughtfully, "My King, this man is a traitor and has been disloyal to your throne. Of that there is no question. At the same time, he is a member of your family albeit by marriage. He is a member of the royal household as are his children and wife whom you love and would not wish to harm. I would not favor death for this reason. Why should his punishment incur severe hurt on members of your family?"

"What would you have me do?" curtly retorted the King.

"My Lord, I recommend banishment to the outer provinces and stripping him of his rank within the Imperial Guard."

Nodding his head in agreement, Amel-Marduk spoke, "Father, I agree with Daniel. As much as Neriglissar deserves to die, why should we continue to hurt our own who are closest to us? I don't want my sister to hate you—or me, for that matter— the rest of our lives. I don't want to face my nephews and niece in the years ahead knowing I was one of those who killed their father. I think Daniel has offered a good solution that duly punishes Neriglissar without also punishing us."

Nebuchadnezzar looked at the three men who sat with him, then at Neriglissar. He struggled with his emotions. No one spoke. For the first time, Neriglissar had a spark of hope his life might be spared but he refused to show it. He could feel the King's eyes staring at him but he refused to return his gaze.

They sat . . . and waited . . . waited for the King to make his decision.

"All right," said Nebuchadnezzar loudly as he stood up. "I will spare his life, but I don't ever want to see your face again," he spit the words out directly in Neriglissar's face. "Make your way to the southwest province to live near my enemies where you rightfully belong."

The King paused, then smiled at an idea that suddenly struck him. "Take a few squads of soldiers and see if you can keep the border secured," Nebuchadnezzar sarcastically snarled. His son-in-law blinked and swallowed, knowing full well he needed to remain silent or this judgment could change in an instant.

"Get him out of here," the King yelled as he headed for the door.

~

No one had changed the lives of the citizens of Babylon for the better than King Nebuchadnezzar. Three generations of

Babylonians had seen first-hand what was once a functional but mundane city flower into a spectacular metropolis known throughout the world for its magnificent buildings and riches. Life had been good even for those dwelling in the outer provinces and rural areas. As the abundance of the city dwellers grew, so did the holdings of those scattered throughout the empire as they fed the budding city's insatiable appetite for good food, beer, clothing and jewelry.

While thousands had seen the King at the bloody massacre of the priesthood on the ziggurat, they were but a tiny part of the city's population. As word filtered throughout the city and into the rural farms and towns surrounding Babylon, excitement at the King's return quickly built. Everyone wanted to see the King for themselves . . . to catch a glimpse of the man-god to whom they owed their bountiful existence. They poured into the city and onto the streets surrounding the palace grounds which began to overflow with citizens who hoped for a glimpse of the long absent King. It was not enough to hear he had returned; they needed to see him for themselves.

Concerned about the growing influx of people on the streets, Zocor asked for an audience with Daniel in the late afternoon three days after the King's public emergence at the ziggurat. He walked into the Governor's office and got right to the point, "Governor, the streets outside the palace walls cannot hold any more people. They are clamoring to see the King for themselves . . . to witness that he is alive."

"Given what we've been through, that's a good thing, isn't it?" replied Daniel looking up from his scattered desk.

"Well . . . yes, but I'm worried about the King's safety," answered Zocor. "At some point, too many people in tight spaces can be dangerous . . . especially if the only way out is through the gates to the palace or over the walls."

"I see your point," mused Daniel. "So, what do we do? Take the Imperial Guard and clear the streets?" He shook his head and added, "That's not going to do any good for this nation's morale . . . not after the past few years."

"I was thinking, Governor, that a large celebration might be in order . . . perhaps a parade led by the King down Procession Way and even across the bridge to the western part of the city . . . the new city. If people can see him, they'll be satisfied. They want to see their King alive, well, and once more in full command of the kingdom."

Daniel looked up at Zocor with surprise, "That's a very good idea, Captain."

He stood and began to pace the room as he mused and talked, "A celebration of the King's recovery from his illness and return to the throne is just what Babylon needs! Not only will the people get to see him, but a celebration will put to rest any remaining resistance harbored by our enemies within our borders and will be a show of strength to foreign powers. I like this."

Pleased that his idea had been well-received, Zocor left the palace and went to shore up the guards at the gates, particularly the main entry off Procession Way.

Daniel called in his aides and began planning a citywide celebration. When he had the details in place, he hurried over to the King's palace and asked to see him. Nebuchadnezzar was still second-guessing himself about the decisions he had made concerning the Governing Council members, especially sparing Neriglissar's life. When he saw Daniel enter his sitting room with a smile on his face, he was eager to hear the good news it portended.

"Daniel, it's good to see a smile on your face again."

"Sire, Zocor has suggested a marvelous idea that I want to share with you," Daniel enthusiastically said, eager to enlist the King's support. As he reviewed the plans he had developed for a massive celebration honoring the King's return to health and the throne, he began to convince Nebuchadnezzar of the value of the idea.

Soon, Nebuchadnezzar was adding to the strategy and taking ownership of the festivities. They worked into the evening, bringing Amel-Marduk into their planning as well as Daniel's key aides. Given that envoys from Egypt and Assyria were presently in the city, they decided that the event should take place soon to take advantage of the presence of their neighbors to the west and north. They also needed time to disseminate the news to those living in the city in addition to the towns within a hundred miles of Babylon. The celebration was set for five days hence.

~

There had never been a party like this in anyone's memory. The closest anything had come was when the city welcomed its victorious troops home from war and, perhaps, the coronation of Nebuchadnezzar when his father died. But that was so many years ago, most people had no memory of it.

The day began with free breakfasts supplied by the King in the eight quadrants of the city. Beer and baked breads and pastries had been set up at over eighty serving stations well before dawn. Throughout the morning, throngs of people crowded the tables. Never did they run out of food or drink even into late morning when the city began to gravitate to Procession Way for the parade and a chance to see the King.

At the palace, a sumptuous meal was served to over one thousand guests in the courtyard surrounding Nebuchadnezzar's private palace on the Euphrates River. The foreign ambassadors who were in the city were in attendance as were the leading citizens of Babylon from all walks of life. Surprisingly, most of the members of the former Governing Council were included, a smart political gesture suggested by Daniel and endorsed by the Crown Prince. Key commanders of the Imperial Guard joined priests from the temple, and both mingled on equal footing with artisans, architects, merchants, growers, and provincial officials who had been invited from out of town. It was a time of merriment, good food, and good will as for the first time in his life the King put aside his warrior face in favor of being the beneficent ruler.

Just before noon, those participating in the parade excused themselves to assemble at the Ishtar Gate on the north central wall outside the palace grounds. There, two thousand premier foot soldiers of the Imperial Guard led by five-hundred troops on horseback were waiting. Banners suspended high on poles carried by the soldiers added a colorful gaiety. Musicians interspersed throughout the troops ensured there was always music in the air as the procession proceeded.

King Nebuchadnezzar insisted that his son ride with him in his chariot and that Daniel be in a chariot directly behind him. If a message was going to be sent, he wanted no one to miss it. They stepped into their chariots waiting on the palace grounds. Usually the King's chariot was a cut above the others, signifying the presence of royalty. Today, however, the artists and craftsmen of the palace had redesigned both. The King's chariot was painted bright red and accented by white decorative scrolls. The symbols of the King's authority—the crown, scepter, and throne—were beautifully carved into the chariot's sides and emblazoned with gold foil on which the sun ricocheted majestically. No less beautiful than the King's chariot, Daniel's vehicle was painted deep blue—the favored color of the Babylonian people. The symbols of his office were affixed to the sides and painted royal red.

Zocor commanded an elite corps of the palace guards surrounding the two vehicles. They moved into the center of the assembled troops and the parade began. The procession traveled the road running beside the north wall until it reached Sin Street, where it turned south. Cheering masses of people crowded both sides of the parade route, waving banners distributed the night before. The crowd screamed as the King rode by. As the parade neared the southern city wall, it turned west on Zababa Street and finally reached Procession Way to head north towards the Temple of Marduk.

As the chariots turned onto Procession Way, Nebuchadnezzar leaned into his son remarking, "You did a great job on this magnificent avenue. The gold lions are outstanding."

Amel beamed as praise from his father had been little and far between throughout his life. "Thank you," he said looking at the King. "I learned from the master."

With so much open space on both sides of this great boulevard, the crowds instantly grew geometrically in size. The noise was deafening as they marched along. An hour into the parade, they arrived at the grand street separating the Temple of Marduk from the ziggurat. They intended to make an appearance in the new city which lay across the Euphrates River, so they proceeded west on Adad Street over the large bridge that spanned the river and crossed into the western half of Babylon. The crowds were equally large and noisy, grateful to see their king.

The afternoon had become long and everyone was tired. But the roar that greeted them once they re-crossed the river and made their final turn onto Procession Way energized the troops and the King. They picked up the pace and shortly found themselves back in front of the palace grounds by the Ishtar Gate where it had all begun.

The crowning event of the day would soon take place. Zocor and his guards smartly made a path for the two chariots which entered the palace gates and stopped at the steps leading up to the royal palace that fronted Procession Way. Waiting palace guards fell in place on foot around Nebuchadnezzar, Amel, and Daniel as they made their way up the massive steps to the imposing entrance. Meanwhile, the Imperial Guard allowed the crowds to swarm onto the large avenue to get a closer view of the King. People pressed from all sides as those standing on the side streets now found opportunity to join others looking up at the King.

The King's special guests for the earlier breakfast had been positioned on the steps to both sides of the central stairway. All were in place as planned. The chant began, "Oh King, live forever. Oh King, live forever." Tens of thousands filled Procession Way and the side streets, picking up the mantra as it echoed in all directions to fill the city.

"Oh King, live forever. Oh King, live forever."
When Nebuchadnezzar reached the top of the stairs, he stepped onto a large podium built for the occasion. Behind him was placed his throne. The Crown Prince stood to his right; Daniel stood to Nebuchadnezzar's left.

It was an amazing sight; thousands of people in every direction . . . chanting and cheering. The rays of the sun now low in the west reflected off the buildings adding to the colorful spectacle of the event. If ever Nebuchadnezzar had a reason to swell with pride, this was it.

The King raised his hands and the crowd responded with a roar. He held them high for a few seconds then began to lower them down, asking for silence. It took a bit of time, but eventually the city quieted. The special megaphone used by the priests for outdoor ceremonies had been brought to the palace and now was placed before the King.

Nebuchadnezzar addressed his subjects telling them he was glad to be back, healthy and fully recovered. He recounted all that had happened during the seven years of his illness . . . how the Crown Prince had led a victorious campaign against Egypt but had stopped short of invading their neighbor as Babylon preferred to live in peace. His eyes burned into those of the Egyptian envoy as he spoke. He hinted that there had been unrest among the higher echelons of government, especially after Amel-Marduk's injury and narrow escape from death. Credit was paid to Daniel's extraordinary skill and wisdom keeping the kingdom on track during this period. He ended by openly reporting on the insurrection led by Antiosyss and how he had dealt with the traitors. The kingdom was secure, he assured his people.

It had been a long day and Nebuchadnezzar sensed it was time to bring the celebration to a close. He stopped speaking for a moment and scanned the vast crowd. He then signaled Amel to join him on the podium. As the Crown Prince stepped up, the crowd began to cheer.

Nebuchadnezzar lifted his arms to ask for quiet. He firmly grasped the arms of his son and said, "This is your next King. When I die, this man will be your ruler. Accord him the honor you give me."

The masses erupted: "Long live the Prince. Long live the Prince." Again, the chant spread quickly throughout the city as everyone joyously joined the refrain. Babylon was safe once again, and promised to be for the years to come with this succession firmly in place.

Nebuchadnezzar looked down at Daniel and smiled. It was his turn. He stepped off the podium and went to stand by his Governor. He motioned for silence. When the crowd had complied, with his left hand he clasped Daniel's right hand and lifted their arms high into the air.

"This is my Governor. Long may he live."

By now, the crowd was ready to pick up any chant and it started immediately, "Long live the Governor. Long live the Governor."

Nebuchadnezzar smiled broadly at the crowd and then at Daniel to whom he quietly said, "Thank you, Daniel, for giving me my kingdom back."

Daniel looked the King straight in the eye and replied, "I was but a tool. Thank Almighty God in heaven, not me."

Nebuchadnezzar slowly nodded, then turned back to face the crowds below. He gestured for silence. By now, they knew the routine and quieted quickly to hear his next words.

"I once thought I was above the gods as I reveled in this magnificent city that I built over the years. Seven years ago, I learned the most important lesson of my life. There is a God greater than me . . . than all of us. I learned about this God from Daniel. It took seven years for it to sink in, but it finally did. For all that we have as Babylonians . . . for all our good fortune . . . I ask you to honor the King of the gods."

The chant began, "Honor to the King of the gods." It swelled in volume as it filtered out onto the streets and to the very walls that surrounded the city. Daniel could not believe what he was hearing. As he listened, tears began to trickle down his cheeks. Not since he had been taken into captivity in Jerusalem almost fifty years ago had he expected to hear his God honored by his captors. He looked up at the sky and smiled: the restoration of Babylon was, indeed, complete.

Chapter Thirteen
THE WINDS OF CHANGE
564 BC

Amel-Marduk was pleased with the progress made on the new central market. He stepped away from the table which held his drawings and plans to stroll into the cavernous atrium that was the centerpiece of the structure. Magnificent, he thought as he swiveled to take in the stalls spreading outward like spokes in a wheel.

After all the starting and stopping that this project had endured the past few years, it was finally taking shape and rising from the ground in grand style. Once his father had regained his sanity and was ruling Babylon, things improved overnight. The complainers had stopped whining, the slackers got back to work, and the priests re-focused on temple ceremonies and rituals rather than politics. The result was an energized population that began to drive commerce once again—just four months since Nebuchadnezzar had returned to the throne.

While Amel was not his father, there were lessons to be learned from a leader who ruled according to his own vision and not by the advice of others. His father was single-minded in how the kingdom should function. He did not waver in his decision-making. Those who produced results were amply rewarded; those who did not failed to curry favor with the King. Amel needed to be as hard as Nebuchadnezzar even if it wasn't in his nature. While he demanded excellence, his empathic nature dictated his behavior . . . not the goals to be achieved. He never failed to see extenuating circumstances that might cause a subordinate to underachieve, and therefore he was too willing to forgive. This had brought him no end of trouble during his father's illness, and he was determined it would not happen again.

Amel greeted the laborers who were working nearby, encouraging them by saying how pleased he was that they were close to completing the job. He was standing physically dead center in the project, so he decided to check on progress at the loading dock on the river where most produce and goods would be off-loaded to merchants and carried to their stalls. The dock was well constructed of stone to ensure it would stand for decades. The craftsmanship was everything he hoped it would be. Even the loading ramps extending like the many legs on a centipede were strongly hinged to accommodate every abuse misdirected barges might subject them to over the course of many years.

As he turned to walk back from the river to his plans table, he saw Daniel entering the construction site with several of his senior administrators.

"If you don't mind, stay there, Sire," called out Daniel. "I want to see the dock for myself."

Amel stopped and waited as the Governor and his party quickened their pace to join him. Both men extended their arms in a clasp of friendship. Ever attentive to the protocol of royalty, Daniel bent down on in one knee in deference to the Prince. He was but an employee; Amel was the blood extension of the King.

Amel pulled Daniel to his feet, always pleased to see him take an interest in his building projects, "To what do I owe the favor of your visit?"

"I always thought building the central market on the banks of the Euphrates was brilliant," replied Daniel. "It makes the transport of goods so much more efficient no matter their origin. I commend you for sticking to your original plans even in the face of the heated opposition that came your way from the merchants."

"Change is difficult," answered Amel with a smile, "but, once we try something new and find it works better than the old, it's easier to swallow."

"I want to see the loading dock," said Daniel.

The men walked back to the river where Amel explained how barges would be channeled into the ramps where their goods would be unloaded onto the docks and, from there, wheeled in carts to the appropriate stalls. Daniel was intrigued with the engineering Amel had used to solve logistical problems while speeding up the movement of product. Following the path of an imaginary product making its way to a retail stall, they explored the back alleyways the carts bearing goods and produce would take to make delivery out of sight of the customers who would fill the wide streets in front of the selling stalls. The intent was that the delivery of goods should never interfere or impinge on the passageways of the buying customers.

"This is incredible!" exclaimed Daniel at the end of the tour. "Just when Babylon's commercial activity is surging forward, this market gives us so much capability to distribute and sell more. We should have many years of growth ahead of us before this reaches its capacity."

"I think you are right," said Amel. "I designed it for the long run. We should be well protected for decades."

"The King will be well pleased when he sees what you have done. You are more than equal to him in design and building prowess," grinned Daniel as he once again bowed before the Crown Prince. Shadrach and Abednego who had accompanied Daniel to the project nodded in agreement, offering their praise and congratulations on a project so well thought out.

As Daniel prepared to leave, Amel grabbed him by the arm and asked him to send his entourage on without him. Nodding his head in agreement, Daniel told his men to go on back to the palace offices . . . that he and the Crown Prince wished to speak alone. A small squad of guards remained behind while the others left the site.

"Let's sit," Amel suggested as he led Daniel to the table bearing all the plans.

Amel called for some refreshment from his staff who accompanied him everywhere he went, and ushered Daniel to one of the chairs by the table. From here, they could see the entire project site which was quite expansive. To the north, the roof was starting to be attached; elsewhere they could see the intricate supporting structure of pillars and columns that defined the sales stalls. They sat in silence for a few minutes, taking it all in.

Maximillan approached with goblets of cold cider, offering them to the two men. Daniel immediately took a sip as the day was hot. "Refreshing," he said. "Thank you, Maximillan. This provides a perfect ending to a perfect visit."

Amel laughed. Maximillan smiled gratefully and slipped off to give the men their privacy.

"What did you wish to speak to me about, my lord?" asked Daniel in between sips.

"It's somewhat delicate," replied Amel. "I don't really know where to start other than to just tell you. I think I have fallen in love with Dorcas."

"What?" choked Daniel who had just swallowed a mouthful of cider. "You are not serious, Sire? I mean . . . this is . . . "

"Inappropriate," Amel finished the sentence. "I know, I know. It's impossible for anyone in the royal bloodline to marry a common citizen let alone a servant . . . or even worse, a Jewish slave. That's why I wanted to speak with you."

"I don't know what to say," mumbled Daniel utterly flummoxed by what he was hearing. He was uncomfortable talking about this. After all, Amel-Marduk was his next King.

"Daniel, I know that my bringing this up to you puts a great stress on you. But you are the wisest man I have ever known. Moreover, you are a man who enjoys a special relationship with the gods . . . even the King of the gods. I could never talk about this to anyone else . . . you know that! I trust no one else."

Amel fell silent. Daniel's mind was racing. He had been asked in a straight forward way for his counsel by the Crown Prince; it was his responsibility to respond in like manner. But there were so many complications to this. How would the King react? How would Babylon react to such a cultural divide within the royal palace? This could start all the trouble up again, and the nation was still fragile.

Finally, Daniel spoke, "My Lord, I well understand your affection for Dorcas. She nursed you back to health when everyone other than your mother had given up on you. She is loyal and trustworthy. There is nothing about her to not love and adore except . . . ."

He left the sentence unfinished, hanging in the air.

"She is a Jewish slave," finished Amel ironically. "She is not of my social standing. She's not worthy of my love."

"Yes and no," said Daniel. "She is worthy of your love. She has earned that. But she is not worthy of being your wife by virtue of her birthright and lowly place in Babylonian culture."

"What about you?" retorted Amel. "You're a Jew! You were a slave! Daniel, look at you now. You are the Governor of the greatest empire in the world. You direct the affairs of Babylonians, powerful and lowly. Are you worthy of this office?"

Daniel hesitated before replying. He turned to Amel, looking him directly in the eyes, "No, I am not. It is only by the will of God."

"So," replied Amel, "can your God will to make my union with Dorcas worthy?"

Again, Daniel waited to respond. They were wading in deep waters. He did not want to send any signals that could be misinterpreted. What to do or say? he thought.

"My Lord, with God anything is possible. I cannot deny or affirm that He might bless your marriage to Dorcas. All I can say is go slow. Be careful. Don't surprise your father, the King. Do not act in haste. Perhaps, this is a union made in heaven . . . or maybe it's not. I don't know."

"I had hoped for better counsel than this, Daniel," said Amel his shoulders drooping disappointed by the results of this conversation.

"I am truly sorry, my Prince," answered Daniel. "Dorcas is a woman of the highest integrity. You can find no better for your wife. I only fear the consequences that might erupt because of the great disparity between you."

"I love her," simply said Amel. "What more is there to a marriage?"

Daniel sat silently, eyes forward. After several minutes, he rose and bowed to the Prince, "I must take my leave. I appreciate your candor with me this afternoon. I will hold this conversation in highest confidence. Let us both give this some thought. The import and consequences of your pending decision are huge. I believe Dorcas would make a wonderful wife and partner for you. I only fear the reaction of everyone else."

He stepped forward and grasped Amel's arm, then concluded, "I honor you as my ruler. I also honor God as my Master. I shall pray for resolution and for your happiness. Meanwhile, go easy. I say this as a friend."

Amel nodded. Then Daniel leaned in and grasped him with both arms in a warm embrace. As much as he tried not to, Amel felt himself tearing up.

~

All was quiet for several weeks. Then one morning, Daniel was abruptly summoned by the King. He went directly to the King's palace where he was ushered into the grand sitting room where the King received family members, friends and special guests. It was curious that Nebuchadnezzar asked to meet him here rather than in the King's quarters in the royal palace as that is where business affairs were conducted. He was a bit startled to see Amel waiting in the room and immediately jumped to the conclusion that the King had found out about his intent to marry Dorcas. This meeting could only be trouble.

"Good morning, Sire," greeted Daniel as he approached the Crown Prince bending on one knee.

"Good morning, Daniel," answered Amel. "I suppose that you, like me, have no idea why we were called here this morning so early."

Daniel nodded, and then stepped closer, "You didn't mention Dorcas to him, did you?"

Amel laughed, "No. That secret is between you and me." He looked quizzically at Daniel and then in the direction of the door that led to King and Queen's private area. "I mean . . . I think it's our secret. Now you have me wondering."

"Good morning, gentlemen," thundered Nebuchadnezzar as he breezed into the room. Daniel immediately bowed deeply as Amel remained standing, merely nodding his head to acknowledge the King. "I've got something very exciting to share with you. Something I've been thinking about for a few months now." He motioned for them to join him in a corner sitting area: "Come. Sit down. I want to hear your ideas on this."

The two men moved as the King directed and took their seats. There were some sweet breads and juice on the small table between them. The King grabbed one and popped it in his mouth, his eyes revealing his delight at the delicious taste it offered. "Try one of these," he said between swallows. "They are incredibly good."

Amel took a roll and joined his father in savoring its flavor. Daniel did not partake, knowing it was not his place to be eating so casually with royalty.

"I have been thinking that I should probably throw the priesthood a bone . . . pat them on the back for their good efforts in re-organizing the affairs of the Temple of Marduk. I'm delighted with the way Ochus has stepped in to replace Antiosyss. He seems loyal and is sticking to priestly business. I think they need to know I am watching them and am pleased."

He reached for another roll, then, looked at the two men, "What do you think?"

"I don't think you need to do anything," replied Amel. "They've been put in their place and you will participate in

Ochus' installation ceremony in the next few weeks. Why worry about doing anything else?" Daniel remained silent.

The King stared hard at his son, displeased by his political naivety.

"I know you are not deaf to what I'm hearing," slowly said Nebuchadnezzar. "As far as the people of Babylon are concerned, the priests have a direct line to the gods. That makes them powerful whether we think so or not. They are regaining their power rather quickly. Better to have them on my side than not. Right, Daniel?"

Daniel nodded his head and agreed, "Yes, sir. They have regained their influence very quickly the past few months."

Nebuchadnezzar turned to his son and smiled, "Maybe you will become more enthusiastic when I tell you what I want to do."

He grabbed a goblet off the table and drained it in one swallow. "I want to build a new temple on the other side of the river in the new city . . . one that faces the current temple on this side." He leaned over and grasped Amel's arm, "And I want you to design and build it."

No one spoke, each man left to his own thoughts as Nebuchadnezzar scooped up a couple more rolls and sat chewing, savoring their sweetness.

"So . . . what do you think?" the King bellowed.

Amel who in an instant had thought of a hundred construction techniques and engineering ideas he wanted to try blurted, "It's a great idea. I'd love to build a temple."

"I thought you would be in favor," said Nebuchadnezzar. "I've built my share of temples. It's time you do one. I think a new project of this magnitude is good for Babylon . . . It will let people see we are growing and moving on. Besides, it is always good to have the priesthood on your side . . . better if they're indebted to you."

Amel rose from his chair and stood by the window that looked across the Euphrates River to the east side of Babylon. "I can almost visualize it," he said, the excitement building in him. He turned back to them, "When do we start?"

"Daniel, we have not heard from you, yet," said the King. "What do you think?"

"My King, may you live forever," started Daniel. "A new major building would indeed be exciting for the people. I am not sure if you necessarily need to go to this extent to appease the priesthood, but I guess it certainly doesn't hurt."

He squirmed, uncomfortable with what he knew he had to say next, "My concern, my King, is the state of the treasury. At the present, we do not have the funds to continue repairing and expanding our roads and waterways that are critical to our commerce let alone finance a new building project."

"Since when did we ever care about money?" snapped Nebuchadnezzar. "If we need more in the treasury, we are not taking enough from the people. They're dependent upon us for their security . . . their livelihood . . . their sustenance. We have no shortage. We will always have what we need."

"I remain concerned, my King," answered Daniel. "Much has changed in the seven years you were ill."

"The temple will be built," roared the King as he rose to his feet glaring at Daniel who averted his gaze. "I did not ask you here to second guess me and to get your advice. I asked you here to tell you what I am planning." He started for the door, then turned back, "Amel, begin drafting some plans. I would like something to show to Ochus to solidify his support." With that, he left the room.

Amel returned to the window to look out onto the new city across the river. Daniel stood to take his leave.

"Daniel," Amel spoke with authority, causing Daniel to stop. Continuing to look out the window with his back to the Governor, he asked, "Is the priesthood rising in power?

"Yes, my Lord. Thankfully, Ochus is not consumed with the thirst for power Antiosyss had, and he is not yet as arrogant. Nonetheless, people are according him much more authority than he seeks or has. Their fear of the gods drives this behavior."

"What do you mean?"

"The priests enjoy a privileged standing—greater than even commended by the leading military commanders with our citizens. To successfully rule Babylon, you must be attentive to this and always manipulate the priesthood to support the throne."

Amel turned away from the window and walked to Daniel. "What you say is a bit frightening. Will we once again be fighting pretenders to the throne from within our own?"

Daniel nodded, his face now very serious.

Amel answered his own question with a question, "The throne rules, but does so with the support and consent of the temple?"

"In the culture of Babylon, that is correct," answered Daniel. "It is an uneasy but necessary alliance."

"And the money?" asked Amel. "Is the treasury that depleted?"

"We are fine if we do not add to our current expenditures," said Daniel. "In fact, we have been gaining ground each month since your father retook his throne. I suspect we will be strong enough to take on new things in another year or two."

"But not now?" asked Amel.

Daniel shook his head, his eyes sad: "I know your father does not want to hear this, but a major project of this size is beyond our ability to fund without a significant increase in contribution to the treasury from every citizen in the kingdom. I fear what this might do just when we have stabilized the economy and growth is on the horizon. Then again, your father is the strongest man I know. Maybe he can weather the storm."

They stood looking at each other, neither knowing what to say. Finally, Amel said, "We'll talk further about this."

"I suspect we shall," replied Daniel bowing, and then exiting through the main door.

~

As he left his father's palace for the central market site where there remained no end to the work that faced him, Amel-Marduk was exhilarated by the prospect of designing and building what could become the most magnificent structure in Babylon. His mind was a jumble of questions and ideas: How do I best site the temple? How high should it be? Do I bridge the old with the new temple across the Euphrates River? What should be its dominant theme? What building materials should I use to make it special?

And yet, he couldn't help but hear Daniel's caution in the back of his mind. He knew that Daniel had been concerned for the past two years about the declining state of the treasury, but he was never able to determine if Daniel was just playing it safe or if the kingdom was truly out of resources. It seemed that when he needed anything for the central market project, capital was always forthcoming At the same time, Daniel's integrity demanded that this be taken seriously. As sole ruler of the empire, his father could always exact more from the merchants, growers and general populace. Replenishing the treasury could be easily done. But at what cost to the King's credibility?

He spent the day at the market construction site solving a myriad of problems, particularly those created by the installation of the roof. His design called for a new approach to the fabrication of the support system which often bewildered the crews. Amel had to personally guide every step of the process, as he had learned the hard way when a section that had been installed in his absence had collapsed.

It was well after nightfall when the workers reached the point where they could quit without endangering the existing structure. Amel's guards brought his horse to the site entry for him to ride back to his palace in the royal compound. As he rode, new design ideas for the temple flooded his mind triggered by the challenges of the day's work. He was eager to find the time to sit at his drafting table to begin giving visual dimension to his thoughts.

Since Maximillan had spent the day at the construction site with Amel-Marduk, Dorcas was responsible for overseeing the evening meal and bath. She greeted the Crown Prince warmly as he entered the foyer, pressing a tankard of cold beer into his hands while directing him to the bath area where two servants waited to assist him. The beer soothed to his dust-caked throat, and tasted even better. He needed no encouragement to clean up and willingly entered the bath that was drawn for him.

Refreshed and dressed in a clean robe, Amel made his way to the dining area where he could smell that a wonderful meal awaited. As soon as he sat down, the food was brought to him in never ending courses. Ravenous, as he had not eaten in over eight hours, the Crown Prince lost himself in the exploding tastes that filled his mouth. By the third course, he slowed, taking time to notice Dorcas standing off to the side carefully watching him.

"Here," he pointed to an empty chair at the table, "Come, sit down and eat with me."

Dorcas embarrassingly laughed, "Oh, I cannot do that, Sire. I cannot sit at the Prince's table."

"Why not?" he demanded. "If I ask you to join me, there is no need to stand on protocol. Now . . . please sit down. I want to tell you about all that happened today."

Dorcas nodded and sat down. Amel took a plate of food, scooped off a portion for her on an empty plate and set it before her. He snapped his fingers to attract the attention of a servant standing quietly at the doorway, "Bring Dorcas some beer, please."

She blushed, but said nothing. When the beer arrived, Amel said, "Dorcas, please, drink . . . eat. This is quite delicious and I suspect you waited until I returned home to eat anything yourself."

"Yes, that is true," she answered. He nodded to her to eat as he took a large mouthful himself. Realizing that he truly meant for her to enjoy dinner with him, she began to eat . . .

slowly at first but then matching his pace as her taste buds enjoyed each bite.

They ate in silence, each relishing the closeness of the other. From time to time, Amel would sneak a look at Dorcas, admiring her beauty and engulfed in her warmth. It was almost more than he could do to not ask her to marry him right then and there. How he loved her. Likewise, Dorcas felt unusually secure and happy to be in the presence of the man she loved although she knew she could never be his equal. But tonight, that didn't matter. Cultures be damned, they were together.

As the servants cleared the dishes and brought out an assortment of fruits for dessert, Amel slid his chair away from the table to get comfortable, "My father surprised Daniel and me this morning with an interesting proposition."

He paused, waiting for her to speak.

"So . . . tell me," she asked. "What is it?"

"He wants to build a new temple for the priesthood in the new city across the river from the current one. And he wants me to design and build it," Amel beamed.

"That's wonderful," said Dorcas reaching over to clasp his hand. "You have been wondering what your next project might be. Now you have it."

"I know," countered Amel. "It's terribly exciting. A building like this allows my imagination to go in so many directions. I'm already fashioning design elements."

She smiled at him, pleased by his genuine excitement. He smiled back, and then became serious.

"There seems to be a down side to this, however. Daniel is concerned that the royal treasury does not have the resources for a new building at this time. He's quite worried that if the King attempts to extract more from the people, there could be a backlash. He doesn't know if the King has the strength and popularity to make this demand without fomenting discontent that we don't need right now."

For the next hour, they spoke at length about what might happen if the King took certain actions. Dorcas was no innocent when it came to Babylonian politics and society. She probed in response to Amel's suppositions of what his father might do. Back and forth they went, attempting to gain a better understanding of the options and the respective political fallout each might cause. Amel's admiration for her intelligence and savvy grew minute by minute. This was a lady of uncommon wisdom who could keep pace with the best minds in Babylon.

"Enough of problems," Dorcas finally said. "Tell me about your vision for the new temple."

Glad to leave a troubling issue, Amel happily plunged into everything he had been thinking about since Nebuchadnezzar asked him to design the building. This was the stuff about which he was passionate. Talking design energized him. He was soon on his feet, animatedly illustrating with his hands the things he was seeing in his head. Before they knew it, they were approaching the midnight hour.

Dorcas stifled a yawn, but didn't want Amel to stop as she delighted in his unbridled passion for his work. It didn't go unseen, however, and Amel stopped to look at her. As she gazed back at him, her beautiful eyes drawing him in, he was filled with desire. He knelt down beside her and took both her hands in his, "I don't know why I'm prattling on like this when I can simply take in your beauty and enjoy the best design the world has ever seen."

She laughed but was deeply pleased. They locked eyes, unspoken thoughts of the heart freely exchanged between them. She finally dropped her gaze and squeezed his hands, "Go on. I love hearing your dreams. I love . . . ."

Dorcas caught herself in mid-sentence. Amel let go her hands to wrap his arms around her, "Let me finish that." He then took her head in his hands bringing it down to within inches of his face, "I think you were going to say, I love you. I love you, too, my beautiful lady." He brought her lips to his in a long and passionate kiss from deep within their beings.

When their lips unclasped, Amel remained on his knees, his head buried against her bosom, his arms tightly hugging her.

The urge to ask her to marry him surged. I want you so badly, he thought. But the better course of wisdom prevailed. He had a few barriers to overcome before he could make this declaration public.

It was not easy to be the Crown Prince of Babylon.

~

The flaming torches that surrounded the ziggurat on each of its seven levels glistened like sparkling gold against the dark night sky. The spectacular scene could be seen from every corner of the city given the three hundred feet that it rose into the heavens above. Musicians ringed the pyramid in such a way that people standing several miles away could hear with clarity each instrument and the beautiful chords they created. On the bottom level were the percussion players; next came the cymbals and tambourines. Level three and four had the horns and trumpets; on levels five and six were the zithers and assorted string instruments. The seventh level, where the shrine was located, was reserved for the priests and the King. This was where the installation ceremony would be conducted.

Nebuchadnezzar had appointed Ochus high priest almost nine months ago. Because he wanted to be sure of Ochus' loyalty to the throne, the King had waited more than a half year before making it official. Tonight was the public declaration of Ochus' ascendance to the role of high priest of the Temple of Marduk, and thus the reigning priest in the empire.

The only way to get to the top was to climb over 400 steps. No one did this in one hike. Frequent rests were requisite, especially for the older priests. Ochus and Nebuchadnezzar began their ascent while the sun was still setting in the west. This would give them a good hour in which to make the journey with sufficient rest stops along the way. Moreover, once at the top, they could rest over some beer and breads that awaited them.

The outer courtyard of the ziggurat was already filled with people. As they climbed higher, they saw thousands more streaming towards them from throughout the city. The last installation of a high priest was twenty-seven years ago, so this was a rare occasion. No one wanted to miss it.

As they rested on the second level, Nebuchadnezzar said, "Now I remember that I vowed never to climb this again after we executed the traitors. This is for young men, not gray hairs like you and me."

Ochus chuckled, "Thankfully, this is my first ascent. I am glad you saw fit that I should miss the last one, my King."

"You have demonstrated your loyalty and know your bounds," said Nebuchadnezzar. "It's for that reason that we are here tonight to celebrate your promotion." He turned in the chair in which he was sitting to look directly at Ochus. "I have another surprise for you that I have been thinking about."

The high priest looked at him curiously as an aide approached to whisper in his ear.

"If you are ready, Sire, we should continue up," said Ochus.

Rising quickly, the King replied: "We shall continue this conversation at our next rest stop. By all means, let's get up there."

Intrigued but also apprehensive at what this surprise might be, Ochus nevertheless avoided asking further about it, focusing on the climb. At level three, they agreed they could go another story before resting. When they reached the fourth level, they were more than ready to take a break. By now, darkness was beginning to consume the sun's fading glow.

They sat quietly, gladly drinking the beer that was again offered.

"About that surprise I mentioned," said Nebuchadnezzar. Ochus stirred in his chair, trying not to reveal his anxiety. "The western part of Babylon has grown far beyond my expectation. There is a whole new city on the other side of the river, and the people who live there should have ready access to a temple. Therefore, I think we should build a new temple across the river from this site . . . one that faces this compound and is, perhaps, more magnificent. I was thinking of building it in your honor as the new high priest of our empire."

Ochus could not contain the grin that covered his face nor his relief. He fell to his knees before the King, grabbing his feet and pressing his head to them: "Oh King, live forever. I am deeply honored and thrilled by this . . . this honor. I am truly overwhelmed."

Nebuchadnezzar laughed, pleased by Ochus's response, "I am glad to do this. It brings me great joy." He leaned forward to take Ochus by the arm to encourage him to stand. "Stand up . . . stand up, please." As Ochus rose, the King signaled for more beer. He touched his tankard against that of Ochus in a toast. Both men drank heavily to celebrate.

"One thing, however," said Nebuchadnezzar, "I have asked my son, the Crown Prince, to design and build this temple. He has already exceeded my accomplishments in design and construction, so the result should be extraordinary. I want you to work with him."

"I would cherish the working relationship," replied Ochus. "The Crown Prince is a strong and brilliant man. This will be a pleasure."

"You know this will take some time, don't you?" asked the King. "It will take many months to design it so everything is right, and then another year to assemble the materials. I think it's going to be two years before you start to see anything . . . I mean, just the outline of the structure."

Ochus nodded, "I understand, Sire. We will take all the time we need to do it right."

It was time to continue upwards. Re-invigorated by the prospect of a new temple, both men rose and climbed the remaining three levels. When they reached the top, they were out of breath and needed to sit for well over thirty minutes. Albeit tired, Ochus glowed with the anticipation of a new temple in his name; this overshadowed even his installation as high priest. Nebuchadnezzar rested easily, pleased that such a simple gesture might solidify the priesthood's support of his throne for many years.

As they regained their energy, the priests participating in the ceremony began to move about, donning their special shrine vestments. They dressed Ochus accordingly and reviewed the ritual with both men. When the King nodded he was ready, the leading archer in the Imperial Guard shot a flaming arrow hundreds of yards into the night sky to signal the start of the ceremony. All music stopped. A hush fell over the tens of thousands of people massed below. With only the sound of the torches, it was almost eerie . . . never had Babylon been this quiet.

Boom . . . boom . . . boom. Three loud beats on the bass drum cued the musicians and the music erupted in glorious celebration. The King, followed by Ochus, stepped out onto the top level of the ziggurat and proceeded to the center facing Procession Way. When the people below recognized them, they responded with a thunderous roar.

The ceremony itself was more ritualistic than dramatic as had been those conducted by Antiosyss and Narseniah. There was no need for spectacle. This was to be a night when the King—the designee of the gods to rule Babylon—conferred on Ochus the office and powers of the high priest of the Temple of Marduk.

Nebuchadnezzar turned to face the altar, and stepped up to stand before it. He ignited the pre-set torches and coals on the altar, shooting flames twenty feet into the sky. As the torches ignited, a gasp went up from the people below. He motioned for Ochus to join him at the altar. The men solemnly faced each other. Bowing to the King, Ochus knelt. An aide handed the King the outer vestment worn only by the high priest. Brilliant colors created intricate river patterns against the white of the garment, and its gold belt sparkled as the flames danced in the darkness.

Nebuchadnezzar placed the vestment on Ochus. Next, he placed an azure blue hat on his head, then, lifted him to his feet.

Ochus turned to face the crowds below while the King descended the altar platform to stand once again center on the edge of the seventh level. Ochus lifted his arms and the music stopped. Silence descended on the city.

Ochus clapped his hands three times.

Whoosh!

The altar exploded in a giant fireball with flames shooting high into the sky. No one was ready for this. The sheer power of the spectacle was enough to send everyone to their knees in fear. It was as though Marduk had confirmed the appointment. There remained no question of who was the new leader of the priesthood.

Nebuchadnezzar smiled, very pleased at how well the ceremony had gone and delighted with the response of Babylon. He brought Ochus forward to stand with him. They stood for well over fifteen minutes looking out onto their grand city as the people celebrated below . . . applauding . . . shouting . . . and dancing.

Babylon was in good hands once more.

~

The journey back to the outer reaches of the Babylonian empire was long and tiring. They had been on the road for twenty-seven days and her new home was finally in sight. I will be so glad to get out of this coach, she thought. I never want to smell another horse again...and the dust! It never stops.

Princess Kassaya had stayed behind in Babylon when her father banished her husband from the city to the southwest province of the kingdom. Neriglissar went on ahead to prepare their new home while she stayed behind. She really did not want to leave Babylon. Nebuchadnezzar made it clear to his daughter that although her husband was not welcome, she could remain in the city and even continue to live in the palace he had built for her within the royal compound. She vacillated between wanting to enjoy the pleasures of royalty—raising her children in the sumptuousness of the royal palaces—and living far from civilized society with her husband whom she still loved. The tension in this struggle was severe . . . so difficult that inertia overcame her, disallowing a decision.

All changed when Ochus was installed as the high priest of the Temple of Marduk. Kassaya could not believe that her father had made this decision, and so she was sure to be among the members of the royal family on the ziggurat the night of the ceremony. She had to see for herself that this was real.

At first the Princess wanted only to send a messenger to Neriglissar telling him the news. On second thought, she felt it would be better for her to go to him and fully explain all that was happening in Babylon. She thought she could make the trip by chariot, but she realized she would need clothes and a few amenities, not to mention servants. This would require a caravan of several wagons.

Within a month of Ochus' installation, Kassaya began the long journey to the north then veered southwest to the Egyptian border. Knowing she would be coming back to Babylon within the year, she had left her children in the care of their nurse and teachers. She had carefully packed only those things she cared little for and would not miss if lost. It had been a terrible trek, but perhaps well worth the pain now that it may be coming to an end.

Neriglissar's guards, posted in concentric circles around his compound, first caught sight of the approaching caravan and rushed to bring him news of the Princess' arrival. Gathering the servants of the household, he stood at the gates waiting for his wife. As her coach pulled up, he ran to greet her. It had been almost a year since they had seen each other. Despite all his other failings, Neriglissar loved Kassaya. He embraced her with an intensity that both surprised and delighted her. They stood for several minutes, relishing the closeness of each other.

The Princess' new house was pleasant and sufficiently large. As she toured it, she was pleased to see it was not a mud brick, rural farmhouse. On the other hand, it was no palace. It would be tough to live here, she thought . . . but if all goes well, this may only be temporary. However, first things first . . . more than anything she wanted a bath to dissolve the dirt that covered her skin from the past four weeks on the road.

She began to feel human once bathed and dressed in clean robes that had been unpacked and carefully hung in the closets of her bed chamber. Neriglissar had gone to check on a disturbance a few miles away and would not be back until sunset. It gave her a few hours to oversee the placement of the furniture, clothing and art pieces that had been unpacked. She had brought with her six of her most trusted servants who were scurrying about trying to make the new house comfortable for their mistress.

Kassaya, however, had no interest in making this place her home. The servants could put things where they wanted, she thought. It was not important to her. This was not her home. Relaxed after a warm bath, she lay back on her bed and drifted off to sleep.

It was dark when she stirred, awakened by her lead servant who informed her that dinner was ready. Her husband awaited her in the dining room.

Kassaya sat alone with Neriglissar in the candle-lit room. So happy to see his wife after a long separation and to have someone to talk to at the evening meal, Neriglissar ate heartily and talked even more. He told her all that he was doing to secure the border and the new plans he had to build this little town into a city in which she would be proud to live. She barely touched her food.

"So tell me what is happening in Babylon," he said, aware that he had monopolized the conversation thus far.

"Ochus has been installed as the high priest," Kassaya replied, looking at him intently.

She could have said anything else and it would not have hit him as hard as this simple declaration. He put his goblet on the table, never taking his eyes off her. Leaning forward to her, he asked, "What did you say?"

"My father appointed Ochus the high priest of the Temple," she stated.

Neriglissar leaned back in his chair, his mind racing. "This changes everything."

"I know," Kassaya smiled. "We could be back in Babylon within a year if we are careful and make the right moves."

"Ochus owes me," whispered Neriglissar. "Antiosyss wanted to drive him out of the priesthood because he had the allegiance of the vast majority of the priests. Ochus was the real power of the temple. Ochus frightened him."

"With good reason," softly said Kassaya. "He well may be the smartest man in the kingdom . . . certainly the most manipulative."

"I convinced Antiosyss to ignore him," continued Neriglissar. "I told him I could take care of any power play he might make; that if he took action against Ochus, it would upset all that we had put in place to take over the throne . . ."

He paused, ". . . and then I told Ochus to be patient . . . to bide his time . . . that I would see he prevailed."

He stopped talking, sinking deep into thought. Kassaya knew enough to remain silent as her husband wrestled through all the thoughts besieging him. He turned to her, a new realization flooding his face, "I do not seek to overthrow your father. I respect and fear him, but he is old. When he finally dies, I know I can rule in his stead better than Amel."

She nodded, "I know that too."

He smiled, "Ochus can bring us back to Babylon."

"Yes," she said. "But we have to set the stage . . . use him to change my father's mind about you. If anyone can do it, he can."

~

Daniel approached the central market construction site eager to see its progress. He had not been there for nine months, and the entry was beginning to take shape. He was glad that Amel-Marduk wanted to meet here rather than at his palace. Daniel needed to get a handle on construction progress. The subject he wished to take up with the Crown Prince depended upon its completion timeline.

He found Amel on the roof deep inside the bowels of the market. The intricate roof that the Crown Prince had designed was still giving the construction crews problems. They were working on the place where the long corridors of the shops connected to the central atrium, like the spokes of a wagon wheel to its hub.

"My Lord," greeted Daniel as he looked up at Amel standing on the roof's rafters twenty-five feet above him.

"Thank you for coming, Daniel," responded Amel. "Let me finish up here and I'll be down to see you. Maximillan, take Daniel through the stall areas. Show him the work we have completed."

"Yes, Sire," replied Maximillan who came quickly to escort Daniel. Daniel did not need a second invitation. He was pleased to have a tour. The two men set off at once.

Thirty minutes later, they returned to find Amel scampering down a ladder to join them. "What do you think?" he asked.

"Your design is absolutely brilliant," answered Daniel. "The efficiencies the merchants and growers and producers will realize in the distribution process alone will impact our commerce for years to come! You obviously took the time to learn their business, and you created a building to improve it."

Amel smiled broadly. Nothing pleased him more than when people he respected admired his architecture and creativity.

"You are right, Daniel," he said. "This new market will revolutionize the way we do business in Babylon."

"How close are you to completing this project?" queried Daniel.

"We're doing very well except for the roof," replied Amel. "But we will sort that out. I think we have finally found the right technique to speed up our progress." He stepped away and slowly turned full circle to take in the vastness of the project. "If we're lucky, we might have this done in nine months. More likely, a year, and it could even be another year and a half. Certainly by then we'll be finished."

"So the next spring's equinox harvest might be traded out of our new market? Is that possible?"

"I would like to say, yes. But don't hold me to it," answered Amel. "We'll give it everything we have, but things happen in the building process."

"This is good news," said Daniel. "You're further along than I suspected. Good for you."

"Well, I know you didn't come out here to talk about the market, laughed Amel. He gestured for Daniel to follow him to an alcove where a bench protruded from the wall. "You asked to speak to me about something of importance. What is it?"

Amel sat down, glad to be off his feet. He patted the bench indicating that Daniel should join him. Not wanting to be so casual with the Crown Prince, Daniel shook his head and remained standing, "Thanks, but I am more comfortable standing."

"So . . . speak," said Amel.

"My Lord, the King has spoken to Ochus about his dream to build a new temple in the new part of the city. I am sure you know how this has excited the high priest, especially as the new temple will be built in his honor. He confronts me regularly, asking when the building will be started. I keep putting him off by saying the central market must be completed first. Not liking my answer, Ochus brought the King into it. The King now wants both projects to proceed simultaneously . . . he says you are phasing out of active on-site supervision of the market and should have ample time to begin work on the temple."

"That's true," nodded Amel. "I can do both, but I thought you wanted us to finish the market first."

"That is the point," said an exasperated Daniel. "Yes, I do prefer that the market be completed before the next project starts. It's all a matter of having sufficient resources in place to time out with expenditures. The treasury cannot support both projects at the same time."

"What happened to extracting more payments from the citizens?" asked Amel.

"Yes, we can do that, but I'm trying to avoid that as long as possible," replied Daniel. "I still think it could jeopardize the current popular status that the King enjoys among his people. If we can segue from one to the other without overlap, then we can maintain the status quo."

"I see what you are saying," said Amel. Daniel made sense, and over the past year he had grown to appreciate Daniel's political savvy. If those driving the economy of Babylon thought the King was acting capriciously to drain more from their profits to simply build things to satisfy his ego, there might be trouble.

"If you could persuade your father to wait to begin the temple for at least another year, we can get through this."

"You make a good case. I will do it," answered Amel. "There should be no problem. Ochus seems to do what he is told. He's a reasonable man. I will slow him down. Together we should present a reasonable front to my father."

Daniel did not respond immediately, but breathed a heavy sigh and looked away. He had to be careful how he said this, "Ochus is not all that harmless and docile. I am afraid he is someone neither you nor the King can necessarily trust."

"Come on," guffawed Amel standing up to end the conversation, ready to get back to his work. "He's glad to have his job and indebted to my father for it. The promise of a new temple only strengthens his loyalty."

Daniel moved closer to the Prince and spoke in a soft voice, "It is my job as Governor to know everything I can about influence peddlers in this city. Since Princess Kassaya left to join her husband two months ago, certain information has been brought to my attention." He looked around to see who was nearby then his voice dropped to a whisper, "Ochus owes allegiance to Neriglissar."

"What are you talking about?"

"Neriglissar prevented Antiosyss from banning Ochus from the priesthood," whispered Daniel. "It seems that Ochus had the allegiance of the vast majority of priests and was on the verge of usurping Antiosyss' power. Neriglissar did not want anything to disturb the insurrection that was in place. A rebellion within the priesthood would have undone his cabal."

This news was like a sword thrust into Amel's bowels. He was stunned and visibly shocked. He looked at Daniel questioningly, his face pale. He sat back down, his body sagging.

"It's not over, is it?" he rhetorically asked.

"No, my Lord," answered Daniel. "It may only be beginning."

Amel nodded in agreement, unable to collect his thoughts and speak.

"We must do everything to contain those who seek the downfall of the throne," urgently spoke Daniel. "That is why we cannot afford any disturbance among those who drive our commerce or even the general citizenry. We must keep things positive and status quo."

Amel nodded again, slowly spitting out six words like flung arrows: "And we must watch Ochus carefully."

"I agree."

Amel sighed and stood again. He reached out his right arm to clasp Daniel's arm in friendship, "Thank the gods for you, Daniel. My father always trusted you, and now he's even got some faith in your God. I think I may do so as well. You are loyal to my family, and we shall not forget this . . . ever."

~

Although she was glad to see her husband, the four weeks Princess Kassaya spent in the outer Babylonian province felt like four years. There was no social life . . . no parties . . . no one with whom she felt at ease to make friends. There were goats and sheep—plenty of them—and more dust than she had ever imagined. When Neriglissar suggested she return to Babylon to align the politics for his return, she could not leave fast enough. She pushed the drivers who pushed the horses to shorten the trip home. They arrived in Babylon twenty-one days later.

Once settled in her palace and again integrating herself into the royal family, Kassaya went to work on behalf of her husband. Getting Ochus in line was easy. He knew Neriglissar was responsible for his ascendancy to the high priest's role. It did not take much to convince him that it was in his best interest to help set the course for Neriglissar's eventual return. He understood that Neriglissar's succession to the throne would make a much better future for him than if Amel-Marduk were to become King. He willingly committed himself to the strategy and course of action outlined by Kassaya; his role was to make the case for Neriglissar's return with Daniel. Meanwhile, she would work on the King.

Ochus had been hounding Daniel for months demanding that work begin on the new temple. So it was not unusual for them to meet frequently. However, rather than simply lobbying for the project to get underway, Ochus changed the tone of their meetings to one that was more conciliatory and collegial, seeking to assist Daniel in governance matters. He apologized for thinking only of his own interests and offered to help Daniel even to the point of proposing strategies to replenish the royal treasury and to do it in such a way that the people would see it as beneficial. Not for one minute did Daniel let his guard down; he knew the character of this man. It was advantageous, however, to have the high priest working with him rather than against him. Thus, the unholy alliance developed into a working relationship.

At every opportunity, Ochus related to Daniel news of Neriglissar's accomplishments on the border. To keep each other informed, Princess Kassaya and her husband employed weekly couriers to make the run from the southwest province to the capital city. Each week, Neriglissar made sure to report an achievement that would be viewed favorably by those in power in Babylon. He was building a new border fortress, increasing the productivity of livestock farmers, and encouraging defectors to re-build their lives within the Babylonian empire, thus strengthening provincial towns. It was hard to ignore these tidbits of information, especially as they bolstered the kingdom. Daniel had to consider the possibility that Neriglissar had changed colors albeit he knew the history of Ochus and Neriglissar would suggest otherwise.

Kassaya, likewise, manipulated her father. If Nebuchadnezzar could be persuaded that Neriglissar was duly repentant for his role in the rebellion and was now focused on the good of the kingdom, she believed his expulsion might be reversed.

In only a few months, attitudes began to change. Word of Neriglissar's achievements got back to the King who was pleased with what he was hearing. He always knew that his son-in-law was a great warrior and commander. Learning that Neriglissar was applying his leadership skills to civic affairs made the King wonder if he erred in banishing him to the hinterlands. On the few times he discussed this thought with Daniel, he was reminded by the Governor of Neriglissar's central role in the cabal that almost seized the throne. Yet, even Daniel had to admit grudgingly that Neriglissar was doing good things rather than sulking in his banishment.

By definition of their roles as appointee of the gods and caretaker of the chief god's temple, the King and high priest regularly met to consult on the intersection of the divine with human affairs. Ochus took these opportunities to inform Nebuchadnezzar of the good work Neriglissar seemed to be doing in the southwest. This added to the growing thought in the King's mind that his son-in-law was truly reforming. He began to consider the possibility of Neriglissar's return.

Chapter Fourteen
SUCCESSION
563-562 BC

The irritating pounding in his head would not stop. Nebuchadnezzar stirred in his bed, and then turned over, bringing the bed covers up over his head. The pounding only became more intense. Angrily he flung off the covers and sat up in bed. Slowly it dawned on him that someone was knocking at his door. He looked towards the window and saw that it was still dark outside. It must be important, he thought, as he yelled out, "I hear you." Nebuchadnezzar got out of bed, put on his robe and shouted, "Enter!"

Zocor opened the door cautiously, knowing the King did not like to be woken. He bowed, "Forgive me, my King, but I have news that cannot wait."

Nebuchadnezzar motioned him to come in as he settled into a chair, "I trust this is important. I was sleeping well until your incessant pounding gave me a headache."

"Nebuzaradan is dead."

"What did you say?" said the King taken back.

"The Supreme Commander, Nebuzaradan, died in the early hours of the morning," replied Zocor.

Nebuchadnezzar absorbed the news slowly as his mind began racing at all the implications the loss of his chief military leader sparked. Without looking at Zocor, he softly said to himself, "I knew he was sick, but I had no idea he was that sick. I should have done something . . . demanded the physicians take this more seriously." He raised his head to stare at Zocor and asked for confirmation, "Was it the illness?"

"Yes, my King."

"Inform the Crown Prince and Daniel at once," Nebuchadnezzar ordered Zocor. "Tell them I want to see them in my chamber mid-morning."

"Yes, my King," Zocor bowed and turned to leave.

"Tell Rabmag and Babsaris . . . also Ochus . . . the news and tell them to join us in the palace as well."

"Yes, Sire," Zocor saluted smartly and exited the room. Nebuchadnezzar sighed deeply. It's always something, he mused. Just when things are going smoothly, the unexpected occurs. At least it wasn't one of those awful dreams, he smiled. I can deal with this.

~

The generals were the first to arrive at the palace. Rabmag and Babsaris walked up the steps together conjecturing what might next happen. They were the highest ranking commanders in Babylon and aware that one of them might soon be promoted. Needless to say, tension ruled their day.

Zocor was waiting for them and escorted them directly into the King's chamber room which was used for smaller, confidential meetings as opposed to the spacious throne room. He invited them to sit to await the arrival of the others, then left the room to return to his post at the entry just in time to greet Ochus whom he also led into the King's chamber.

Before he had time to leave, Amel and Daniel entered the room and greeted those present. The moment was solemn, but also anxious as each speculated on the King's successor for Nebuzaradan and whatever other action he might choose to take.

The doors were flung open as the King entered. The five men rose and, with the exception of Amel, bowed to the King as he crossed to take his seat, a smaller replica of the throne in the larger room.

"Sit," he commanded. "This is a sad day. A great warrior has died. Nebuzaradan was a man I trusted with my life both on and off the battlefield. As all of you know, he was my surrogate on many battlefields and in many nations which we defeated. It will be difficult to replace him, but replace him I must. The Imperial Guard must have a Supreme Commander whom they respect and will die for if our armed forces are to remain strong."

There was a stirring around the room as all in attendance murmured their agreement. Babsaris and Rabmag glanced at each other knowingly. Amel smiled at both of them to relieve the tension each was feeling at the imminent announcement.

"I am bringing Neriglissar back to Babylon to take command of the Imperial Guard."

It was as though a massive bolt of lightning pierced the room. All but Ochus were dumbfounded by the King's decision. Rabmag's and Babsaris's tension turned to hostility, albeit they did not show it. Amel's shock turned to anger. The smile that crossed Ochus's face did not go unnoticed by Daniel who was greatly disturbed at the King's news.

"You cannot be serious, father," blurted Amel. "Neriglissar is a traitor. He's fortunate to be alive!"

"You can stop it right there!" thundered Nebuchadnezzar. "I still sit on this throne, and I still make the decisions in this kingdom. You are not privy to the reformation in Neriglissar's character that has taken place during the past year." His voice grew in volume and intensity, "He has risen to new leadership heights, even out in the most remote province of our empire. And he is proving his loyalty to this throne."

Amel sat shaking his head violently in disbelief and opposition, "I cannot believe this." He pointed at the two generals sitting across from him, "Certainly either of these great commanders can do the job, and you are assured of their loyalty."

Nebuchadnezzar abruptly stood, angry that his son would question his decision. He looked at the generals who had risen with him and said, "Commanders, I think very highly of both of you. You have served well, and I continue to expect you to serve well. You have heard my decision. You are excused."

The two men bowed and hastily made their exit. Nebuchadnezzar paced the room before turning to Ochus. "I know how the Crown Prince feels. What about you, Ochus? Do you think my bringing Neriglissar back to command the Imperial Guard will anger the gods or our people?"

"No, my King," answered Ochus. "From all the reports I am hearing, Neriglissar is quite repentant and eager to get back into your good graces. I think he has learned an invaluable lesson. I cannot imagine he would be anything but grateful for a second chance. This should guarantee his allegiance."

Nebuchadnezzar smiled, pleased that someone agreed with him. Encouraged, he looked at Daniel, "Well?"

"It is your decision to make, oh King," said Daniel looking directly at Nebuchadnezzar.

"Is it a good one?" asked the King.

"All your decisions are good," replied Daniel. "In this case, however, I suggest you think about this . . . see how you feel a few months from now." The King nodded as Daniel paused. He looked at the King, "Does a leopard lose his spots? I think not."

"I will take your advice, Governor," said Nebuchadnezzar. "It is wise to reflect before taking action. I, too, ask you to think about this. Perhaps you will be more persuaded as time goes by." He turned to Amel, "The same goes for you. Give the man a chance."

Amel did not respond.

Not wishing the mood to darken further, Daniel changed the subject, "My Lord, you would be pleased to see the progress that has been made on the new central market. The Crown Prince has designed a structure that will change the way we conduct commerce. The efficiencies that will be gained will greatly profit everyone."

"That's good to hear," said Nebuchadnezzar. "I should go see for myself what you are doing there, Amel."

The Crown Prince lifted his head, a slight smile on his face, "I'd be honored to show you, father. Like Daniel said, I think the new building will benefit everyone."

"Speaking of benefits and profits," said Nebuchadnezzar looking at Daniel, "is the treasury in a position to initiate work on the new temple?"

"My King," replied Daniel, "if we can wait six to twelve months—whenever the central market is finished—we can move into the temple project with no problem. Right now, having two projects under way will place undue stress on the treasury."

"When do you think the market will be completed?" the King asked Amel.

"Maybe in six months," he replied. "Things are going well right now. We seem to have solved the difficult engineering problems."

"Ochus," the King looked at the high priest, "you can wait six months, can't you?"

"I will abide by your decision, my King," replied the high priest.

"Here it is then," said the King. "We will finish the market and then start the temple. That should keep you happy, Daniel."

Nebuchadnezzar stepped towards the doors leading out of the chamber which were opened by his guards. He paused, and without turning to face the three remaining men in the room, said very slowly, "I am seriously persuaded that Neriglissar is the best man to command the Imperial Guard."

No one spoke. The King turned to look at them with a smile, "Perhaps each of us can have what we want."

He was gone.

"Thank you for agreeing to wait until the market is finished," Daniel said to Ochus.

"Like the King said," smiled Ochus, "perhaps we can all have what we each want. I am pleased to do what is best for the kingdom."

Ochus nodded to Daniel, bowed to Amel, and then left the room. After a few moments Amel looked at Daniel and said, "Bringing the snake back into the tent could be disastrous."

Daniel shrugged, knowing the King had made his decision. He was resigned to the King's impulses . . . he had lived through many before. He quietly said, "We must be more cautious and knowing than ever before if the King follows through on this decision. We must never let any mutinous thought grow into action."

He clasped Amel's arm in friendship, "You will be the next king so you will be in control. Until then, you must not anger your father by opposing him; rather, you must be his colleague . . . his alter ego . . . and guide him wisely."

Amel nodded: "You are truly a wise man, Daniel."

He walked out of the room, leaving Daniel alone in the King's chamber. Daniel stood for a moment, gathering his thoughts, then slowly exited . . . the burdens of the empire grew ever more heavier on his shoulders.

~

Amel-Marduk turned his attention to the final push to complete the central market. His father's enthusiasm for his new design and construction techniques energized him as they toured the project site. The King was an accomplished architect and builder in his own right. He had, after all, created the incredible hanging gardens for his wife and built the massive ziggurat acclaimed throughout the known world. It was no small measure of Amel's talent and creative ability for Nebuchadnezzar to accord him high praise.

As hard as he pushed his crews, Amel missed his goal of opening the market within the six months timeline he had set for himself. In fact, it took seven months which still pleased the King and Daniel to no end. With the market open and in place, the commerce of the kingdom would get a much needed jolt. Even within the two weeks' shakedown period during which the merchants, growers and artisans were introduced to the building and made familiar with how business would be conducted, news of its potential spread like wildfire into the surrounding towns and provinces. More people wanted to set up shop than ever before in the history of Babylon. The smell of profit and success permeated the air of the city and the surrounding provinces.

The grand opening was a major event . . . a spectacle that attracted tens of thousands of people. The King had declared a holiday in honor of the new central market. Musicians and dancers filled the day with songs and theatrics to delight the ever-changing masses who came. Food vendors set up stands on the streets making it unnecessary for anyone to leave what had become a great party.

At midday, the King formally opened the venue with plenty of pomp and circumstance supplied by the Imperial Guard. Amel-Marduk was the hero of the day as dignitary after dignitary paid him homage for his remarkable vision. As Ochus and Daniel stood on the platform for the opening ceremony, Nebuchadnezzar faced the crowd and hailed his son as the next great king of the Babylonian empire. He was effusive in praising Amel as a gifted heir to the throne. Ochus had no choice but to join in with unwavering affirmation. Nebuchadnezzar used the day to establish beyond any doubt Amel's succession to the throne and his divine appointment by the gods.

The people concurred . . . their cheering loud and hearty. The merrymaking continued well into the night as Babylon celebrated not only a new market but a new royalty.

~

That night the King and Queen hosted a banquet honoring Amel-Marduk in celebration of the completion of the central market. Anybody who was somebody attended. It had been years since the King opened the palace for such a lavish event. Military leaders, officials, leading merchants, major growers, the cognoscenti and the priesthood had wrestled for invitations. The large banquet hall at the palace was so full that many attendees spilled out into the anteroom and adjoining sitting rooms.

Flattered by the recognition, especially from his father, Amel's joy was nonetheless dampened because he was unable to share the night with the one person who meant the most to him. How he longed for Dorcas to be at his side. If not for her, he would not be alive. If not for her encouragement, he would not have taken the risks he did in his design employing untested technologies. She deserved the accolades that were thrown at him throughout the night, and as the evening wore on it was more and more difficult to contain his feelings.

When the King and Queen finally exited the hall in the wee hours of the morning, Amel took his leave as well. The revelry was still in full swing, but it had been a long day and, in his heart, he wanted to be in his own palace. He bid goodnight to the ranking people who were still present and quietly left the building.

Maximillan was waiting for him as he entered his palace. Anticipating that the Crown Prince might want a bath before retiring, he had the servants standing by with hot water ready to pour into the tub. Gratefully Amel accepted the offer and sank back in the bath taking pleasure in the warmth that encased him. His thoughts were on Dorcas as they had been most of the night. He wished that he could talk to her right now, but she had long since retired.

He toweled himself off and put on the clean robe that was offered. Adrenalin still coursing through his veins from the excitement of the day, he wasn't ready to retire for the evening. He asked Maximillan for some fruit and juice. He had had enough beer to last a month and now sought only the sweetness of nectar.

Amel walked into the small sitting room off his bedchamber where several candles created a romantic glow. He plopped down in his favorite chair enjoying the enveloping cushions as he recreated the day's events in his mind. A knock at the door startled him out of his reverie. He called out, "Come in."

Expecting Maximillan but seeing Dorcas startled him. Was it an apparition? Was she real? As much as he wanted to see her and talk with her, she was the last person he thought would come through that doorway tonight.

"My Lord," said Dorcas, "I asked Maximillan if I could bring you the fruit and juice you requested. I hope you do not mind."

"Mind?" he blurted out, rising to sit up in his chair. "No I do not mind. In fact, I cannot tell you how glad I am to see you." As she walked towards him to set the tray on a small table at his side, he continued, "Do you know that you are all I have been thinking about all night."

"My Lord is joking," Dorcas stepped back. "Never has there been such a feast and banquet to honor a man in Babylon as tonight. No, Sire, I had no presence there."

Amel rose and pulled a chair up next to his. He patted the seat and said, "Dorcas, please come . . . sit with me. I so wanted to talk with you tonight . . . to share all that happened to me."

They sat looking at each other in silence, drinking from each other's eyes. Finally, Dorcas looked away. She did not want him to see that she had lost her composure, but her heaving shoulders gave her away.

Amel leaned towards her and took one of her hands in his, "Dorcas, why are you crying? Did I do something wrong?"

"I was so proud of you today and of all that you have accomplished for this city. The esteem that the people—even your father—had for you was thrilling for me to see." She turned to look at him, tears trickling from her eyes, "I'm crying because I care so much for you. I wanted to be near you all day . . . to support you."

"Oh, Dorcas," Amel knelt beside her, holding her hands in his. "If you only knew how much I wanted that as well. Today should have been yours to share with me. You gave me my very life. I would not be alive without you."

"That is not true," she managed a laugh through her tears. "Maybe I helped a bit, but God brought you through the storm and gave you your life back."

"Yes," nodded Amel, "I believe that."

They did not move, their eyes refusing to unlock from each other. So much was shared between them in the next two minutes—all of it unspoken. Finally overwhelmed, Amel gripped her hands tightly and softly whispered, "Dorcas, I want you to marry me."

Her eyes sprang wide open in surprise. These were not the words she expected to hear. "Please do not joke with me, my Lord. Not tonight."

"I mean it. I want you to marry me."

"It is impossible," she answered. "Even if I want to and said yes, it could not happen. You are the next king of Babylon and I'm . . . I'm a simple servant."

"It is possible," he said fiercely. "I can make it possible. I never thought I would want a woman again to share my life once my wife died. But you've changed that. You have served me so lovingly over the years. Your integrity . . . your gentleness . . . your love is something I have grown to admire and adore. There is no one I would rather share the rest of my life with than you."

He took her shoulders in both of his hands and drew her close, "I love you, Dorcas. Say you will marry me."

She could not speak. All she could think of was the great social divide between them and the scorn that would be heaped on Amel if such an alliance happened. She shook her head, "There is nothing I want more, but I cannot see how it can happen."

"Do you love me?" he asked.

"Yes. Of course, I love you," she began to cry, burying her head in his shoulder.

"Am I to be the next king of Babylon?" he asked.

"Yes . . . yes you are," she answered.

"Then I can make anything happen. Right?" Amel chuckled.

"Yes . . . I suppose you can," Dorcas began to laugh, seeing where he was going.

"So it's done. Marriage between you and me is not a problem . . . not for the King."

"Are you sure the people will accept me? I mean, I don't seek their favor, but I don't want you to get hurt."

"Dorcas," Amel said firmly. "Enough. Say yes."

She looked longingly at him, never happier in her life than right now as she answered, "Yes."

Amel drew her to him in an embrace. Their lips met . . . and then their passion exploded. He finally had the life partner he long sought . . . the object of a burning love for several years. She no longer needed to conceal her love—a love that had been growing for many years. They had each other. The rest of the city . . . the empire . . . the world . . . none of it mattered.

~

It was as though he was walking in the clouds, thousands of feet in the air, his feet never touching the ground below. Amel-Marduk had risen early and busied himself with drawings of the new temple that was next on his plate. He knew he should wait until mid-morning to visit with his father who in his later years enjoyed sleeping a little longer than was his custom for the majority of his life. Furthermore, the King had celebrated well into the night and Amel knew he would have little resolve for a serious discussion early in the morning.

Finally, as the sun approached its zenith in the sky, he left his palace and was now floating—or at least it felt so—toward the King's palace on the Euphrates River. Another beautiful day in paradise, he thought. No, he reconsidered. It was *the* most beautiful day in the world and he intended to drink of its fullness.

He was met at the entry by the King's chief servant who asked the Crown Prince to wait in the King's receiving chamber while he went to announce his visit. Within minutes, the King strode through the door and warmly embraced his son.

"That was quite a party last night! I think the entire kingdom attended."

"I was deeply honored by you, Sire," replied Amel. "To be given such a banquet . . . what can I say? It defies words."

"You well deserved it all," his father said. "The ingenuity you brought to the new central market charts a new course in architecture. I am proud of you, son. You are going to make a fine ruler when I am gone." He held Amel's shoulders with his large hands. "I know the entire kingdom attended."

"Again, I am greatly honored. Thank you."

Nebuchadnezzar laughed, pleased with the relationship he enjoyed with his eldest son. He eased into his favorite chair and gestured for Amel to sit across from him.

"I know you didn't come here to make small talk," the King chuckled. "That's not your style. So what brought you here to see me this morning?"

Amel hesitated, and then slowly began, his eyes cast downward, "Probably the most important thing in my life."

He paused, and looked directly at his father, "I never thought it would happen, but I have found the woman I wish to marry. I am here to ask your blessing."

"Wonderful," beamed Nebuchadnezzar. "It's about time!"

They sat in silence, beaming at each other, waiting for the other to speak.

"Well . . . so who is it?" thundered the King exasperated that he had to wait for Amel to speak.

"Father, I want you to listen to me carefully . . . to know the depth of my love for this lady. In all the years that have passed since my wife died, I never believed I would again have such deep feelings for any woman. But in the past few years I guess the seed was planted and over time the tree of love has bloomed to full maturity. Last night, after the party, I asked her to marry me and she accepted."

"Who is it? roared Nebuchadnezzar, eager to know.

"Dorcas. The woman in my household who has served me faithfully for many years."

Dumbfounded, Nebuchadnezzar looked at him. So many thoughts and words collided in his mind he could not speak at first.

"You cannot be serious!" he finally exclaimed. "Dorcas is a servant. She's not of royal lineage or anything close to it! It's just not right. You must have a wife of high standing . . . one worthy of being the queen of Babylon."

"She is most worthy, Sire," replied Amel as he slid from his chair to fall on his knees before his father. "She is a woman of impeccable integrity, devotion and intelligence. But all that doesn't even matter because I am incredibly in love with her."

Nebuchadnezzar rose and walked the length of the room before responding. He chose his words carefully, "Amel-Marduk, how will it look to our people to have you marrying a servant? No, it's even worse," he whirled to face his son. "She's a Jewish slave! The scorn will be palpable."

Refusing to back down, Amel stepped to him pressing his case, "Father, I have thought all that through. I am confident that Dorcas is of such character that she will rise above initial reaction and, in short order, command the respect and loyalty of the empire."

The King looked at him hard, "You realize that this marriage will jeopardize your authority to rule . . . that you are elevating a Jew to be the queen."

"You have already done that," retorted Amel. "You made a Jew governor of the kingdom. Did anyone refuse to accept the authority you gave him?"

"What do you mean?" stammered Nebuchadnezzar.

"Daniel! I am speaking of Daniel. He is the highest-ranking man in Babylon next to you. In only a short time, his wisdom and integrity have garnered the respect and obedience of our people."

Nebuchadnezzar stood staring at his son. Amel had successfully countered his argument, albeit he was not happy about it. They faced off like two stallions, each waiting for the other to make the next move. Nebuchadnezzar, knowing that his son was resolute, relaxed his shoulders first. Amel also lowered his guard.

Nebuchadnezzar wearily returned to his chair and sat, looking at Amel. He was not pleased, but he was not going to oppose his son's wish.

"I remain very concerned about your decision. But you have earned my respect. You have been victorious in many battles for me. You have a curious mind that knows no end to its limits. Now you are a builder who surpasses even my abilities. You have always served the kingdom—and me—well."

He paused, looking intently at his son, every facial muscle tense. Then he shrugged, opting to let it go, "I don't like it, but I will accept your judgment and your bride to be."

Relieved, but unhappy that his father had not received Dorcas more enthusiastically, Amel crossed to Nebuchadnezzar to take his arm in a clasp of agreement, "Thank you, Father. Thank you for your affirmation of what I seek most. I will not let you down."

Nebuchadnezzar waved his hand, directing Amel to take his seat. "Now, I have something I want to talk to you about," he said.

Looking at his father quizzically, the Crown Prince slowly took his seat. He felt the tenor of the room changing and it alarmed him.

They looked at each other in silence. This time, Amel broke first. "So what is it?" he asked.

"I have made my decision on the Supreme Commander of the Imperial Guard," replied the King speaking slowly.

Amel tensed, knowing he was not going to like what was coming next.

"I'm bringing Neriglissar back to Babylon. I have no other man as capable as he to ensure the safety of our empire."

Nebuchadnezzar had found no other candidate who had the military genius and leadership skills demanded by the position. At the same time, he realized he was returning to the fold a man who nearly usurped his throne. But the King was fully recovered and back in control of his empire. He felt confident that his power base would not be challenged again; moreover, there had been extenuating circumstances for Neriglissar's actions. He was, in some part, a member of the royal family by his marriage to the King's daughter, and therefore his ambition could be justified.

Amel waited before speaking. He did not want to anger his father but he did want him to listen to his logic, "I think it is a bad decision. Not because Neriglissar is not the man for the job. You are right. He is the best man to command our military. My concern is that I don't think he can be trusted. He proved his disloyalty once. Does a lion lose his hunger? Does a snake cease to hunt? No, Father. You will be bringing back into our innermost circle a man who despises Daniel, who seeks my demise, and who eventually will usurp you."

"Those are strong words," softly uttered the King. "Is he really all that bad?"

"I think so."

More silence. The two men were lost in their respective thoughts.

"I disagree," suddenly said Nebuchadnezzar, rising to take his leave. Amel quickly rose from his chair out of respect for his father, the King.

"I will watch him carefully," Nebuchadnezzar said reinforcing his decision. "We will both watch him carefully. While we give him our trust, we will not give him our hearts."

Realizing there was nothing else he could do, Amel swallowed hard and nodded.

"Here it is, then," declared the King. "You have made a decision I don't agree with, and I have made one you don't agree with. We shall each accept the judgment of the other, and we will be unified in agreement to all outside this room."

"I hope we are not wrong," whispered Amel.
"If you are wrong, you could lose the throne," said Nebuchadnezzar looking hard at his son.
"If you are wrong," answered Amel, "we could both lose the throne."

~

The timing had to be right. Amel-Marduk was sufficiently sensitive to the dynamics of Babylonian culture as they interplayed with the power brokers of society to know he had to introduce the idea of marrying Dorcas to the right people in the right order to avoid hostile opposition. While Dorcas insisted on a Judaic ceremony, Amel knew beyond a doubt that they needed to be married in the Temple of Marduk to have the blessing of the priesthood. The Jewish ceremony could be private and take place anytime. He was grateful that Dorcas saw the wisdom of this move and that she agreed.

The wedding of the Crown Prince demanded a major celebration requiring careful planning. While he was happy to involve Dorcas in all that she wanted to participate, a royal event was beyond her experience and understanding. A battery of planners was required to handle the logistics. Most importantly, they needed time to ensure all went according to plan. The wedding was scheduled to be six months from the night of their engagement. This aligned perfectly with the climate of Babylon as it put the event in the early fall when the weather was at its best. The spring floods would be long over, the fall harvesting completed, and the summer's blistering heat would give way to comfortable sunny days and warm, breezy evenings allowing for an outdoor celebration on the palace grounds.

The time flew for Amel as he went from one meeting to another to convince Babylon's opinion makers to endorse their union. Ochus, the high priest of the Temple of Marduk, was the first and key person he had to persuade. Telling Ochus that he wanted the high priest to marry them in the temple went a long ways to incur the priest's blessing. The event would heighten the import of the priesthood within the empire. Moreover, it did not hurt that Amel let Ochus know he was thinking of designing an elaborate gold trim on the exterior of the new temple to be built on the west side of the Euphrates River. This opulent trim would reflect the rays of the sun to every corner of the old and new cities. He suggested that the temple would be a glorious monument to Ochus for centuries to come.

Once Ochus bought in, Amel made his way through the wise men and astrologers of the court, the leading merchants and growers, the major land owners, and the key leadership of the Imperial Guard. Although he had to wait a few weeks for Neriglissar to return to the capital city to take up his new post, he nevertheless met with Rabmag and Babsaris, important generals in the Imperial Guard who could sway the opinion of the very soldiers he counted on to defend his throne. They needed to understand that he was in no way suggesting an alliance with what remained of Israel by marrying a Jew. He considered Dorcas a Babylonian and made the point emphatically that she had spent her entire adult life in Babylon.

It took over a month before Neriglissar arrived. He was immediately installed as Supreme Commander and eagerly assumed his duties. For the most part, the commanders and troops liked Neriglissar and admired his fearlessness in battle. They knew they were getting the best.

Amel-Marduk was surprised at how readily Neriglissar endorsed his marriage to Dorcas, but then realized his brother-in-law needed to be in his debt as he worked his way back from banishment. Knowing he had to mend broken fences with the Crown Prince and Daniel, Neriglissar dutifully met with each man to report on his plans and actions to strengthen the Imperial Guard. He made it a point to regularly invite them to social events at his home and meeting with them weekly in the royal palace. Although wary, Daniel was pleased to see Neriglissar making an effort to restore his credibility. Everything was a quid pro quo.

Amel was not oblivious of the Jewish community which had become a substantial part of the city's population over the years. They were pleased to see one of their own ascend to the royal palace, but skeptical that they might be played as pawns in some covert scheme that could work to nullify the gains they had made. It was essential to gain the blessing of Daniel and his senior administrators. As much as Daniel was concerned about a push-back to this unequal union from certain sectors in Babylonian society, he knew first-hand how much in love Amel and Dorcas were with each other and so he agreed to publicly support them. Daniel met with the few rabbis that still remained within the Jewish community, encouraging them to lend their support which they did.

Plans for the wedding proceeded as Amel maneuvered through the political hoops of Babylon. The wedding itself would take place at noon in the Temple of Marduk. Ochus, the high priest, would officiate at the ceremony, preceded by a private Jewish ceremony in Amel's palace conducted by Daniel and the city's senior rabbi. Following the temple rite, the royal couple and family would join thousands of guests for a banquet and celebration. The guest list was so extensive, no interior space was suitable. The festivities would take place on the royal palace grounds.

~

Amel woke to the early morning's sun beams dancing on the walls of his bedchamber. He was instantly awake but chose to lie in bed for a few moments to savor the beginning of a very special day. This was it . . . the day he would finally be joined in marriage to the love of his life. All the preparations had been made. Now, it was theirs to enjoy.

In her new bedchamber located in the King's palace where Amytis had insisted she move once the engagement was publicly announced, Dorcas enjoyed the same dance of light on the walls. Unlike Amel, she had not slept a wink, all consumed by the excitement and apprehension of how her life was going to change that day. She was thrilled the day had finally arrived as more than anything in life she wanted to be one with Amel. But this was going to be life-changing for her in more ways than one. She was grateful that her God was sovereign and decided there and then to embrace the day.

Several attendants who now looked after her every want brought Dorcas to the Crown Prince's palace at mid-morning. As she entered, she saw Amel waiting along with the rest of the royal family including King Nebuchadnezzar and the Queen. She was pleased to see Nebudaren and Marduk-Sum-Lisir standing by their father but had to force a smile when her eyes settled on Neriglissar and Princess Kassaya. No matter how Amel tried to assure her that he was a different man, Neriglissar would forever be a traitor to her.

A substantial showing from the Jewish community caught her eye which pleasantly diverted her thoughts from Neriglissar. She was pleased to see Daniel, Meshach, Abednego and Shadrach among the group along with many men and women she had known for years. So many of them had been captured and taken out of Jerusalem years ago. She could not believe these same people now stood in the palace of the next King of Babylon witnessing her marriage and ultimate ascendance to become the next queen of the world's most powerful empire.

From that point, Dorcas entered a dream world, not to wake up until the afternoon celebration was well underway. The traditional Jewish wedding ceremony was conducted by the rabbi and Daniel. Once they were proclaimed a union of one, the rest did not matter. She was now the wife of the man she had adored for years, never hoping that this could ever be a reality.

The couple together with the royal family and court entourage made their way down Procession Way to a fanfare of trumpets and hundreds of thousands of people longing to catch a glimpse of them. As they entered the gates to the Temple of Marduk and began the long ascendance up the massive stairs to the main entry of the building, the crowds began to cheer wildly.

Taken back by their overwhelming display of affection, Amel waved excitedly to them until he heard his father behind him telling him to behave like a king.

The temple ceremony was long. Ochus had pulled out all the stops in an effort to milk everything to highlight his central role in this royal event. Unlike Antiosyss, he did not inject any demonology and supernatural effects into the ritual, but he did prolong it as much as possible to make it a memorable event. It was only when he heard Nebuchadnezzar hiss under his breath that this had gone on long enough and he was no longer going to endure it did Ochus bring the rite to a close.

The afternoon was magical . . . the fulfillment of every bride's fantasy of what it would be like to marry the man of her dreams. Brilliantly colored banners and lanterns festooned the grounds of the royal compound. Tables bedecked with flowers had been set up throughout the campus, providing a festive atmosphere for almost five thousand guests. The food was bountiful and the beer and wine plentiful. From the start, there was music, dancing and all sorts of entertainment to captivate and enthrall the guests. There was no shortage perceived in the royal treasury that afternoon.

As dusk began to settle on the grounds, lanterns were lit and the party kicked up another notch. No one wanted to go home; no one wanted the fantasy to end.

And then . . . it crashed!

King Nebuchadnezzar who had been enjoying himself immensely throughout the day and who had imbibed in too much beer and wine stood to join the dancers performing on a stage before them. He got up without assistance and went to the steps that led up to the outdoor stage that had been constructed for the party. He mounted the stage steadily enough, and as he reached out to take the hand of a young dancer to become part of the swirling circle, he suddenly blacked out and careened off the stage, falling to the ground where he lay motionless.

Screams erupted from the first few tables who saw what had happened and recognized the seriousness of his collapse.

The guards who had been stationed nearby ran to the King as did Amel. Dorcas and Amytis were a step behind, fearing the worst.

~

It was not the fall that did damage. Nebuchadnezzar had managed to hit the ground on his side, his shoulder and buttock taking most of the impact. Something else—deeply internal—had triggered the blackout. Two days after the wedding, the King was walking without any aid and back to his normal routine, but there was a gnawing pain in his lower back and side that he began to notice which had not been there before. He gave it little thought for a month, supposing it would go away as most of his pains did. This one, however, persisted.

For the first two weeks following their wedding, Amel and Dorcas spent the time enjoying their new found lives together as husband and wife. For the first time in as long as both could remember, they spent hours in the lush countryside that was bordered by the Euphrates and Tigris rivers simply enjoying the beauty of nature's wonders. If they weren't on a boat drifting on the river, they were riding among the vegetation on horses from the King's prize herd. It was an idyllic time in their lives . . . one they embraced and enjoyed.

The demands of the kingdom soon encroached on their fantasy world. Ochus was eager for the completed designs for the new temple so that work could begin. Now that he had done the Crown Prince a favor, he vigorously forced him to his drawing board. Moreover, things were piling up on Daniel's desk which needed Amel's counsel. The King, also Amel's mentor, was trying to ease Amel into assuming more and more of the empire's governing responsibilities.

Concerned about the growing intensity of the pain spreading within his abdomen, Nebuchadnezzar began to consult with his physicians who applied a variety of remedies, all to no avail. Not wanting others to know he was suffering, the King took only Amytis into his confidence. She managed the comings and goings of the court physicians and personally monitored all the medicines they were giving her husband topically as well as internally. As his situation deteriorated, she sought the help of healers from the temple to work their mystical magic. The parade of doctors and mystics into and out of the King's palace did not go unnoticed. Eventually, word came to Dorcas that something strange was afoot.

~

The winter was uncharacteristically warm. It was as though the climate had shifted one-hundred and eighty degrees. There was no relief from the heat, no matter where one stood or sat. Amel's crew had pitched a large canopy on the site of the new temple as close to the river as possible in the hope of channeling cool breezes from the flowing water. Their strategy did not work. There were no breezes. Being under the canopy merely shielded one from the direct rays of the sun, but there was no escaping its biting heat.

Amel was finally ready to unveil his plan for the new temple; he wanted his father to be present. Ochus and his coterie of priests were already there. They were waiting for the King who made his way towards them in his chariot. It had been three months since the wedding.

Upon the King's arrival, Amel began his presentation. He was obviously excited by his new building project and animatedly described what was going to be built where as he gestured to certain areas on the grounds. He augmented his drawings which were held up for all to see with miniature samples of architectural and decorative elements. On occasion, he left the shade of the canopy to outline the location of walls or walkways. It was quite a show. His audience quickly caught his exuberance and applauded enthusiastically when he finished. There was no question that this was going to be the piece de resistance of Babylon's burgeoning building projects and skyscape.

Amel had his assistants take Ochus and the priests on a tour of the grounds so they could see for themselves the enormity of the project. He had noticed that his father did not seem to be feeling well that morning and wanted to help him get back to the palace. He asked Nebuchadnezzar if everything was all right as he escorted the King to his chariot. Rather than answer him, Nebuchadnezzar patted him on the shoulder and asked him to come by his palace that afternoon . . . that he had something he wished to discuss with Amel and Daniel.

~

Even though it was late afternoon, the sun remained high in the sky and the temperature high as well as Amel walked up the steps to the palace his father had built for his mother on the banks of the Euphrates. He could not wait to be inside where it was cool, thanks in large part to the cooling breezes blowing through the hanging gardens into the palace. He might be able to build grander and bigger buildings than his father, but the brilliance of the King's mind never beamed so brightly as in the magnificent hanging gardens he had built for his Queen. The palace was an oasis in the desert.

Zocor was waiting for him and brought him immediately to the King's sitting room. He was surprised to see Daniel and his mother present. He had presumed this was a private discussion with his father about the temple designs . . . an opportunity for him to get some constructive input from the man who had virtually created the magnificent city in which they lived.

Daniel quickly rose and went forward to greet Amel, bowing as he spoke, "My Lord, I was just told about your wonderful presentation today. Congratulations."

Amel smiled gratefully, "Thank you Daniel. Yes, it did go rather well. I think everyone was pleased."

He bussed his mother then approached Nebuchadnezzar, "How about you, father? You never told me what you thought about my work."

The King chuckled and waved his arm in a sort of salute, "Superb! That's the best word I can think of. Your designs and plans are nothing short of superb. You have moved far beyond my abilities."

"Thank you, Sire," beamed Amel, caught somewhat off guard by the accolades thrown his way. "I mean . . . you are very gracious, sir. It means a lot to hear this from you." He bowed low to his father, "I truly thank you."

"That's not why I asked the three of you to meet with me today," gruffly spoke Nebuchadnezzar. He gestured to the chairs surrounding his, "Sit down. We have a situation we must deal with that is quite serious, and this will take some time."

Amel looked questioningly at his father, then at his mother who averted his glance by looking down. His eyes quickly moved to Daniel who, likewise, did not return his look. He was obviously the only person in the room who did not know what was going on. Rather than force the issue, he slowly settled into the chair directly across from the King and waited for him to speak.

"Amel, my son," his father started, "I am very ill."

"What?" erupted the Crown Prince, looking at everyone for answers. "What are you talking about?"

"Hear me out," sternly ordered his father, still very much the King in control. "I did not fall at your wedding because I was drunk. There has been something wrong deep inside me for many months. The combination of the excitement of the day, the foods and the drinks and I suppose my illness . . . well, it all worked to cause me to lose consciousness. From that day on, things have been getting progressively worse."

"Why haven't you told me before now?" asked Amel incredulously. "Why keep this a secret?"

"I didn't want to dampen your happiness, son. I thought this pain would go away. I didn't tell your mother until a month ago . . . and only then because I wanted to consult with our physicians to see if I really was seriously sick. And it was not the time to raise concern among our people. The last thing this city needs is more speculation on who is in control."

"Son," Amytis leaned forward to pat his arm, "we had to know more before you or others could be told your father was ill. We needed to know how serious it was."

"How serious?" blurted out Amel.

Amytis and Nebuchadnezzar hesitated, looking at each other as to who should answer. The King nodded at his wife to take the lead as he clutched his side.

"Very serious," she said. "It seems to worsen each day."

Amel was dumbstruck. He looked from one person to the next, his eyes pleading for understanding and help.

"Son," said Nebuchadnezzar now revealing some degree of pain in his voice, "we have been talking and are in agreement about succession to the throne. You need to take the throne right now . . . before I die. There must be no lapse in power."

Amel looked at him, "What? What are you saying?"

"I'm saying that I want you to be crowned King of Babylon within the next week or two. I will abdicate my throne in favor of you."

"Daniel, have you been involved in this conversation?" asked Amel as he turned to look hard into Daniel's eyes. "Do you agree with this?"

"Yes, my Lord," answered Daniel. "I believe it is the right thing to do if we are to maintain order in the empire. If your father recovers—which we all pray he will—no harm is done. He is old in years and ready to let you rule, whether he is in good or bad health."

He paused to look deep into Amel's eyes, then continued, each word a sentence unto itself, "Your becoming King now prevents disruption in our land and does no harm. It only brings good."

"Mother?" Amel stared at Amytis.

She raised her head to look back. The steeliness in her eyes revealed her answer. She nodded in affirmation, then stifled a sob.

"So . . . when? When does this happen? How does it happen?"

Nebuchadnezzar smiled, glad to know this was finally over and all were in agreement. Regaining control of the conversation, he said, "We must plan a coronation which means we need to bring Ochus and Neriglissar into this immediately. We cannot afford to give them any time to consider alternatives as we know they could quickly fall into collusion . . . and then we will have real trouble."

~

He blinked.

Amel-Marduk relished the movement of the early morning sun's beams on the bedroom's walls. The last time he remembered waking like this was on his wedding day. Did the sun's rays dance like this on the day he married Dorcas? He slowly shifted his body upwards to rest on his elbows as he looked at Dorcas lying next to him. His eyes took in her whole body beginning with her feet and moving upwards until he realized he was staring into her open eyes looking directly back at him. She smiled.

"This is a big day," she said softly as her hand lifted to stroke his cheek gently. "You're going to be crowned the King of Babylon today."

The thought should have brought him joy. Instead, he was filled with apprehension. How would he be received, especially by those who dared to cross swords with him before? Was he up to carrying the burdens his father had shouldered all these years? Could he maintain Babylon's dominance in the world? Would the enemies of his country sense an opportunity to test his inexperience and attack? So many questions . . . so many worries. And all he wanted to do was design and construct great buildings.

Amel smiled at Dorcas, and bent down to kiss her on the lips. Swinging his legs out of bed, he stretched and stood, "It's time to get up and get on with the day."

Four months ago, he greeted his wedding day with much anticipation. He had little enthusiasm today for what should be the highest achievement of his life. Then, he was consumed with the joy of becoming one with the love of his life. Today, he felt sadness at the imminent loss of his father and ambivalence toward assuming a role that would compete with his passion for architecture. He shook his head and grimaced, then told himself: it was time to grow up and do what he had been placed on earth to do.

The royal family was in agreement to keep the coronation a modest event. But Ochus would have none of it. It was another opportunity for the priesthood to take center stage in Babylonian society and he was not going to miss it. As soon as he was told of Nebuchadnezzar's plan to crown Amel King, he put the ceremonial wheels in motion. He planned the festivities to take place on the ziggurat where a majority of the city's population could witness the event and watch him perform.

At first Ochus wanted the coronation to take place on the uppermost level where visibility would be best. Nebuchadnezzar insisted on being present but he was in no condition to walk up the four hundred feet of steps. Moreover, it would have been difficult for his guards to carry him that far. They compromised. The ceremony would take place on the third level where an expanded stage would be built to accommodate dignitaries and the rites Ochus had planned.

Like most major events in Babylon, the coronation was set for noon when the sun was at its high point in the sky. Eager to have a good view of the proceedings, people had already filled Procession Way, the side streets and the courtyard of the ziggurat by dawn. By mid-morning, the weather had turned and the day had become overcast and grey. The priests appeared on the platform to light torches which heightened the ceremony's dramatic effect.

The procession of the royal family and dignitaries left the palace grounds thirty minutes before the appointed hour and made its way to the adjoining ziggurat. Nebuchadnezzar led in a sedan chair, carried on two long poles by six husky servants as the palace guards cleared the way before him. He was followed by Amel, then Amytis and Dorcas, Marduk-Sum-Lisir and Nebudaren, and, lastly, by Princess Kassaya and Neriglissar. The roars of the crowd were deafening as they cheered their old and new Kings.

Nebuchadnezzar was in such pain that a recliner had been placed on the stage for him to lie upon. Amytis was seated next to him. On the other side sat the remainder of the family. Amel and Dorcas were seated in two throne-like chairs at the rear of the stage facing out to the crowds below.

The ceremony was spectacular. Ochus took a page from Antiosyss's book and incorporated everything he could think of to enthrall his audience. Ceremonial dances, virtuoso musical performances, leaping fire pots, and even the occasional supernatural spectacle. Amel had to give Ochus due credit for a grand show; he would have been amused if it were not for his ailing father.

That it was his coronation had not yet registered in him. That is, not until Ochus had him rise and walk to take the hand of the god Bel as required by tradition. They continued to walk to the outside edge of the platform where Ocus took the scepter from the hands of Nebuchadnezzar and placed it in Amel's. For the first time that day, a jolt ran through the Crown Prince's body as he cradled one of the key symbols of royal authority never held by anyone other than the King.

As the crowd roared, Amel began to sense for the first time that his life had now changed. He was to be the King. He was now their leader. His previous ambivalence faded away to be replaced by the regency of the authority he was assuming. By the time Ochus took the crown from Nebuchadnezzar and placed it upon the Crown Prince's head, the transformation was complete. He—Amel-Marduk—was now King of Babylon. He stood, enjoying the accolades of the screaming city below. He could not move. The moment was riveting, and he had been transformed by a higher power.

The masses were ecstatic! The young King energized them. Fear and acceptance of the inevitable status quo of Nebuchadnezzar's reign was replaced by joy and exuberance for a new royalty they could love and endear. The celebratory spirit was contagious, spreading quickly throughout the city as parties and parades went well into the night.

But the dark side was coming to life as well. The muttering, sneering and grumbling began the moment the coronation ended. Amel did not have the fierce personality of his father. Those around him admired him for his creativity and for his courage in battle, but they did not fear him. This made it easy to snipe and question his authority.

On his way down the ziggurat, Neriglissar grabbed Ochus' arm and whispered in his ear, "Remember . . . you owe me. I will soon see you to collect." Others, more circumspect, waited to speculate on the new King's failings until they were away from the crowds and safely within the confines of their own homes.

Later that evening, back in their quarters within the palace, the newly appointed wise men and court magicians gathered to eat and review the day. Mysonus had long been replaced by Mister as the spokesman for the courtiers. He quipped to his colleague, "He better treat us with more respect than his father."

There was unanimous concurrence as their prestige in the King's court had greatly diminished since Daniel began interpreting the King's dreams and had become his single advisor. A wise man who was caught up in the intrigue of regaining the power they once held in the King's court added, "There's only one thing we need to do, and that is get rid of

Daniel . . . move him out of the palace." The group
enthusiastically concurred.

And on it went as those who had risen to leadership
positions in the dismantled Governing Council saw for the first
time a chink in the armor that protected the throne.

~

Six months later King Amel-Marduk and his Queen,
Dorcas, strolled in the very same hanging gardens where
Nebuchadnezzar and Amytis were reunited following his seven
years' exile in the pastures. The splendor of the large trees and
lushness of the shrubbery and flowers were a treat they regularly
enjoyed. Not wishing to displace his mother, Amel insisted that
she continue to live in the primary palace her husband had built
for her while he and Dorcas resided in the palace that had been
built for him as Crown Prince of Babylon. Since all five palaces
of the royal family were within a single campus, it didn't matter
to the public where each was housed. All that was important was
that the royal palace—the building which housed the offices of
the nation's administrative staff and the King's public
chambers—continue to function as before.

As Dorcas and Amytis spent more time together, their
friendship deepened far beyond that of a mother-in-law to
daughter-in-law relationship. Much of their time together was
spent in the gardens Nebuchadnezzar had built for the Queen.
Her love for the gardens was easily absorbed by Dorcas who, too,
missed the mountains and hills of her homeland. It was only
natural that she often brought Amel here when they had time by
themselves, much to the delight of Amytis.

In years past, Amel had wandered in the vast gardens to
please his mother—especially when they were first constructed—
but as a young man he never had time for natural beauty. So
consumed with man-made design and structures, he could not
enjoy a tree for its innate splendor. At first, he resisted Dorcas'
wish to take late afternoon walks in the gardens. He would much

rather sit on a patio looking down on the gardens, enjoying the cooling breezes that the irrigation system provided while enjoying a beer. As she took the time to point out to him the individual characteristics of the plantings, he started to awaken to the incredible designs of nature and quickly began a quest to know more and different plants to broaden his awareness.

He looked forward to this time of the day when he could release the burdens of the kingdom and simply enter a world of beauty with his treasured partner. They stood on the second level looking down on the river banks where the magnificent cypress trees were planted.

"To think these trees are over one hundred years old," he said in admiration as they watched the orange and pink light of the sunset skip on the branches. "They've seen more life than we ever will."

They watched in silence, nature's light show mesmerizing them.

"I'd love to hear their stories," he continued. "They must have fascinating stories of all the intrigue and political shenanigans they've been witness to through the decades." He smiled at Dorcas, "We would learn a lot."

"Come," she said, taking his hand, "let's sit."

She led him to an oasis hidden within the gardens where she surprised him with some fruits and sweet breads as well as a pitcher of beer.

"I just love you," Amel laughed as he grabbed Dorcas to give her a kiss and hug. "You are always surprising me."

"Well, you need a pleasant surprise every now and then. I am glad I can still do something you haven't been told about . . . all knowing King."

They sat in two pillowed chairs that she had arranged to be brought into the gardens. The magic of the sun's light continued to captivate them, their pleasure heightened by the cool beer and fruit.

"It's been a fast six months since the day you were crowned King," said Dorcas. "I cannot believe all that has happened. I wonder if even these trees can absorb it all."

Amel laughed. They sat in silence, caught up in the vastness of the forest in which they were sitting.

"Your father went very fast once you were on the throne," mused Dorcas. "I wish he had lived longer. I was scared to death of him, but I know I would have liked what I didn't know about him."

"He lived to be seventy-two," replied Amel. "That is a long life, especially the way he lived it with all the wars and battles he seemed to be immersed in for decades." He let that thought sit in their minds for a few seconds then added, "Another year would have been good. Just his presence would have stopped a lot of the chicanery that we now face."

"What do you mean?" Dorcas turned to him suddenly. "What's going on that I don't know about?"

"It's the usual," Amel waved his hand dismissing any anxieties he may have triggered. "Neriglissar is difficult to keep contained. He's changed his senior commanders so often that I don't believe there is a division leader I know any more in the Imperial Guard."

"He's obviously putting men loyal to him in leadership positions. The less they know you, the better for him."

"I can't quarrel with you," Amel chuckled, amused at his wife's political instincts. "If I didn't have Zocor keeping me informed, I wouldn't know their names let alone their faces. I make it a point to have them come to the palace as soon as I get word of their promotions. They need to know their King first hand."

"Have you been using the wise men as advisors?" she suddenly asked, changing the subject. "They were very unhappy with your father and Daniel, and probably you, because they were ignored for so long. I hope you're conferring with them."

"Funny you should mention them," said Amel, his voice taking on a more serious tone. "We've tried to bring them in on our decisions but all they want is for Daniel to be removed as Governor. They will twist any subject or issue around to the need for Daniel to be relieved of his duties."

"So how do you placate them?"

"I can't . . . because I will not discharge Daniel. Now, they are aligning with Ochus and the priests. Ochus is openly criticizing my edict that released King Jehoichim from prison. The man has been imprisoned for many years and is impotent as a leader. It made no sense for me to keep him jailed."

"I'm glad you finally did that," said Dorcas as she reached out to pat his arm affectionately. "Freeing the former King of Israel made a positive statement to the Jewish community in Babylon."

Starting to feel the tension of the day returning to his body, Amel stood and took Dorcas' hand to lift her from her chair, "Come, I don't want to sit anymore. Let's walk."

He led the way to a staircase hidden to the side of the level they were on. She followed him as he began climbing upward.

"You're not treating Jehoichim any different than the other captive kings you have freed in Babylon are you?" she had to shout as he was moving quickly ahead of her.

"Well, I trust him more than the others so . . . yes . . . he's probably held a little higher in the regard of my senior people."

"Be careful, Amel," cautioned Dorcas who finally caught up with him as he stood on the third level where the branches of the Cypress trees extended to where they could touch them. "Ochus and Neriglissar are aligned. Angering Ochus could make for a lot of trouble."

Amel grabbed her hand and they began walking through a grove of fruit trees. He reached out to grab a pear off its branch and took a big, juicy bite. The sweetness of its juice brought a smile to his face as it dribbled down onto his chin. "Here," he handed it to Dorcas, "take a bite. This is delicious!"

She readily complied, savoring the taste as well. Like two adolescent children, they were lost in the moment. Between the two of them, the pear disappeared in seconds. Dorcas reached over to wipe Amel's mouth, laughing as she did. He, likewise, cleaned off her face with his sleeve.

"If only all of life were this delicious . . . free of sour and full of sweet," Amel exclaimed.

Dorcas frowned. His cavalier comment abruptly brought her back to the realities they were discussing. While she wanted it all to be sweet, she knew there was always something bubbling on the horizon.

"I shouldn't ask," she said, "but how is the new central market doing? Is our commerce doing well? I guess more to the point, is the treasury regaining its former strength?"

Amel stopped in his tracks and turned to look at Dorcas, his hands on his hips, "You must be the only woman in Babylon who even knows to ask about the workings of commerce and trade. You amaze me! I should put you in charge of the market."

Dorcas did not smile but stood her ground, "I mean it. How are things going?"

Knowing he was up against a woman who would not be put off until her question was answered, he told her the truth, "Things are not well. The new market has brought all sorts of efficiencies. We are able to process so much more goods and foodstuffs, but the business does not seem to warrant it."

"And the merchants and growers? How are they taking it?"

"They're unhappy, of course," Amel replied. He turned to continue walking, then, looked back at her, "Well . . . really . . . they're in a bit of an uproar. That's a whole other battle that we are fighting."

They walked in silence, arms around each other. The sun had almost set and the gardens were dark. What had just looked warm and inviting a few minutes ago was now a sea of shadows, almost forbidding.

A lighted torch appeared above them carried by one of the palace guards who never let the royal couple out of their sight.

"I guess it's time we get back to our own palace," chuckled Amel. He could see Dorcas was disturbed. The political storms he faced daily had become a normal way of life for him. He wanted to protect her from them. He needed to change the mood.

"You haven't asked me about my favorite project," he mockingly scolded her.

It took her a moment to clear out the dark clouds of Babylonian politics before she realized what he was talking about.

"Oh, yes," she replied eager to talk about something cheerful. "How is the new temple going? I want to hear what you did today."

Amel loved sharing with her his creative impulses and discoveries no matter how small. She soaked up all he had to say like a sponge, delighted to share in his joy. They made their way to the guard with the torch who led them to their own palace. They fed off each other, their excitement ever increasing as they dreamed together the always-unfolding design of Babylon's newest and most magnificent building.

They entered their palace where Dorcas was met by her servants and taken to her bath before the evening meal. Amel made his way to the rooftop off his bedchamber where he could look down on the grandest city in the world . . . one that he, his father, and his grandfather had created. The sight should have brought great joy. But a nagging thought would not leave him: the political storms that began with Nebuchadnezzar's transformation into a bull in his own pasture continued to rage and seemed never to be put to rest.

The lions were still roaring.

The thought was terrifying. Where would it all end? How do I rule? He lifted his eyes to the starry skies and prayed, "Oh, God . . . and I mean the God of all gods . . . guide me as you do Daniel."

The Reigning Kings of the Neo-Babylon Empire

Neboplassar (father of Nebuchadnezzar II)
Reigned 626 to 605 BC

Nebuchadnezzar (aka Nebuchadnezzar II)
Reigned 605 to 562 BC

Amel-Marduk
Reigned 562 to 560 BC

Neriglissar
Reigned 560 to 556 BC

Labashi-Marduk
Reigned 556 BC

Nabonidus
Reigned 556 to 553 BC

Belshazzer
Reigned 553 to 539 BC

Cyrus the Great conquered the Babylonian Empire
in 539 BC

Daniel
The time and circumstances of Daniel's death have not been recorded; however, tradition maintains that Daniel was still alive in the third year of Cyrus according to the Tanakh (Daniel 10:1). He would have been almost 100 years old at that point.

10094929R00252

Made in the USA
San Bernardino, CA
05 April 2014